THE HERO AND THE DRAGON

John bent from the saddle and touched Jenny's lips with his own. Then he drove in his spurs. The crack of iron-shod hooves as they shot forward was like the chip of distant lightning.

Jenny took two steps down the loose, rocky slope after him, watching the gray horse and the pewter-dark shape of the man as they plunged through the labyrinth of gaping foundations, broken beams, and standing water, slipping down drifts of charred wood chips and racing towards the open mouth of the gnomes' cavern.

Her heart hammering achingly in her chest, Jenny stretched her mageborn senses, straining to hear. The cold air seemed to breathe with the dragon's mind. Somewhere in that darkness was the slithery drag of metallic scales on stone...

Morkaleb, greatest and wisest of dragons, was coming out to meet his puny challenger!

Also by Barbara Hambly
Published by Ballantine Books:

THE DARWATH TRILOGY
   The Time of the Dark
   The Walls of Air
   The Armies of Daylight

THE LADIES OF MANDRIGYN

DRAGONSBANE

BARBARA HAMBLY

A Del Rey Book

BALLANTINE BOOKS • NEW YORK

Library of Congress Catalog Card Number: 85–90837

ISBN 0–345–31572–3

Manufactured in the United States of America

First Edition: January 1986

Maps by Shelly Shapiro
Cover Art by Michael Whelan

For information regarding reproduction of art work by Michael
Whelan, contact Glass Onion Graphics, P.O. Box 88, Brookfield,
CT 06804

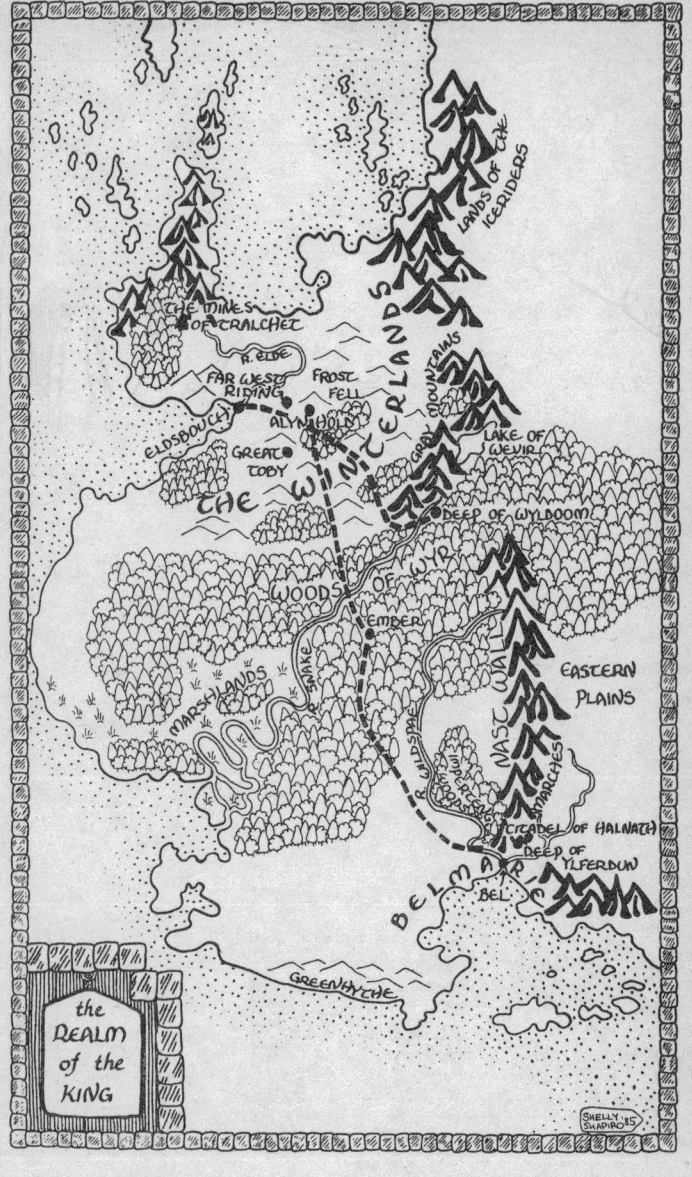

THE WINTERLANDS

LANDS OF THE ICERIDERS

THE MINES OF TRALCHET

R. ELDE

FAR WEST RIDING

FROST FELL

ELDSBOUCH

ALYN HOLD

GREAT TOBY

GREY MOUNTAINS

LAKE OF WEVIR

DEEP OF WYLDOOM

WOODS OF WYR

EMBER

SNAKE

MARSHLANDS

R. WILDSPAE

NAST WALL

EASTERN PLAINS

WILDSPAE MARCHES

CITADEL OF HALNATH

DEEP OF YLFERDUN

BELMARIE

BEL

GREENHYTHE

the REALM of the KING

SHELLY SHAPIRO '85

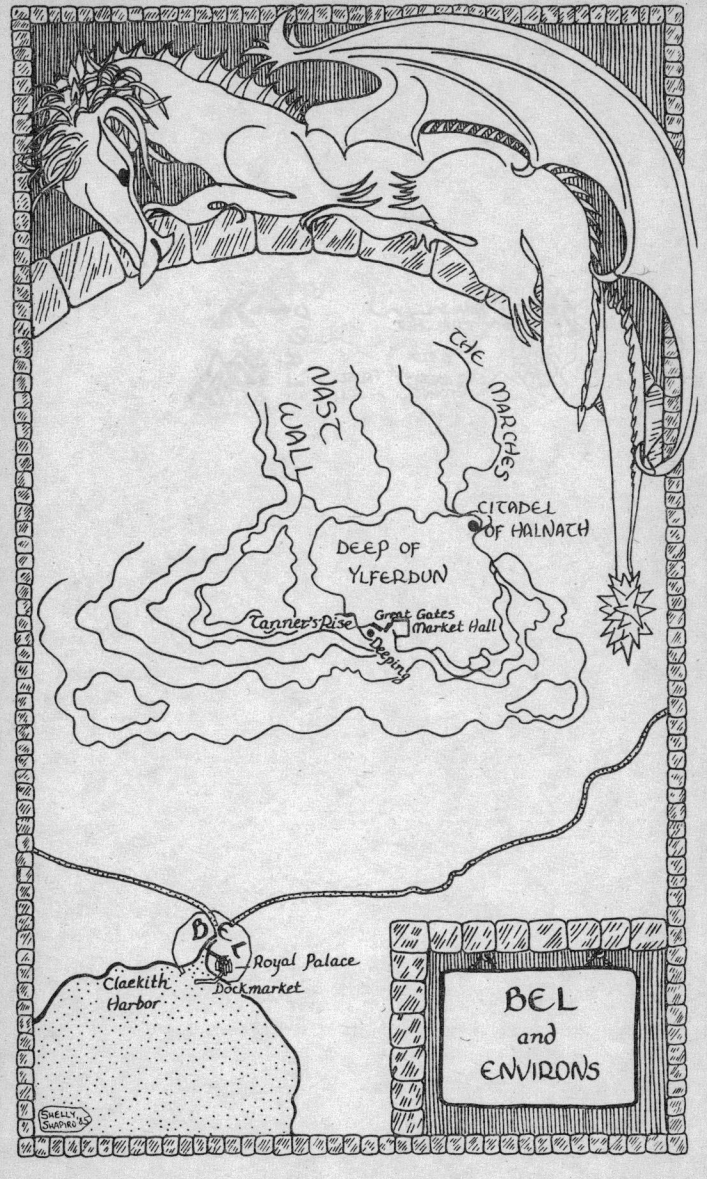

THE MARCHES

NASC WALL

DEEP OF YLFERDUN

CITADEL OF HALNATH

Tanner's Rise

Great Gates
Market Hall

Deeping

BEL

Royal Palace

Dockmarket

Claekith Harbor

BEL
and
ENVIRONS

SHELLY SHAPIRO '85

CHAPTER I

BANDITS OFTEN LAY in wait in the ruins of the old town at the fourways—Jenny Waynest thought there were three of them this morning.

She was not sure any more whether it was magic which told her this, or simply the woodcraftiness and instinct for the presence of danger that anyone developed who had survived to adulthood in the Winterlands. But as she drew rein short of the first broken walls, where she knew she would still be concealed by the combination of autumn fog and early morning gloom beneath the thicker trees of the forest, she noted automatically that the horse droppings in the sunken clay of the roadbed were fresh, untouched by the frost that edged the leaves around them. She noted, too, the silence in the ruins ahead; no coney's foot rustled the yellow spill of broomsedge cloaking the hill slope where the old church had been, the church sacred to the Twelve Gods beloved of the old Kings. She thought she smelled the smoke of a concealed fire near the remains of what had been a crossroads inn, but honest men would have gone there straight and left a track in the nets of dew that covered the weeds all around. Jenny's white mare Moon Horse pricked her long ears at the scent of other beasts, and Jenny wind-whispered to her for silence, smoothing the raggedy mane against the long neck. But she had been looking for all those signs before she saw them.

She settled into stillness in the protective cloak of fog and shadow, like a partridge blending with the brown of the woods. She was a little like a partridge herself, dark and small and nearly invisible in the dull, random plaids of the northlands; a thin, compactly built woman, tough as the roots of moorland heather. After a moment of silence, she wove her magic into a rope of mist and cast it along the road toward the nameless ruins of the town.

It was something she had done even as a child, before the old wander-mage Caerdinn had taught her the ways of power. All her thirty-seven years, she had lived in the Winterlands—she knew the smells of danger. The late-lingering birds of autumn, thrushes and blackbirds, should have been waking in the twisted brown mats of ivy that half-hid the old inn's walls—they were silent. After a moment, she caught the scent of horses, and the ranker, dirtier stench of men.

One bandit would be in the stumpy ruin of the old tower that commanded the south and eastward roads, part of the defenses of the ruined town left from when the prosperity of the King's law had given it anything to defend. They always hid there. A second, she guessed, was behind the walls of the old inn. After a moment she sensed the third, watching the crossroads from a yellow thicket of seedy tamarack. Her magic brought the stink of their souls to her, old greeds and the carrion-bone memories of some cherished rape or murder that had given a momentary glow of power to lives largely divided between the giving and receiving of physical pain. Having lived all her life in the Winterlands, she knew that these men could scarcely help being what they were; she had to put aside both her hatred of them, and her pity for them, before she could braid the spells that she laid upon their minds.

Her concentration deepened further. She stirred judiciously at that compost of memories, whispering to their blunted minds of the bored sleepiness of men who have watched too long. Unless every illusion and Limitation was wrought correctly, they would see her when she moved. Then she loosened her halberd in its holster upon her saddle-tree, settled her sheepskin jacket a little more closely about her shoulders and, with scarcely breath or movement, urged Moon Horse forward toward the ruins.

The man in the tower she never saw at all, from first to last. Through the browning red leaves of a screen of hawthorn, she glimpsed two horses tethered behind a ruined wall near the inn, their breath making plumes of white in the dawn cold; a moment later she saw the bandit crouching behind the crumbling wall, a husky man in greasy old leathers. He had been watching the road, but started suddenly and cursed; looking down, he began scratching his crotch with vigor and annoyance but no particular surprise. He did not see Jenny as she ghosted past. The third bandit, sitting his rawboned black horse between a broken corner of a wall and a spinney of raggedy birches, simply stared out ahead of him, lost in the daydreams she had sent.

She was directly in front of him when a boy's voice shouted from down the southward road, "LOOK OUT!"

Jenny whipped her halberd clear of its rest as the bandit woke with a start. He saw her and roared a curse. Peripherally Jenny was aware of hooves pounding up the road toward her; the other traveler, she thought with grim annoyance, whose well-meant warning had snapped the man from his trance. As the bandit bore down upon her, she got a glimpse of a young man riding out of the mist full-pelt, clearly intent upon rescue.

The bandit was armed with a short sword, but swung

at her with the flat of it, intending to unhorse her without damaging her too badly to rape later. She feinted with the halberd to bring his weapon up, then dipped the long blade on the pole's end down under his guard. Her legs clinched to Moon Horse's sides to take the shock as the weapon knifed through the man's belly. The leather was tough, but there was no metal underneath. She ripped the blade clear as the man doubled up around it, screaming and clawing; both horses danced and veered with the smell of the hot, spraying blood. Before the man hit the muddy bed of the road, Jenny had wheeled her horse and was riding to the aid of her prospective knight-errant, who was engaged in a sloppy, desperate battle with the bandit who had been concealed behind the ruined outer wall.

Her rescuer was hampered by his long cloak of ruby red velvet, which had got entangled with the basketwork hilt of his jeweled longsword. His horse was evidently better trained and more used to battle than he was: the maneuverings of the big liver-bay gelding were the only reason the boy hadn't been killed outright. The bandit, who had gotten himself mounted at the boy's first cry of warning, had driven them back into the hazel thickets that grew along the tumbled stones of the inn wall, and, as Jenny kicked Moon Horse into the fray, the boy's trailing cloak hung itself up on the low branches and jerked its wearer ignominiously out of the saddle with the horse's next swerve.

Using her right hand as the fulcrum of a swing, Jenny swept the halberd's blade at the bandit's sword arm. The man veered his horse to face her; she got a glimpse of piggy, close-set eyes under the rim of a dirty iron cap. Behind her she could hear her previous assailant still screaming. Evidently her current opponent could as well, for he ducked the first slash and swiped at Moon Horse's face to cause the mare to shy, then spurred past Jenny and away up the road, willing neither to face a weapon that so outreached his own, nor to stop for his comrade who had done so.

There was a brief crashing in the thickets of briar as the man who had been concealed in the tower fled into the raw mists, then silence, save for the dying bandit's hoarse, bubbling sobs.

Jenny dropped lightly from Moon Horse's back. Her young rescuer was still thrashing in the bushes like a stoat in a sack, half-strangled on his bejeweled cloak strap. She used the hook on the back of the halberd's blade to twist the long court-sword from his hand, then stepped in to pull the muffling folds of velvet aside. He struck at her with his hands, like a man swatting at wasps. Then he seemed to see her for the first time and stopped, staring up at her with wide, myopic gray eyes.

After a long moment of surprised stillness, he cleared his throat and unfastened the chain of gold and rubies that held the cloak under his chin. "Er—thank you, my lady," he gasped in a slightly winded voice, and got to his feet. Though Jenny was used to people being taller than she, this young man was even more so than most. "I—uh—" His skin was as fine-textured and fair as his hair, which was already, despite his youth, beginning to thin away toward early baldness. He couldn't have been more than eighteen, with a natural awkwardness increased tenfold by the difficult task of thanking the intended object of a gallant defense for saving his life.

"My profoundest gratitude," he said, and performed a supremely graceful Dying Swan, the like of which had not been seen in the Winterlands since the nobles of the Kings had departed in the wake of the retreating royal armies. "I am Gareth of Magloshaldon, a traveler upon errantry in these lands, and I wish to extend my humblest expressions of . . ."

Jenny shook her head and stilled him with an upraised hand. "Wait here," she said, and turned away.

Puzzled, the boy followed her.

The first bandit who had attacked her still lay in the clay muck of the roadbed. The soaking blood had turned it into a mess of heel gouges, strewn with severed entrails; the stink was appalling. The man was still groaning weakly. Against the matte pallor of the foggy morning, the scarlet of the blood stood out shockingly bright.

Jenny sighed, feeling suddenly cold and weary and unclean, looking upon what she had done and knowing what it was up to her yet to do. She knelt beside the dying man, drawing the stillness of her magic around her again. She was aware of Gareth's approach, his boots threshing through the dew-soaked bindweed in a hurried rhythm that broke when he tripped on his sword. She felt a tired stirring of anger at him for having made this necessary. Had he not cried out, both she and this poor, vicious, dying brute would each have gone their ways...

...And he would doubtless have killed Gareth after she passed. And other travelers besides.

She had long since given up trying to unpick wrong from right, present *should* from future *if*. If there was a pattern to all things, she had given up thinking that it was simple enough to lie within her comprehension. Still, her soul felt filthy within her as she put her hands to the dying man's clammy, greasy temples, tracing the proper runes while she whispered the death-spells. She felt the life go out of him and tasted the bile of self-loathing in her mouth.

Behind her, Gareth whispered, "You—he's—he's dead."

She got to her feet, shaking the bloody dirt from her skirts. "I could not leave him for the weasels and foxes," she replied, starting to walk away. She could hear the small carrion-beasts already, gathering at the top of the bank above the misty slot of the road, drawn to the blood-smell and waiting impatiently for the killer to abandon her prey. Her voice was brusque—she had always hated the death-spells. Having grown up in a land without law, she had killed her first man when she was fourteen, and six since, not counting the dying she had helped from life as the only midwife and healer from the Gray Mountains to the sea. It never got easier.

She wanted to be gone from the place, but the boy Gareth put a staying hand on her arm, looking from her to the corpse in a kind of nauseated fascination. He had never seen death, she thought. At least, not in its raw form. The pea green velvet of his travel-stained doublet, the gold stampwork of his boots, the tucked embroidery of his ruffled lawn shirt, and the elaborate, feathered crestings of his green-tipped hair all proclaimed him for a courtier. All things, even death, were doubtless done with a certain amount of style where he came from.

He gulped. "You're—you're a witch!"

One corner of her mouth moved slightly; she said, "So I am."

He stepped back from her in fear, then staggered, clutching at a nearby sapling for support. She saw then that among the decorative slashings of his doublet sleeve was an uglier opening, the shirt visible through it dark and wet. "I'll be fine," he protested faintly, as she moved to support him. "I just need . . ." He made a fumbling effort to shake free of her hand and walk, his myopic gray eyes peering at the ankle-deep drifts of moldering leaves that lined the road.

"What you need is to sit down." She led him away to a broken boundary stone and forced him to do so and unbuttoned the diamond studs that held the sleeve to the body of the doublet. The wound did not look deep, but it was bleeding badly. She pulled loose the leather thongs that bound the wood-black knots of her hair and used them as a tourniquet above the wound. He winced and gasped and tried to loosen it as she tore a strip from the hem of her shift for a bandage, so that she slapped at his fingers like a child's. Then, a moment later, he tried to get up again. "I have to find..."

"I'll find them," Jenny said firmly, knowing what it was that he sought. She finished binding his wound and walked back to the tangle of hazel bushes where Gareth and the bandit had struggled. The frosty daylight glinted on a sharp reflection among the leaves. The spectacles she found there were bent and twisted out of shape, the bottom of one round lens decorated by a star-fracture. Flicking the dirt and wetness from them, she carried them back.

"Now," she said, as Gareth fumbled them on with hands shaking from weakness and shock. "You need that arm looked to. I can take you..."

"My lady, I've no time." He looked up at her, squinting a little against the increasing brightness of the sky behind her head. "I'm on a quest, a quest of terrible importance."

"Important enough to risk losing your arm if the wound turns rotten?"

As if such things could not happen to him, did she only have the wits to realize it, he went on earnestly, "I'll be all right, I tell you. I am seeking Lord Aversin the Dragonsbane, Thane of Alyn Hold and Lord of Wyr, the greatest knight ever to have ridden the Winterlands. Have you heard of him hereabouts? Tall as an angel, handsome as song... His fame has spread through the southlands the way the floodwaters spread in the spring, the noblest of chevaliers... I must find Alyn Hold, before it is too late."

Jenny sighed, exasperated. "So you must," she said. "It is to Alyn Hold that I am going to take you."

The squinting eyes got round as the boy's mouth fell open. "To—to Alyn Hold? Really? It's near here?"

"It's the nearest place where we can get your arm seen to," she said. "Can you ride?"

Had he been dying, she thought, amused, he would

still have sprung to his feet as he did. "Yes, of course. I—do you know Lord Aversin, then?"

Jenny was silent for a moment. Then, softly, she said, "Yes. Yes, I know him."

She whistled up the horses, the tall white Moon Horse and the big liver-bay gelding, whose name, Gareth said, was Battlehammer. In spite of his exhaustion and the pain of his roughly bound wound, Gareth made a move to offer her totally unnecessary assistance in mounting. As they reined up over the ragged stone slopes to avoid the corpse in its rank-smelling puddles of mud, Gareth asked, "If— if you're a witch, my lady, why couldn't you have fought them with magic instead of with a weapon? Thrown fire at them, or turned them into frogs, or struck them blind..."

She had struck them blind, in a sense, she thought wryly—at least until he shouted.

But she only said, "Because I cannot."

"For reasons of honor?" he asked dubiously. "Because there are some situations in which honor cannot apply..."

"No." She glanced sidelong at him through the astonishing curtains of her loosened hair. "It is just that my magic is not that strong."

And she nudged her horse into a quicker walk, passing into the vaporous shadows of the forest's bare, overhanging boughs.

Even after all these years of knowing it, she found the admission still stuck in her throat. She had come to terms with her lack of beauty, but never with her lack of genius in the single thing she had ever wanted. The most she had ever been able to do was to pretend that she accepted it, as she pretended now.

Ground fog curled around the feet of the horses; through the clammy vapors, tree roots thrust from the roadbanks like the arms of half-buried corpses. The air here felt dense and smelled of mold, and now and then, from the woods above them, came the furtive crackle of dead leaves, as if the trees plotted among themselves in the fog.

"Did you—did you see him slay the dragon?" Gareth asked, after they had ridden in silence for some minutes. "Would you tell me about it? Aversin is the only living Dragonsbane—the only man who has slain a dragon. There are ballads about him everywhere, about his courage and his noble deeds . . . That's my hobby. Ballads, I mean, the ballads of Dragonsbanes, like Selkythar the White back in the reign of Ennyta the Good and Antara Warlady and her brother, during the Kinwars. They say her brother slew . . ." By the way he caught himself up Jenny guessed he could have gone on about the great Dragonsbanes of the past for hours, only someone had told him not to bore people with the subject. "I've always wanted to see such a thing—a true Dragonsbane—a glorious combat. His renown must cover him like a golden mantle."

And, rather to her surprise, he broke into a light, wavery tenor:

> Riding up the hillside gleaming,
> Like flame in the golden sunlight streaming;
> Sword of steel strong in hand,
> Wind-swift hooves spurning land,
> Tall as an angel, stallion-strong,
> Stern as a god, bright as song . . .
>
> In the dragon's shadow the maidens wept,
> Fair as lilies in darkness kept.
> 'I know him afar, so tall is he,
> His plumes as bright as the rage of the sea,'
> Spake she to her sister, 'fear no ill . . .'

Jenny looked away, feeling something twist inside inside her at the memory of the Golden Dragon of Wyr.

She remembered as if it were yesterday instead of ten

years ago the high-up flash of gold in the wan northern sky, the plunge of fire and shadow, the boys and girls screaming on the dancing floor at Great Toby. They were memories she knew should have been tinted only with horror; she was aware that she should have felt only gladness at the dragon's death. But stronger than the horror, the taste of nameless grief and desolation came back to her from those times, with the metallic stench of the dragon's blood and the singing that seemed to shiver the searing air . . .

Her heart felt sick within her. Coolly, she said, "For one thing, of the two children who were taken by the dragon, John only managed to get the boy out alive. I think the girl had been killed by the fumes in the dragon's lair. It was hard to tell from the state of the body. And if she hadn't been dead, I still doubt they'd have been in much condition to make speeches about how John looked, even if he had come riding straight up the hill—which of course he didn't."

"He didn't?" She could almost hear the shattering of some image, nursed in the boy's mind.

"Of course not. If he had, he would have been killed immediately."

"Then how . . ."

"The only way he could think of to deal with something that big and that heavily armored. He had me brew the most powerful poison that I knew of, and he dipped his harpoons in that."

"*Poison*?" Such foulness clearly pierced him to the heart. "*Harpoons?* Not a sword at all?"

Jenny shook her head, not knowing whether to feel amusement at the boy's disappointed expression, exasperation at the way he spoke of what had been for her and hundreds of others a time of sleepless, nightmare horror, or only a kind of elder-sisterly compassion for the naïveté that would consider taking a three-foot steel blade against twenty-five feet of spiked and flaming death. "No," she only said, "John came at it from the overhang of the gully in which it was laired—it wasn't a cave, by the way; there are no caves that large in these hills. He slashed its wings first, so that it couldn't take to the air and fall on him from above. He used poisoned harpoons to slow it down, but he finished it off with an ax."

"An *ax*?!" Gareth cried, utterly aghast. "That's—that's the most horrible thing I've ever heard! Where is the glory in that? Where is the honor? It's like hamstringing your opponent in a duel! It's cheating!"

"He wasn't fighting a duel," Jenny pointed out. "If a dragon gets into the air, the man fighting it is lost."

"But it's dishonorable!" the boy insisted passionately, as if that were some kind of clinching argument.

"It might have been, had he been fighting a man who had honorably challenged him—something John has never been known to do in his life. Even fighting bandits, it pays to strike from behind when one is outnumbered. As the only representative of the King's law in these lands, John generally *is* outnumbered. A dragon is upward of twenty feet long and can kill a man with a single blow of its tail. You said yourself," she added with a smile, "that there are situations in which honor does not apply."

"But that's different!" the boy said miserably and lapsed into disillusioned silence.

The ground beneath the horses' feet was rising; the vague walls of the misty tunnel through which they rode were ending. Beyond, the silvery shapes of the round-backed hills could be dimly seen. As they came clear of the trees, the winds fell upon them, clearing the mists and nipping their clothes and faces like ill-trained dogs. Shaking the blowing handfuls of her hair out of her eyes, Jenny got a look at Gareth's face as he gazed about him at the moors. It wore a look of shock, disappointment, and puz-

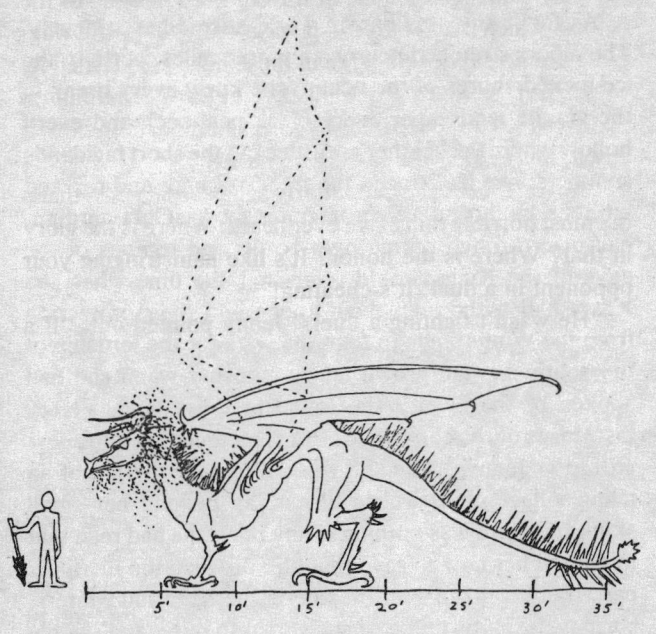

Scale and Structure of a Dragon
(From John Aversin's notes)

1) Mane structure and spikes at joints are thicker than shown. A bone "shield" extends from the back of the skull beneath the mane to protect the nape of the neck.

2) Golden Dragon of Wyr measured approx. 27′ of which 12′ was tail; there are rumors of dragons longer than 50′

zlement, as if he had never thought to find his hero in this bleak and trackless world of moss, water, and stone.

As for Jenny, this barren world stirred her strangely. The moors stretched nearly a hundred miles, north to the ice-locked shores of the ocean; she knew every break in the granite landscape, every black peat-beck and every hollow where the heather grew thick in the short highlands summers; she had traced the tracks of hare and fox and kitmouse in three decades of winter snows. Old Caerdinn, half-mad through poring over books and legends of the days of the Kings, could remember the time when the Kings had withdrawn their troops and their protection from the Winterlands to fight the wars for the lordship of the south; he had grown angry with her when she had spoken of the beauty she found in those wild, silvery fastnesses of rock and wind. But sometimes his bitterness stirred in Jenny, when she worked to save the life of an ailing village child whose illness lay beyond her small skills and there was nothing in any book she had read that might tell her how to save that life; or when the Iceriders came raiding down over the floe-ice in the brutal winters, burning the barns that cost such labor to raise, and slaughtering the cattle that could only be bred up from such meager stock. However, her own lack of power had taught her a curious appreciation for small joys and hard beauties and for the simple, changeless patterns of life and death. It was nothing she could have explained; not to Caerdinn, nor to this boy, nor to anyone else.

At length she said softly, "John would never have gone after the dragon, Gareth, had he not been forced to it. But as Thane of Alyn Hold, as Lord of Wyr, he is the only man in the Winterlands trained to and living by the arts of war. It is for this that he is the lord. He fought the dragon as he would have fought a wolf, as a vermin which was harming his people. He had no choice."

"But a dragon isn't vermin!" Gareth protested. "It is

the most honorable and greatest of challenges to the manhood of a true knight. You must be wrong! He *couldn't* have fought it simply—simply out of *duty*. He *can't* have!"

There was a desperation to believe in his voice that made Jenny glance over at him curiously. "No," she agreed. "A dragon isn't vermin. And this one was truly beautiful." Her voice softened at the recollection, even through the horror-haze of death and fear, of its angular, alien splendor. "Not golden, as your song calls it, but a sort of amber, grading to brownish smoke along its back and ivory upon its belly. The patterns of the scales on its sides were like the beadwork on a pair of slippers, like woven irises, all shades of purple and blue. Its head was like a flower, too; its eyes and maw were surrounded with scales like colored ribbons, with purple horns and tufts of white and black fur, and with antennae like a crayfish's tipped with bobs of gems. It was butcher's work to slay it."

They rounded the shoulder of a tor. Below them, like a break in the cold granite landscape, spread a broken line of brown fields where the mists lay like stringers of dirty wool among the stubble of harvest. A little further along the track lay a hamlet, disordered and trashy under a bluish smear of woodsmoke, and the stench of the place rose on the whipping ice-winds: the lye-sting of soap being boiled; an almost-visible murk of human and animal waste; the rotted, nauseating sweetness of brewing beer. The barking of dogs rose to them like churchbells in the air. In the midst of it all a stumpy tower stood, the tumbledown remnant of some larger fortification.

"No," said Jenny softly, "the dragon was a beautiful creature, Gareth. But so was the girl it carried away to its lair and killed. She was fifteen—John wouldn't let her parents see the remains."

She touched her heels to Moon Horse's sides and led the way down the damp clay of the track.

* * *

"Is this village where you live?" Gareth asked, as they drew near the walls.

Jenny shook her head, drawing her mind back from the bitter and confusing tangle of the memories of the slaying of the dragon. "I have my own house about six miles from here, on Frost Fell—I live there alone. My magic is not great; it needs silence and solitude for its study." She added wryly, "Though I don't have much of either. I am midwife and healer for all of Lord Aversin's lands."

"Will—will we reach his lands soon?"

His voice sounded unsteady, and Jenny, regarding him worriedly, saw how white he looked and how, in spite of the cold, sweat ran down his hollow cheeks with their faint fuzz of gold. A little surprised at his question, she said, "These are Lord Aversin's lands."

He raised his head to look at her, shocked. *"These?"* He stared around him at the muddy fields, the peasants shouting to one another as they shocked up the last of the corn, the ice-scummed waters of the moat that girdled the rubble fill and fieldstone patches of the shabby wall. "Then—that is one of Lord Aversin's villages?"

"That," Jenny said matter-of-factly as the hooves of their horses rumbled hollowly on the wood of the drawbridge, "is Alyn Hold."

The town huddled within the curtain wall—a wall built by the present lord's grandfather, old James Standfast, as a temporary measure and now hoary with fifty winters— was squalid beyond description. Through the archway beneath the squat gatehouse untidy houses were visible, clustered around the wall of the Hold itself as if the larger building had seeded them, low-built of stone and rubble upon the foundations of older walls, thatched with river reed-straw and grubby with age. From the window-turret of the gatehouse old Peg the gatekeeper stuck her head out, her long, gray-streaked brown braids hanging down like bights of half-unraveled rope, and she called out to Jenny, "You're in luck," in the glottal lilt of the north-country speech. "Me lord got in last night from ridin' the bounds. He'll be about."

"She wasn't—was she talking about *Lord Aversin?*" Gareth whispered, scandalized.

Jenny's crescent-shaped eyebrows quirked upward. "He's the only lord we have."

"Oh." He blinked, making another mental readjustment. "'Riding the bounds'?"

"The bounds of his lands. He patrols them, most days of the month, he and militia volunteers." Seeing Gareth's face fall, she added gently, "That is what it is to be a lord."

"It isn't, you know," Gareth said. "It is chivalry, and honor, and..." But she had already ridden past him, out of the slaty darkness of the gatehouse passage and into the heatless sunlight of the square.

With all its noise and gossipy squalor, Jenny had always liked the village of Alyn. It had been the home of her childhood; the stone cottage in which she had been born and in which her sister and brother-in-law still lived—though her sister's husband discouraged mention of the relationship—still stood down the lane, against the curtain wall. They might regard her with awe, these hard-working people with their small lives circumscribed by the work of the seasons, but she knew their lives only a little less intimately than she knew her own. There was not a house in the village where she had not delivered a child, or tended the sick, or fought death in one of the myriad forms that it took in the Winterlands; she was familiar with them, and with the long-spun, intricate patterns of their griefs and joys. As the horses sloshed through mud and standing water to the center of the square, she saw Gareth looking about him with carefully concealed dismay at the pigs and chickens that shared the fetid lanes

so amicably with flocks of shrieking children. A gust of
wind blew the smoke of the forge over them, and with it
a faint wash of heat and a snatch of Muffle the smith's
bawdy song; in one lane laundry flapped, and in another,
Deshy Werville, whose baby Jenny had delivered three
months ago, was milking one of her beloved cows half-
in, half-out of her cottage door. Jenny saw how Gareth's
disapproving gaze lingered upon the shabby Temple, with
its lumpish, crudely carved images of the Twelve Gods,
barely distinguishable from one another in the gloom, and
then went to the circled cross of Earth and Sky that was
wrought into the stones of so many village chimneys. His
back got a little stiffer at this evidence of paganism, and
his upper lip appeared to lengthen as he regarded the
pigpen built out from the Temple's side and the pair of
yokels in scruffy leather and plaids who leaned against
the railings, gossiping.

"Course, pigs see the weather," one of them was saying, reaching with a stick across the low palings to scratch
the back of the enormous black sow who reposed within.
"That's in Clivy's *On Farming*, but I've seen them do it.
And they're gie clever, cleverer than dogs. My aunt
Mary—you remember Aunt Mary?—used to train them
as piglets and she had one, a white one, who'd fetch her
shoes for her."

"Aye?" the second yokel said, scratching his head as
Jenny drew rein near them, with Gareth fidgeting impatiently at her side.

"Aye." The taller man made kissing sounds to the sow,
who raised her head in response with a slurping grunt of
deepest affection. "It says in Polyborus' *Analects* that the
Old Cults used to worship the pig, and not as a devil,
either, as Father Hiero would have it, but as the Moon
Goddess." He pushed his steel-rimmed spectacles a little
higher on the bridge of his long nose, a curiously profes-
sorial gesture for a man ankle-deep in pig-muck.

"That a fact, now?" the second yokel said with interest. "Now you come to speak on it, this old girl—when she were young and flighty, that is—had it figured to a *T* how to get the pen gate open, and would be after . . . Oh!" He bowed hastily, seeing Jenny and the fuming Gareth sitting their horses quietly.

The taller of the two men turned. As the brown eyes behind the thick spectacle lenses met Jenny's, they lost their habitual guarded expression and melted abruptly into an impish brightness. Middle-sized, unprepossessing, shaggy and unshaven in his scruffy dark leather clothing, his old wolfskin doublet patched with bits of metal and scraps of chain mail to protect his joints—after ten years, she wondered, what was there about him that still filled her with such absurd joy?

"Jen." He smiled and held out his hands to her.

Taking them, she slid from the white mare's saddle into his arms, while Gareth looked on in disapproving impatience to get on with his quest. "John," she said, and turned back to the boy. "Gareth of Magloshaldon—this is Lord John Aversin, the Dragonsbane of Alyn Hold."

For one instant, Gareth was shocked absolutely speechless. He sat for a moment, staring, stunned as if struck over the head; then he dismounted so hastily that he clutched his hurt arm with a gasp. It was as if, Jenny thought, in all his ballad-fed fantasies of meeting the Dragonsbane, it had never occurred to him that his hero would be afoot, not to say ankle-deep in mud beside the local pigsty. In his face was plain evidence that, though he himself was over six-foot-three, and must be taller than anyone else he knew, he had never connected this with the fact that, unless his hero was a giant, he would perforce be shorter also. Neither, she supposed, had any ballad mentioned spectacles.

Still Gareth had not spoken. Aversin, interpreting his silence and the look on his face with his usual fiendish accuracy, said, "I'd show you my dragon-slaying scars to prove it, but they're placed where I can't exhibit 'em in public."

It said worlds for Gareth's courtly breeding—and, Jenny supposed, the peculiar stoicism of courtiers—that, even laboring under the shock of his life and the pain of a wounded arm, he swept into a very creditable salaam of greeting. When he straightened up again, he adjusted the set of his cloak with a kind of sorry hauteur, pushed his bent spectacles a little more firmly up onto the bridge of his nose, and said in a voice that was shaky but oddly determined, "My lord Dragonsbane, I have ridden here on errantry from the south, with a message for you from the King, Uriens of Belmarie." He seemed to gather strength from these words, settling into the heraldic sonority of his ballad-snatch of golden swords and bright plumes in spite of the smell of the pigsty and the thin, cold rain that had begun to patter down.

"My lord Aversin, I have been sent to bring you south. A dragon has come and laid waste the city of the gnomes in the Deep of Ylferdun; it lairs there now, fifteen miles from the King's city of Bel. The King begs that you come to slay it ere the whole countryside is destroyed."

The boy drew himself up, having delivered himself of his quest, a look of noble and martyred serenity on his face, very like, Jenny thought, someone out of a ballad himself. Then, like all good messengers in ballads, he collapsed and slid to the soupy mud and cowpies in a dead faint.

CHAPTER II

RAIN DRUMMED STEADILY, drearily, on the walls of Alyn Hold's broken-down tower. The Hold's single guest room was never very bright; and, though it was only mid-afternoon, Jenny had summoned a dim ball of bluish witchfire to illuminate the table on which she had spread the contents of her medicine satchel; the rest of the little cubbyhole was curtained in shadow.

In the bed, Gareth dozed restlessly. The air was sweet with the ghosts of the long-dried fragrances of crushed herbs; the witchlight threw fine, close-grained shadows around the dessicated mummies of root and pod where they lay in the circles Jenny had traced. Slowly, rune by rune, she worked the healing spells over them, each with its own Limitation to prevent a too-quick healing that might harm the body as a whole, her fingers patiently tracing the signs, her mind calling down the qualities of the universe particular to each, like separate threads of unheard music. It was said that the great mages could see the power of the runes they wrought glowing like cold fire in the air above the healing powders and sense the touch of it like plasmic light drawn from the fingertips.

After long years of solitary meditation, Jenny had come to accept that, for her, magic was a depth and a stillness rather than the moving brilliance that it was for the great. It was something she would never quite become reconciled to, but at least it kept her from the resentment that would block what powers she did have. Within her narrow bounds, she knew she worked well.

The key to magic is magic, Caerdinn had said. To be a mage, you must be a mage. There is no time for anything else, if you will come to the fullness of your power.

So she had remained in the stone house on Frost Fell after Caerdinn had died, studying his books and measuring the stars, meditating in the crumbling circle of ancient standing stones that stood on the hillcrest above. Through the slow years her powers had grown with meditation and study, though never to what his had been. It was a life that had contented her. She had looked no further than the patient striving to increase her powers, while she healed others where she could and observed the turning of the seasons.

Then John had come.

The spells circled to their conclusion. For a time silence hung on the air, as if every hearth brick and rafter shadow, the fragrance of the applewood fire and the guttural trickle of the rain, had been preserved in amber for a thousand years. Jenny swept the spelled powders together into a bowl and raised her eyes. Gareth was watching her fearfully from the darkness of the curtained bed.

She got to her feet. As she moved toward him, he recoiled, his white face drawn with accusation and loathing. "You are his mistress!"

Jenny stopped, hearing the hatred in that weak voice. She said, "Yes. But it has nothing to do with you."

He turned his face away, fretful and still half-dreaming. "You are just like her," he muttered faintly. "Just like Zyerne . . ."

She stepped forward again, not certain she had heard clearly. "Who?"

"You've snared him with your spells—brought him down into the mud," the boy whispered and broke off with a feverish sob. Disregarding his repulsion, she came worriedly to his side, feeling his face and hands; after a moment, he ceased his feeble resistance, already sinking back to sleep. His flesh felt neither hot nor overly chilled; his pulse was steady and strong. But still he tossed and murmured, "Never—I never will. Spells—you have laid spells on him—made him love you with your witcheries..." His eyelids slipped closed.

Jenny sighed and straightened up, looking down into the flushed, troubled face. "If only I had laid spells on him," she murmured. "Then I could release us both— had I the courage."

She dusted her hands on her skirt and descended the narrow darkness of the turret stair.

She found John in his study—what would have been a fair-sized room, had it not been jammed to overflowing with books. For the most part, these were ancient volumes, left at the Hold by the departing armies or scavenged from the cellars of the burned-out garrison towns of the south; rat-chewed, black with mildew, unreadable with waterstains, they crammed every shelf of the labyrinth of planks that filled two walls and they spilled off to litter the long oak table and heaped the floor in the corners. Sheets of notes were interleaved among their pages and between their covers, copied out by John in the winter evenings. Among and between them were jumbled at random the tools of a scribe—prickers and quills, knives and inkpots, pumice stones—and stranger things besides: metal tubes and tongs, plumb-bobs and levels, burning-glasses and pendulums, magnets, the blown shells of eggs, chips of rock, dried flowers, and a half-disassembled clock. A vast spiderweb of hoists and pulleys occupied the rafters in one corner, and battalions of guttered and decaying candles angled along the edges of every shelf and sill. The room was a magpie-nest of picked-at knowledge, the lair of a tinkerer to whom the universe was one vast toyshop of intriguing side issues. Above the hearth, like a giant iron pinecone, hung the tail-knob of the dragon of Wyr—fifteen inches long and nine through, covered with stumpy, broken spikes.

John himself stood beside the window, gazing through the thick glass of its much-mended casement out over the barren lands to the north, where they merged with the bruised and tumbled sky. His hand was pressed to his side, where the rain throbbed in the ribs that the tail-knob had cracked.

Though the soft buckskin of her boots made no sound on the rutted stone of the floor, he looked up as she came in. His eyes smiled greeting into hers, but she only leaned her shoulder against the stone of the doorpost and asked, "Well?"

He glanced ceilingward where Gareth would be lying. "What, our little hero and his dragon?" A smile flicked the corners of his thin, sensitive mouth, then vanished like the swift sunlight of a cloudy day. "I've slain one dragon, Jen, and it bloody near finished me. Tempting as the promise is of getting more fine ballads written of my deeds, I think I'll pass this chance."

Relief and the sudden recollection of Gareth's ballad made Jenny giggle as she came into the room. The whitish light of the windows caught in every crease of John's leather sleeves as he stepped forward to meet her and bent to kiss her lips.

"Our hero never rode all the way north by himself, surely?"

Jenny shook her head. "He told me he took a ship from the south to Eldsbouch and rode east from there."

"He's gie lucky he made it that far," John remarked,

and kissed her again, his hands warm against her sides. "The pigs have been restless all day, carrying bits of straw about in their mouths—I turned back yesterday even from riding the bounds because of the way the crows were acting out on the Whin Hills. It's two weeks early for them, but it's in my mind this'll be the first of the winter storms. The rocks at Eldsbouch are shipeaters. You know, Dotys says in Volume Three of his *Histories*—or is it in that part of Volume Five we found at Ember?—or is it in Clivy?—that there used to be a mole or breakwater across the harbor there, back in the days of the Kings. It was one of the Wonders of the World, Dotys—or Clivy—says, but nowhere can I find any mention of the engineering of it. One of these days I'm minded to take a boat out there and see what I can find underwater at the harbor mouth . . ."

Jenny shuddered, knowing John to be perfectly capable of undertaking such an investigation. She had still not forgotten the stone house he had blown up, after reading in some moldering account about the gnomes using blasting powder to tunnel in their Deeps, nor his experiments with water pipes.

Sudden commotion sounded in the dark of the turret stair, treble voices arguing, "She is, too!" and "Let go!" A muted scuffle ensued, and a moment later a red-haired, sturdy urchin of four or so exploded into the room in a swirl of grubby sheepskin and plaids, followed immediately by a slender, dark-haired boy of eight. Jenny smiled and held out her arms to them both. They flung themselves against her; small, filthy hands clutched delightedly at her hair, her skirt, and the sleeves of her shift, and she felt again the surge of ridiculous and illogical delight at being in their presence.

"And how are my little barbarians?" she asked in her coolest voice, which fooled neither of them.

"Good—we been good, Mama," the older boy said,

clinging to the faded blue cloth of her skirt. "*I* been good— Adric hasn't."

"Have, too," retorted the younger one, whom John had lifted into his arms. "Papa had to whip Ian."

"Did he, now?" She smiled down into her older son's eyes, heavy-lidded and tip-tilted like John's, but as summer blue as her own. "He doubtless deserved it."

"With a big whip," Adric amplified, carried away with his tale. "A hundred cuts."

"Really?" She looked over at John with matter-of-fact inquiry in her expression. "All at one session, or did you rest in between?"

"One session," John replied serenely. "And he never begged for mercy even once."

"Good boy." She ruffled Ian's coarse black hair, and he twisted and giggled with pleasure at the solemn make-believe.

The boys had long ago accepted the fact that Jenny did not live at the Hold, as other boys' mothers lived with their fathers; the Lord of the Hold and the Witch of Frost Fell did not have to behave like other adults. Like puppies who tolerate a kennelkeeper's superintendence, the boys displayed a dutiful affection toward John's stout Aunt Jane, who cared for them and, she believed, kept them out of trouble while John was away looking after the lands in his charge and Jenny lived apart in her own house on the Fell, pursuing the solitudes of her art. But it was their father they recognized as their master, and their mother as their love.

They started to tell her, in an excited and not very coherent duet, about a fox they had trapped, when a sound in the doorway made them turn. Gareth stood there, looking pale and tired, but dressed in his own clothes again, bandages making an ungainly lump under the sleeve of his spare shirt. He'd dug an unbroken pair of spectacles from his baggage as well; behind the thick lenses, his eyes were filled with sour distaste and bitter disillusion as he looked at her and her sons. It was as if the fact that John and she had become lovers—that she had borne John's sons—had not only cheapened his erstwhile hero in his eyes, but had made her responsible for all those other disappointments that he had encountered in the Winterlands as well.

The boys sensed at once his disapprobation. Adric's pugnacious little jaw began to come forward in a miniature version of John's. But Ian, more sensitive, only signaled to his brother with his eyes, and the two took their silent leave. John watched them go; then his gaze returned, speculative, to Gareth. But all he said was, "So you lived, then?"

Rather shakily, Gareth replied, "Yes. Thank you—" He turned to Jenny, with a forced politeness that no amount of animosity could uproot from his courtier's soul. "Thank you for helping me." He took a step into the room and stopped again, staring blankly about him as he saw the place for the first time. Not something from a ballad, Jenny thought, amused in spite of herself. But then, no ballad could ever prepare anyone for John.

"Bit crowded," John confessed. "My dad used to keep the books that had been left at the Hold in the storeroom with the corn, and the rats had accounted for most of 'em before I'd learned to read. I thought they'd be safer here."

"Er . . ." Gareth said, at a loss. "I—I suppose . . ."

"He was a stiff-necked old villain, my dad," John went on conversationally, coming to stand beside the hearth and extend his hands to the fire. "If it hadn't been for old Caerdinn, who was about the Hold on and off when I was a lad, I'd never have got past the alphabet. Dad hadn't much use for written things—I found half an act of Luciard's *Firegiver* pasted over the cracks in the walls of the cupboard my granddad used to store winter clothes in. I could have gone out and thrown rocks at his grave,

I was that furious, because of course there's none of the play to be found now. God knows what they did with the rest of it—kindled the kitchen stoves, I expect. What we've managed to save isn't much—Volumes Three and Four of Dotys' *Histories*; most of Polyborus' *Analects* and his *Jurisprudence*; the *Elucidus Lapidarus*; Clivy's *On Farming*—in its entirety, for all that's worth, though it's pretty useless. I don't think Clivy was much of a farmer, or even bothered to talk to farmers. He says that you can tell the coming of storms by taking measurements of the clouds and their shadows, but the grannies round the villages say you can tell just watching the bees. And when he talks about the mating habits of pigs . . ."

"I warn you, Gareth," Jenny said with a smile, "that John is a walking encyclopedia of old wives' tales, granny-rhymes, snippets of every classical writer he can lay hands upon, and trivia gleaned from the far corners of the hollow earth—encourage him at your peril. He also can't cook."

"I can, though," John shot back at her with a grin.

Gareth, still gazing around him in mystification at the cluttered room, said nothing, but his narrow face was a study of mental gymnastics as he strove to adjust the ballads' conventionalized catalog of perfections with the reality of a bespectacled amateur engineer who collected lore about pigs.

"So, then," John went on in a friendly voice, "tell us of this dragon of yours, Gareth of Magloshaldon, and why the King sent a boy of your years to carry his message, when he's got warriors and knights that could do the job as well."

"Er . . ." Gareth looked completely taken aback for a moment—messengers in ballads never being asked for their credentials. "That is—but that's just it. He hasn't got warriors and knights, not that can be spared. And I came because I knew where to look for you, from the ballads."

He fished from the pouch at his belt a gold signet ring, whose bezel flashed in a spurt of yellow hearthlight—Jenny glimpsed a crowned king upon it, seated beneath twelve stars. John looked in silence at it for a moment, then bent his head and drew the ring to his lips with archaic reverence.

Jenny watched his action in silence. The King was the King, she thought. It was nearly a hundred years since he withdrew his troops from the north, leaving that to the barbarians and the chaos of lands without law. Yet John still regarded himself as the subject of the King.

It was something she herself had never understood—either John's loyalty to the King whose laws he still fought to uphold, or Caerdinn's sense of bitter and personal betrayal by those same Kings. To Jenny, the King was the ruler of another land, another time—she herself was a citizen only of the Winterlands.

Bright and small, the gold oval of the ring flashed as Gareth laid it upon the table, like a witness to all that was said. "He gave that to me when he sent me to seek you," he told them. "The King's champions all rode out against the dragon, and none of them returned. No one in the Realm has ever slain a dragon—nor even seen one up close to know how to attack it, really. And there is nothing to tell us. I know, I've looked, because it was the one useful thing that I *could* do. I know I'm not a knight, or a champion . . ." His voice stammered a little on the admission, breaking the armor of his formality. "I know I'm no good at sports. But I've studied all the ballads and all their variants, and no ballad really tells that much about the actual how-to of killing a dragon. We need a Dragonsbane," he concluded helplessly. "We need someone who knows what he's doing. We need your help."

"And we need yours." The light timbre of Aversin's smoky voice suddenly hardened to flint. "We've needed your help for a hundred years, while this part of the Realm, from the River Wildspae north, was being laid waste by bandits and Iceriders and wolves and worse things, things we haven't the knowledge anymore to deal with: marsh-devils and Whisperers and the evils that haunt the night woods, evils that steal the blood and souls of the living. Has your King thought of that? It's a bit late in the day for him to be asking favors of us."

The boy stared at him, stunned. "But the dragon..."

"Pox blister your dragon! Your King has a hundred knights and my people have only me." The light slid across the lenses of his specs in a flash of gold as he leaned his broad shoulders against the blackened stones of the chimney-breast, the spikes of the dragon's tail-knob gleaming evilly beside his head. "Gnomes never have just one entrance to their Deeps. Couldn't your King's knights have gotten the surviving gnomes to guide them through a secondary entrance to take the thing from behind?"

"Uh..." Visibly nonplussed by the unheroic practicality of the suggestion, Gareth floundered. "I don't think they could have. The rear entrance of the Deep is in the fortress of Halnath. The Master of Halnath—Polycarp, the King's nephew—rose in revolt against the King not long before the dragon's coming. The Citadel is under siege."

Silent in the corner of the hearth to which she had retreated, Jenny heard the sudden shift in the boy's voice, like the sound of a weakened foundation giving under strain. Looking up, she saw his too-prominent Adam's apple bob as he swallowed.

There was some wound there, she guessed to herself, some memory still tender to the touch.

"That's—that's one reason so few of the King's champions could be spared. It isn't only the dragon, you see." He leaned forward pleadingly. "The whole Realm is in danger from the rebels as well as the dragon. The Deep tunnels into the face of Nast Wall, the great mountain-ridge that divides the lowlands of Belmarie from the north-eastern Marches. The Citadel of Halnath stands on a cliff on the other side of the mountain from the main gates of the Deep, with the town and the University below it. The gnomes of Ylferdun were our allies against the rebels, but now most of them have gone over to the Halnath side. The whole Realm is split. You must come! As long as the dragon is in Ylferdun we can't keep the roads from the mountains properly guarded against the rebels, or send supplies to the besiegers of the Citadel. The King's champions went out..." He swallowed again, his voice tightening with the memory. "The men who brought back the bodies said that most of them never even got a chance to draw their swords."

"Gah!" Aversin looked away, anger and pity twisting his sensitive mouth. "Any fool who'd take a sword after a dragon in the first place..."

"But they didn't know! All they had to go on were the songs!"

Aversin said nothing to this; but, judging by his compressed lips and the flare of his nostrils, his thoughts were not pleasant ones. Gazing into the fire, Jenny heard his silence, and something like the chill shadow of a wind-driven cloud passed across her heart.

Half against her will, she saw images form in the molten amber of the fire's heart. She recognized the winter-colored sky above the gully, the charred and brittle spears of poisoned grass fine as needle-scratches against it, John standing poised on the gully's rim, the barbed steel rod of a harpoon in one gloved hand, an ax gleaming in his belt. Something rippled in the gully, a living carpet of golden knives.

Clearer than the sharp, small ghosts of the past that she saw was the shiv-twist memory of fear as she saw him jump.

They had been lovers then for less than a year, still

burningly conscious of one another's bodies. When he had sought the dragon's lair, more than anything else Jenny had been aware of the fragility of flesh and bone when it was pitted against steel and fire.

She shut her eyes; when she opened them again, the silken pictures were gone from the flame. She pressed her lips taut, forcing herself to listen without speaking, knowing it was and could be none of her affair. She could no more have told him not to go—not then, not now—than he could have told her to leave the stone house on Frost Fell and give up her seeking, to come to the Hold to cook his meals and raise his sons.

John was saying, "Tell me about this drake."

"You mean you'll come?" The forlorn eagerness in Gareth's voice made Jenny want to get up and box his ears.

"I mean I want to hear about it." The Dragonsbane came around the table and slouched into one of the room's big carved chairs, sliding the other in Gareth's direction with a shove of his booted foot. "How long ago did it strike?"

"It came by night, two weeks ago. I took ship three days later, from Claekith Harbor below the city of Bel. The ship is waiting for us at Eldsbouch."

"I doubt that." John scratched the side of his long nose with one scarred forefinger. "If your mariners were smart they'll have turned and run for a safe port two days ago. The storms are coming. Eldsbouch will be no protection to them."

"But they said they'd stay!" Gareth protested indignantly. "I paid them!"

"Gold will do them no good weighting their bones to the bottom of the cove," John pointed out.

Gareth sank back into his chair, shocked and cut to the heart by this final betrayal. "They can't have gone ..."

There was a moment's silence, while John looked down

at his hands. Without lifting her eyes from the heart of the fire, Jenny said softly, "They are not there, Gareth. I see the sea, and it is black with storms; I see the old harbor at Eldsbouch, the gray river running through the broken houses there; I see the fisher-folk making fast their little boats to the ruins of the old piers and all the stones shining under the rain. There is no ship there, Gareth."

"You're wrong," he said hopelessly. "You have to be wrong." He turned back to John. "It'll take us weeks to get back, traveling overland..."

"*Us?*" John said softly, and Gareth blushed and looked as frightened as if he had uttered mortal insult. After a moment John went on, "How big is this dragon of yours?"

Gareth swallowed again and drew his breath in a shaky sigh. "Huge," he said dully.

"How huge?"

Gareth hesitated. Like most people, he had no eye for relative size. "It must have been a hundred feet long. They say the shadow of its wings covered the whole of Deeping Vale."

"Who says?" John inquired, shifting his weight sideways in the chair and hooking a knee over the fornicating sea-lions that made up the left-hand arm. "I thought it came at night, and munched up anyone close enough to see it by day."

"Well..." He floundered in a sea of third-hand rumor.

"Ever see it on the ground?"

Gareth blushed and shook his head.

"It's gie hard to judge things in the air," John said kindly, pushing up his specs again. "The drake I slew here looked about a hundred feet long in the air, when I first saw it descending on the village of Great Toby. Turned out to be twenty-seven feet from beak to tail." Again his quick grin illuminated his usually expressionless face. "It comes of being a naturalist. The first thing we did, Jenny and I, when I was on my feet again after killing it, was to go out there with cleavers and see how the thing was put together, what there was left of it."

"It could be bigger, though, couldn't it?" Gareth asked. He sounded a little worried, as if, Jenny thought dryly, he considered a twenty-seven foot dragon somewhat paltry. "I mean, in the Greenhythe variant of the Lay of Selkythar Dragonsbane and the Worm of the Imperteng Wood, they say that the Worm was sixty feet long, with wings that would cover a battalion."

"Anybody measure it?"

"Well, they must have. Except—now that I come to think of it, according to that variant, when Selkythar had wounded it unto death the dragon fell into the River Wildspae; and in a later Belmarie version it says it fell into the sea. So I don't see how anyone could have."

"So a sixty-foot dragon is just somebody's measure of how great Selkythar was." He leaned back in his chair, his hands absentmindedly tracing over the lunatic carvings—the mingled shapes of all the creatures of the Book of Beasts. The worn gilding still caught in the chinks flickered with a dull sheen in the stray glints of the fire. "Twenty-seven feet doesn't sound like a lot, 'til it's there spitting fire at you. You know their flesh will decompose almost as soon as they die? It's as if their own fire consumes them, as it does everything else."

"Spitting fire?" Gareth frowned. "All the songs say they breathe it."

Aversin shook his head. "They sort of spit it—it's liquid fire, and nearly anything it touches'll catch. That's the trick in fighting a dragon, you see—to stay close enough to its body that it won't spit fire at you for fear of burning itself, and not get rolled on or cut to pieces with its scales whilst you're about it. They can raise the scales along their sides like a blowfish bristling, and they're edged like razors."

"I never knew that," Gareth breathed. Wonder and curiosity lessened, for a moment, the shell of his offended dignity and pride.

"Well, the pity of it is, probably the King's champions didn't either. God knows, I didn't when I went after the dragon in the gorge. There was nothing about it in any book I could find—Dotys and Clivy and them. Only a few old granny-rhymes that mention dragons—or drakes or worms, they're called—and they weren't much help. Things like:

> "Cock by its feet, horse by its hame,
> Snake by its head, drake by its name.

"Or what Polyborus had in his *Analects* about certain villages believing that if you plant loveseed—those creeper-things with the purple trumpet-flowers on them—around your house, dragons won't come near. Jen and I used bits of that kind of lore—Jen brewed a poison from the loveseed to put on my harpoons, because it was obvious on the face of it that no fiddling little sword was going to cut through those scales. And the poison did slow the thing down. But I don't know near as much about them as I'd like."

"No." Jenny turned her eyes at last from the fire's throbbing core and, resting her cheek upon her hand where it lay on her up-drawn knees, regarded the two men on either side of the book-cluttered table. She spoke softly, half to herself. "We know not where they come from, nor where they breed; why of all the beasts of the earth they have six limbs instead of four..."

"'Maggots from meat,'" quoted John, "'weevils from rye, dragons from stars in an empty sky.' That's in Terens' *Of Ghosts.* Or Caerdinn's 'Save a dragon, slave a dragon.' Or why they say you should never look into a dragon's eyes—and I'll tell you, Gar, I was gie careful not to do that. We don't even know simple things, like why magic and illusion won't work on them; why Jen couldn't call the dragon's image in that jewel of hers, or use a cloaking-spell against his notice—nothing."

"Nothing," Jenny said softly, "save how they died, slain by men as ignorant of them as we."

John must have heard the strange sorrow that underlay her voice, for she felt his glance, worried and questioning. But she turned her eyes away, not knowing the answer to what he asked.

After a moment, John sighed and said to Gareth, "It's all knowledge that's been lost over the years, like Luciard's *Firegiver* and how they managed to build a breakwater across the harbor mouth at Eldsbouch—knowledge that's been lost and may never be recovered."

He got to his feet and began to pace restlessly, the flat, whitish gray reflections from the window winking on spike and mail-scrap and the brass of dagger-hilt and buckle. "We're living in a decaying world, Gar; things slipping away day by day. Even you, down south in Bel—you're losing the Realm a piece at a time, with the Winterlands tearing off in one direction and the rebels pulling away the Marches in another. You're losing what you had and don't even know it, and all that while knowledge is leaking out the seams, like meal from a ripped bag, because there isn't time or leisure to save it.

"I would never have slain the dragon, Gar—slay it, when we know nothing about it? And it was beautiful in itself, maybe the most beautiful thing I've ever laid eyes on, every color of it perfect as sunset, like a barley field in certain lights you get on summer evenings."

"But you must—you have to slay ours!" There was sudden agony in Gareth's voice.

"Fighting it and slaying it are two different things." John turned back from the window, his head tipped slightly to one side, regarding the boy's anxious face. "And I haven't yet said I'd undertake the one, let alone accomplish the other."

"But you have to." The boy's voice was a forlorn whisper of despair. "You're our only hope."

"Am I?" the Dragonsbane asked gently. "I'm the only hope of all these villagers, through the coming winter, against wolves and bandits. It was because I was their only hope that I slew the most perfect creature I'd ever seen, slew it dirtily, filthily, chopping it to pieces with an ax—it was because I was their only hope that I fought it at all and near had my flesh shredded from my bones by it. I'm only a man, Gareth."

"No!" the boy insisted desperately. "You're the Dragonsbane—the only Dragonsbane!" He rose to his feet, some inner struggle plain upon his thin features, his breathing fast as if forcing himself to some exertion. "The King..." He swallowed hard. "The King told me to make whatever terms I could, to bring you south. If you come..." With an effort he made his voice steady. "If you come, we will send troops again to protect the northlands, to defend them against the Iceriders; we will send books, and scholars, to bring knowledge to the people again. I swear it." He took up the King's seal and held it out in his trembling palm, and the cold daylight flashed palely across its face. "In the King's name I swear it."

But Jenny, watching the boy's white face as he spoke, saw that he did not meet John's eyes.

As night came on the rain increased, the wind throwing it like sea-breakers against the walls of the Hold. John's Aunt Jane brought up a cold supper of meat, cheese, and beer, which Gareth picked at with the air of one doing his duty. Jenny, sitting cross-legged in the corner of the hearth, unwrapped her harp and experimented with its tuning pegs while the men spoke of the roads that led south, and of the slaying of the Golden Dragon of Wyr.

"That's another thing that wasn't like the songs," Gareth said, resting his bony elbows amid the careless scatter of John's notes on the table. "In the songs the dragons are all gay-colored, gaudy. But this one is black, dead-black all over save for the silver lamps of its eyes."

"Black," repeated John quietly, and looked over at Jenny. "You had an old list, didn't you, love?"

She nodded, her hands resting in the delicate maneuverings of the harp pegs. "Caerdinn had me memorize many old lists," she explained to Gareth. "Some of them he told me the meaning of—this one he never did. Perhaps he didn't know himself. It was names, and colors . . ." She closed her eyes and repeated the list, her voice falling into the old man's singsong chant, the echo of dozens of voices, back through the length of years. "Teltrevir heliotrope; Centhwevir is blue knotted with gold; Astirith is primrose and black; Morkeleb alone, black as night . . . The list goes on—there were dozens of names, if names they are." She shrugged and linked her fingers over the curve of the harp's back. "But John tells me that the old dragon that was supposed to haunt the shores of the lake of Wevir in the east was said to have been blue as the waters, marked all over his back with patterns of gold so that he could lie beneath the surface of the lake in summer and steal sheep from the banks."

"Yes!" Gareth almost bounced out of his chair with enthusiasm as he recognized the familiar tale. "And the Worm of Wevir was slain by Antara Warlady and her brother Darthis Dragonsbane in the last part of the reign of Yvain the Well-Beloved, who was . . ." He caught himself up again, suddenly embarrassed. "It's a popular tale," he concluded, red-faced.

Jenny hid her smile at the abrupt checking of his ebullience. "There were notes for the harp as well—not tunes, really. He whistled them to me, over and over, until I got them right."

She put her harp to her shoulder, a small instrument that had also been Caerdinn's, though he had not played it; the wood was darkened almost black with age. By daylight it appeared perfectly unadorned, but when fire-light glanced across it, as it did now, the circles of the air and sea were sometimes visible, traced upon it in faded gold. Carefully, she picked out those strange, sweet knots of sound, sometimes two or three notes only, sometimes a string of them like a truncated air. They were individual in the turns of their timing, hauntingly half-familiar, like things remembered from childhood; and as she played she repeated the names: Teltrevir heliotrope, Centhwevir is blue knotted with gold ... It was part of the lost knowledge, like that from John's scatterbrained, jackdaw quest in the small portion of his time not taken up with the brutal demands of the Winterlands. Notes and words were meaningless now, like a line from a lost ballad, or a few torn pages from the tragedy of an exiled god, pasted to keep wind from a crack—the echoes of songs that would not be heard again.

From them her hands moved on, random as her passing thoughts. She sketched vagrant airs, or snatches of jigs and reels, slowed and touched with the shadow of an inevitable grief that waited in the hidden darkness of future time. Through them she moved to the ancient tunes that held the timeless pull of the ocean in their cadences; sorrows that drew the heart from the body, or joys that called the soul like the distant glitter of stardust banners in the summer night. In time John took from its place in a hole by the hearth a tin pennywhistle, such as children played in the streets, and joined its thin, bright music to hers, dancing around the shadowed beauty of the harp like a thousand-year-old child.

Music answered music, joining into a spell-circle that banished, for a time, the strange tangle of fear and grief and dragonfire in Jenny's heart. Whatever would come to pass, this was what they were and had now. She tossed back the cloudy streams of her hair and caught the bright flicker of Aversin's eyes behind his thick spectacles, the pennywhistle luring the harp out of its sadness and into dance airs wild as hay-harvest winds. As the evening deepened, the Hold folk drifted up to the study to join them, sitting where they could on the floor or the hearth or in the deep embrasures of the windows: John's Aunt Jane and Cousin Dilly and others of the vast tribe of his female relatives who lived at the Hold; Ian and Adric; the fat, jovial smith Muffle; all part of the pattern of the life of the Winterlands that was so dull-seeming at first, but was in truth close-woven and complex as its random plaids. And among them Gareth sat, ill at ease as a bright southern parrot in a rookery. He kept looking about him with puzzled distaste in the leaping restlessness of the red firelight that threw into momentary brightness the moldery rummage of decaying books, of rocks and chemical experiments, and that glowed in the children's eyes and made amber mirrors of the dogs'—wondering, Jenny thought, how a quest as glorious as his could possibly have ended in such a place.

And every now and then, she noticed, his eyes returned to John. There was in them not only anxiety, but a kind of nervous dread, as if he were haunted by a gnawing guilt for something he had done, or something he knew he must yet do.

"Will you go?" Jenny asked softly, much later in the night, lying in the warm nest of bearskins and patchwork with her dark hair scattered like sea-wrack over John's breast and arm.

"If I slay his dragon for him, the King will have to listen to me," John said reasonably. "If I come at his calling, I must be his subject, and if I am—we are—his subjects, as King he owes us the protection of his troops.

If I'm not his subject..." He paused, as he thought over what his next words would mean about the Law of the Realm for which he had so long fought. He sighed and let the thought go.

For a time the silence was broken only by the groan of wind in the tower overhead and the drumming of the rain on the walls. But even had she not been able to see, catlike, in the dark, Jenny knew John did not sleep. There was a tension in all his muscles, and the uneasy knowledge of how narrow had been the margin between living and dying, when he had fought the Golden Dragon of Wyr. Her hand under his back could still feel the rucked, hard ridges of scar.

"Jenny," he said at last, "my father told me that his dad used to be able to raise four and five hundred of militia when the Iceriders came. They fought pitched battles on the edge of the northern ocean and marched in force to break the strongholds of the bandit-kings that used to cover the eastward roads. When that band of brigands attacked Far West Riding the year before last, do you remember how many men we could come up with, the mayor of Riding, the mayor of Toby, and myself among us? Less than a hundred, and twelve of those we lost in that fight."

As he moved his head, the banked glow of the hearth on the other side of the small sanctum of their bedchamber caught a thread of carnelian from the shoulder-length mop of his hair. "Jen, we can't go on like this. You know we can't. We're weakening all the time. The lands of the King's law, the law that keeps the stronger from enslaving the weaker, are shrinking away. Every time a farm is wiped out by wolves or brigands or Iceriders, it's one less shield in the wall. Every time some family ups and goes south to indenture themselves as serfs there, always provided they make it that far, it weakens those of us that are left. And the law itself is waning, as fewer and fewer people even know why there is law. Do you realize that because I've read a handful of volumes of Dotys and whatever pages of Polyborus' *Jurisprudence* I could find stuck in the cracks of the tower I'm accounted a scholar? We need the help of the King, Jen, if we're not to be feeding on one another within a generation. I can buy them that help."

"With what?" asked Jenny softly. "The flesh off your bones? If you are killed by the dragon, what of your people then?"

Beneath her cheek she felt his shoulder move. "I could be killed by wolves or bandits next week—come to that, I could fall off old Osprey and break my neck." And when she chuckled, unexpectedly amused at that, he added in an aggrieved voice, "It's exactly what my father did."

"Your father knew no better than to ride drunk." She smiled a little in spite of herself. "I wonder what he would have made of our young hero?"

John laughed in the darkness. "Gaw, he'd have eaten him for breakfast." Seventeen years, ten of which had been spent knowing Jenny, had finally given him a tolerance of the man he had grown up hating. Then he drew her closer and kissed her hair. When he spoke again, his voice was quiet. "I have to do it, Jen. I won't be gone long."

A particularly fierce gust of wind shivered in the tower's ancient bones, and Jenny drew the worn softness of quilts and furs up over her bare shoulders. A month, perhaps, she calculated; maybe a little more. It would give her a chance to catch up on her neglected meditations, to pursue the studies that she too often put aside these days, to come to the Hold to be with him and their sons.

To be a mage you must be a mage, Caerdinn had said. *Magic is the only key to magic.* She knew that she was not the mage that he had been, even when she had known him first, when he was in his eighties and she a skinny, wretched, ugly girl of fourteen. She sometimes wondered whether it was because he had been so old, at the end of his strength, when he came to teach her, the last of his pupils, or because she was simply not very good. Lying awake in the darkness, listening to the wind or to the terrible greatness of the moor silence which was worse, she sometimes admitted the truth to herself—that what she gave to John, what she found herself more and more giving to those two little boys snuggled together like puppies upstairs, she took from the strength of her power.

All that she had, to divide between her magic and her love, was time. In a few years she would be forty. For ten years she had scattered her time, sowing it broadcast like a farmer in summer sunshine, instead of hoarding it and pouring it back into meditation and magic. She moved her head on John's shoulder, and the warmth of their long friendship was in the tightening of his arm around her. Had she forgone this, she wondered, would she be as powerful as Caerdinn had once been? As powerful as she sometimes felt she could be, when she meditated among the stones on her lonely hill?

She would have that time, with her mind undistracted, time to work and strive and study. The snow would be deep by the time John returned.

If he returned.

The shadow of the dragon of Wyr seemed to cover her again, blotting the sky as it swooped down like a hawk over the autumn dance floor at Great Toby. The sickening jam of her heart in her throat came back to her, as John ran forward under that descending shadow, trying to reach the terrified gaggle of children cowering in the center of the floor. The metallic stink of spat fire seemed to burn again in her nostrils, the screams echoing in her ears . . .

Twenty-seven feet, John had said. What it meant was that from the top of the dragon's shoulder to the ground was the height of a man's shoulder, and half again that to the top of its tall haunches, backed by all that weight and strength and speed.

And for no good reason she could think of, she remembered the sudden shift of the boy Gareth's eyes.

After a long time of silence she said, "John?"

"Aye, love?"

"I want to go with you, when you ride south."

She felt the hardening of the muscles of his body. It was nearly a full minute before he answered her, and she could hear in his voice the struggle between what he wanted and what he thought might be best. "You've said yourself it'll be a bad winter, love. I'm thinking one or the other of us should be here."

He was right, and she knew it. Even the coats of her cats were thick this fall. A month ago she had been troubled to see how the birds were departing, early and swiftly, anxious to be gone. The signs pointed to famine and sleet, and on the heels of those would come barbarian raids from across the ice-locked northern sea.

And yet, she thought . . . and yet . . . Was this the weakness of a woman who does not want to be parted from the man she loves, or was it something else? Caerdinn would have said that love clouded the instincts of a mage.

"I think I should go with you."

"You think I can't handle the dragon myself?" His voice was filled with mock indignation.

"Yes," Jenny said bluntly, and felt the ribs vibrate under her hand with his laughter. "I don't know under what circumstances you'll be meeting it," she went on. "And there's more than that."

His voice was thoughtful in the darkness, but not surprised. "It strikes you that way too, does it?"

That was something people tended not to notice about John. Behind his facade of amiable barbarism, behind his frivolous fascination with hog-lore, granny-rhymes, and how clocks were made lurked an agile mind and an almost feminine sensitivity to nuances of situations and relationships. There was not much that he missed.

"Our hero has spoken of rebellion and treachery in the south," she said. "If the dragon has come, it will ruin the harvest, and rising bread-prices will make the situation worse. I think you'll need someone there whom you can trust."

"I've been thinking it, too," he replied softly. "Now, what makes you think I won't be able to trust our Gar? I doubt he'd betray me out of pique that the goods aren't as advertised."

Jenny rolled up onto her elbows, her dark hair hanging in a torrent down over his breast. "No," she said slowly, and tried to put her finger on what it was that troubled her about that thin, earnest boy she had rescued in the ruins of the old town. At length, she said, "My instincts tell me he can be trusted, at heart. But he's lying about something, I don't know what. I think I should go with you to the south."

John smiled and drew her down to him again. "The last time I went against your instincts, I was that sorry," he said. "Myself, I'm torn, for I can smell there's going to be danger here later in the winter. But I think you're right. I don't understand why the King would have given his word and his seal into the keeping of the likes of our young hero, who by the sound of it has never done more than collect ballads in all his life, and not to some proven warrior. But if the King's pledged his word to aid us, then I'd be a fool not to take the chance to pledge mine. Just the fact that there's only the two of us, Jen, shows how close to the edge of darkness all this land lies. Besides," he added, sudden worry in his voice, "you've got to come."

Her thoughts preoccupied by her nameless forebodings, Jenny turned her head quickly. "What is it? Why?"

"We'll need someone to do the cooking."

With a cat-swift move she was on top of him, smothering his face under a pillow, but she was laughing too much to hold him. They tussled, giggling, their struggles blending into lovemaking. Later, as they drifted in the warm aftermath, Jenny murmured, "You make me laugh at the strangest times."

He kissed her then and slept, but Jenny sank no further than the uneasy borderlands of half-dreams. She found herself standing once again on the lip of the gully, the heat from below beating at her face, the poisons scouring her lungs. In the drifting vapors below, the great shape was still writhing, heaving its shredded wings or clawing ineffectually with the stumps of its forelegs at the small figure braced like an exhausted woodcutter over its neck, a dripping ax in his blistered hands. She saw John moving mechanically, half-asphyxiated with the fumes and swaying from the loss of the blood that gleamed stickily on his armor. The small stream in the gully was clotted and red with the dragon's blood; gobbets of flesh choked it; the stones were blackened with the dragon's fire. The dragon kept raising its dripping head, trying to snap at John; even in her dream, Jenny felt the air weighted with the strange sensation of singing, vibrant with a music beyond the grasp of her ears and mind.

The singing grew stronger as she slid deeper into sleep. She saw against the darkness of a velvet sky the burning white disc of the full moon, her private omen of power, and before it the silver-silk flash of membranous wings.

She woke in the deep of the night. Rain thundered against the walls of the Hold, a torrent roaring in darkness. Beside her John slept, and she saw in the darkness what she had noticed that morning in daylight: that for all his thirty-four years, he had a thread or two of silver in his unruly brown hair.

A thought crossed her mind. She put it aside firmly, and just as firmly it reintruded itself. It was not a daylight thought, but the nagging whisper that comes only in the dark hours, after troubled sleep. Don't be a fool, she told herself; the times you have done it, you have always wished you hadn't.

But the thought, the temptation, would not go away.

At length she rose, careful not to wake the man who slept at her side. She wrapped herself in John's worn, quilted robe and padded from the bedchamber, the worn floor like smooth ice beneath her small, bare feet.

The study was even darker than the bedchamber had been, the fire there nothing more than a glowing line of rose-colored heat above a snowbank of ash. Her shadow passed like the hand of a ghost over the slumbering shape of the harp and made the sliver of reflected red wink along the pennywhistle's edge. At the far side of the study, she raised a heavy curtain and passed into a tiny room that was little more than a niche in the Hold's thick wall. Barely wider than its window, in daylight it was coolly bright, but now the heavy bull's-eye glass was black as ink, and the witchlight she called into being above her head glittered coldly on the rain streaming down outside.

The phosphorescent glow that illuminated the room outlined the shape of a narrow table and three small shelves. They held things that had belonged to the cold-eyed ice-witch who had been John's mother, or to Caerdinn—simple things, a few bowls, an oddly shaped root, a few crystals like fragments of broken stars sent for mending. Pulling her robe more closely about her, Jenny took from its place a plain pottery bowl, so old that whatever designs had once been painted upon its outer surface had long since been rubbed away by the touch of mages' hands. She dipped it into the stone vessel of water that stood in a corner and set it upon the table, drawing up before it a tall, spindle-legged chair.

For a time she only sat, gazing down into the water. Slips of foxfire danced on its black surface; as she slowed

her breathing, she became aware of every sound from the
roaring of the rain gusts against the tower's walls to the
smallest drip of the eaves. The worn tabletop was like
cold glass under her fingertips; her breath was cold against
her own lips. For a time she was aware of the small flaws
and bubbles in the glaze of the bowl's inner surface; then
she sank deeper, watching the colors that seemed to swirl
within the endless depths. She seemed to move down
toward an absolute darkness, and the water was like ink,
opaque, ungiving.

Gray mists rolled in the depths, then cleared as if wind
had driven them, and she saw darkness in a vast place,
pricked by the starlike points of candleflame. An open
space of black stone lay before her, smooth as oily water;
around it was a forest, not of trees, but of columns of
stone. Some were thin as silk, others thicker than the
most ancient of oaks, and over them swayed the shadows
of the dancers on the open floor. Though the picture was
silent, she could feel the rhythm to which they danced—
gnomes, she saw, their long arms brushing the floor as
they bent, the vast, cloudy manes of their pale hair catching rims of firelight like sunset seen through heavy smoke.
They danced around a misshapen stone altar, the slow
dances that are forbidden to the eyes of the children of
men.

The dream changed. She beheld a desolation of charred
and broken ruins beneath the dark flank of a tree-covered
mountain. Night sky arched overhead, wind-cleared and
heart-piercingly beautiful. The waxing moon was like a
glowing coin; its light touching with cold, white fingers
the broken pavement of the empty square below the hillside upon which she stood, edging the raw bones that
moldered in puddles of faintly smoking slime. Something
flashed in the velvet shadow of the mountain, and she
saw the dragon. Starlight gleamed like oil on the lean,

sable sides; the span of those enormous wings stretched for a moment like a skeleton's arms to embrace the moon's stern face. Music seemed to drift upon the night, a string of notes like a truncated air, and for an instant her heart leaped toward that silent, dangerous beauty, lonely and graceful in the secret magic of its gliding flight.

Then she saw another scene by the low light of a dying fire. She thought she was in the same place, on a rise overlooking the desolation of the ruined town before the gates of the Deep. It was the cold hour of the tide's ebbing, some hours before dawn. John lay near the fire, dark blood leaking from the clawed rents in his armor. His face was a mass of blisters beneath a mask of gore and grime; he was alone, and the fire was dying. Its light caught a spangle of red from the twisted links of his torn mail shirt and glimmered stickily on the upturned palm of one blistered hand. The fire died, and for a moment only starlight glittered on the pooling blood and outlined the shape of his nose and lips against the darkness.

She was underground once more, in the place where the gnomes had danced. It was empty now, but the hollow silences beneath the earth seemed filled with the inchoate murmur of formless sound, as if the stone altar whispered to itself in the darkness.

Then she saw only the small flaws in the glaze of the bowl, and the dark, oily surface of the water. The witchlight had long ago failed above her head, which ached as it often did when she had overstretched her power. Her body felt chilled through to the bones, but she was for a time too weary to move from where she sat. She stared before her into the darkness, listening to the steady drum of the rain, hurting in her soul and wishing with all that was in her that she had not done what she had done.

All divination was chancy, she told herself, and water

CHAPTER III

THEY SET FORTH two days later and rode south through a maelstrom of wind and water.

In the days of the Kings, the Great North Road had stretched from Bel itself northward like a gray stone serpent, through the valley of the Wildspae River and across the farm and forest lands of Wyr, linking the southern capital with the northern frontier and guarding the great silver mines of Tralchet. But the mines had flagged, and the Kings had begun to squabble with their brothers and cousins over the lordship of the south. The troops who guarded the Winterlands' forts had been withdrawn—temporarily, they said, to shore up the forces of one contender against another. They had never returned. Now the gray stone serpent was disintegrating slowly, like a shed skin; its stones were torn up to strengthen house walls against bandits and barbarians, its ditches choked with decades of detritus, and its very foundations forced apart by the encroaching tree roots of the forest of Wyr. The Winterlands had destroyed it, as they destroyed all things.

Traveling south along what remained of the road was

slow, for the autumn storms swelled the icy becks of the moors to white-toothed torrents and reduced the ground in the tree-tangled hollows to sodden, nameless mires. Under the flail of the wind, Gareth could no longer argue that the ship upon which he had come north would still be waiting at Eldsbouch to waft them south in relative comfort and speed, but Jenny suspected he still felt in his heart that it should have been, and, illogically, blamed her that it was not.

They rode for the most part in silence. Sometimes when they halted, as they frequently did for John to scout the tumbled rocks or dense knots of woodland ahead, Jenny looked across at Gareth and saw him gazing around him in a kind of hurt bewilderment at the desolation through which they rode: at the barren downs with their weed-grown lines of broken walls; at the old boundary stones, lumpish and melted-looking as spring snowmen; and at the stinking bogs or the high, bare tors with their few twisted trees, giant balls of mistletoe snagged weirdly in their naked branches against a dreary sky. It was a land that no longer remembered law or the prosperity of ordered living that comes with law, and sometimes she could see him struggling with the understanding of what John was offering to buy at the stake of his life.

But usually it was plain that Gareth simply found the halts annoying. "We're never going to get there at this rate," he complained as John appeared from the smoke-colored tangle of dead heather that cloaked the lower flanks of a promontory that hid the road. A watchtower had once crowned it, now reduced to a chewed-looking circle of rubble on the hill's crest. John had bellied up the slope to investigate it and the road ahead and now was shaking mud and wet out of his plaid. "It's been twenty days since the dragon came," Gareth added resentfully. "Anything can have happened."

"It can have happened the day after you took ship, my

hero," John pointed out, swinging up to the saddle of his spare riding horse, Cow. "And if we don't look sharp and scout ahead, we *are* never going to get there."

But the sullen glance the boy shot at John's back as he reined away told Jenny more clearly than words that, though he could not argue with this statement, he did not believe it, either.

That evening they camped in the ragged birches of the broken country where the downs gave place to the hoary densities of the Wyrwoods. When camp was set, and the horses and mules picketed, Jenny moved quietly along the edge of the clearing, the open ground above the high bank of a stream whose noisy rushing blended with the sea-sound of the wind in the trees. She touched the bark of the trees and the soggy mast of acorns, hazelnuts, and decaying leaves underfoot, tracing them with the signs that only a mage could see—signs that would conceal the camp from those who might pass by outside. Looking back toward the fluttering yellow light of the new fire, she saw Gareth hunkered down beside it, shivering in his damp cloak, looking wretched and very forlorn.

Her square, full lips pressed together. Since he had learned she was his erstwhile hero's mistress, he had barely spoken to her. His resentment at her inclusion in the expedition was still obvious, as was his unspoken assumption that she had included herself out of a combination of meddling and a desire not to let her lover out of her sight. But Gareth was alone in an alien land, having clearly never been away from the comforts of his home before, lonely, disillusioned, and filled with a gnawing fear of what he would return to find.

Jenny sighed and crossed the clearing to where he sat.

The boy looked up at her suspiciously as she dug into her jacket pocket and drew out a long sliver of smoky crystal on the chain that Caerdinn had used to hang around his neck. "I can't see the dragon in this," she said, "but if you'll tell me the name of your father and something about your home in Bel, at least I should be able to call their images and tell you if they're all right."

Gareth turned his face away from her. "No," he said. Then, after a moment, he added grudgingly, "Thank you all the same."

Jenny folded her arms and regarded him for a moment in the jumpy orange firelight. He huddled a little deeper into his stained crimson cloak and would not meet her eyes.

"Is it because you think I can't?" she asked at last. "Or because you won't take the aid of a witch?"

He didn't answer that, though his full lower lip pinched up a bit in the middle. With a sigh of exasperation, Jenny walked away from him to where John stood near the oil-skin-covered mound of the packs, looking out into the darkening woods.

He glanced back as she came near, the stray gleams of firelight throwing glints of dirty orange on the metal of his patched doublet. "D'you want a bandage for your nose?" he inquired, as if she'd tried to pet a ferret and gotten nipped for her trouble. She laughed ruefully.

"He didn't have any objections to me before," she said, more hurt than she had realized by the boy's enmity.

John put an arm around her and hugged her close. "He feels cheated, is all," he said easily. "And since God forbid he should have cheated himself with his expectations, it must have been one of us that did it, mustn't it?" He leaned down to kiss her, his hand firm against the bare nape of her neck beneath the coiled ridge of her braided hair. Beyond them, among the ghostly birches, the thin underbrush rustled harshly; a moment later a softer, steadier rushing whispered in the bare branches overhead. Jenny smelled the rain almost before she was conscious of its light fingers upon her face.

Behind them, she heard Gareth cursing. He squelched

across the clearing to join them a moment later, wiping raindroplets from his spectacles, his hair in lank strings against his temples.

"We seem to have outsmarted ourselves," he said glumly. "Picked a nice place to camp—only there's no shelter. There's a cave down under the cut of the streambank..."

"Above the highest rise of the water?" inquired John, a mischievous glint in his eye.

Gareth said defensively, "Yes. At least—it isn't so very far down the bank."

"Big enough to put the horses in, always supposing we could get them down there?"

The boy bristled. "I could go see."

"No," said Jenny. Gareth opened his mouth to protest this arbitrariness, but she cut him off with, "I've laid spells of ward and guard about this camp—I don't think they should be crossed. It's almost full-dark now..."

"But we'll get *wet*!"

"You've been wet for days, my hero," John pointed out with cheerful brutality. "Here at least we know we're safe from the side the stream's on—unless, of course, it rises over its bank." He glanced down at Jenny, still in the circle of his arm; she was conscious, too, of Gareth's sulky gaze. "What about the spell-ward, love?"

She shook her head. "I don't know," she said. "Sometimes the spells will hold against the Whisperers, sometimes they don't. I don't know why—whether it's because of something about the Whisperers, or because of something about the spells." Or because, she added to herself, her own powers weren't strong enough to hold even a true spell against them.

"Whisperers?" Gareth demanded incredulously.

"A kind of blood-devil," said John, with an edge of irritation in his voice. "It doesn't matter at the moment, my hero. Just stay inside the camp."

"Can't I even go *look* for shelter? I won't go far."

"If you leave the camp, you'll never find your way back to it," John snapped. "You're so bloody anxious not to lose time on this trip, you wouldn't want to have us spend the next three days looking for your body, would you? Come on, Jen—if you're not after making supper, I'll do it..."

"I'll do it, I'll do it," Jenny agreed, with a haste that wasn't entirely jest. As she and John walked back to the smoky, sheltered campfire, she glanced back at Gareth, still standing on the edge of the faintly gleaming spell-circle. His vanity stinging from John's last words, the boy picked up an acorn and hurled it angrily out into the wet darkness. The darkness whispered and rustled, and then fell still again under the ceaseless pattern of the rain.

They left the folded lands of rock hills and leaping streams for good after that and entered the ruinous gloom of the great Forest of Wyr. Here crowded oaks and haw-thorn pressed close upon the road, catching the faces of the travelers with warty, overhanging boughs and dirty moss and their horses' hooves with scabrous roots and soggy drifts of dead leaves. The black lattices of bare branches above them admitted only a fraction of the pallid daylight, but rain still leaked through, pattering in an end-less, dreary murmur in the dead fern and hazel thickets. The ground was worse here, sodden and unsteady, or flooded in meres of silver water in which the trees stood, knee-deep and rotting; and Aversin remarked that the marshes of the south were spreading again. In many places the road was covered, or blocked with fallen trees, and the labor of clearing it or beating a path through the thick-ets around these obstacles left them all cold and exhausted. Even for Jenny, used to the hardships of the Winterlands, this was tiring, and the more so because there was no respite; she lay down weary at night and rose weary in the bleak grayness before dawn to travel on once again.

What it was to Gareth she could well imagine. As he grew more weary, his temper shortened, and he complained bitterly at every halt.

"What's he looking for now?" he demanded one afternoon, when John ordered their fifth halt in three hours and, armed with his heavy horn hunting-bow, dismounted and vanished into the choking tangle of hazel and blackthorn beside the road.

It had been raining most of the forenoon, and the tall boy drooped miserably on the back of The Stupid Roan, one of the spare horses they'd brought from the Hold. The other spare, Jenny's mount, John had christened The Stupider Roan, a name that was unfortunately apt. Jenny suspected that, in his wearier moments, Gareth even blamed her for the generally poor quality of the Hold's horseflesh. The rain had ceased now, but cold wind still probed through the very weave of their garments; every now and then a gust shook the branches above them and splattered them with leftover rain and an occasional sodden oak leaf that drifted down like a dead bat.

"He's looking for danger." Jenny herself was listening, her nerves queerly on edge, searching the silence that hung like an indrawn breath among the dark, close-crowded trees.

"He didn't find any last time, did he?" Gareth tucked his gloved hands under his cloak for warmth and shivered. Then he looked ostentatiously upward, scanning what sky was visible, calculating the time of day, and from there going on to remember how many days they had been on the road. Under his sarcasm she could hear fear. "Or the time before that, either."

"And lucky for us that he didn't," she replied. "I think you have little understanding of the dangers in the Winterlands..."

Gareth gasped, and his gaze fixed. Turning her head quickly, Jenny followed his eyes to the dark shape of

Aversin, his plaids making him nearly invisible in the gloom among the trees. With a single slow movement he had raised his bow, the arrow nocked but not yet pulled.

She tracked the trajectory of the arrow's flight to the source of the danger.

Just visible through the trees, a skinny little old man was stooping arthritically to scrape the dry insides from a rotting log for kindling. His wife, an equally lean, equally rag-clad old woman whose thin white hair hung lankly about her narrow shoulders, was holding a reed basket to receive the crumbling chips. Gareth let out a cry of horror. "NO!"

Aversin moved his head. The old woman, alerted also, looked up and gave a thin wail, dropping her basket to shield her face futilely with her arms. The dry, woody punk spilled onto the marshy ground about her feet. The old man caught her by the arm and the two of them began to flee dodderingly into the deeper forest, sobbing and covering their heads with their arms, as if they supposed that the broad-tipped iron war arrow would be stopped by such slack old flesh.

Aversin lowered his bow and let his targets stumble unshot into the wet wilderness of trees.

Gareth gasped, "He was going to kill them! Those poor old people..."

Jenny nodded, as John came back to the road. "I know." She understood why; but, as when she had killed the dying robber in the ruins of the old town, she still felt unclean.

"Is that all you can say?" Gareth raged, horrified. "You *know*? He would have shot them in cold blood..."

"They were Meewinks, Gar," John said quietly. "Shooting's the only thing you can do with Meewinks."

"I don't care what you call them!" he cried. "They were old and harmless! All they were doing was gathering kindling!"

A small, straight line appeared between John's reddish

brows, and he rubbed his eyes. Gareth, Jenny thought, was not the only one upon whom this trip was telling.

"I don't know what you call them in your part of the country," Aversin said tiredly. "Their people used to farm all the valley of the Wildspae. They..."

"John." Jenny touched his arm. She had followed this exchange only marginally; her senses and her power were diffused through the damp woods, and in the fading light she scented danger. It seemed to prickle along her skin— a soft plashing movement in the flooded glades to the north, a thin chittering that silenced the small restive noises of fox and weasel. "We should be moving. The light's already going. I don't remember this part of the woods well but I know it's some distance from any kind of camping place."

"What is it?" His voice, like hers, dropped to a whisper.

She shook her head. "Maybe nothing. But I think we should go."

"Why?" Gareth bleated. "What's wrong? For three days you've been running away from your own shadows..."

"That's right," John agreed, and there was a dangerous edge to his quiet voice. "You ever think what might happen to you if your own shadow caught you? Now ride— and ride silent."

It was nearly full night when they made camp, for, like Jenny, Aversin was nervous, and it took some time for him to find a camping place that his woodsmanship judged to be even relatively safe. One of them Jenny rejected, not liking the way the dark trees crowded around it; another John passed by because the spring could not be seen from where the fire would be. Jenny was hungry and tired, but the instincts of the Winterlands warned her to keep moving until they found a place that could be defended, though against what she could not tell.

When Aversin ruled against a third place, an almost-circular clearing with a small, fern-choked spring gurgling through one side of it, Gareth's hunger-frayed temper snapped. "What's wrong with it?" he demanded, dismounting and huddling on the lee-side of The Stupid Roan for warmth. "You can take a drink without getting out of sight of the fire, and it's bigger than the other place was."

Annoyance glinted like the blink of drawn steel in John's voice. "I don't like it."

"Well, why in the name of Sarmendes not?"

Aversin looked around him at the clearing and shook his head. The clouds had parted overhead enough to admit watery moonlight to glint on his specs, on the water droplets in his hair when he pushed back his hood, and on the end of his long nose. "I just don't. I can't say why."

"Well, if you can't say why, what would you like?"

"What I'd like," the Dragonsbane retorted with his usual devastating accuracy, "is not to have some snirp of a silk-lined brat telling me a place is safe because he wants his supper."

Because that was obviously Gareth's first concern, the boy exploded, "That isn't the reason! I think you've lived like a wolf for so long you don't trust anything! I'm not going to trek through the woods all night long because . . ."

"Fine," said Aversin grimly. "You can just bloody well stay here, then."

"That's right! Go ahead, abandon me! Are you going to take a shot at me if I try to come after you and you hear the bushes rustle?"

"I might."

"John!" Jenny's cool, slightly gravelly voice cut across his next words. "How much longer can we travel without lights of some kind? Clouds are moving up. It won't rain, but you won't be able to see a foot ahead of you in two hours."

"*You* could," he pointed out. He felt it, too, she thought—that growing sensation that had begun back along the road; the uneasy feeling of being watched.

"I could," she agreed quietly. "But I don't have your woodsmanship. And I know this part of the road—there isn't a better place ahead. I don't like this place either, but I'm not sure that staying here wouldn't be safer than showing up our position by traveling with lights, even a very dim magelight. And even that might not show up signs of danger."

John looked about him at the dark woods, now barely visible in the cold gloom. Wind stirred at the bare boughs interlaced above their heads, and somewhere before them in the clearing Jenny could hear the whisper of the ferns and the rushing voice of the rain-fed stream. No sound of danger, she thought. Why then did she subconsciously watch with her peripheral vision; why this readiness to flee?

Aversin said quietly, "It's too good."

Gareth snapped, "First you don't like it and then you say it's too good..."

"They'll know all the camping places anyway," Jenny replied softly across his words.

Furious, Gareth sputtered, "Who'll know?"

"The Meewinks, you stupid oic," snapped John back at him.

Gareth flung up his hands. "Oh, fine! You mean you don't want to camp here because you're afraid of being attacked by a little old man and a little old lady?"

"And about fifty of their friends, yes," John retorted. "And one more word out of you, my hero, and you're going to find yourself slammed up against a tree."

Thoroughly roused now, Gareth retorted, "Good! Prove how clever you are by thrashing someone who disagrees with you! If you're afraid of being attacked by a troop of forty four-foot-tall septuagenarians..."

He never even saw Aversin move. The Dragonsbane might not have the appearance of a hero, Jenny thought, but he nevertheless had the physical reflexes of one. Gareth gasped as he was literally lifted off his feet by a double-handful of cloak and doublet, and Jenny strode forward to catch John's spike-studded forearm. With softness as definite as an assassin's footfall, she said, "Be quiet! And drop him."

"Got a cliff handy?" But she felt the momentum of his rage slack. After a pause he pushed—almost threw—Gareth from him. "Right." Behind his anger he sounded embarrassed. "Thanks to our hero, it's well too dark now to be moving on. Jen, can you do anything with this place? Spell it?"

Jenny thought for a few moments, trying to analyze what it was that she feared. "Not against the Meewinks, no," she replied at last. She added acidly, "They'll have tracked you gentlemen by your voices."

"It wasn't me who..."

"I didn't ask who it was." She took the reins of the horses and mules and led them on into the clearing, anxious now to get a camp set and circled with the spells of ward before they were seen from the outside. Gareth, a little shamefaced at his outburst, followed sulkily, looking at the layout of the clearing.

In the voice of one who sought to mollify by pretending that the disagreement never happened, he asked, "Does this hollow look all right for the fire?"

Irritation still crackled in Aversin's voice. "No fire. We're in for a cold camp tonight—and you'll take the first watch, my hero."

Gareth gasped in protest at this arbitrary switch. Since leaving the Hold, Gareth had always taken the last watch, the dawn watch, because at the end of a day's riding he wanted nothing more than to lie down and sleep; Jenny had always taken second; and John, used to the habits of wolves who hunted in the early part of the night, took the first. The boy began, "But I ... " and Jenny swung around to look at them in the somber gloom.

"One more word out of either of you and I will lay a spell of dumbness upon you both."

John subsided at once. Gareth started to speak again, then thought better of it. Jenny pulled the picket rope out of the mule Clivy's pack and looped it around a sapling. Half to herself, she added, "Though God knows it couldn't make you any dumber."

Throughout their meager dinner of dried beef, cold cornmeal mush, and apples, Gareth remained ostentatiously silent. Jenny scarcely noticed, and John, seeing her preoccupied, said little to her, not wanting to disturb her concentration. She was not sure how much he felt of the danger she sensed in the woods all around them—she didn't know how much of it was only the product of her own weariness. But she wove all her concentration, all her abilities, into the spell-circle that she put around the camp that night: spells of ward that would make their campsite unnoticeable from the outside, that would thwart the eye of any who were not actually within the circle. They would not be much help against the Meewinks, who would know where the clearing was, but they might provide a delay that would buy time. To these she added other spells against other dangers, spells that Caerdinn had taught her against the blood-devils and Whisperers that haunted the Woods of Wyr, spells whose efficacy she privately doubted because she knew that they sometimes failed, but the best spells that she—or anyone to whom she had spoken—knew.

She had long suspected that the Lines of magic were thinning and that every generation attenuated the teaching of magic that had been passed down from the old times, the times before the Realm of Belmarie had united all the West under itself and the glittering worship of the Twelve Gods. Caerdinn had been one of the mightiest of the Line of Herne, but, when she had first met him at fourteen, he was already very old, feeble, and a little crazy. He had

taught her, trained her in the secrets of the Line passed
from master to pupil over a dozen generations. But since
his death she had found two instances where his knowledge
had been incorrect and had heard of spells from her Line-
kindred, the pupils' pupils of Caerdinn's master Spaeth
Skywarden, which Caerdinn had either not bothered to
teach her, or had not known himself. The spells of guard
against the Whisperers that had more and more come to
haunt the Wyrwoods were ineffective and sporadic, and she
knew of no spell that would drive them or the blood-devils
out of an area to render it safe for humans again. Such things
might reside somewhere in a book, written down by the mage
who discovered them, but neither Jenny, nor any mage she
had met, had known of them.

She slept that night uneasily, exhausted in body and
troubled by strange shapes that seemed to slide in and
out through the cracks in her dreams. She seemed to be
able to hear the whistling chitter of the blood-devils as
they flitted from tree to tree in the marshy woods across
the stream and below them the soft murmurs of the Whisperers in the darkness beyond the barrier of spells. Twice
she pulled herself painfully from the sucking darkness of
sleep, fearing some danger, but both times she only saw
Gareth sitting propped against a pile of packsaddles, nodding in the misty blackness.

The third time she woke up, Gareth was gone.

It had been a dream that woke her; a dream of a woman
standing half-hidden among the trees. She was veiled, like
all the women of the south; the lace of that veil was like
a cloak of flowers scattered over her dark curls. Her soft
laughter was like silver bells, but there was a husky note
in it, as if she never laughed save with pleasure at something gained. She held out small, slender hands, and whispered Gareth's name.

Leaves and dirt were scuffed where he had crossed
the flickering lines of the protective circles.

Jenny sat up, shaking back the coarse mane of her hair, and touched John awake. She called the witchlight into being, and it illuminated the still, silent camp and glowed in the eyes of the wakened horses. The voice of the spring was loud in the hush.

Like John, she had slept in her clothes. Reaching over to the bundle of her sheepskin jacket, her plaids, her boots and her belt that lay heaped at one side of their blankets, she pulled from its pouch the small scrying-crystal and angled it to the witchlight while John began, without a word, to pull on his boots and wolfskin-lined doublet.

Of the four elements, scrying earth—crystal—was easiest and most accurate, though the crystal itself had to be enchanted beforehand. Scrying fire needed no special preparation, but what it showed was what it would, not always what was sought; water would show both future and past, but was a notorious liar. Only the very greatest of mages could scry the wind.

The heart of Caerdinn's crystal was dark. She stilled her fears for Gareth's safety, calming her mind as she summoned the images; they gleamed on the facets, as if reflected from somewhere else. She saw a stone room, extremely small, with the architecture of some place half-dug into the ground; the only furnishing was a bed and a sort of table formed by a block of stone projecting from the wall itself. A wet cloak was thrown over the table, with a puddle of half-dried water about it—swamp weeds clung to it like dark worms. A much-bejeweled longsword was propped nearby, and on top of the table and cloak lay a pair of spectacles. The round lenses caught a spark of greasy yellow lamplight as the door of the room opened.

Someone in the corridor held a lamp high. Its light showed small, stooped forms crowding in the broad hall beyond. Old and young, men and women, there must have been forty of them, with white, sloped, warty faces and round, fishlike eyes. The first through the doorway were the old man and the old woman, the Meewinks whom John had nearly shot that afternoon.

The old man held a rope; the woman, a cleaver.

The house of the Meewinks stood where the land lay low, on a knoll above a foul soup of mud and water from whose surface rotting trees projected like half-decayed corpses. Squat-built, it was larger than it looked—stone walls behind it showed one wing half-buried underground. In spite of the cold, the air around the place was fetid with the smell of putrefying fish, and Jenny closed her teeth hard against a queasiness that washed over her at the sight of the place. Since first she had known what they were, she had hated the Meewinks.

John slid from his dapple war horse Osprey's back and looped his rein and Battlehammer's over the limb of a sapling. His face, in the rainy darkness, was taut with a mingling of hatred and disgust. Twice households of Meewinks had tried to establish themselves near Alyn Hold; both times, as soon as he had learned of them, he had raised what militia he could and burned them out. A few had been killed each time, but he had lacked the men to pursue them through the wild lands and eradicate them completely. Jenny knew he still had nightmares about what he had found in their cellars.

He whispered, "Listen," and Jenny nodded. From the house she could detect a faint clamor of voices, muffled, as if half-below the ground, thin and yammering like the barking of beasts. Jenny slid her halberd from the holster on Moon Horse's saddle and breathed to all three mounts for stillness and silence. She sketched over them the spells of ward, so that the casual eye would pass them by, or think they were something other than horses—a hazel thicket, or the oddly shaped shadow of a tree. It was these same spells upon the camp, she knew, that had prevented

Gareth from finding his way back to it, once what must have been the Whisperer had led him away.

John tucked his spectacles into an inner pocket. "Right," he murmured. "You get Gar—I'll cover you both."

Jenny nodded, feeling cold inside, as she did when she emptied her mind to do some great magic beyond her power, and steeled herself for what she knew was coming. As they crossed the filthy yard and the strange, muffled outcry in the house grew stronger, John kissed her and, turning, smashed his booted foot into the small house's door.

They broke through the door like raiders robbing Hell. A hot, damp fetor smote Jenny in the face as she barged through on John's heels, the putrid stink of the filth the Meewinks lived in and of the decaying fish they ate— above it all was the sharp, copper-bright stench of new-shed blood. The noise was a pandemonium of yammering screams; after the darkness outside, even the smoky glow of the fire in the unnaturally huge hearth seemed blinding. Bodies seethed in a heaving mob around the small door at the opposite side of the room; now and then sharp flashes of light glinted from the knives clutched in moist little hands.

Gareth was backed to the doorpost in the midst of the mob. He had evidently fought his way that far but knew if he descended into the more open space of the big room he would be surrounded. His left arm was wrapped, shieldlike, in a muffling tangle of stained and filthy bedding; in his right hand was his belt, the buckle-end of which he was using to slash at the faces of the Meewinks all around him. His own face was streaming with blood from knife-cuts and bites—mixed with sweat, it ran down and encrimsoned his shirt as if his throat had been cut. His naked gray eyes were wide with a look of sickened, nightmare horror.

The Meewinks around him were gibbering like the souls

of the damned. There must have been fifty of them, all armed with their little knives of steel, or of sharpened shell. As John and Jenny broke in, Jenny saw one of them crawl in close to Gareth and slash at the back of his knee. His thighs were already gashed with a dozen such attempts, his boots sticky with runnels of blood; he kicked his attacker in the face, rolling her down a step or two into the mass of her fellows. It was the old woman he had kept John from shooting.

Without a word, John plunged down into the heaving, stinking mob. Jenny sprang after him, guarding his back; blood splattered her from the first swing of his sword, and around them the noise rose like the redoubling of a storm at sea. The Meewinks were a small folk, though some of the men were as tall as she; it made her cringe inside to cut at the slack white faces of people no bigger than children and to slam the weighted butt of the halberd into those pouchy little stomachs and watch them fall, gasping, vomiting, and choking. But there were so many of them. She had kilted her faded plaid skirts up to her knees to fight and she felt hands snatch and drag at them, as one man caught up a cleaver from among the butcher's things lying on the room's big table, trying to cripple her. Her blade caught him high on the cheekbone and opened his face down to the opposite corner of his jaw. His scream ripped the cut wider. The stench of blood was everywhere.

It seemed to take only seconds to cross the room. Jenny yelled, "Gareth!" but he swung at her with the belt—she was short enough to be a Meewink, and he had lost his spectacles. She flung up the halberd; the belt wrapped itself around the shaft, and she wrenched it from his hands. "It's Jenny!" she shouted, as John's sword strokes came down, defending them both as it splattered them with flying droplets of gore. She grabbed the boy's bony wrist, jerking him down the steps into the room. "Now, run!"

"But we can't . . ." he began, looking back at John, and she shoved him violently in the direction of the door. After what appeared to be a momentary struggle with a desire not to seem a coward by abandoning his rescuers, Gareth ran. They passed the table and he caught up a meat hook in passing, swinging at the pallid, puffy faces all around them and at the little hands with their jabbing knives. Three Meewinks were guarding the door, but fell back screaming before the greater length of Jenny's weapon. Behind her, she could hear the squeaky cacophony around John rising to a crescendo; she knew he was outnumbered, and her instincts to rush back to fight at his side dragged at her like wet rope. It was all she could do to force herself to hurl open the door and drag Gareth at a run across the clearing outside.

Gareth balked, panicky. "Where are the horses? How are we . . .?"

For all her small size, she was strong; her shove nearly toppled him. "Don't ask questions!" Already small, slumped forms were running about the darkness of the woods ahead. The ooze underfoot soaked through her boots as she hauled Gareth toward where she, at least, could see the three horses, and she heard Gareth gulp when they got close enough for the spells to lose their effectiveness.

While the boy scrambled up to Battlehammer's back, Jenny flung herself onto Moon Horse, caught Osprey's lead-rein, and spurred back toward the house in a porridgey spatter of mud. Pitching her voice to cut through the screaming clamor within, she called out, "JOHN!" A moment later a confused tangle of figures erupted through the low doorway, like a pack of dogs trying to bring down a bear. The white glare of the witchlight showed Aversin's sword bloody to the pommel, his face streaked and run-

ning with his own blood and that of his attackers, his
breath pouring like a ribbon of steam from his mouth.
Meewinks clung to his arms and his belt, hacking and
chewing at the leather of his boots.

With a screaming battle cry like a gull's, Jenny rode
down upon them, swinging her halberd like a scythe. Meewinks scattered, mewing and hissing, and John wrenched
himself free of the last of them and flung himself up to
Osprey's saddle. A tiny Meewink child hurled up after
him, clinging to the stirrup leather and jabbing with its
little shell knife at his groin; John swung his arm downward and caught the child across its narrow temple with
the spikes of his armband, sweeping it off as he would
have swept a rat.

Jenny wheeled her horse sharply, spurring back to where
Gareth still clung to Battlehammer's saddle on the edge
of the clearing. With the precision of circus riders, she
and John split to grab the big gelding's reins, one on either
side, and, with Gareth in tow between them, plunged back
into the night.

"There." Aversin dipped one finger into a puddle of
rainwater and flicked a droplet onto the iron griddle balanced over the fire. Satisfied with the sizzle, he patted
cornmeal into a cake and dropped it into place. Then he
glanced across at Gareth, who was struggling not to cry
out as Jenny poured a scouring concoction of marigold-
simple into his wounds. "Now you can say you've seen
Aversin the Dragonsbane run like hell from a troop of
forty four-foot-tall septuagenarians." His bitten, bandaged hands patted another cake into shape, and the dawn
grayness flashed off his specs as he grinned.

"Will they be after us?" Gareth asked faintly.

"I doubt it." He picked a fleck of cornmeal off the
spikes of his armbands. "They'll have enough of their
own dead to keep them fed awhile."

The boy swallowed queasily, though having seen the instruments laid out on the table in the Meewinks' house, there could be little doubt what they had meant for him.

At Jenny's insistence, after the rescue, they had shifted their camp away from the garnered darkness of the woods. Dawn had found them in relatively open ground on the formless verges of a marsh, where long wastes of ice-scummed, standing water reflected a steely sky among the black pen strokes of a thousand reeds. Jenny had worked, cold and weary, to lay spells about the camp, then had occupied herself with the contents of her medicine satchel, leaving John, somewhat against her better judgment, to make breakfast. Gareth had dug into his packs for the bent and battered spectacles that had survived the fight in the ruins up north, and they perched forlornly askew now on the end of his nose.

"They were always a little folk," John went on, coming over to the packs where the boy sat, letting Jenny finish binding up his slashed knees. "After the King's troops left the Winterlands, their villages were forever being raided by bandits, who'd steal whatever food they raised. They never were a match for an armored man, but a village of 'em could pull one down—or, better still, wait till he was asleep and hack him up as he lay. In the starving times, a bandit's horse could feed a whole village for a week. I expect it started out as only the horses."

Gareth swallowed again and looked as if he were going to be ill.

John put his hands through his metal-plated belt. "They generally strike right before dawn, when sleep is deepest—it's why I switched the watches, so I'd be the one they dealt with, instead of you. It was a Whisperer that got you away from the camp, wasn't it?"

"I—I suppose so." He looked at the ground, a shadow crossing his thin face. "I don't know. It was something..." Jenny felt him shudder.

"I've seen them on my watch, once or twice . . . Jen?"

"Once." Jenny spoke shortly, hating the memory of those crying shapes in the darkness.

"They take all forms," John said, sitting on the ground beside her and wrapping his arms about his knees. "One night one even took Jen's, with her lying beside me . . . Polyborus says in his *Analects*—or maybe it's in that half-signature of Terens' *Of Ghosts*—that they read your dreams and take on the forms that they see there. From Terens—or is it Polyborus? Or maybe it's in Clivy, though it's a bit accurate for Clivy—I get the impression they used to be much rarer than they are now, whatever they are."

"I don't know," Gareth said quietly. "They must have been, because I'd never heard of them, or of the Meewinks, either. After it—it lured me into the woods, it attacked me. I ran, but I couldn't seem to find the camp again. I ran and ran . . . and then I saw the light from that house . . ." He fell silent again with a shudder.

Jenny finished wrapping Gareth's knee. The wounds weren't deep, but, like those on John's face and hands, they were vicious, not only the knife cuts, but the small, crescent-shaped tears of human teeth. Her own body bore them, too, and experience had taught her that such wounds were filthier than poisoned arrows. For the rest, she was aching and stiff with pulled muscles and the general fatigue of battle, something she supposed Gareth's ballads neglected to mention as the inevitable result of physical combat. She felt cold inside, too, as she did when she worked the death-spells, something else they never mentioned in ballads, where all killing was done with serene and noble confidence. She had taken the lives of at least four human beings last night, she knew, for all that they had been born and raised into a cannibal tribe; had maimed others who would either die when their wounds turned septic in that atmosphere of festering decay, or would be killed by their brothers.

To survive in the Winterlands, she had become a very competent killer. But the longer she was a healer, the more she learned about magic and about life from which all magic stemmed, the more she loathed what she did. Living in the Winterlands, she had seen what death did to those who dealt it out too casually.

The gray waters of the marsh began to brighten with the remote shine of daybreak beyond the clouds. With a soft winnowing of a thousand wings, the wild geese rose from the black cattail beds, seeking again the roads of the colorless sky. Jenny sighed, weary to her bones and knowing that they could not afford to rest—knowing that she would have no rest until they crossed the great river Wildspae and entered the lands of Belmarie.

Quietly, Gareth said, "Aversin—Lord John—I—I'm sorry. I didn't understand about the Winterlands." He looked up, his gray eyes tired and unhappy behind their cracked specs. "And I didn't understand about you. I— I hated you, for not being what—what I thought you should be."

"Oh, aye, I knew that," John said with a fleet grin. "But what you felt about me was none of my business. My business was to see you safe in a land you had no knowledge of. And as for being what you expected—Well, you can only know what you know, and all you knew were those songs. I mean, it's like Polyborus and Clivy and those others. I know bears aren't born completely shapeless for their mothers to sculpt with their tongues, like Clivy says, because I've seen newborn bear cubs. But for all I know, lions *may* be born dead, although personally I don't think it's likely."

"They aren't," Gareth said. "Father had a lioness once

as a pet, when I was very little—her cubs were born live, just like big kittens. They were spotted."

"Really?" Aversin looked genuinely pleased for one more bit of knowledge to add to the lumber room of his mind. "I'm not saying Dragonsbanes aren't heroic, because Selkythar and Antara Warlady and the others might have been, and may have gone about it all with swords in golden armor and plumes. It's just that I know I'm not. If I'd had a choice, I'd never have gone near the bloody dragon, but nobody asked me." He grinned and added, "I'm sorry you were disappointed."

Gareth grinned back. "I suppose it had to rain on my birthday sometime," he said, a little shyly. Then he hesitated, as if struggling against some inner constraint. "Aversin, listen," he stammered. Then he coughed as the wind shifted, and smoke swept over them all.

"God's Grandmother, it's the bloody cakes!" John swore and dashed back to the fire, cursing awesomely. "Jen, it isn't my fault..."

"It is." Jenny walked in a more leisurely manner to join him, in time to help him pick the last pitiful black lump from the griddle and toss it into the waters of the marsh with a milky plash. "I should have known better than to trust you with this. Now go tend the horses and let me do what you brought me along to do." She picked up the bowl of meal. Though she kept her face stern, the touch of her eyes upon his was like a kiss.

CHAPTER IV

IN THE DAYS that followed, Jenny was interested to notice the change in Gareth's attitude toward her and toward John. For the most part he seemed to return to the confiding friendliness he had shown her after she had rescued him from the bandits among the ruins, before he had learned that she was his hero's mistress, but it was not quite the same. It alternated with a growing nervousness and with odd, struggling silences in his conversation. If he had lied about something at the Hold, Jenny thought, he was regretting it now—but not regretting it enough yet to confess the truth.

Whatever the truth was, she felt that she came close to learning it the day after the rescue from the Meewinks. John had ridden ahead to scout the ruinous stone bridge that spanned the torrent of the Snake River, leaving them alone with the spare horses and mules in the louring silence of the winter woods. "Are the Whisperers real?" he asked her softly, glancing over his shoulder as if he feared to see last night's vision fading into daytime reality from the mists between the trees.

"Real enough to kill a man," Jenny said, "if they can

75

lure him away from his friends. Since they drink blood, they must be fleshly enough to require sustenance; but, other than that, no one knows much about them. You had a narrow escape."

"I know," he mumbled, looking shamefacedly down at his hands. They were bare, and chapped with cold—as well as his cloak and sword, he had lost his gloves in the house of the Meewinks; Jenny suspected that later in the winter the Meewinks would boil them and eat the leather. One of John's old plaids was draped on over the boy's doublet and borrowed jerkin. With his thin hair dripping with moisture down onto the lenses of his cracked spectacles, he looked very little like the young courtier who had come to the Hold.

"Jenny," he said hesitantly, "thank you—this is the second time—for saving my life. I—I'm sorry I've behaved toward you as I have. It's just that . . ." His voice tailed off uncertainly.

"I suspect," said Jenny kindly, "that you had me mistaken for someone else that you know."

Ready color flooded to the boy's cheeks. Wind moaned through the bare trees—he startled, then turned back to her with a sigh. "The thing is, you saved my life at the risk of your own, and I endangered you both stupidly. I should have known better than to trust the Meewinks; I should never have left the camp. But . . ."

Jenny smiled and shook her head. The rain had ceased, and she had put back her hood, letting the wind stir in her long hair; with a touch of her heels, she urged The Stupider Roan on again, and the whole train of them moved slowly down the trail.

"It is difficult," she said, "not to believe in the illusions of the Whisperers. Even though you know that those whom you see cannot possibly be there outside the spell-circle crying your name, there is a part of you that needs to go to them."

"What—what shapes have you seen them take?" Gareth asked in a hushed voice.

The memory was an evil one, and it was a moment before Jenny answered. Then she said, "My sons. Ian and Adric." The vision had been so real that even calling their images in Caerdinn's scrying-crystal to make sure that they were safe at the Hold had not entirely banished her fears for them from her mind. After a moment's thought she added, "They have an uncanny way of taking the shape that most troubles you; of knowing, not only your love, but your guilt and your longing."

Gareth flinched at that, and looked away. They rode on in silence for a few moments; then he asked, "How do they know?"

She shook her head. "Perhaps they do read your dreams. Perhaps they are themselves only mirrors and, like mirrors, have no knowledge of what they reflect. The spells we lay upon them cannot be binding because we do not know their essence."

He frowned at her, puzzled. "Their what?"

"Their essence—their inner being." She drew rein just above a long, flooded dip in the road where water lay among the trees like a shining snake. "Who are you, Gareth of Magloshaldon?"

He startled at that, and for an instant she saw fright and guilt in his gray eyes. He stammered, "I—I'm Gareth of—of Magloshaldon. It's a province of Belmarie..."

Her eyes sought his and held them in the gray shadows of the trees. "And if you were not of that province, would you still be Gareth?"

"Er—yes. Of course. I..."

"And if you were not Gareth?" she pressed him, holding his gaze and mind locked with her own. "Would you still be you? If you were crippled, or old—if you became a leper, or lost your manhood—who would you be then?"

"I don't know—"

"You know."

"Stop it!" He tried to look away and could not. Her grip upon him tightened, as she probed at his mind, showing him it through her eyes: a vivid kaleidoscope of the borrowed images of a thousand ballads, burning with the overwhelming physical desires of the adolescent; the raw wounds left by some bitter betrayal, and over all, the shadowing darkness of a scarcely bearable guilt and fear.

She probed at that darkness—the lies he had told her and John at the Hold, and some greater guilt besides. A true crime, she wondered, or only that which seemed one to him? Gareth cried, "Stop it!" again, and she heard the despair and terror in his voice; for a moment, through his eyes, she saw herself—pitiless blue eyes in a face like a white wedge of bone between the cloud-dark streams of her hair. She remembered when Caerdinn had done this same thing to her, and released Gareth quickly. He turned away, covering his face, his whole body shivering with shock and fright.

After a moment Jenny said softly, "I'm sorry. But this is the inner heart of magic, the way all spells work—with the essence, the true name. It is true of the Whisperers and of the greatest of mages as well." She clucked to the horses and they started forward again, their hooves sinking squishily into the tea-colored ooze. She went on, "All you can do is ask yourself if it is reasonable that those you see would be there in the woods, calling to you."

"But that's just it," said Gareth. "It was reasonable. Zyerne . . ." He stopped himself.

"Zyerne?" It was the name he had muttered in his dreams at the Hold, when he had flinched aside from her touch.

"The Lady Zyerne," he said hesitantly. "The—the King's mistress." Under its streaking of rain and mud his face was bright carnation pink. Jenny remembered her strange and cloudy dream of the dark-haired woman and her tinkling laughter.

"And you love her?"

Gareth blushed even redder. In a stifled voice he repeated, "She is the King's mistress."

As I am John's, Jenny thought, suddenly realizing whence his anger at her had stemmed.

"In any case," Gareth went on after a moment, "we're all in love with her. That is—she's the first lady of the Court, the most beautiful... We write sonnets to her beauty..."

"Does she love you?" inquired Jenny, and Gareth fell silent for a time, concentrating on urging his horse through the mud and up the stony slope beyond.

At length he said, "I—I don't know. Sometimes I think..." Then he shook his head. "She frightens me," he admitted. "And yet—she's a witch, you see."

"Yes," said Jenny softly. "I guessed that, from what you said at the Hold. You feared I would be like her."

He looked stricken, as if caught in some horrible social gaffe. "But—but you're not. She's very beautiful..." He broke off, blushing in earnest, and Jenny laughed.

"Don't worry. I learned a long time ago what a mirror was for."

"But you *are* beautiful," he insisted. "That is—Beautiful isn't the right word."

"No." Jenny smiled. "I do think 'ugly' *is* the word you're looking for."

Gareth shook his head stubbornly, his honesty forbidding him to call her beautiful and his inexperience making it impossible to express what he did mean. "Beauty—beauty really doesn't have anything to do with it," he said at last. "And she's nothing like you—for all her beauty, she's crafty and hard-hearted and cares for nothing save the pursuit of her powers."

"Then she is like me," said Jenny. "For I am crafty—

skilled in my crafts, such as they are—and I have been called hard-hearted since I was a little girl and chose to sit staring at the flame of a candle until the pictures came, rather than play at house with the other little girls. And as for the rest . . ." She sighed. "The key to magic is magic; to be a mage you must be a mage. My old master used to say that. The pursuit of your power takes all that you have, if you will be great—it leaves neither time, nor energy, for anything else. We are born with the seeds of power in us and driven to be what we are by a hunger that knows no slaking. Knowledge—power—to know what songs the stars sing; to center all the forces of creation upon a rune drawn in the air—we can never give over the seeking of it. It is the stuff of loneliness, Gareth."

They rode on in silence for a time. The woods about them were pewter and iron, streaked here and there with the rust of the dying year. In the wan light Gareth looked older than he had when they began, for he had lost flesh on the trip, and lack of sleep had left permanent smudges of bister beneath his eyes. At length he turned to her again and asked, "And do the mageborn love?"

Jenny sighed again. "They say that a wizard's wife is a widow. A woman who bears a wizard's child must know that he will leave her to raise the child alone, should his powers call him elsewhere. It is for this reason that no priest will perform the wedding ceremony for the mageborn, and no flute player will officiate upon the rites. And it would be an act of cruelty for a witch to bear any man's child."

He looked across at her, puzzled both by her words and by the coolness of her voice, as if the matter had nothing to do with her.

She went on, looking ahead at the half-hidden road beneath its foul mire of tangled weeds, "A witch will always care more for the pursuit of her powers than for her child, or for any man. She will either desert her child, or come to hate it for keeping her from the time she needs to meditate, to study, to grow in her arts. Did you know John's mother was a witch?"

Gareth stared at her, shocked.

"She was a shaman of the Iceriders—his father took her in battle. Your ballads said nothing of it?"

He shook his head numbly. "Nothing—in fact, in the Greenhythe variant of the ballad of Aversin and the Golden Worm of Wyr, it talks about him bidding farewell to his mother in her bower, before going off to fight the dragon—but now that I think of it, there is a scene very like it in the Greenhythe ballad of Selkythar Dragonsbane and in one of the late Halnath variants of the Song of Antara Warlady. I just thought it was something Dragonsbanes did."

A smile brushed her lips, then faded. "She was my first teacher in the ways of power, when I was six. They used to say of her what you thought of me—that she had laid spells upon her lord to make him love her, tangling him in her long hair. I thought so, too, as a little child—until I saw how she fought for the freedom that he would not give her. When I knew her, she had already borne his child; but when John was five, she left in the screaming winds of an icestorm, she and the frost-eyed wolf who was her companion. She was never seen in the Winterlands again. And I . . ."

There was long silence, broken only by the soft squish of hooves in the roadbed, the patter of rain, and the occasional pop of the mule Clivy's hooves as he overreached his own stride. When she went on, her voice was low, as if she spoke to herself.

"He asked me to bear his children, for he wanted children, and he wanted those children to be mine also. He knew I would never live with him as his wife and devote my time to his comfort and that of his sons. I knew it, too." She sighed. "The lioness bears her cubs and then goes back to the hunting trail. I thought I could do the same. All my life I have been called heartless—would that it were really so. I hadn't thought that I would love them."

Through the trees, the dilapidated towers of the Snake River bridge came into view, the water streaming high and yellow beneath the crumbling arches. Before them, a dark figure sat his horse in the gloomy road, spectacles flashing like rounds of dirty ice in the cold daylight, signaling that the way was safe.

They made camp that night outside the ruined town of Ember, once the capital of the province of Wyr. Nothing remained of it now save a dimpled stone mound, overgrown with birch and seedling maple, and the decaying remains of the curtain wall. Jenny knew it of old, from the days when she and Caerdinn had searched for books in the buried cellars. He had beaten her, she remembered, when she had spoken of the beauty of the skeleton lines of stone that shimmered through the dark cloak of the fallow earth.

As dusk came down, they pitched their camp outside the walls. Jenny gathered the quick-burning bark of the paper birch for kindling and fetched water from the spring nearby. Gareth saw her coming and broke purposefully away from his own tasks to join her. "Jenny," he began, and she looked up at him.

"Yes?"

He paused, like a naked swimmer on the bank of a very cold pool, then visibly lost his courage. "Er—is there some reason why we didn't camp in the ruins of the town itself?"

It was patently not what he had been about to say, but she only glanced back toward the white bones of the town, wrapped in shadow and vine. "Yes."

His voice dropped. "Is there—is there *something* that haunts the ruins?"

The corners of her mouth tucked a little. "Not that I know of. But the entire town is buried under the biggest patch of poison ivy this side of the Gray Mountains. Even so," she said, kneeling beside the little dry firewood they had been able to find and arranging the birchbark beneath it, "I have laid spells of ward about the camp, so take care not to leave it."

He ducked his head a little at this gentle teasing and blushed.

A little curiously, she added, "Even if this Lady Zyerne of yours is a sorceress—even if she is fond of you—she would never have come here from the south, you know. Mages only transform themselves into birds in ballads, for to change your essence into the essence of some other life form—which is what shapeshifting is—aside from being dangerous, requires an incredible amount of power. It is not something done lightly. When the mageborn go, they go upon their two feet."

"But..." His high forehead wrinkled in a frown. Having decided to be her champion, he was unwilling to believe there was anything beyond her powers. "But the Lady Zyerne does it all the time. I've seen her."

Jenny froze in the act of arranging the logs, cut by an unexpected pang of a hot jealousy she had thought that she had long outgrown—the bitter jealousy of her youth toward those who had greater skills than she. All her life she had worked to rid herself of it, knowing it crippled her from learning from those more powerful. It was this that made her tell herself, a moment later, that she ought not to be shocked to learn of another's use of power.

Yet in the back of her mind she could hear old Caerdinn speaking of the dangers of taking on an alien essence, even if one had the enormous power necessary to perform the transformation and of the hold that another form could take on the minds of all but the very greatest.

"She must be a powerful mage indeed," she said, rebuking her own envy. With a touch of her mind, she called fire to the kindling, and it blazed up hotly beneath the logs. Even that small magic pricked her, like a needle carelessly left in a garment, with the bitter reflection of the smallness of her power. "What forms have you seen her take?" She realized as she spoke that she hoped he would say he had seen none himself and that it was, in fact, only rumor.

"Once a cat," he said. "And once a bird, a swallow. And she's taken other shapes in—in dreams I've had. It's odd," he went on rather hastily. "In ballads they don't make much of it. But it's hideous, the most horrible thing I've ever seen—a woman, and a woman I—I—" He stumbled in his words, barely biting back some other verb that he replaced with, "—I know, twisting and withering, changing into a beast. And then the beast will watch you with her eyes."

He folded himself up cross-legged beside the fire as Jenny put the iron skillet over it and began to mix the meal for the cakes. Jenny asked him, "Is she why you asked the King to send you north on this quest? To get away from her?"

Gareth turned his face from her. After a moment he nodded. "I don't want to betray—to betray the King." His words caught oddly as he spoke. "But sometimes I feel I'm destined to do so. And I don't know what to do.

"Polycarp hated her," he went on, after a few moments during which John's voice could be heard, cheerfully cursing the mules Clivy and Melonhead as he unloaded the last of the packs. "The rebel Master of Halnath. He always told me to stay away from her. And he hated her influence over the King."

"Is that why he rebelled?"

"It might have had something to do with it. I don't know." He toyed wretchedly with a scrap of meal left in the bowl. "He—he tried to murder the King and—and the Heir to the throne, the King's son. Polycarp is the next heir, the King's nephew. He was brought up in the palace as a sort of a hostage after his father rebelled. Polycarp stretched a cable over a fence in the hunting field on a foggy morning when he thought no one would see until it was too late." His voice cracked a little as he added, "I was the one who saw him do it."

Jenny glanced across at his face, broken by darkness and the leaping light of the flames into a harsh mosaic of plane and shadows. "You loved him, didn't you?"

He managed to nod. "I think he was a better friend to me than anyone else at Court. People—people our age there—Polycarp is five years older than I am—used to mock at me, because I collect ballads and because I'm clumsy and can't see without my spectacles; they'd mock at him because his father was executed for treason and because he's a philosopher. Many of the Masters have been. It's because of the University at Halnath—they're usually atheists and troublemakers. His father was, who married the King's sister. But Polycarp was always like a son to the King." He pushed back the thin, damp weeds of his hair from his high forehead and finished in a strangled voice, "Even when I saw him do it, I couldn't believe it."

"And you denounced him?"

Gareth's breath escaped in a defeated sigh. "What could I do?"

Had this, Jenny wondered, been what he had hidden from them? The fact that the Realm itself was split by threat of civil war, like the Kinwars that had drawn the King's troops away from the Winterlands to begin with? Had he feared that if John knew that there was a chance the King would refuse to lend him forces needed at home, he would not consent to make the journey?

Or was there something else?

It had grown fully dark now. Jenny picked the crisp mealcakes from the griddle and set them on a wooden plate at her side while she cooked salt pork and beans. While Gareth had been speaking, John had come to join them, half-listening to what was said, half-watching the woods that hemmed them in.

As they ate, Gareth went on, "Anyway, Polycarp managed to get out of the city before they came for him. The King's troops were waiting for him on the road to Halnath, but we think he went to the Deep, and the gnomes took him through to the Citadel that way. Then they—the gnomes—bolted up the doors leading from the Deep to the Citadel and said they would not meddle in the affairs of men. They wouldn't admit the King's troops through the Deep to take the Citadel from the rear, but they wouldn't let the rebels out that way, either, or sell them food. There was some talk of them using blasting powder to close up the tunnels to Halnath completely. But then the dragon came."

"And when the dragon came?" asked John.

"When the dragon came, Polycarp opened the Citadel gates that led into the Deep and let the gnomes take refuge with him. At least, a lot of the gnomes *did* take refuge with him, though Zyerne says they were the ones who were on the Master's side to begin with. And she should know—she was brought up in the Deep."

"Was she, now?" John tossed one of the small pork bones into the fire and wiped his fingers on a piece of corncake. "I thought the name sounded like the tongue of the gnomes."

Gareth nodded. "The gnomes used to take a lot of the children of men as apprentices in the Deep—usually children from Deeping, the town that stands—stood—in the vale before the great gates of the Deep itself, where the smelting of the gold and the trade in foodstuffs went on. They haven't done so in the last year or so—in fact in the last year they forbade men to enter the Deep at all."

"Did they?" asked John, curious. "Why was that?"

Gareth shrugged. "I don't know. They're strange creatures, and tricky. You can't ever tell what they're up to, Zyerne says."

As the night deepened, Jenny left the men by the fire and silently walked the bounds of the camp, checking the spell-circles that defended it against the blood-devils, the Whisperers, and the sad ghosts that haunted the ruins of the old town. She sat on what had been a boundary stone, just beyond the edge of the fire's circle of light, and sank into her meditations, which for some nights now she had neglected.

It was not the first time she had neglected them—she was too well aware of the nights she had let them go by while she was at the Hold with John and her sons. Had she not neglected them—had she not neglected the pursuit of her power—would she be as powerful as this Zyerne, who could deal in shapeshifting at a casual whim? Caerdinn's strictures against it returned to her mind, but she wondered if that was just her own jealousy speaking, her own spite at another's power. Caerdinn had been old, and there had been nowhere in the Winterlands that she could turn for other instruction after he had died. Like John, she was a scholar bereft of the meat of scholarship; like the people of the village of Alyn, she was circumscribed by the fate that had planted her in such stony soil.

Against the twisting yellow ribbons of the flames, she could see John's body swaying as he gestured, telling Gareth some outrageous story from his vast collection of tales about the Winterlands and its folk. The Fattest Bandit in the Winterlands? she wondered. Or one about his incredible Aunt Mattie? It occurred to her for the first time that it was for her, as well as for his people, that he had undertaken the King's command—for the things that she had never gotten, and for their sons.

It's not worth his life! she thought desperately, watching him. *I do well with what I have!* But the silent ruins of Ember mocked at her, their naked bones veiled by darkness, and the calm part of her heart whispered to her that it was his to choose, not hers. She could only do what she was doing—make her choice and abandon her studies to ride with him. The King had sent his command and his promise, and John would obey the King.

Five days south of Ember, the lands opened up once more. The forests gave way to the long, flat, alluvial slopes that led down to the Wildspae, the northern boundary of the lands of Belmarie. It was an empty countryside, but without the haunted desolation of the Winterlands; there were farms here, like little walled fortresses, and the road was at least passably drained. Here for the first time they met other travelers, merchants going north and east, with news and rumor of the capital—of the dread of the dragon that gripped the land, and the unrest in Bel due to the high price of grain.

"Stands to reason, don't it?" said a foxlike little trader, with his cavalcade of laden mules behind him. "What with the dragon ruining the harvest, and the grain rotting in the fields; yes, and the gnomes what took refuge in Bel itself hoarding the stuff, taking it out of the mouths of honest folk with their ill-got gold."

"Ill-got?" asked John curiously. "They mined and smelted it, didn't they?" Jenny, who wanted news without irritating its bearer, kicked him surreptitiously in the shin.

The merchant spat into the brimming ditch by the roadside and wiped his grizzled reddish beard. "That gives them no call to buy grain away from folks that needs it," he said. "And word has it that they're trafficking regular with their brothers up in Halnath—yes, and that they and the Master between them kidnapped the King's Heir, his only child, to hold for ransom."

"Could they have?" John inquired.

"Course they could. The Master's a sorcerer, isn't he? And the gnomes have never been up to any good, causing riot and mayhem in the capital..."

"Riot and mayhem?" Gareth protested. "But the gnomes have been our allies for time out of mind! There's never been trouble between us."

The man squinted up at him suspiciously. But he only grumbled, "Just goes to show, doesn't it? Treacherous little buggers." Jerking on his lead mule's bridle, he passed them by.

Not long after this they met a company of the gnomes themselves, traveling banded together, surrounded by guards for protection, with their wealth piled in carts and carriages. They peered up at John with wary, shortsighted eyes of amber or pale blue beneath low, wide brows, and gave him unwilling answers to his questions about the south.

"The dragon? Aye, it lairs yet in Ylferdun, and none of the men the King has sent have dislodged it." The gnome leader toyed with the soft fur trim of his gloves, and the thin winds billowed at the silk of his strangely cut garments. Behind him, the guards of the cavalcade watched the strangers in deepest suspicion, as if fearing an attack from even that few. "As for us, by the heart of the Deep, we have had enough of the charity of the sons of men, who charge us four times the going price for rooms the household servants would scorn and for food retrieved from the rats." His voice, thin and high like that of all the gnomes, was bitter with the verjuice of hate given back for hate. "Without the gold taken from the Deep, their city would never have been built, and yet not a man will speak to us in the streets, save to curse. They say in the city now that we plot with our brethren who fled through the back ways of the Deep into the Citadel of Halnath. By the Stone, it is lies; but such lies are believed now in Bel."

From the carts and carriages and curtained litters, a murmur of anger went up, the rage of those who have never before been helpless. Jenny, sitting quietly on Moon Horse, realized that it was the first time she had ever seen gnomes by daylight. Their eyes, wide and nearly colorless, were ill-attuned for its glare; the hearing that could catch the whispers of the cave bats would be daily tortured by the clamor of the cities of men.

Aversin asked, "And the King?"

"The King?" The gnome's piping voice was vicious, and his whole stooping little body bristled with the raw hurt of humiliation. "The King cares nothing for us. With all our wealth mewed up in the Deep, where the dragon sits hoarding over it, we have little to trade upon but promises, and with each day that passes those promises buy less in a city where bread is dear. And all this, while the King's whore sits with his head in her lap and poisons his mind as she poisons everything she touches—as she poisoned the very heart of the Deep."

Beside her, Jenny heard the hissing of Gareth's indrawn breath and saw the anger that flashed in his eyes, but he said nothing. When her glance questioned him, he looked away in shame.

As the gnomes moved out of sight once again into the mists, John remarked, "Sounds a proper snakes' nest. *Could* this Master really have kidnapped the King's child?"

"No," Gareth said miserably, as the horses resumed their walk toward the ferry, invisible in the foggy bottomlands to the south. "He couldn't have left the Citadel. He isn't a sorcerer—just a philosopher and an atheist. I—don't worry about the King's Heir." He looked down at his hands, and the expression on his face was the one that Jenny had seen in the camp outside Ember that night—a struggle to gather his courage. "Listen," he began shakily. "I have to . . ."

"Gar," said John quietly, and the boy startled as if burned. There was an ironic glint in John's brown eyes and an edge like chipped flint to his voice. "Now—the King wouldn't by any chance have sent for me for some other reason than the dragon, would he?"

"No," Gareth said faintly, not meeting his eyes. "No, he—he didn't."

"Didn't what?"

Gareth swallowed, his pale face suddenly very strained. "He—he didn't send for you—for any other reason. That is . . ."

"Because," John went on in that quiet voice, "if the King happened to send me his signet ring to get me involved in rescuing that child of his, or helping him against this Master of Halnath I hear such tell of, or for his dealings with the gnomes, I do have better things to do. There are real problems, not just money and power, in my own lands, and the winter closing in looks to be a bad one. I'll put my life at risk against the dragon for the sake of the King's protection to the Winterlands, but if there's aught else in it . . ."

"No!" Gareth caught his arm desperately, a terrible fear in his face, as if he thought that with little more provocation the Dragonsbane would turn around then and there and ride back to Wyr.

And perhaps, Jenny thought, remembering her vision in the water bowl, it might be better if they did.

"Aversin, it isn't like that. You are here to slay the dragon—because you're the only Dragonsbane living. That's the only reason I sought you out, I swear it. I swear it! Don't worry about politics and—and all that." His shortsighted gray eyes pleaded with Aversin to believe, but in them there was a desperation that could never have stemmed from innocence.

John's gaze held his for a long moment, gauging him. Then he said, "I'm trusting you, my hero."

In dismal silence, Gareth touched his heels to Battle-hammer's sides, and the big horse moved out ahead of them, the boy's borrowed plaids making them fade quickly into no more than a dark, cut-out shape in the colorless fogs. John, riding a little behind, slowed his horse so that he was next to Jenny, who had watched in speculative silence throughout.

"Maybe it's just as well you're with me after all, love."

She glanced from Gareth up to John, and then back. Somewhere a crow called, like the voice of that melancholy land. "I don't think he means us ill," she said softly.

"That doesn't mean he isn't gormless enough to get us killed all the same."

The mists thickened as they approached the river, until they moved through a chill white world where the only sound was the creak of harness leather, the pop of hooves, the faint jingle of bits, and the soughing rattle of the wind in the spiky cattails growing in the flooded ditches. From that watery grayness, each stone or solitary tree emerged, silent and dark, like a portent of strange events. More than all else, Jenny felt the weight of Gareth's silence, his fear and dread and guilt. John felt it, too, she knew; he watched the tall boy from the corner of his eye and listened to the hush of those empty lands like a man waiting for ambush. As evening darkened the air, Jenny called a blue ball of witchfire to light their feet, but the soft, opalescent walls of the mist threw back the light at them and left them nearly as blind as before.

"Jen." John drew rein, his head cocked to listen. "Can you hear it?"

"Hear what?" Gareth whispered, coming up beside them

at the top of the slope which dropped away into blankets of moving fog.

Jenny flung her senses wide through the dun-colored clouds, feeling as much as hearing the rushing voice of the river below. There were other sounds, muffled and altered by the fog, but unmistakable. "Yes," she said quietly, her breath a puff of white in the raw air. "Voices— horses—a group of them on the other side."

John glanced sharply sidelong at Gareth. "They could be waiting for the ferry," he said, "if they had business in the empty lands west of the river at the fall of night."

Gareth said nothing, but his face looked white and set. After a moment John clucked softly to Cow, and the big, shaggy sorrel plodded forward again down the slope to the ferry through the clammy wall of vapor.

Jenny let the witchlight ravel away as John pounded on the door of the squat stone ferry house. She and Gareth remained in the background while John and the ferryman negotiated the fare for three people, six horses, and two mules. "Penny a leg," said the ferryman, his squirrel-dark eyes darting from one to the other with the sharp interest of one who sees all the world pass his doorstep. "But there'll be supper here in an hour, and lodging for the night. It's growing mortal dark, and there's chowder fog."

"We can get along a few miles before full dark; and besides," John added, with an odd glint in his eye as he glanced back at the silent Gareth, "we may have someone waiting for us on the far bank."

"Ah." The man's wide mouth shut itself like a trap. "So it's you they're expecting. I heard 'em out there a bit ago, but they didn't ring no bell for me, so I bided by my stove where it's warm."

Holding up the lantern and struggling into his heavy quilted jacket, he led the way down to the slip, while Jenny followed silently behind, digging in the purse at her belt for coin.

The great horse Battlehammer had traveled north with Gareth by ship and, in any case, disdained balking at anything as sheer bad manners; neither Moon Horse nor Osprey nor any of the spares had such scruples, with the exception of Cow, who would have crossed a bridge of flaming knives at his customary phlegmatic plod. It took Jenny much whispered talk and stroking of ears before any of them would consent to set foot upon the big raft. The ferryman made the gate at the raft's tail fast and fixed his lantern on the pole at its head; then he set to turning the winch that drew the wide, flat platform out across the opaque silk of the river. The single lantern made a woolly blur of yellowish light in the leaden smoke of the fog; now and then, on the edge of the gleam, Jenny could see the brown waters parting around a snagged root or branch that projected from the current like a drowned hand.

From somewhere across the water she heard the jingle of metal on metal, the soft blowing of a horse, and men's voices. Gareth still said nothing, but she felt that, if she laid a hand upon him, she would find him quivering, as a rope does before it snaps. John came quietly to her side, his fingers twined warm and strong about hers. His spectacles flashed softly in the lanternlight as he slung an end of his voluminous plaid around her shoulders and drew her to his side.

"John," Gareth said quietly, "I—I have something to tell you."

Dimly through the fog came another sound, a woman's laugh like the tinkling of silver bells. Gareth twitched, and John, a dangerous flicker in his lazy-lidded eyes, said, "I thought you might."

"Aversin," Gareth stammered and stopped. Then he forced himself on with a rush, "Aversin, Jenny, listen. I'm sorry. I lied to you—I betrayed you, but I couldn't help it; I had no other choice. I'm sorry."

"Ah," said John softly. "So there was something you forgot to mention before we left the Hold?"

Unable to meet his eyes, Gareth said, "I meant to tell you earlier, but—but I couldn't. I was afraid you'd turn back and—and I couldn't let you turn back. We need you, we really do."

"For a lad who's always on about honor and courage," Aversin said, and there was an ugly edge to his quiet voice, "you haven't shown very much of either, have you?"

Gareth raised his head, and met his eyes, "No," he said. "I—I've been realizing that. I thought it was all right to deceive you in a good cause—that is—I had to get you to come..."

"All right, then," said John. "What is the truth?"

Jenny glanced from the faces of the two men toward the far shore, visible dimly now as a dark blur and a few lights moving like fireflies in the mist. A slightly darker cloud beyond would be the woodlands of Belmarie. She touched John's spiked elbow warningly, and he looked quickly in that direction. Movement stirred there, shapes crowding down to wait for the ferry to put in. The horse Battlehammer flung up his head and whinnied, and an answering whinny trumpeted back across the water. The Dragonsbane's eyes returned to Gareth and he folded his hands over the hilt of his sword.

Gareth drew a deep breath. "The truth is that the King didn't send for you," he said. "In fact, he—he forbade me to come looking for you. He said it was a foolish quest, because you probably didn't exist at all and, even if you did, you'd have been killed by another dragon long ago. He said he didn't want me to risk my life chasing a phantom. But—but I had to find you. He wasn't going to send anyone else. And you're the only Dragonsbane, as it was in all the ballads..." He stammered uncertainly. "Except that I didn't know then that it wasn't like the ballads. But I knew you had to exist. And I knew we needed someone.

I couldn't stand by and let the dragon go on terrorizing the countryside. I had to come and find you. And once I found you, I had to bring you back..."

"Having decided you knew better about the needs of my people and my own choice in the matter than I did?" John's face never showed much expression, but his voice had a sting to it now, like a scorpion's tail.

Gareth shied from it, as from a lash. "I—I thought of that, these last days," he said softly. He looked up again, his face white with an agony of shame. "But I couldn't let you turn back. And you will be rewarded, I swear I'll see that you get the reward somehow."

"And just how'll you manage that?" John's tone was sharp with disgust. The deck jarred beneath their feet as the raft ground against the shoals. Lights like marsh candles bobbed down toward them through the gloom. "With a mage at the Court, it couldn't have taken them long to figure out who'd pinched the King's seal, nor when he'd be back in Belmarie. I expect the welcoming committee..." he gestured toward the dark forms crowding forward from the mists. "...is here to arrest you for treason."

"No," Gareth said in a defeated voice. "They'll be my friends from Court."

As if stepping through a door the forms came into visibility; lanternlight danced over the hard gleam of satin, caressed velvet's softer nap, and touched edges of stiffened lace and the cloudy gauze of women's veils, salted all over with the leaping fire of jewels. In the forefront of them all was a slender, dark-haired girl in amber silk, whose eyes, golden as honey with a touch of gray, sought Gareth's and caused the boy to turn aside with a blush. One man was holding a cloak for her of ermine-tagged velvet; another her golden pomander ball. She laughed, a sound at once silvery and husky, like an echo from a troubled dream.

It could be no one but Zyerne.

John looked inquiringly back at Gareth.

"That seal you showed me was real," he said. "I've seen it on the old documents, down to the little nicks on its edges. They're taking its theft a bit casually, aren't they?"

He laid hold of Cow's bridle and led him down the short gangplank, forcing the others to follow. As they stepped ashore, every courtier on the bank, led by Zyerne, swept in unison into an elaborate Phoenix Rising salaam, touching their knees in respect to the clammy, fish-smelling mud.

Crimson-faced, Gareth admitted, "Not really. Technically it wasn't theft. The King is my father. I'm the missing Heir."

CHAPTER V

"So that's your Dragonsbane, is it?"

At the sound of Zyerne's voice, Jenny paused in the stony blue dimness of the hall of the enchantress's hunting lodge. From the gloom in which she stood, the little antechamber beyond the hall glowed like a lighted stage; the rose-colored gauze of Zyerne's gown, the whites and violets of Gareth's doublet, sleeves, and hose, and the pinks and blacks of the rugs beneath their feet all seemed to burn like the hues of stained glass in the ember-colored lamplight. The instincts of the Winterlands kept Jenny to the shadows. Neither saw her.

Zyerne held her tiny goblet of crystal and glass up to one of the lamps on the mantel, admiring the blood red lights of the liqueur within. She smiled mischievously. "I must say, I prefer the ballad version myself."

Seated in one of the gilt-footed ivory chairs on the opposite side of the low wine table, Gareth only looked unhappy and confused. The dimple on the side of Zyerne's curving, shell pink lips deepened, and she brushed a corner of her lace veils aside from her cheek. Combs of crystal and sardonyx flashed in her dark hair as she tipped her head.

When Gareth didn't speak, her smile widened a little, and she moved with sinuous grace to stand near enough to him to envelop him in the faint aura of her perfume. Like shooting stars, the lamplight jumped from the crystal facets of Gareth's goblet with the involuntary tremor of his hand.

"Aren't you even going to thank me for coming to meet you and offering you the hospitality of my lodge?" Zyerne asked, her voice teasing.

Because she was jealous of Zyerne's greater powers, Jenny had forced herself to feel, upon meeting her at the ferry, nothing but surprise at the enchantress's youth. She looked no more than twenty, though at the lowest computation—which Jenny could not keep herself from making, though the cattiness of her reaction distressed her—her age could not have been much less than twenty-six. Where there was jealousy, there could be no learning, she had told herself; and in any case she owed this girl justice.

But now anger stirred in her. Zyerne's closeness and the hand that she laid with such artless intimacy on Gareth's shoulder, so that less than a half-inch of her fingertip touched the flesh of his neck above his collar-lace could be nothing but calculated temptations. From what he had told her—from every tense line of his face and body now—Jenny knew he was struggling with all that was in him against his desire for his father's mistress. Judging by her expression in the lamplight, Gareth's efforts to resist amused Zyerne very much.

"Lady—Lady Jenny?"

Jenny's head turned quickly at the hesitant voice. The stairway of the lodge was enclosed in an elaborate latticework of pierced stone; in the fretted shadows, she could make out the shape of a girl of sixteen or so. Only a little taller than Jenny herself, she was like an exquisitely dressed doll, her hair done up in an exaggeration of Zyerne's elaborate coiffure and dyed like white-and-purple taffy.

The girl curtseyed. "My name is Trey, Trey Clerlock." She glanced nervously at the two forms framed in the lighted antechamber, then back up the stair, as if fearing that one of Zyerne's other guests would come down and overhear. "Please don't take this wrongly, but I came to offer to lend you a dress for dinner, if you'd like one."

Jenny glanced down at her own gown, russet wool with a hand like silk, banded with embroideries of red and blue. In deference to custom which dictated that no woman in polite society was ever seen with her hair uncovered, she had even donned the white silk veil John had brought back to her from the east. In the Winterlands she would have been accounted royally clad.

"Does it matter so much?"

The girl Trey looked as embarrassed as years of deportment lessons would let her. "It shouldn't," she said frankly. "It doesn't, really, to me, but . . . but some people at Court can be very cruel, especially about things like being properly dressed. I'm sorry," she added quickly, blushing as she stepped out of the checkered darkness of the stair. Jenny could see now that she carried a bundle of black and silver satin and a long, trailing mass of transparent gauze veils, whose random sequins caught stray spangles of light.

Jenny hesitated. Ordinarily the conventions of polite society never had bothered her, and her work left her little time for them in any case. Knowing she would be coming to the King's court, she had brought the best gown she had—her only formal gown, as a matter of fact—aware that it would be out of date. It had been no concern to her what others thought of her for wearing it.

But from the moment she had stepped from the ferry earlier that evening, she had had the feeling of walking among unmarked pitfalls. Zyerne and her little band of courtiers had been all polite graciousness, but she had sensed the covert mockery in their language of eyebrows and glances. It had angered her and puzzled her, too, reminding her too much of the way the other children in the village had treated her as a child. But the child in her was alive enough to feel a morbid dread of their sport.

Zyerne's sweet laughter drifted out into the hall. "I vow the fellow was looking about him for a bootscraper as he crossed the threshold . . . I didn't know whether to offer him a room with a bed or a pile of nice, comfortable rushes on the floor—you know a good hostess must make her guests feel at home . . ."

For a moment Jenny's natural suspicion made her wonder if the offer of a gown itself might be part of some scheme to make her look ridiculous. But Trey's worried blue eyes held nothing but concern for her—and a little for herself, lest she be spotted in the act of spoiling sport. Jenny considered for a moment defying them, then discarded the idea—whatever gratification it might bring was scarcely worth the fight. She had been raised in the Winterlands, and every instinct she possessed whispered for the concealment of protective coloration.

She held out her hands for the slithery armfuls of satin.

"You can change in the little room beneath the stairs," Trey offered, looking relieved. "It's a long way back to your rooms."

"And a longer one back to your own home," Jenny pointed out, her hand on the latch of the concealed door. "Did you send for this specially, then?"

Trey regarded her with guileless surprise. "Oh, no. When Zyerne knew Gareth was returning, she told us all we'd come here for a welcome dinner: my brother Bond and myself, the Beautiful Isolde, Caspar of Walfrith and Merriwyn of Longcleat, and all the others. I always bring two or three different dinner gowns. I mean, I didn't know two days ago what I might want to wear."

She was perfectly serious, so Jenny repressed her smile.

She went on, "It's a little long, but I thought it looked like your colors. Here in the south, only servants wear brown."

"Ah." Jenny touched the folds of her own gown, which caught a cinnamon edge in the glow from the antechamber's lamps. "Thank you, Trey, very much—and Trey? Could I ask yet another favor?"

"Of course," the girl said generously. "I can help..."

"I think I can manage. John—Lord Aversin—will be down in a few moments..." She paused, thinking of the somewhat old-fashioned but perfectly decent brown velvet of his doublet and indoor cloak. But it was something about which she could do nothing, and she shook her head. "Ask him to wait, if you would."

The room beneath the stairs was small, but showed evidence of hasty toilettes and even hastier romantic assignations. As she changed clothes, Jenny could hear the courtiers assembling in the hall to await the summons for dinner. Occasionally she could catch some of the muted bustling from the servants in the dining hall beyond the antechamber, laying the six cloths and undercover so necessary, according to Gareth, to the proper conduct of a meal; now and then a maid would laugh and be rebuked by the butler. Nearer, soft voices gossiped and teased: "...well, really, what can you say about someone who still wears those awful smocked sleeves—and she's so *proud* of them, too!"... "Yes, but in broad daylight? *Outdoors?* And with her *husband?*"... "Well, of course it's all a plot by the gnomes..." "Did you hear the joke about why gnomes have flat noses?"

Closer, a man's voice laughed, and asked, "Gareth, are you sure you found the right man? I mean, you didn't mistake the address and fetch someone else entirely?"

"Er—well—" Gareth sounded torn between his loyalty to his friends and his dread of mockery. "I suppose you'd call him a bit barbaric, Bond..."

"A bit!" The man Bond laughed richly. "That is to say that the dragon has caused 'a bit' of trouble, or that old Polycarp tried to murder you 'a bit.' And you're taking him to Court? Father *will* be pleased."

"Gareth?" There was sudden concern in Zyerne's lilting voice. "You did get his credentials, didn't you? Membership in the Guild of Dragonsbanes, Proof of Slaughter..."

"Testimonials from Rescued Maidens," Bond added. "Or is that one of his rescued maidens he has with him?"

Above her head, Jenny felt rather than heard a light descending tread on the steps. It was the tread of a man raised to caution and it stopped, as her own had stopped for a moment, at the point on the stairs just behind where the light fell from the room beyond. As she hastened to pull on the stiffened petticoats, she could feel his silence in the entwining shadows of the latticed staircase.

"Of course!" Bond was saying, in the voice of a man suddenly enlightened. "He has to carry her about with him because nobody in the Winterlands can read a written testimonial! It's similar to the barter system, you see..."

"Well," another woman's voice purred, "if you ask me, she isn't much of a maiden."

With teasing naughtiness, Zyerne giggled. "Perhaps it wasn't much of a dragon."

"She must be thirty if she's a day," someone else added.

"Now, my dear," Zyerne chided, "let us not be catty. That rescue was a long time ago."

In the general laugh, Jenny was not sure, but she thought she heard the footsteps overhead soundlessly retreat. Zyerne went on, "I do think, if this Dragonsbane of yours was going to cart a woman along, he might at least have picked a pretty one, instead of someone who looks like a gnome—a short little thing with all that hair. She scarcely needs a veil for modesty."

"That's probably why she doesn't wear one."

"If you're going to be charitable, my dear..."

"She isn't..." began Gareth's voice indignantly.

"Oh, Gareth, don't take everything so seriously!" Zyerne's laughter mocked him. "It's such a bore, darling, besides giving you wrinkles. There. Smile. Really, it's all in jest—a man who can't take a little joking is only a short step from far more serious sins, like eating his salad with a fish fork. I say, you don't think..."

Her hands shaking with a queerly feelingless anger, Jenny straightened her veils. The mere touch of the stiffened gauze fired a new spurt of irritation through her, annoyance at them and that same sense of bafflement she had felt before. The patterns of human relationships interested her, and this one, shot through with a web of artificiality and malice, explained a good deal about Gareth. But the childishness of it quelled her anger, and she was able to slip soundlessly from her cubbyhole and stand among them for several minutes before any of them became aware of her presence.

Lamps had been kindled in the hall. In the midst of a small crowd of admiring courtiers, Zyerne seemed to sparkle bewitchingly under a powdering of diamonds and lace. "I'll tell you," she was saying. "However much gold Gareth was moved to offer the noble Dagonsbane as a reward, I think we can offer him a greater one. We'll show him a few of the amenities of civilization. How does that sound? He slays our dragon and we teach him how to eat with a fork?"

There was a good deal of appreciative laughter at this. Jenny noticed the girl Trey joining in, but without much enthusiasm. The man standing next to her must be her brother Bond, she guessed; he had his sister's fine-boned prettiness, set off by fair hair of which one lovelock, trailing down onto a lace collar, was dyed blue. Beside his graceful slimness, Gareth looked—and no doubt felt—gangly, overgrown, and miserably out of place; his expression was one of profound unhappiness and embarrassment.

It might have been merely because he wasn't wearing his spectacles—they were doubtless hideously unfashionable—but he was looking about him at the exquisite carvings of the rafters, at the familiar glimmer of lamplit silk and stiffened lace, and at the faces of his friends, with a weary confusion, as if they had all become strangers to him.

Even now, Bond was saying, "And is your Dragonsbane as great as Silkydrawers the Magnificent, who slew the Crimson-and-Purple-Striped Dragon in the Golden Woods back in the Reign of Potpourri the Well-Endowed—or was it Kneebiter the Ineffectual? Do enlighten me, Prince."

But before the wretched Gareth could answer, Zyerne said suddenly, "My dears!" and came hurrying to Jenny, her small white hands stretched from the creamy lace of her sleeve ruffles. The smile on her face was as sweet and welcoming as if she greeted a long-lost friend. "My dearest Lady Jenny—forgive me for not seeing you sooner! You look exquisite! Did darling Trey lend you her black-and-silver? How very charitable of her..."

A bell rang in the dining room, and the minstrels in the gallery began to play. Zyerne took Jenny's arm to lead in the guests—first women, then men, after the custom of the south—to dinner. Jenny glanced quickly around the hall, looking for John but knowing he would not be there. A qualm crossed her stomach at the thought of sitting through this alone.

Beside her, the light voice danced on. "Oh, yes, you're a mage, too, aren't you?... You know I did have some very good training, but it's the sort of thing that has always come to me by instinct. You must tell me about using your powers to make a living. I've never had to do that, you know..." Like the prick of knives in her back, she felt the covert smiles of those who walked in procession behind.

Yet because they were deliberate, Jenny found that the younger woman's slights had lost all power to wound her. They stirred in her less anger than Zyerne's temptation of Gareth had. Arrogance she had expected, for it was the besetting sin of the mageborn and Jenny knew herself to be as much prey to it as the others and she sensed the enormous power within Zyerne. But this condescension was a girl's ploy, the trick of one who was herself insecure.

What, she wondered, did Zyerne have to feel insecure about?

As they took their places at the table, Jenny's eyes traveled slowly along its length, seeing it laid like a winter forest with snowy linen and the crystal icicles of candelabra pendant with jewels. Each silver plate was inlaid with traceries of gold and flanked with a dozen little forks and spoons, the complicated armory of etiquette; all these young courtiers in their scented velvet and stiffened lace were clearly her slaves, each more interested in carrying on a dialogue, however brief, with her, than with any of their neighbors. Everything about that delicate hunting lodge was designed to speak her name, from the entwined Zs and Us carved in the corners of the ceiling to the delicate bronze of the horned goddess of love Hartemgarbes, wrought in Zyerne's image, in its niche near the door. Even the delicate music of hautbois and hurdygurdy in the gallery was a proclamation, a boast that Zyerne had and would tolerate nothing but the very finest.

Why then the nagging fear that lay behind pettiness?

She turned to look at Zyerne with clinical curiosity, wondering about the pattern of that girl's life. Zyerne's eyes met hers and caught their expression of calm and slightly pitying question. For an instant, the golden orbs narrowed, scorn and spite and anger stirring in their depths. Then the sweet smile returned, and Zyerne asked, "My dear, you haven't touched a bite. Do you use forks in the north?"

There was a sudden commotion in the arched doorway of the hall. One of the minstrels in the gallery, shocked, hit a glaringly wrong squawk out of his recorder; the others stumbled to silence.

"Gaw," Aversin's voice said, and every head along the shimmering board turned, as if at the clatter of a dropped plate. "Late again."

He stepped into the waxlight brightness of the hall with a faint jingle of scraps of chain mail and stood looking about him, his spectacles glinting like steel-rimmed moons. He had changed back into the battered black leather he'd worn on the journey, the wolfhide-lined jerkin with its stray bits of mail and metal plates and spikes and the dark leather breeches and scarred boots. His plaids were slung back over his shoulder like a cloak, cleaned of mud but frayed and scruffy, and there was a world of bright mischief in his eyes.

Gareth, at the other end of the table, went red with mortification to the roots of his thinning hair. Jenny only sighed, momentarily closed her eyes, and thought resignedly, *John*.

He strode cheerily into the room, bowing with impartial goodwill to the courtiers along the board, not one of whom seemed capable of making a sound. They had, for the most part, been looking forward to baiting a country cousin as he tried unsuccessfully to ape his betters; they had scarcely been prepared for an out-and-out barbarian who obviously wasn't even going to bother to try.

With a friendly nod to his hostess, he settled into his place on the opposite side of Zyerne from Jenny. For a moment, he studied the enormous battery of cutlery arrayed on both sides of his plate and then, with perfect neatness and cleanliness, proceeded to eat with his fingers.

Zyerne recovered her composure first. With a silky smile, she picked up a fish fork and offered it to him. "Just as a suggestion, my lord. We *do* do things differently here."

Somewhere down the board, one of the ladies tittered. Aversin regarded Zyerne with undisguised suspicion. She speared a scallop with the fish fork and held it out to him, by way of demonstration, and he broke into his sunniest smile. "Ah, so that's what they're for," he said, relieved. Removing the scallop from the tines with his fingers, he took a neat bite out of it. In a north-country brogue six times worse than anything Jenny had ever heard him use at home, he added, "And here I was thinking I'd been in your lands less than a night, and already challenged to a duel with an unfamiliar weapon, and by the local magewife at that. You had me gie worrit."

On his other side, Bond Clerlock nearly choked on his soup, and John thumped him helpfully on the back.

"You know," he went on, gesturing with the fork in one hand and selecting another scallop with the other, "we did uncover a great box of these things—all different sizes they were, like these here—in the vaults of the Hold the year we looked out the bath for my cousin Kat's wedding. We hadn't a clue what they were for, not even Father Hiero—Father Hiero's our priest—but the next time the bandits came down raiding from the hills, we loaded the lot into the ballistas instead of stone shot and let fly. Killed one of 'em dead on the spot and two others went riding off over the moor with all these little spikey things sticking into their backs . . ."

"I take it," Zyerne said smoothly, as stifled giggles skittered around the table, "that your cousin's wedding was an event of some moment, if it occasioned a bath?"

"Oh, aye." For someone whose usual expression was one of closed watchfulness, Aversin had a dazzling smile. "She was marrying this southern fellow..."

It was probably, Jenny thought, the first time that anyone had succeeded in taking an audience away from Zyerne, and, by the glint in the sorceress's eyes, she did not like it. But the courtiers, laughing, were drawn into the circle of Aversin's warm and dotty charm; his exaggerated barbarity disarmed their mockery as his increasingly outrageous tale of his cousin's fictitious nuptials reduced them to undignified whoops. Jenny had enough of a spiteful streak in her to derive a certain amount of enjoyment from Zyerne's discomfiture—it was Zyerne, after all, who had mocked Gareth for not being able to take jests—but confined her attention to her plate. If John was going to the trouble of drawing their fire so that she could finish her meal in peace, the least she could do was not let his efforts go to waste.

On her other side, Trey said softly, "He doesn't look terribly ferocious. From Gareth's ballads, I'd pictured him differently—stern and handsome, like the statues of the god Sarmendes. But then," she added, winkling the meat from an escargot with the special tongs to show Jenny how it was done, "I suppose it would have been a terrific bore for you to ride all the way back from the Winterlands with someone who just spent his time 'scanning th'encircling welkin with his eagle-lidded eyes,' as the song says."

In spite of Zyerne's disapproving glances, her handsome cicisbeo Bond was wiping tears of laughter from his eyes, albeit with great care for his makeup. Even the servants were having a hard time keeping their faces properly expressionless as they carried in peacocks roasted and resplendent in all their feathers and steaming removes of venison in cream.

"... so the bridegroom looked about for one of those

wood things such as you have here in my rooms," John was continuing, "but as he couldn't find one, he hung his clothes over the armor-stand, and damned if Cousin Kat didn't wake in the night and set about it with her sword, taking it for a bandit..."

Trust John, Jenny thought, that if he couldn't make an impression on them on their own grounds, he wouldn't try to do it on the grounds of Gareth's ballads, either. They had succumbed to the devil of mischief in him, the devil that had drawn her from the first moment they had met as adults. He had used his outrageousness as a defense against their scorn, but the fact that he had been able to use it successfully made her think a little better of these courtiers of Zyerne's.

She finished her meal in silence, and none of them saw her go.

"Jenny, wait." A tall figure detached itself from the cluster of bright forms in the antechamber and hurried across the hall to catch her, tripping over a footstool half-way.

Jenny paused in the enclosing shadow of the stair lattice. From the anteroom, music was already lilting—not the notes of the hired musicians, this time, but the complex tunes made to show off the skill of the courtiers themselves. To play well, it seemed, was the mark of a true gentleperson; the music of the cwrdth and the double-dulcimer blended into a counterpoint like lace, from which themes would emerge like half-familiar faces glimpsed in a crowd. Over the elaborate harmonies, she heard the blithe, unrepentant air of the pennywhistle, following the melody by ear, and she smiled. If the Twelve Gods of the Cosmos came down, they would be hard put to disconcert John.

"Jenny, I—I'm sorry." Gareth was panting a little from his haste. He had resumed his battered spectacles; the

fracture in the bottom of the right-hand lens glinted like
a star. "I didn't know it would be like that. I thought—
he's a Dragonsbane..."

She was standing a few steps up the flight; she put out
her hand and touched his face, nearly on level with her
own. "Do you remember when you first met him?"

He flushed with embarrassment. In the illuminated
antechamber, John's scruffy leather and plaids made him
look like a mongrel in a pack of lapdogs. He was exam-
ining a lute-shaped hurdy-gurdy with vast interest, while
the red-haired, Beautiful Isolde of Greenhythe told the
latest of her enormous stock of scatalogical jokes about
the gnomes. Everyone guffawed but John, who was far
too interested in the musical instrument in his lap to notice;
Jenny saw Gareth's mouth tighten with something between
anger and confused pain. He went north seeking a dream,
she thought; now he had neither that which he had sought
nor that to which he had thought he would return.

"I shouldn't have let them bait you like that," he said
after a moment. "I didn't think Zyerne..."

He broke off, unable to say it. She saw bitterness harden
his mouth, and a disillusion worse than the one John had
dealt him beside the pigsty at Alyn. He had probably
never seen Zyerne being petty before, she thought; or
perhaps he had only seen her in the context of the world
she had created, never having been outside of it himself.
He took a deep breath and went on, "I know I should
have taken up for you somehow, but...but I didn't
know how!" He spread his hands helplessly. With the first
rueful humor at himself that Jenny had seen, he added,
"You know, in ballads it's so easy to rescue someone. I
mean, even if you're defeated, at least you can die grace-
fully and not have everyone you know laugh at you for
the next three weeks."

Jenny laughed and reached out to pat his arm. In the
gloom, his features were only an edge of gold along the

awkward cheekline, and the twin circles of glass were opaque with the lamplight's reflection that glinted on a few flame-caught strands of hair and formed a spiky illumination along the edges of his lace collar. "Don't worry about it." She smiled. "Like slaying dragons, it's a special art."

"Look," said Gareth, "I—I'm sorry I tricked you. I wouldn't have done it, if I'd known it would be like this. But Zyerne sent a messenger to my father—it's only a day's ride to Bel, and a guest house is being prepared for you in the Palace. I'll be with you when you present yourselves to him, and I know he'll be willing to make terms . . ." He caught himself, as if remembering his earlier lying assurances. "That is, I really *do* know it, this time. Since the coming of the dragon, there's been a huge standing reward for its slaying, more than the pay of a garrison for a year. He has to listen to John."

Jenny leaned one shoulder against the openwork of the newel post, the chips of reflected lamplight filtering through the lattice and dappling her black and silver gown with gold. "Is it so important to you?"

He nodded. Even with the fashionable padding of his white-and-violet doublet, his narrow shoulders looked stooped with tiredness and defeat. "I didn't tell very much truth at the Hold," he said quietly. "But I did tell this: that I know I'm not a warrior, or a knight, and I know I'm not good at games. And I'm not stupid enough to think that the dragon wouldn't kill me in a minute, if I went there. But—I know everyone around here laughs when I talk about chivalry and honor and a knight's duty, and you and John do, too . . . But that's what makes John the Thane of the Winterlands and not just another bandit, doesn't it? He didn't *have* to kill that first dragon." The boy gestured wearily, a half-shrug that sent fragments of luminosity slithering along the white stripes of his slashed sleeves to the diamonds at his cuffs. "I couldn't not do something. Even if I did muff it up."

Jenny felt she had never liked him so well. She said, "If you had truly muffed it up, we wouldn't be here."

She climbed the stairs slowly and crossed the gallery that spanned the hall below. Like the stair, it was enclosed in a stone trellis cut into the shapes of vines and trees, and the shadows flickered in a restless harlequin over her gown and hair. She felt tired and cold from holding herself braced all evening—the sly baiting and lace-trimmed malice of Zyerne's court had stung more than she cared to admit. She pitied them, a little, for what they were, but she did not have John's brass hide.

She and John had been given the smaller of the two rooms at the end of the wing; Gareth, the larger, next door to theirs. Like everything else in Zyerne's lodge, they were beautifully appointed. The red damasked bed hangings and alabaster lamps were designed both as a setting for Zyerne's beauty and a boast of her power to get what she wanted from the King. No wonder, thought Jenny, Gareth distrusted and hated any witch who held sway over a ruler's heart.

As she left the noise of the gallery behind her and turned down the corridor toward her room, she became conscious of the stiff rustling of her borrowed finery upon the inlaid wood of the floor and, with her old instinct for silence, gathered the heavy skirts up in her hands. Lamplight from a half-opened door laid a molten trapezoid of brightness across the darkness before her. Zyerne, Jenny knew, was not downstairs with the others, and she felt uneasy about meeting that beautiful, spoiled, powerful girl, especially here in her own hunting lodge where she held sole dominion. Thus Jenny passed the open doorway in a drift of illusion; and, though she paused in the shadows at what she saw by the lights within, she remained herself unseen.

It would have been so, she thought later, even had she not been cloaked in the spells that thwart the casual eye. Zyerne sat in an island of brightness, the glow of a night-lamp stroking the gilt-work of her blackwood chair, so still that not even the rose-point shadows of her lace veils stirred upon her gown. Her hands were cupped around the face of Bond Clerlock, who knelt at her feet, and such was his immobility that not even the sapphires pinning his hair glinted, but burned steadily with a single reflection. Though he looked up toward her face, his eyes were closed; his expression was the contorted, intent face of a man in ecstasy so strong that it borders pain.

The room smoked with magic, the weight of it like a glittering lour in the air. As a mage, Jenny could feel it, smell it like an incense; but it was an incense tainted with rot. She stepped back, repelled. Though the touch of Zyerne's hands upon Bond's face was the only contact between their two bodies, she had the sickened sensation of having looked upon that which was obscene. Zyerne's eyes were closed, her childlike brow puckered in slight concentration; the smile that curved her lips was one of physical and emotional satisfaction, like a woman's after the act of love.

Not love, thought Jenny, drawing back from the scene and moving soundlessly down the hall once more, but some private satiation.

She sat for a long time in the dark window embrasure of her room and thought about Zyerne. The moon rose, flecking the bare tips of the trees above the white carpet of ground mists; she heard the clocks strike downstairs and the drift of voices and laughter. The moon was in its first quarter, and something about that troubled her, though she could not for the moment think what. After a long time she heard the door open softly behind her and turned to see John silhouetted in the dim lamplight from the hall, its reflection throwing a scatter of metallic glints from his doublet and putting a rough halo on the coarse wool of his plaids.

Into the darkness he said softly, "Jen?"

"Here."

Moonlight flashed across his specs. She moved a little—the barring of the casement shadows on her black and silver gown made her nearly invisible. He came cautiously across the unfamiliar terrain of the floor, his hands and face pale blurs against his dark clothing.

"Gaw," he said in disgust as he slung off his plaids. "To come here to risk my bones slaying a dragon and end up playing dancing bear for a pack of children." He sat on the edge of the curtained bed, working at the heavy buckles of his doublet.

"Did Gareth speak to you?"

His spectacles flashed again as he nodded.

"And?"

John shrugged. "Seeing the pack he runs with, I'm not surprised he's a gammy-handed chuff with less sense than my Cousin Dilly's mulberry bushes. And he did take the risk to search for me, I'll give him that." His voice was muffled as he bent over to pull off his boots. "Though I'll wager all the dragon's gold to little green apples he had no idea how dangerous it would be. God knows what I'd have done in his shoes, and him that desperate to help and knowing he hadn't a chance against the dragon himself." He set his boots on the floor and sat up again. "However we came here, I'd be a fool not to speak with the King and see what he'll offer me, though it's in my mind that we'll run up against Zyerne in any dealings we have with him."

Even while playing dancing bear, thought Jenny as she drew the pins from her hair and let her fashionable veils slither to the floor, John didn't miss much. The stiffened silk felt cold under her fingers, from the touch of the window's nearness, even as her hair did when she unwound its thick coil and let it whisper dryly down over her bony, half-bared shoulders.

At length she said, "When Gareth first spoke to me of her, I was jealous, hating her without ever having seen her. She has everything that I wanted, John: genius, time ...and beauty," she added, realizing that that, too, mattered. "I was afraid it was that, still."

"I don't know, love." He got to his feet, barefoot in breeches and creased shirt, and came to the window where she sat. "It doesn't sound very like you." His hands were warm through the stiff, chilly satins of her borrowed gown as he collected the raven weight of her hair and sorted it into columns that spilled down through his fingers. "I don't know about her magic, for I'm not mageborn myself, but I do know she is cruel for the sport of it—not in the big things that would get her pointed at, but in the little ones—and she leads the others on, teaching them by example and jest to be as cruel as she. Myself, I'd take a whip to Ian, if he treated a guest as she treated you. I see now what that gnome we met on the road meant when he said she poisons what she touches. But she's only a mistress, when all's said. And as for her being beautiful..." He shrugged. "If I was a bit shapecrafty, I'd be beautiful, too."

In spite of herself Jenny laughed and leaned back into his arms.

But later, in the darkness of the curtained bed, the memory of Zyerne returned once more to her thoughts. She saw again the enchantress and Bond in the rosy aura of the nightlamp and felt the weight and strength of the magic that had filled the room like the silent build of thunder. Was it the magnitude of the power alone that had frightened her, she wondered. Or had it been some sense of filthiness that lay in it, like the back-taste of souring milk? Or had that, in its turn, been only the wormwood of her own jealousy of the younger woman's greater arts?

John had said that it didn't sound very like her, but she knew he was wrong. It was like her, like the part of herself she fought against, the fourteen-year-old girl still buried in her soul, weeping with exhausted, bitter rage when the rains summoned by her teacher would not disperse at her command. She had hated Caerdinn for being stronger than she. And although the long years of looking after the irascible old man had turned that hatred to affection, she had never forgotten that she was capable of it. Even, she added ironically to herself, as she was capable of working the death-spells on a helpless man, as she had on the dying robber in the ruins of the town; even as she was capable of leaving a man and two children who loved her, because of her love of the quest for power.

Would I have been able to understand what I saw tonight if I had given all my time, all my heart, to the study of magic? Would I have had power like that, mighty as a storm gathered into my two hands?

Through the windows beyond the half-parted bedcurtains, she could see the chill white eye of the moon. Its light, broken by the leading of the casement, lay scattered like the spangles of a fish's mail across the black and silver satin of the gown that she had worn and over the respectable brown velvet suit that John had not. It touched the bed and picked out the scars that crossed John's bare arm, glimmered on the upturned palm of his hand, and outlined the shape of his nose and lips against the darkness. Her vision in the water bowl returned to her again, an icy shadow on her heart.

Would she be able to save him, she wondered, if she were more powerful? If she had given her time to her powers wholly, instead of portioning it between them and him? Was that, ultimately, what she had cast unknowingly away?

Somewhere in the night a hinge creaked. Stilling her breathing to listen, she heard the almost soundless pat of bare feet outside her door and the muffled vibration of a shoulder blundering into the wall.

She slid from beneath the silken quilts and pulled on her shift. Over it she wrapped the first garment she laid hands on, John's voluminous plaids, and swiftly crossed the blackness of the room to open the door.

"Gar?"

He was standing a few feet from her, gawky and very boyish-looking in his long nightshirt. His gray eyes stared out straight ahead of him, without benefit of spectacles, and his thin hair was flattened and tangled from the pillow. He gasped at the sound of her voice and almost fell, groping for the wall's support. She realized then that she had waked him.

"Gar, it's me, Jenny. Are you all right?"

His breathing was fast with shock. She put her hand gently on his arm to steady him, and he blinked myopically down at her for a moment. Then he drew a long breath. "Fine," he said shakily. "I'm fine, Jenny. I . . ." He looked around him and ran an unsteady hand through his hair. "I—I must have been walking in my sleep again."

"Do you often?"

He nodded and rubbed his face. "That is . . . I didn't in the north, but I do sometimes here. It's just that I dreamed . . ." He paused, frowning, trying to recall. "Zyerne . . ."

"Zyerne?"

Sudden color flooded his pallid face. "Nothing," he mumbled, and avoided her eyes. "That is—I don't remember."

After she had seen him safely back to the dark doorway of his room, Jenny stood for a moment in the hall, hearing the small sounds of bedcurtains and sheets as he returned to his rest. How late it was, she could not guess. The hunting lodge was deathly silent about her, the smells of long-dead candles, spilled wine, and the frowsty residue of spent passions now flat and stale. All the length of the corridor, every room was dark save one, whose door stood ajar. The dim glow of a single nightlamp shone within, and its light lay across the silky parquet of the floor like a dropped scarf of luminous gold.

CHAPTER VI

"HE'LL HAVE TO listen to you." Gareth perched himself in the embrasure of one of the tall windows that ran the length of the southern wall of the King's Gallery, the wan sunlight shimmering with moony radiance in the old-fashioned jewels he wore. "I've just heard that the dragon destroyed the convoy taking supplies out to the siege troops at Halnath last night. Over a thousand pounds of flour and sugar and meat destroyed—horses and oxen dead or scattered—the bodies of the guards burned past recognition."

He nervously adjusted the elaborate folds of his ceremonial mantlings and peered shortsightedly at John and Jenny, who shared a carved bench of ebony inlaid with malachite. Due to the exigencies of court etiquette, formal costume had been petrified into a fashion a hundred and fifty years out of date, with the result that all the courtiers and petitioners assembled in the long room had the stilted, costumed look of characters in a masquerade. Jenny noticed that John, though he might persist in playing the barbarian in his leather and plaids among the admiring younger courtiers, was not about to do so in the presence of the King. Gareth had draped John's blue-and-cream satin mantlings for him—a valet's job. Bond Clerlock had offered to do it but, Jenny gathered, there were rigid sartorial rules governing such matters; it would have been very like Bond to arrange the elaborate garment in some ridiculous style, knowing the Dragonsbane was unable to tell the difference.

Bond was present among the courtiers who awaited the arrival of the King. Jenny could see him, further down the King's Gallery, standing in one of the slanting bars of pale, platinum light. As usual, his costume outshone every other man's present; his mantlings were a miracle of complex folds and studied elegance, so thick with embroidery that they glittered like a snake's back; his flowing sleeves, six generations out of date, were precise to a quarter-inch in their length and hang. He had even painted his face in the archaic formal fashion, which some of the courtiers did in preference to the modern applications of kohl and rouge—John had flatly refused to have anything to do with either style. The colors accentuated the pallor of young Clerlock's face, though he looked better, Jenny noted, than he had yesterday on the ride from Zyerne's hunting lodge to Bel—less drawn and exhausted.

He was looking about him now with nervous anxiety, searching for someone—probably Zyerne. In spite of how ill he had seemed yesterday, he had been her most faithful attendant, riding at her side and holding her whip, her pomander ball, and the reins of her palfrey when she dismounted. Small thanks, Jenny thought, he had gotten for it. Zyerne had spent the day flirting with the unresponsive Gareth.

It was not that Gareth was immune to her charms. As a nonparticipant, Jenny had an odd sense of unobserved leisure, as if she were watching squirrels from a blind. Unnoticed by the courtiers, she could see that Zyerne was deliberately teasing Gareth's senses with every touch and smile. Do the mageborn love? he had asked her once, back in the bleak Winterlands. Evidently he had come to his own conclusions about whether Zyerne loved him, or he her. But Jenny knew full well that love and desire were two different things, particularly to a boy of eighteen. Under her innocently minxish airs, Zyerne was a woman skilled at manipulating the passions of men.

Why? Jenny wondered, looking up at the boy's awkward profile against the soft cobalt shadows of the gallery. For the amusement of seeing him struggle not to betray his father? Somehow to use his guilt to control him so that one day she could turn the King against him by crying rape?

A stir ran the length of the gallery, like wind in dry wheat. At the far end, voices murmured, "The King! The King!" Gareth scrambled to his feet and hastily checked the folds of his mantlings again. John rose, pushing his anachronistic specs a little more firmly up on the bridge of his nose. Taking Jenny's hand, he followed more slowly, as Gareth hurried toward the line of courtiers that was forming up in the center of the hall.

At the far end, bronze doors swung inward. The Chamberlain Badegamus stepped through, stout, pink, and elderly, emblazoned in a livery of crimson and gold that smote the eye with its splendor. "My lords, my ladies— the King."

Her arm against Gareth's in the press, Jenny was aware of the boy's shudder of nervousness. He had, after all, stolen his father's seal and disobeyed his orders—and he was no longer as blithely unaware of the consequences of his actions as the characters of most ballads seemed to be. She felt him poised, ready to step forward and execute the proper salaam, as others down the rank were already doing, and receive his father's acknowledgment and invitation to a private interview.

The King's head loomed above all others, taller even

than his son; Jenny could see that his hair was as fair as Gareth's but much thicker, a warm barley-gold that was beginning to fade to the color of straw. Like the steady murmuring of waves on the shore, voices repeated "My lord . . . my lord . . ."

Her mind returned briefly to the Winterlands. She supposed she should have felt resentment for the Kings who had withdrawn their troops and left the lands to ruin, or awe at finally seeing the source of the King's law that John was ready to die to uphold. But she felt neither, knowing that this man, Uriens of Bel, had had nothing to do with either withdrawing those troops or making the Law, but was merely the heir of the men who had. Like Gareth before he had traveled to the Winterlands, he undoubtedly had no more notion of those things than what he had learned from his tutors and promptly forgotten.

As he approached, nodding to this woman or that man, signing that he would speak to them in private, Jenny felt a vast sense of distance from this tall man in his regal crimson robes. Her only allegiance was to the Winterlands and to the individuals who dwelt there, to people and a land she knew. It was John who felt the ancient bond of fealty; John who had sworn to this man his allegiance, his sword, and his life.

Nevertheless, she felt the tension as the King approached them, tangible as a color in the air. Covert eyes were on them, the younger courtiers watching, waiting to see the reunion between the King and his errant son.

Gareth stepped forward, the oak-leaf-cut end of his mantlings gathered like a cloak between the second and third fingers of his right hand. With surprising grace, he bent his long, gangly frame into a perfect Sarmendes-in-Splendor salaam, such as only the Heir could make, and then only to the monarch. "My lord."

King Uriens II of Belmarie, Suzerain of the Marches,

High Lord of Wyr, Nast, and the Seven Islands, regarded his son for a moment out of hollow and colorless eyes set deep within a haggard, brittle face. Then, without a word, he turned away to acknowledge the next petitioner.

The silence in the gallery would have blistered the paint from wood. Like black poison dumped into clear water, it spread to the farthest ends of the room. The last few petitioners' voices were audible through it, clearer and clearer, as if they shouted; the closing of the gilded bronze doors as the King passed on into his audience room sounded like the booming of thunder. Jenny was conscious of the eyes of all the room looking anywhere but at them, then sliding back in surreptitious glances, and of Gareth's face, as white as his collar lace.

A soft voice behind them said, "Please don't be angry with him, Gareth."

Zyerne stood there, in plum-colored silk so dark it was nearly black, with knots of pink-tinted cream upon her trailing sleeves. Her mead-colored eyes were troubled. "You did take his seal, you know, and depart without his permission."

John spoke up. "Bit of an expensive slap on the wrist, though, isn't it? I mean, there the dragon is and all, while we're here waiting for leave to go after it."

Zyerne's lips tightened a little, then smoothed. At the near end of the King's Gallery, a small door in the great ones opened, and the Chamberlain Badegamus appeared, quietly summoning the first of the petitioners whom the King had acknowledged.

"There really is no danger to us here, you know. The dragon has been confining his depredations to the farmsteads along the feet of Nast Wall."

"Ah," John said comprehendingly. "That makes it all right, then. And is this what you've told the people of those farmsteads to which, as you say, the dragon's been confining his depredations?"

The flash of anger in her eyes was stronger then, as if no one had ever spoken to her so—or at least, thought Jenny, observing silently from John's side, not for a long time. With visible effort, Zyerne controlled herself and said with an air of one reproving a child, "You must understand. There are many more pressing concerns facing the King..."

"More pressing than a dragon sitting on his doorstep?" demanded Gareth, outraged.

She burst into a sweet gurgle of laughter. "There's no need to enact a Dockmarket drama over it, you know. I've told you before, darling, it isn't worth the wrinkles it will give you."

He pulled his head back from her playful touch. "Wrinkles! We're talking about people being killed!"

"Tut, Gareth," Bond Clerlock drawled, strolling languidly over to them. "You're getting as bad as old Polycarp used to be."

Under the paint, his face looked even more washed-out next to Zyerne's sparkling radiance. With a forced effort at his old lightness, he went on, "You shouldn't grudge those poor farmers the only spice in their dull little lives."

"Spice..." Gareth began, and Zyerne squeezed his hand chidingly.

"Don't tell me you're going to go all dull and altruistic on us. What a bore that would be." She smiled. "And I will tell you this," she added more soberly. "Don't do anything that would further anger your father. Be patient—and try to understand."

Halfway down the long gallery, the Chamberlain Badegamus was returning, passing the small group of gnomes who sat, an island of isolation, in the shadow of one of the fluted ornamental arches along the east wall. As the Chamberlain walked by, one of them rose in a silken whisper of flowing, alien robes, the cloudy wisps of his milk-white hair floating around his slumped back. Gareth had pointed him out to Jenny earlier—Azwylcartusherands, called Dromar by the folk of men who had little patience with the tongue of gnomes, longtime ambassador from the Lord of the Deep to the Court of Bel. Badegamus saw him and checked his stride, then glanced quickly at Zyerne. She shook her head. Badegamus averted his face and walked past the gnomes without seeing them.

"They grow impudent," the enchantress said softly. "To send envoys here, when they fight on the side of the traitors of Halnath."

"Well, they can hardly help that, can they, if the back way out of the Deep leads into the Citadel," John remarked.

"They could have opened the Citadel gates to let the King's troops in."

John scratched the side of his long nose. "Well, being a barbarian and all, I wouldn't know how things are done in civilized lands," he said. "In the north, we've got a word for someone who'd do that to a man who gave him shelter when he was driven from his home."

For an instant Zyerne was silent, her power and her anger seeming to crackle in the air. Then she burst into another peal of chiming laughter. "I swear, Dragonsbane, you do have a refreshingly naïve way of looking at things. You make me feel positively ancient." She brushed a tendril of her hair aside from her cheek as she spoke; she looked as sweet and guileless as a girl of twenty. "Come. Some of us are going to slip away from this silliness and go riding along the sea cliffs. Will you come, Gareth?" Her hand stole into his in such a way that he could not avoid it without rudeness—Jenny could see his face color slightly at the touch. "And you, our barbarian? You know the King won't see you today."

"Be that as it may," John said quietly. "I'll stay here on the off chance."

Bond laughed tinnily. "There's the spirit that won the Realm!"

"Aye," John agreed in a mild voice and returned to the carved bench where he and Jenny had been, secure in his established reputation for barbarous eccentricity.

Gareth drew his hand from Zyerne's and sat down nearby, catching his mantlings in the lion's-head arm of the chair. "I think I'll stay as well," he said, with as much dignity as one could have while disentangling oneself from the furniture.

Bond laughed again. "I think our Prince has been in the north too long!" Zyerne wrinkled her nose, as if at a joke in doubtful taste.

"Run along, Bond." She smiled. "I must speak to the King. I shall join you presently." Gathering up her train, she moved off toward the bronze doors of the King's antechamber, the opals that spangled her veils giving the impression of dew flecking an apple blossom as she passed the pale bands of the windowlight. As she came near the little group of gnomes, old Dromar rose again and walked toward her with the air of one steeling himself for a loathed but necessary encounter. But she turned her glance from him and quickened her step, so that, to intercept her, he would have to run after her on his short, bandy legs. This he would not do, but stood looking after her for a moment, smoldering anger in his pale amber eyes.

"I don't understand it," said Gareth, much later, as the three of them jostled their way along the narrow lanes of the crowded Dockmarket quarter. "She said Father was angry, yes—but he knew whom I'd be bringing with me. And he must have known about the dragon's latest attack." He hopped across the fish-smelling slime of the gutter to avoid a trio of sailors who'd come staggering out of one of the taverns that lined the cobbled street and nearly tripped over his own cloak.

When Badegamus had announced to the nearly empty gallery that the King would see no one else that day, John and Jenny had taken the baffled and fuming Gareth back with them to the guest house they had been assigned in one of the outer courts of the Palace. There they had changed out of their borrowed court dress, and John had announced his intention of spending the remainder of the afternoon in the town, in quest of gnomes.

"Gnomes?" Gareth said, surprised.

"Well, if it hasn't occurred to anyone else, it has occurred to me that, if I'm to fight this drake, I'm going to need to know the layout of the caverns." With surprising deftness, he disentangled himself from the intricate crisscross folds of his mantlings, his head emerging from the double-faced satin like a tousled and unruly weed. "And since it didn't seem the thing to address them at Court . . ."

"But they're plotting!" Gareth protested. He paused in his search for a place to dump the handful of old-fashioned neck-chains and rings among the already-accumulating litter of books, harpoons, and the contents of Jenny's medical pouch on the table. "Speaking to them at Court would have been suicide! And besides, you're not going to fight him in the Deep, are you? I mean . . ." He barely stopped himself from the observation that in all the ballads the Dragonsbanes had slain their foes in front of their lairs, not in them.

"If I fight him outside and he takes to the air, it's all over," John returned, as if he were talking about backgammon strategy. "And though it's crossed my mind we're walking through a morass of plots here, it's to no one's advantage to have the dragon stay in the Deep. The rest of it's all none of my business. Now, are you going to guide us, or do we go about the streets asking folk where the gnomes might be found?"

To Jenny's surprise and probably a little to his own, Gareth offered his services as a guide.

"Tell me about Zyerne, Gar," Jenny said now, thrusting her hands deep into her jacket pockets as she walked. "Who is she? Who was her teacher? What Line was she in?"

"Teacher?" Gareth had obviously never given the matter a thought. "Line?"

"If she is a mage, she must have been taught by someone." Jenny glanced up at the tall boy towering beside her, while they detoured to avoid a gaggle of passersby around a couple of street-corner jugglers. Beyond them, in a fountain square, a fat man with the dark complexion of a southerner had set up a waffle stand, bellowing his wares amid clouds of steam that scented the raw, misty air for yards.

"There are ten or twelve major Lines, named for the mages that founded them. There used to be more, but some have decayed and died. My own master Caerdinn, and therefore I and any other pupils of his, or of his teacher Spaeth, or Spaeth's other students, are all in the Line of Herne. To a mage, knowing that I am of the Line of Herne says—oh, a hundred things about my power and my attitude toward power, about the kinds of spells that I know, and about the kind that I will not use."

"Really?" Gareth was fascinated. "I didn't know it was anything like that. I thought that magic was just something—well, something you were born with."

"So is the talent for art," Jenny said. "But without proper teaching, it never comes to fullest fruition; without sufficient time given to the study of magic, sufficient striving..." She broke off, with an ironic smile at herself. "All power has to be paid for," she continued after a moment. "And all power must come from somewhere, have been passed along by someone."

It was difficult for her to speak of her power; aside

from the confusion of her heart about her own power, there was much in it that any not mageborn simply did not understand. She had in all her life met only one who did, and he was presently over beside the waffle stand, getting powdered sugar on his plaids.

Jenny sighed and came to a halt to wait for him at the edge of the square. The cobbles were slimy here with sea air and offal; the wind smelled of fish and, as everywhere in the city of Bel, of the intoxicating wildness of the sea. This square was typical of the hundreds that made up the interlocking warrens of Bel's Dockmarket, hemmed in on three-and-a-half sides by the towering, rickety tenements and dominated by the moldering stones of a slate-gray clock tower, at whose foot a neglected shrine housed the battered image of Quis, the enigmatic Lord of Time. In the center of the square bubbled a fountain in a wide basin of chip-edged granite, the stones of its rim worn smooth and white above and clotted beneath with the black-green moss that seemed to grow everywhere in the damp air of the city. Women were dipping water there and gossiping, their skirts hiked up almost to their thighs but their heads modestly covered in clumsy wool veils tied in knots under their hair to keep them out of the way.

In the mazes of stucco and garish color of the Dock-market, John's outlandishness hadn't drawn much notice. The sloping, cobbled streets were crowded with sojourn-ers from three-fourths of the Realm and all the Southern Lands: sailors with shorn heads and beards like coconut husks; peddlers from the garden province of Istmark in their old-fashioned, bundly clothes, the men as well as the women wearing veils; moneychangers in the black gabardine and skullcaps that marked them out as the Wan-derer's Children, forbidden to own land; whores painted to within an inch of their lives; and actors, jugglers, scarf sellers, rat killers, pickpockets, cripples, and tramps. A few women cast looks of dismissive scorn at Jenny's uncovered head, and she was annoyed at the anger she felt at them.

She asked, "How much do you know about Zyerne? What was she apprenticed as in the Deep?"

Gareth shrugged. "I don't know. My guess would be in the Places of Healing. That was where the greatest power of the Deep was supposed to lie—among their healers. People used to journey for days to be tended there, and I know most of the mages were connected with them."

Jenny nodded. Even in the isolated north, among the children of men who knew virtually nothing of the ways of the gnomes, Caerdinn had spoken with awe of the power that dwelled within the Places of Healing in the heart of the Deep of Ylferdun.

Across the square, a religious procession came into view, the priests of Kantirith, Lord of the Sea, walking with their heads muffled in their ceremonial hoods, lest an unclean sight distract them, the ritual wailing of the flutes all but drowning out their murmured chants. Like all the ceremonials of the Twelve Gods, both the words and the music of the flutes had been handed down by rote from ancient days; the words were unintelligible, the music like nothing Jenny had heard at Court or elsewhere.

"And when did Zyerne come to Bel?" she asked Gareth, as the muttering train filed past.

The muscles of the boy's jaw tightened. "After my mother died," he said colorlessly. "I—I suppose I shouldn't have been angry at Father about it. At the time I didn't understand the way Zyerne can draw people, sometimes against their will." He concentrated his attention upon smoothing the ruffles of his sleeve for some moments, then sighed. "I suppose he needed someone. I wasn't particularly good to him about Mother's death."

Jenny said nothing, giving him room to speak or hold his peace. From the other end of the square, another

religious procession made its appearance, one of the
southern cults that spawned in the Dockmarket like rabbits; dark-complexioned men and women were clapping
their hands and singing, while skinny, androgynous priests
swung their waist-length hair and danced for the little idol
borne in their midst in a carrying shrine of cheap, pink
chintz. The priests of Kantirith seemed to huddle a little
more closely in their protecting hoods, and the wailing of
the flutes increased. Gareth spared the newcomers a disapproving glance, and Jenny remembered that the King
of Bel was also Pontifex Maximus of the official cult;
Gareth had no doubt been brought up in the most careful
orthodoxy.

But the din gave them the illusion of privacy. For all
any of the crowd around them cared, they might have
been alone; and after a time Gareth spoke again.

"It was a hunting accident," he explained. "Father and
I both hunt, although Father hasn't done so lately. Mother
hated it, but she loved my father and would go with him
when he asked her to. He teased her about it, and made
little jokes about her cowardice—but he wasn't really
joking. He can't stand cowards. She'd follow him over
terrible country, clinging to her sidesaddle and staying up
with the hunt; after it was over, he'd hug her and laugh
and ask her if it wasn't worth it that she'd plucked up her
courage—that sort of thing. She did it for as long as I
can remember. She used to lie and tell him she was starting
to learn to enjoy it; but when I was about four, I remember
her in her hunting habit—it was peach-colored velvet with
gray fur, I remember—just before going out, throwing up
because she was so frightened."

"She sounds like a brave lady," Jenny said quietly.

Gareth's glance flicked up to her face, then away again.
"It wasn't really Father's fault," he went on after a moment.
"But when it finally did happen, he felt that it was. The
horse came down with her over some rocks—in a side-

saddle you can't fall clear. She died four or five days later. That was five years ago. I—" He hesitated, the words sticking in his throat. "I wasn't very good to him about it."

He adjusted his specs in an awkward and unconvincing cover for wiping his eyes on his sleeve ruffle. "Now that I look back on it, I think, if she'd been braver, she'd probably have had the courage to tell him she didn't want to go—the courage to risk his mockery. Maybe that's where I get it," he added, with the shy flash of a grin. "Maybe I should have seen that I couldn't possibly blame him as much as he blamed himself—that I didn't say anything to him that he hadn't already thought." He shrugged his bony shoulders. "I understand now. But when I was thirteen, I didn't. And by the time I did understand, it had been too long to say anything to him. And by that time, there was Zyerne."

The priests of Kantirith wound their way out of sight up a crooked lane between the drunken lean of crazy buildings. Children who had stopped to gawk after the procession took up their games once more; John resumed his cautious way across the moss-edged, herringbone pattern of the wet cobbles toward them, stopping every few paces to stare at some new marvel—a chair-mender pursuing his trade on the curbstone, or the actors within a cheap theater gesticulating wildly while a crier outside shouted tidbits of the plot to the passersby around the door. He would never, Jenny reflected with rueful amusement, learn to comport himself like the hero of legend that he was.

"It must have been hard for you," she said.

Gareth sighed. "It was easier a few years ago," he admitted. "I could hate her cleanly then. Later, for a while I—I couldn't even do that." He blushed again. "And now..."

A commotion in the square flared suddenly, like the

noise of a dogfight; a woman's jeering voice yelled, "Whore!" and Jenny's head snapped around.

But it was not she and her lack of veils that was the target. A little gnome woman, her soft mane of hair like an apricot cloud in the wan sunlight, was making her hesitant way toward the fountain. Her black silk trousers were hitched up over her knees to keep them out of the puddles in the broken pavement, and her white tunic, with its flowing embroideries and carefully mended sleeves, proclaimed that she was living in poverty alien to her upbringing. She paused, peering around her with a painful squint in the too-bright daylight; then her steps resumed in the direction of the fountain, her tiny, round hands clutching nervously at the handle of the bucket that she inexpertly bore.

Somebody else shouted, "Come slumming, have we, m'lady? Tired of sitting up there on all that grain you got hid? Too cheap to hire servants?"

The woman stopped again, swinging her head from side to side as if seeking her tormentors, half-blind in the outdoor glare. Someone caught her with a dog turd on the arm. She hopped, startled, and her narrow feet in their soft leather shoes skidded on the wet, uneven stones. She dropped the bucket as she fell, and groped about for it on hands and knees. One of the women by the fountain, with the grinning approbation of her neighbors, sprang down to kick it beyond her reach.

"That'll learn you to hoard the bread you've bought out of honest folks' mouths!"

The gnome made a hasty scrabble around her. A faded, fat woman who'd been holding forth the loudest in the gossip around the fountain kicked the pail a little further from the searching hands.

"And to plot against the King!"

The gnome woman raised herself to her knees, peering about her, and one of the children darted out of the gathering crowd behind her and pulled the long wisps of her hair. She spun around, clutching, but the boy had gone. Another took up the game and sprang nimbly out to do the same, too engrossed in the prospect of fun to notice John.

At the first sign of trouble, the Dragonsbane had turned to the man next to him, a blue-tattooed easterner in a metalsmith's leather apron and not much else, and handed him the three waffles he held stacked in his hands. "Would you ever hold these?" Then he made his way unhurriedly through the press, with a courteous string of "Excuse me ... pardon..." in time to catch the second boy who'd jumped out to take up the baiting where the first had begun it.

Gareth could have told them what to expect—Zyerne's courtiers weren't the only ones deceived by John's appearance of harmless friendliness. The bully, caught completely offguard from behind, didn't even have time to shriek before he hit the waters of the fountain. A huge splash doused every woman on the steps and most of the surrounding idlers. As the boy surfaced, spitting and gasping, Aversin turned from picking up the bucket and said in a friendly tone, "Your manners are as filthy as your clothes—I'm surprised your mother lets you out like that. They'll be a bit cleaner now, won't they?"

He dipped the bucket full and turned back to the man who was holding his waffles. For an instant Jenny thought the smith would throw them into the fountain, but John only smiled at him, bright as the sun on a knifeblade, and sullenly the man put the waffles into his free hand. In the back of the crowd a woman sneered, "Gnome lover!"

"Thanks." John smiled, still at his brass-faced friend-liest. "Sorry I threw offal in the fountain and all." Balancing the waffles in his hand, he descended the few steps and walked beside the little gnome woman across the square toward the mouth of the alley whence she had come. Jenny, hurrying after him with Gareth at her heels, noticed that none followed them too closely.

"John, you are incorrigible," she said severely. "Are you all right?" This last was addressed to the gnome, who was hastening along on her short, bowed legs, clinging to the Dragonsbane's shadow for protection.

She peered up at Jenny with feeble, colorless eyes. "Oh, yes. My thanks. I had never—always we went out to the fountain at night, or sent the girl who worked for us, if we needed water during the day. Only she left." The wide mouth pinched up on the words, at the taste of some unpleasant memory.

"I bet she did, if she was like that lot," John remarked, jerking his thumb back toward the square. Behind them, the crowd trailed menacingly, yelling, "Traitors! Hoarders! Ingrates!" and fouler things besides. Somebody threw a fish head that flicked off Jenny's skirts and shouted something about an old whore and her two pretty-boys; Jenny felt the bristles of rage rise along her spine. Others took up this theme. She felt angry enough to curse them, but in her heart she knew that she could lay no greater curse upon them than to be what they already were.

"Have a waffle?" John offered disarmingly, and the gnome lady took the proferred confection with hands that shook.

Gareth, carmine with embarrassment, said nothing.

Around a mouthful of sugar, John said, "Gie lucky for us fruit and vegies are a bit too dear these days to fling, isn't it? Here?"

The gnome ducked her head quickly as she entered the shadows of a doorway to a huge, crumbling house wedged between two five-storey tenements, its rear wall dropping straight to the dank brown waters of a stagnant canal. The windows were tightly shuttered, and the crumbling stucco was written over with illiterate and filthy scrawls, splattered with mud and dung. From every shutter Jenny could sense small, weak eyes peering down in apprehension.

The door was opened from within, the gnome taking her bucket and popping through like a frightened mole into its hill. John put a quick hand on the rotting panels to keep them from being shut in his face, then braced with all his strength. The doorkeeper was determined and had the prodigious muscles of the gnomes.

"Wait!" John pleaded, as his feet skidded on the wet marble of the step. "Listen! I need your help! My name's John Aversin—I've come from the north to see about this dragon of yours, but I can't do it without your aid." He wedged his shoulder into the narrow slit that was all that was left. "Please."

The pressure on the other side of the door was released so suddenly that he staggered inward under his own momentum. From the darkness beyond a soft, high voice like a child's said in the archaic High Speech that the gnomes used at Court, "Come in, thou others. It does thee no good to be thus seen at the door of the house of the gnomes."

As they stepped inside, John and Gareth blinked against the dimness, but Jenny, with her wizard's sight, saw at once that the gnome who had admitted them was old Dromar, ambassador to the court of the King.

Beyond him, the lower hall of the house stretched in dense shadow. It had once been grand in the severe style of a hundred years ago—the old manor, she guessed, upon whose walled grounds the crowded, stinking tenements of the neighborhood had later been erected. In places, rotting frescoes were still dimly visible on the stained walls; and the vastness of the hall spoke of gracious furniture now long since chopped up for firewood and of an aristocratic carelessness about the cost of heating fuel. The place was like a cave now, tenebrous and damp, its boarded windows letting in only a few chinks of watery light to outline stumpy pillars and the dry mosaics of the impluvium. Above the sweeping curve of the old-fashioned, open stair she saw movement in the gallery. It was crowded with gnomes, watching warily these intruders from the hostile world of men.

In the gloom, the soft, childlike voice said, "Thy name is not unknown among us, John Aversin."

"Well, that makes it easier," John admitted, dusting off his hands and looking down at the round head of the gnome who stood before him and into sharp, pale eyes under the flowing mane of snowy hair. "Be a bit awkward if I had to explain it all, though I imagine Gar here could sing you the ballads."

A slight smile tugged at the gnome's mouth—the first, Jenny suspected, in a long time—as he studied the incongruous, bespectacled reality behind the glitter of the legends. "Thou art the first," he remarked, ushering them into the huge, chilly cavern of the room, his mended silk robes whispering as he moved. "How many hast thy father sent out, Prince Gareth? Fifteen? Twenty? And none of them came here, nor asked any of the gnomes what they might know of the dragon's coming—we, who saw it best."

Gareth looked disconcerted. "Er—that is—the wrath of the King..."

"And whose fault was that, Heir of Uriens, when rumor had been noised abroad that we had made an end of thee?"

There was an uncomfortable silence as Gareth reddened under that cool, haughty gaze. Then he bent his head and said in a stifled voice, "I am sorry, Dromar. I never thought of—of what might be said, or who would take the blame for it, if I disappeared. Truly I didn't know. I behaved rashly—I seem to have behaved rashly all the way around."

The old gnome sniffed. "So." He folded his small hands before the complicated knot of his sash, his gold eyes studying Gareth in silence for a time. Then he nodded, and said, "Well, better it is that thou fall over thine own feet in the doing of good than sit upon thy hands and let it go undone, Gareth of Magloshaldon. Another time thou shalt do better." He turned away, gesturing toward the inner end of the shadowed room, where a blackwood table could be distinguished in the gloom, no more than a foot high, surrounded by burst and patched cushions set on the floor in the fashion of the gnomes. "Come. Sit. What is it that thou wish to know, Dragonsbane, of the coming of the dragon to the Deep?"

"The size of the thing," John said promptly, as they all settled on their knees around the table. "I've only heard rumor and story—has anybody got a good, concrete measurement?"

From beside Jenny, the high, soft voice of the gnome woman piped, "The top of his haunch lies level with the frieze carved above the pillars on either side of the doorway arch, which leads from the Market Hall into the Grand Passage into the Deep itself. That is twelve feet, by the measurements of men."

There was a moment's silence, as Jenny digested the meaning of that piece of information. Then she said, "If the proportions are the same, that makes it nearly forty feet."

"Aye," Dromar said. "The Market Hall—the first cavern of the Deep, that lies just behind the Great Gates that lead into the outer world—is one hundred and fifty feet from the Gates to the inner doors of the Grand Passage at the rear. The dragon was nearly a third of that length."

John folded his hands on the table before him. Though his face remained expressionless, Jenny detected the slight quickening of his breath. Forty feet was half again the size of the dragon that had come so close to killing him in Wyr, with all the dark windings of the Deep in which to hide.

"D'you have a map of the Deep?"

The old gnome looked affronted, as if he had inquired about the cost of a night with his daughter. Then his face darkened with stubborn anger. "That knowledge is forbidden to the children of men."

Patiently, John said, "After all that's been done you here, I don't blame you for not wanting to give out the secrets of the Deep; but I need to know. I can't take the thing from the front. I can't fight something that big head-on. I need to have some idea where it will be lairing."

"It will be lairing in the Temple of Sarmendes, on the first level of the Deep." Dromar spoke grudgingly, his pale eyes narrow with the age-old suspicion of a smaller, weaker race that had been driven underground millennia ago by its long-legged and bloodthirsty cousins. "It lies just off the Grand Passage that runs back from the Gates. The Lord of Light was beloved by the men who dwelt within the Deep—the King's ambassadors and their households, and those who had been apprenticed among our people. His Temple is close to the surface, for the folk of men do not like to penetrate too far into the bones of the Earth. The weight of the stone unnerves them; they find the darkness disquieting. The dragon will lie there. There he will bring his gold."

"Is there a back way into it?" John asked. "Through the priests' quarters or the treasuries?"

Dromar said, "No," but the little gnome woman said, "Yes, but thou would never find it, Dragonsbane."

"By the Stone!" The old gnome whirled upon her, smoldering rage in his eyes. "Be silent, Mab! The secrets of the Deep are not for his kind!" He looked viciously at Jenny and added, "Nor for hers."

John held up his hand for silence. "Why wouldn't I find it?"

Mab shook her head. From beneath a heavy brow, her round, almost colorless blue eyes peered up at him, kindly and a little sad. "The ways lead through the warrens," she said simply. "The caverns and tunnels there are a maze that we who dwell there can learn, in twelve or fourteen years of childhood. But even were we to tell thee the turnings thou must take, one false step would condemn thee to a death by starvation and to the madness that falls upon men in the darkness under the earth. We filled the mazes with lamps, but those lamps are quenched now."

"Can you draw me a map, then?" And, when the two gnomes only looked at him with stubborn secrets in their eyes, he said, "Dammit, I can't do it without your help! I'm sorry it has to be this way, but it's trust me or lose the Deep forever; and those are your only choices!"

Dromar's long, outward-curling eyebrows sank lower over the stub of his nose. "So be it, then," he said.

But Miss Mab turned resignedly and began to rise. The ambassador's eyes blazed. "No! By the Stone, is it not enough that the children of men seek to steal the secrets of the Deep? Must thou give them up freely?"

"Tut," Mab said with a wrinkled smile. "This Dragonsbane will have problems enow from the dragon, without going seeking in the darkness for others."

"A map that is drawn may be stolen!" Dromar insisted. "By the Stone that lies in the heart of the Deep . . ."

Mab got comfortably to her feet, shaking out her patched silken garments, and pottered over to the scroll-rack that filled one corner of the dim hall. She returned with a reed pen and several sheets of tattered papyrus paper in her hand. "Those whom you fear would steal it know the way to the heart of the Deep already," she pointed out gently. "If this barbarian knight has ridden all the way from the Winterlands to be our champion, it would be paltry not to offer him a shield."

"And her?" Dromar jabbed one stumpy finger, laden with old-fashioned, smooth-polished gems, at Jenny. "She is a witch. What surety have we that *she* will not go snooping and spying, delving out our secrets, turning them against us, defiling them, poisoning them, as others have done?"

The gnome woman frowned down at Jenny for a moment, her wide mouth pursed up with thought. Then she knelt beside her again and pushed the writing things across the table at Dromar. "There," she said. "Thou may draw the maps, and put upon them what thou will, and leave from them what thou will."

"And the witch?" There was suspicion and hatred in his voice, and Jenny reflected that she was getting very tired of being mistaken for Zyerne.

"Ah," said Miss Mab, and reaching out, took Jenny's small, scratched, boyish brown hands in her own. For a long moment she looked into her eyes. As if the small, cold fingers clasping hers stirred at the jewel heap of her dreams, Jenny felt the gnome woman's mind probing at her thoughts, as she had probed at Gareth's, seeking to see the shape of her essence. She realized that Miss Mab was a mage, like herself.

Reflex made her stiffen. But Mab smiled gently and held out to her the depths of her own mind and soul— gentle and clear as water, and stubborn as water, too, containing none of the bitterness, resentments, and doubts that Jenny knew clotted the corners of her own heart. She relaxed, feeling as ashamed as if she had struck out at an inquiry kindly made, and felt some of her own angers dissolving under that wise scrutiny. She felt the other woman's power, much greater than her own, but gentle and warm as sunlight.

When Miss Mab spoke, it was not to Dromar, but to her. "Thou art afraid for him," she said softly. "And perhaps thou should be." She put out one round little hand, to pat Jenny's hair. "But remember that the dragon is not the greatest of evils in this land, nor is death the worst that can befall; neither for him, nor for thee."

CHAPTER VII

IN THE WEEK that followed, Jenny returned many times to the crumbling house in the Dockmarket. Twice John accompanied her, but John, for the most part, spent his days in the King's Gallery with Gareth, waiting for a sign from the King. His evenings he spent with the wild young courtiers who surrounded Zyerne, playing dancing bear, as he called it, and dealing as best he could with the slow torture of waiting for a combat that could cost his life. Being John, he did not speak of it, but Jenny felt it when they made love and in his silences when they were alone together, this gradual twisting of the nerves that was driving him nearly mad.

She herself avoided the Court for the most part and spent her days in the city or in the house of the gnomes. She went there quietly, wrapped in spells to conceal her from the folk in the streets, for, as the days ground by, she could feel the ugly miasma of hate and fear spreading through the streets like poisoned fog. On her way through the Dockmarket quarter, she would pass the big taverns—the Lame Ox, the Gallant Rat, the Sheep in the Mire—where the unemployed men and women who had come in off the ruined farms gathered daily, hoping for a few hours' hire. Those in need of cheap labor knew to go there to find people who would move furniture or clean out stables for a few coppers; but with the winter storms making the shipping scarce and the high price of bread taking all the spare funds to be had, there were few enough who could afford to pay even that. None of the gnomes still living in the city—and there were many of them, in spite of the hardships—dared go by the Sheep in the Mire after noontime, for by that hour those within would have given up hope of work that day and would be concentrating what little energy they had on getting drunk.

So Jenny moved in her shadowy secrets, as she had moved through the lawless Winterlands, to visit the Lady Taseldwyn, who was called Miss Mab in the language of men.

From the first, she had been aware that the gnome woman was a more powerful mage than she. But, rather than jealousy and resentment, she felt only gladness that she had found someone to teach her after all those years.

In most things, Mab was a willing teacher, though the shape of the gnomes' wizardry was strange to Jenny, alien, as their minds were alien. They had no Lines, but seemed to transmit their power and knowledge whole from generation to generation of mages in some fashion that Jenny did not understand. Mab told her of the healing spells for which the Deep was famous, of the drugs now sequestered there, lost to them as surely as the dragon's gold was lost, of the spells that could hold the soul, the essence of life, to the flesh, or of the more dangerous spells by which the life-essence of one person could be drawn to strengthen the crumbling life of another. The gnome woman taught her other spells of the magic underground—spells of crystal and stone and spiraling darkness, whose meaning Jenny could only dimly comprehend. These she could only memorize by rote, hoping that with later meditation, skill and understanding would come. Mab spoke also to her of the secrets of the earth, the movement of water, and how stones thought; and she spoke of the dark realms of the Deep itself, cavern beneath cavern in endless succession of hidden glories that had never seen light.

Once, she spoke of Zyerne.

"Aye, she was apprenticed among us Healers." She sighed, putting aside the three-stringed dulcimer upon which she had been outlining to Jenny the song-spells of their craft. "She was a vain little girl, vain and spoiled. She had her talent for mockery even then—she would listen to the Old Ones among us, the great Healers, who had more power at their command than she could ever dream of, nodding that sleek little head of hers in respect, and then go and imitate their voices to her friends in Deeping."

Jenny remembered the silvery chime of the sorceress's laughter at dinner and the way she had hurried her steps to make Dromar run after her if he would speak.

It was early evening. For all its cold, the great hall of the gnomes' house was stuffy, the air stagnant beneath its massive arches and along the faded pavement of its checkered corridors. The noises of the streets had fallen to their dinnertime lull, save for the chiming of the clock towers all over the city and one lone kindling-peddler crying his wares.

Mab shook her head, her voice low with remembrance of times past. "She was greedy for secrets, as some girls are greedy for sweets—covetous for the power they could give her. She studied out the hidden ways around the Places of Healing so that she could sneak and spy, hiding to listen in darkness. All power must be paid for, but she took the secrets of those greater than she and defiled them, tainted them—poisoned them as she poisoned the very heart of the Deep—yes, she did poison it!—and turned all our strength against us."

Jenny shook her head, puzzled. "Dromar said something of the kind," she said. "But how can you taint spells? You can spoil your own magic, for it colors your soul as you wield it, but you cannot spoil another's. I don't understand."

Mab glanced sharply at her, as if remembering her presence and remembering also that she was not one of the folk of the gnomes. "Nor should thou," she said in her soft, high voice. "These are things that concern the magic of gnomes only. They are not human things."

"Zyerne seems to have made them human things." Jenny moved her weight on her heels, easing her knees on the hardness of the stone floor through the shabby cushion. "If it is, indeed, from the Places of Healing that she learned the arts that have made her the most powerful mage in the land."

"Pah!" the gnome mage said in disgust. "The Healers of the Deep were more powerful than she—by the Stone, *I* was more powerful!"

"Was?" Jenny said, perplexed. "I know that most of the Healers in the Deep were killed with the coming of the dragon; I had thought none of sufficient strength survived to defy her. The magic of gnomes is different from the spells of men, but power is power. How could Zyerne have lessened yours?"

Mab only shook her head furiously, so that her pale, web-colored hair whipped back and forth, and said, "These are the things of the gnomes."

In those days Jenny did not see much of Zyerne, but the enchantress was often on her mind. Zyerne's influence pervaded the court like the faint waft of her cinnamon perfume; when Jenny was in the Palace confines, she was always conscious of her. However Zyerne had acquired her power and whatever she had done with it since, Jenny never forgot that it was so much greater than hers. When she neglected what tomes of magic John was able to pilfer from the Palace library to sit with her scrying-stone, watching the tiny, soundless images of her sons skylarking perilously along the snow-covered battlements of the Hold, she felt a pang of guilt. Zyerne was young, at least ten years younger than she; her power shone from her like the sun. Jenny no longer felt jealousy and she could not, in all honesty, feel anger at Zyerne for having what she herself did not, as long as she was not willing to do what was needful to obtain that power. But she did feel envy, the envy of a traveler on a cold night who saw into the warmth of a lighted room.

But when she asked Mab about Zyerne—about the powers that had once been less than Mab's, but now were greater; about why the gnomes had forbidden her to enter the Deep—the little mage would only say stubbornly, "These are the things of the gnomes. They have naught to do with men."

In the meantime John went his own way, a favorite of the younger courtiers who laughed at his extravagant barbarism and called him their tame savage, while he held forth about engineering and the mating customs of pigs, or quoted classical authors in his execrable north-country drawl. And still, every morning, the King passed them by in the gallery, turning his dull eyes aside from them, and the etiquette of the Court forbade Gareth to speak.

"What's his delay?" John demanded as he and Gareth emerged from the arched porticoes of the gallery into the chill, fleet sunlight of the deserted terrace after yet another futile day's waiting. Jenny joined them quietly, coming up the steps from the deserted garden below, carrying her harp. She had been playing it on the rocks above the sea wall, waiting for them and watching the rainclouds scud far out over the sea. It was the season of winds and sudden gales, and in the north the weather would be sleety and cold, but here days of high, heatless sunlight alternated with fogs and blowing rains. The matte, white day-moon was visible, sinking into the cloud wrack over the sea; Jenny wondered what it was that troubled her about its steady waxing toward its half. Against the loamy colors of the fallow earth, the clothes of Zyerne and her court stood out brightly as they passed on down into the garden, and Jenny could hear the enchantress's voice lifted in a wickedly accurate imitation of the gnomes' shrill speech.

John went on, "Is he hoping the dragon will fall on the Citadel and spare him the trouble of the siege?"

Gareth shook his head. "I don't think so. I'm told Polycarp has catapults for slinging naphtha set up on the highest turrets. The dragon keeps his distance." In spite of the Master's treason, Jenny could hear in the Prince's voice a trace of pride in his former friend.

Unlike John, who had rented a Court costume from a shop outside the palace gates which specialized in such things for petitioners to the King, Gareth owned at least a dozen of them—like all Court costumes, criminally expensive. The one he wore today was parakeet green and primrose and, in the uncertain light of the afternoon, it turned his rather sallow complexion yellow.

John pushed his specs a little further up on the bridge of his nose. "Well, I tell you, I'm not exactly ettling to go on kicking my heels here like a rat catcher waiting for the King to decide he wants my services. I came here to protect my lands and my people, and right now they're getting nothing from the King who's supposed to guard them, nor from me."

Gareth had been gazing down into the garden at the little group around the leaf-stained marble statue of the god Kantirith absently, as if not aware of where he looked; now he turned his head quickly. "You can't go," he said, worry and fear in his voice.

"And why not?"

The boy bit his lip and did not answer, but his glance darted nervously back down to the garden. As if she felt the touch of it, Zyerne turned and blew him a playful kiss, and Gareth looked away. He looked tired and hagridden, and Jenny suddenly wondered if he still dreamed of Zyerne.

The uncomfortable silence was broken, not by him, but by the high voice of Dromar.

"My lord Aversin..." The gnome stepped out onto the terrace and blinked painfully in the wan, overcast light. His words came haltingly, as if they were unfamiliar in his mouth. "Please—do not go."

John glanced down at him sharply. "You haven't precisely extended your all in welcome and help, either, have you?"

The old ambassador's gaze challenged him. "I drew thee the maps of the Deep. By the Stone, what more canst thou want?"

"Maps that don't lie," John said coolly. "You know as well as I do the maps you drew have sections of 'em left blank. And when I put them together, the maps of the various levels and the up-and-down map, damned if it wasn't the same place on all of them. I'm not interested in the secrets of your bloody Deep, but I can't know what's going to happen, nor where I may end up playing catch-me in the dark with the dragon, and I'd just as soon have an accurate map to do it with."

There was an edge of anger on his level voice, and an edge of fear. Dromar must have heard both, for the answering blaze died out of his own countenance, and he looked down at his hands, clasped over the knots of his sash. "This is a matter that has nothing to do with the dragon, nothing to do with thee," he said quietly. "The maps are accurate—I swear it by the Stone in the heart of the Deep. What is left off is the affair of the gnomes, and the gnomes only—the very secret of the heart of the Deep. Once, one of the children of men spied out that heart, and since then we have had cause to regret it bitterly."

He lifted his head again, pale eyes somber under the long shelf of snowy brow. "I beg that thou trust me, Dragonsbane. It goes against our ways to ask the aid of the children of men. But thou must help us. We are miners and traders; we are not warriors, and it is a warrior that we need. Day by day, more of our folk are forced to leave this city. If the Citadel falls, many of the people of the Deep will be slaughtered with the rebels who have given them not only the shelter of their walls, but the very bread of their rations. The King's troops will not let them leave the Citadel, even if they would—and believe me, many have tried. Here in Bel, the cost of bread rises, and soon we shall be starved out, if we are not murdered by the mobs from the taverns. In a short time we shall be too few to hold the Deep, even should we be able to pass its gates."

He held out his hands, small as a child's and grotesquely knotted with age, pallidly white against the soft black layerings of his strangely cut sleeves. "If thou dost not help us, who among the children of men will?"

"Oh, run along, Dromar, do." Clean and sweet as a silver knife, Zyerne's voice cut across his last words. She came mounting the steps from the garden, light as an almond blossom floating on the breeze, her pink-edged veils blown back over the dark and intricate cascades of her hair. "Isn't it enough that you try to foist your way into the King's presence day after day, without troubling these poor people with politics out of season? Gnomes may be vulgar enough to talk business and buttonhole their betters in the evening, but here we feel that once the day is done, it should be a time for enjoyment." She made shooing gestures with her well-kept hands and pouted in impatience. "Now run along," she added in a teasing tone, "or I shall call the guards."

The old gnome stood for a moment, his eyes upon hers, his cloudy white hair drifting like cobwebs around his wrinkled face in the stir of the sea winds. Zyerne wore an expression of childlike pertness, like a well-loved little girl demanding her own way. But Jenny, standing behind her, saw the delighted arrogance of her triumph in every line and muscle of her slim back. She had no doubt that Zyerne would, in fact, call the guards.

Evidently Dromar hadn't, either. Ambassador from the court of one monarch to another for thirty years, he turned and departed at the behest of the King's leman. Jenny watched him stump away down the gray and lavender stonework of the path across the garden, with Bond Clerlock, pale and brittle-looking, imitating his walk behind his back.

Ignoring Jenny as she generally did, Zyerne slid one hand through Gareth's arm and smiled up at him. "Backbiting old plotter," she remarked. "I must present myself to your father at supper in an hour, but there's time for a stroll along the sea wall, surely? The rains won't start until then."

She could say it with surety, thought Jenny; at the touch of her spells, the clouds would come and depart like lapdogs waiting to be fed.

Still holding Gareth's arm and leaning her suppleness against his height, she drew him toward the steps leading down into the garden; the courtiers there were already dispersing, and its walks were empty under the wind-driven scurry of fugitive leaves. Gareth cast a despairing glance back at John and Jenny, standing together on the terrace, she in the plaids and sheepskin jacket of the north, and he in the ornate blue-and-cream satins of the Court, his schoolboy spectacles balanced on his nose.

Jenny nudged John gently. "Go after them."

He looked down at her with a half-grin. "So from a dancing bear I'm being promoted to a chaperon for our hero's virtue?"

"No," Jenny said, her voice low. "A bodyguard for his

safety. I don't know what it is about Zyerne, but he feels it, too. Go after them."

John sighed and bent to kiss her lips. "The King had better pay me extra for this." His hug was like being embraced by a satin lion. Then he was off, trotting down the steps and calling to them in horrible north-country brogue, the wind billowing his mantlings and giving him the appearance of a huge orchid in the gray garden.

In all, it was just over a week, before the King finally sent for his son.

"He asked me where I'd been," Gareth said quietly. "He asked me why I hadn't presented myself to him before." Turning, he struck the side of his fist against the bedpost, his teeth gritted to fight tears of rage and confusion. "Jenny, in all these days he hasn't even *seen* me!"

He swung angrily around. The faded evening light, falling through the diamond-shaped panes of the window where Jenny sat, brushed softly across the citron-and-white satins of his Court mantlings and flickered eerily in the round, facetless old jewels on his hands. His hair had been carefully curled for the audience with his father and, as was the nature of fine hair, hung perfectly straight around his face again, except for a stray lock or two. He'd put on his spectacles after the audience, cracked and bent and unlikely-looking with his finery; the lenses were speckled with the fine blowing rain that chilled the windowglass.

"I don't know what to do," he said in a strangulated voice. "He said—he said we'd talk about the dragon the next time he saw me. I don't understand what's going on . . ."

"Was Zyerne there?" John inquired. He was sitting at the spindly desk, which, like the rest of the upper floor of his and Jenny's guest house, was heaped with books. The whole room, after eight days, had the appearance of a ransacked library; volumes were propped against one another, places marked by pages of John's notes or odd articles of clothing or other books—and in one case a dagger—slipped between the leaves.

Gareth nodded miserably. "Half the time when I asked him things, she'd answer. Jenny, could she be holding him under some kind of spell?"

Jenny started to say, "Possibly..."

"Well, of course she is," John said, tipping back his high stool to lean the small of his back against the desk. "And if you hadn't been so bloody determined to do that slick little baggage justice, Jen, you'd have seen it a week ago. Come!" he added, as a soft tapping sounded at the door.

It opened wide enough for Trey Clerlock to put her head around the doorframe. She hesitated a moment; then, when John gestured, she came in, carrying a pearwood hurdy-gurdy with ivory stars scattered at random over its stubby neck box and playing pegs. John beamed with delight as he took it, and Jenny groaned.

"You're not going to play that thing, are you? You'll frighten the cattle for miles around, you know."

"I'll not," John retorted. "And besides, there's a trick to making it louder or softer..."

"Do you know it?"

"I can learn. Thank you, Trey, love—some people just haven't any appreciation for the sound of fine music."

"Some people haven't any appreciation for the sound of a cat being run through a mangle," Jenny replied. She turned back to Gareth. "Zyerne could be holding him under a spell, yes—but from what you've told me of your father's stubbornness and strength of will, I'm a little surprised that her influence is that great."

Gareth shook his head. "It isn't only that," he said. "I—I don't know how to put this, and I can't be sure, because I wasn't wearing my spectacles during the interview, but it almost seems that he's *faded* since I've been gone. That's a stupid idea," he recanted at once, seeing Jenny's puzzled frown.

"No," said Trey unexpectedly. The other three looked at her, and she blushed a little, like a flustered doll. "I don't think it's stupid. I think it's true, and *faded* is a good word for it. Because I—I think the same thing is happening to Bond."

"Bond?" Jenny said, and the memory of the King's face flashed across her mind; how hollow and brittle he had looked, and how, like Bond, the paint on his face had seemed to stand out from the waxiness beneath.

Trey appeared to concentrate for a moment on carefully straightening the lace on her left cuff. An opal flickered softly in the particolored coils of her hair as she looked up. "I thought it was just me," she said in a small voice. "I know he's gotten heavier-handed, and less funny about his jests, the way he is when his mind is on something else. Except that his mind doesn't seem to *be* on anything else; it just isn't on what he's doing, these days. He's so absentminded, the way your father's gotten." Her gaze went to Jenny's, imploring. "But why would Zyerne put a spell on my brother? She's never needed to hold him to her. He's always squired her around. He was one of the first friends she had at Court. He—he loved her. He used to dream about her..."

"Dream about her how?" Gareth demanded sharply.

Trey shook her head. "He wouldn't tell me."

"Did he sleepwalk?"

The surprise in the girl's eyes answered the question before she spoke. "How did you know?"

The fitful rain outside had ceased; in the long silence, the voices of the palace guards in the court below the guest house windows could be heard clearly, telling a story about a gnome and a whore in town. Even the hazy light of the afternoon was failing, and the room was cold and slate gray. Jenny asked, "Do you dream about her still, Gareth?"

The boy turned red as if scalded. He stammered, shook his head, and finally said, "I—I don't love her. I truly don't. I try—I don't want to be alone with her. But . . ." He gestured helplessly, unable to fight the traitor dreams.

Jenny said softly, "But she is calling you. She called you that first night we were in her hunting lodge. Had she done so before?"

"I—I don't know." He looked shaken and ill and very frightened, as he had when Jenny had probed at his mind, as if looking at things that he did not want to see. Trey, who had gone to take a spill from the fire and was lighting the small ivory lamps on the edge of John's desk, shook out her taper, went quietly over to him, and got him to sit down beside her on the edge of the curtained bed.

At length Gareth said, "She might have. A few months ago she asked me to dine with her and my father in her wing of the palace. I didn't go. I was afraid Father would be angry at me for slighting her, but later on he said something that made me wonder whether he'd even known about it. I wondered then. I thought . . ." He blushed still more hotly. "That was when I thought she might have been in love with me."

"I've seen loves like that between wolves and sheep, but the romance tends to be a bit one-sided," John remarked, scratching his nose. "What prevented you from going?"

"Polycarp." He toyed with the folds of his mantlings, which caught a soft edge of brightness where the angle of the lamplight came down past the curtains of the bed. "He was always telling me to beware of her. He found out about the dinner and talked me out of going."

"Well, I don't know much about magic and all that, but just offhand, lad, I'd say he might have saved your life." John braced his back against the desk's edge and fingered a silent run of melody up the hurdy-gurdy's keys.

Gareth shook his head, puzzled. "But why? It wasn't a week before he tried to kill us—me and my father both."

"If that was him."

The boy stared at him, slowly-growing horror and realization in his face. He whispered, "But I saw him."

"If she could take the shape of a cat or a bird, putting on the form of the Master of Halnath wouldn't be beyond her—Jen?" He glanced across the room to where she sat silent, her arm resting across one up-drawn knee, her chin upon her wrist.

"She wouldn't have taken on his actual being," she said quietly. "An illusion would have served. Shape-shifting requires enormous power—but then, Zyerne *has* enormous power. However she did it, the act itself is logical. If Polycarp had begun to suspect her intentions toward Gareth, it would dispose of and discredit him at once. By making you the witness, Gar, she removed all chance of your helping him. She must have known how bitter a betrayal it would be."

Numbly, Gareth whispered, "No!" struck by the horror of what he had done.

Trey's voice was soft in the stillness. "But what does she want with Gareth? I can understand her holding the King, because without his support she'd—she wouldn't exactly be nothing, but she certainly wouldn't be able to live as she does now. But why entrap Gareth as well? And what does she want with Bond? He's no good to her ... We're really only a very minor family, you know. I mean, we haven't any political power, and not that much money." A rueful smile touched one corner of her lips as she fingered the rose-point lace of her cuff. "All this ... One must keep up appearances, of course, and Bond is trying to marry me off well. But we really haven't anything Zyerne would want."

"And why destroy them?" Gareth asked, desperate concern for his father in his voice. "Do all spells do that?"

"No," Jenny said. "That's what surprises me about this—I've never heard of a spell of influence that would waste the body of the victim as it holds the mind. But neither have I heard of one holding as close as the one which she has upon your father, Gareth; nor of one that lasts so long. But her magic is the magic of the gnomes and unlike the spells of men. It may be that among their secrets is one that will hold the very essence of another, twining around it like the tendrils of a morning-glory vine, which can tear the foundations of a stone house asunder. But then," she went on, her voice low, "it is almost certain that to have that kind of control over him, at the first, she had to obtain his consent."

"His consent?" Trey cried, horrified. "But how could he? How could anyone?"

Gareth, Jenny was interested to note, said nothing to this. He had seen, however briefly, on the road in the north, the mirror of his own soul—and he also knew Zyerne.

Jenny explained, "To tamper that deeply with another's essence always requires the consent of the victim. Zyerne is a shapeshifter—the principle is the same."

Trey shook her head. "I don't understand."

Jenny sighed and, rising to her feet, crossed to where the two young people sat side-by-side. She put her hand on the girl's shoulder. "A shapeshifter can change someone else's essence, even as she can change her own. It requires enormous power—and first she must in some fashion obtain the victim's consent. The victim can resist, unless the shapeshifter can find some chink of consenting, some hidden demon within—some part of the essence that wills to be changed."

The deepening darkness outside made the lamplight even more golden, like honey where it lay over the girl's face. Under the shadows of the long, thick lashes, Jenny could read both fear and fascination, that half-understanding that is the first whisper of consent.

"I think you would resist me if I tried to transform you into a lapdog, had I the power to do so. There is very little of the lapdog in your soul, Trey Clerlock. But if I were to transform you into a horse—a yearling filly, smoke-gray and sister to the sea winds—I think I could obtain your consent to that."

Trey jerked her eyes away, hiding them against Gareth's shoulder, and the young man put a protective arm around her as well as he could, considering that he was sitting on the trailing ends of his extravagant sleeves.

"It is the power of shapeshifting and the danger," Jenny said, her voice low in the silence of the room. "If I transformed you into a filly, Trey, your essence would be the essence of a horse. Your thoughts would be a horse's thoughts, your body a mare's body; your loves and desires would be those of a young, swift beast. You might remember for a time what you were, but you could not find your way back to be it once again. I think you would be happy as a filly."

"Stop it," Trey whispered, and covered her ears. Gareth's hold about her tightened. Jenny was silent. After a moment the girl looked up again, her eyes dark with the stirred depths of her dreams. "I'm sorry," she said, her voice small. "It's not you I'm afraid of. It's me."

"I know," Jenny replied softly. "But do you understand now? Do you understand what she might have done to your father, Gareth? It is sometimes less painful to give over striving and let another mind rule yours. When Zyerne first came to power she couldn't have acquired that kind of hold over you, because you would not come near enough for her to do it. You hated her, and you were only a boy— she could not draw you as she draws men. But when you became a man . . ."

"I think that's loathsome." It was Trey's turn to put a protective arm around Gareth's satin shoulders.

"But a damn good way to keep her power," John pointed out, leaning one arm across the hurdy-gurdy resting upon his knees.

"I still can't be sure that this is what she did," Jenny said. "And it still wouldn't explain why she did the same thing to Bond. I would not know for certain until I could see the King, speak to him..."

"God's Grandmother, he'll scarcely speak to his own son, love, let alone me or thee." John paused, listening to his own words. "Which might be a good reason for not speaking to me or thee, come to that." His eyes flickered to Gareth. "You know, Gar, the more I see of this, the more I think I'd like to have a few words with your dad."

CHAPTER VIII

IN THE DEATHLY hush that hung over the gardens, Gareth's descent from the wall sounded like the mating of oxen in dry brush. Jenny winced as the boy crashed down the last few feet into the shrubbery; from the shadows of the ivy on the wall top at her side she saw the dim flash of spectacle lenses and heard a voice breathe, "You forgot to shout 'Eleven o'clock and all's well,' my hero!"

A faint slur of ivy followed. She felt John land on the ground below more than she heard him. After a last check of the dark garden half-visible through the woven branches of the bare trees, she slipped down to join them. In the darkness, Gareth was a gawky shadow in rust-colored velvet, John barely to be seen at all, the random pattern of his plaids blending into the colors of the night.

"Over there," Gareth whispered, nodding toward the far side of the garden where a light burned in a niche between two trefoil arches. Its brightness spangled the wet grass like pennies thrown by a careless hand.

He started to lead the way, but John touched his arm and breathed, "I think we'd better send a scout, if it's burglary and all we're after. I'll work round the three sides through the shadows of the wall; when I get there, I'll whistle once like a nightjar. Right?"

Gareth caught his sleeve as he started to move off. "But what if a real nightjar whistles?"

"What, at this time of the year?" And he melted like a cat into the darkness. Jenny could see him, shifting his way through the checkered shadows of the bare topiary that decorated the three sides of the King's private court; by the way Gareth moved his head, she could tell he had lost sight of him almost at once.

Near the archways there was a slither of rosy lamplight on a spectacle frame, the glint of spikes, and the brief outline of brightness on the end of a long nose. Gareth, seeing him safe, started to move, and Jenny drew him soundlessly back again. John had not yet whistled.

An instant later, Zyerne appeared in the doorway arch.

Though John stood less than six feet from her, she did not at first see him, for he settled into stillness like a snake in leaves. The enchantress's face, illuminated in the warm apricot light, wore that same sated look Jenny had seen in the upstairs room at the hunting lodge near the Wildspae—the look of deep content with some wholly private pleasure. Now, as then, it raised the hackles on Jenny's neck, and at the same time she felt a cold shudder of fear.

Then Zyerne turned her head. She startled, seeing John motionless so near to her; then she smiled. "Well. An enterprising barbarian." She shook out her unbound, unveiled hair, straying tendrils of it lying against the hollow of her cheek, like an invitation to a caress. "A little late, surely, to be paying calls on the King."

"A few weeks late, by all I've heard." Aversin scratched his nose self-consciously. "But better late than never, as Dad said at Granddad's wedding."

Zyerne giggled, a sweet and throaty sound. Beside her,

Jenny felt Gareth shiver, as if the seductive laughter brought memories of evil dreams.

"And impudent as well. Did your mistress send you along to see if Uriens had been entangled in spells other than his own stupidity and lust?"

Jenny heard the hiss of Gareth's breath and sensed his anger and his shock at hearing the guttersnipe words fall so casually from those pink lips. Jenny wondered why she herself was not surprised.

John only shrugged and said mildly, "No. It's just I'm no dab hand at waiting."

"Ah." Her smile widened, lazy and alluring. She seemed half-drunk, but not sleepy as drunkards are; she glowed, as she had on that first morning in the King's Gallery, bursting with life and filled with the casual arrogance of utter well-being. The lamp in its tiled niche edged her profile in amber as she stepped toward John, and Jenny felt again the grip of fear, as if John stood unknowingly in deadly danger. "The barbarian who eats with his hands— and doubtless makes love in his boots."

Her hands touched his shoulders caressingly, shaping themselves to the muscle and bone beneath the leather and plaid. But Aversin stepped back a pace, putting distance between them, rather as she had done in the gallery to Dromar. Like Dromar, she would not relax her self-consequence enough to pursue.

In a deliberately deepened north-country drawl, he said, "Aye, my lack of manners does give me sleepless nights. But it weren't to eat prettily nor yet to make love that I came south. I was told you had this dragon eating folks hereabouts."

She giggled again, an evil trickle of sound in the night. "You shall have your chance to slay it when all is ready. Timing is a civilized art, my barbarian."

"Aye," John's voice agreed, from the dark cutout of his silhouette against the golden light. "And I've had buckets of time to study it here, along with all them other civilized arts, like courtesy and kindness to suppliants, not to speak of honor, and keeping one's faith with one's lover, instead of rubbing up against his son."

There were perhaps three heartbeats of silence before she spoke. Jenny saw her back stiffen; when she spoke again, her voice, though still sweet, had a note to it like a harp string taken a half-turn above its true note. "What is it to you, John Aversin? It is how things are done here in the south. None of it shall interfere with your chance of glory. That is all that should concern you. I shall tell you when it is right for you to go.

"Listen to me, Aversin, and believe me. I know this dragon. You have slain one worm—you have not met Morkeleb the Black, the Dragon of Nast Wall. He is mightier than the worm you slew before, mightier than you can ever know."

"I'd guessed that." John pushed up his specs, the rosy light glancing off the spikes of his armbands as from spearpoints. "I'll just have to slay him how I can, seemingly."

"No." Acid burned through the sweetness of her voice like poisoned candy. "You can not. I know it, if you and that slut of yours don't. Do you think I don't know that those stinking offal-eaters, the gnomes, have lied to you? That they refused to give you true maps of the Deep? I know the Deep, John Aversin—I know every tunnel and passage. I know the heart of the Deep. Likewise I know every spell of illusion and protection, and believe me, you will need them against the dragon's wrath. You will need my aid, if you are to have victory—you will need my aid if you are to come out of that combat with your life. Wait, I say, and you shall have that aid; and afterward, from the spoils of the Deep, I shall reward you beyond the dreams of any man's avarice."

John tilted his head a little to one side. "*You'll* reward me?"

In the silence of the sea-scented night, Jenny heard the other woman's breath catch.

"How is it you'll be the one to divvy up the gnomes' treasure?" John asked. "Are you anticipating taking over the Deep, once the dragon's out of the way?"

"No," she said, too quickly. "That is—surely you know that the insolence of the gnomes has led them to plot against his Majesty? They are no longer the strong folk they were before the coming of Morkeleb. Those that were not slain are divided and weak. Many have left this town, forfeiting all their rights, and good riddance to them."

"Were I treated as I've seen them treated," John remarked, leaning one shoulder against the blue-and-yellow tiles of the archway, "I'd leave, myself."

"They deserved it." Her words stung with sudden venom. "They kept me from..." She stopped herself, then added, more reasonably, "You know they are openly in league with the rebels of Halnath—or you should know it. It would be foolish to dispose of the dragon before their plots are uncovered. It would only give them a strong place and a treasure to return to, to engage in plotting further treason."

"I know the King and the people have heard nothing but how the gnomes are plotting," Aversin replied in a matter-of-fact voice. "And from what I hear, the gnomes up at the Citadel haven't much choice about whose side they're on. Gar's being gone must have been a real boon to you there; with the King half-distracted, he'd have been about ready to believe anything. And I suppose it would be foolish to get rid of the dragon before so many of the gnomes have left the Realm—or some reason can be found for getting rid of the rest of 'em—that they can't reoccupy their stronghold, if so be it happened someone else wanted the place, that is."

There was a moment's silence. Jenny could see the light slither quickly along the silk facing of Zyerne's sleeve, where her small hand clenched it in anger, leaving a print of wrinkles like the track of invisible thoughts. "These are matters of high polity, Dragonsbane. It is nothing to you, after all. I tell you, be patient and wait until I tell you it is time for us to ride together to the Deep, you and I. I promise that you shall not be cheated of this slaying."

She stepped close to him again, and the diamonds on her hands threw little spits of fire against the dullness of leather and plaid.

"No," Aversin said, his voice low. "Nor shall you be cheated of the Deep, after I've done your butchering for you. You summoned the dragon, didn't you?"

"No." The word was brittle as the snap of a frost-killed twig. "Of course not."

"Didn't you, love? Then it's gie lucky for you that it came along just when it did, when you were wanting a power base free of the King, in case he tired of you or died; not to speak of all that gold."

Jenny felt the scorch of her wrath like an invisible explosion across the garden, even as Zyerne raised her hand. Jenny's throat closed on a cry of fear and warning, knowing she could never have moved in time to help and could not have stood against the younger woman's magic, if she did; Aversin, his back to the stone of the arch, could only throw his arm before his eyes as the white fire snaked from Zyerne's hand. The hissing crackle of it in the air was like lightning; the blaze of it, so white it seemed edged in violet, seared over every stone chink and moss tuft in the pavement and outlined each separate, waxy petal of the winter roses in colorless glare. In its aftermath, the air burned with the smell of ozone and scorched leaves.

After a long moment, John raised his face from his protecting arms. Even across the garden, Jenny could see he was shaking; her own knees were so weak from shock and fear she felt she could have collapsed, except for her greater fear of Zyerne; and she cursed her own lack of power. John, standing before Zyerne, did not move.

It was Zyerne who spoke, her voice dripping with triumph. "You get above yourself, Dragonsbane. I'm not that snaggle-haired trollop of yours, that you can speak to me with impunity. I am a true sorceress."

Aversin said nothing, but carefully removed his spectacles and wiped his eyes. Then he replaced them and regarded her silently in the dim light of the garden lamp.

"I am a true sorceress," she repeated softly. She held out her hands to him, the small fingers plucking at his sleeves, and a husky note crept into her sweet voice. "And who says our alliance must be so truculent, Dragonsbane? You need not spend your time here tugging with impatience to be gone. I can make the wait pleasant."

As her delicate hands touched his face, however, Aversin caught the fragile wrists, forcing her away at arm's length. For an instant they stood so, facing one another, the silence absolute but for the racing draw of their breath. Her eyes were fixed upon his, probing at his mind, Jenny knew, the same way she had probed at Gareth's earlier, seeking some key of consent.

With a curse she twisted free of his grip. "So," she whispered. "That raddled bitch can at least get her rutting-spells right, can she? With her looks, she'd have to. But let me tell you this, Dragonsbane. When you ride to meet the dragon, like it or not, it will be me who rides with you, not her. You shall need my aid, and you shall ride forth when I say so, when I tell the King to give you leave, and not before. So learn a little of the civilized art of patience, my barbarian—for without my aid against Morkeleb, you shall surely die."

She stepped away from him and passed under the lamp-lit arch, reaching out to take the light with her as she went. In its honeyed brightness her face looked as gentle and guileless as that of a girl of seventeen, unmarked by rage or perversion, pettiness or spite. John remained where he was, watching her go, sweat beading his face like a mist of diamonds, motionless save where he rubbed the thin, sharp flashburns on his hands.

A moment later, the window behind him glowed into soft life. Through the fretted screen of scented shrubs and vine that twined its filigreed lattice, Jenny got a glimpse of the room beyond. She had an impression of half-seen frescoes on the walls, of expensive vessels of gold and silver, and of the glint of bullion embroidery thickly edging the hangings of the bed. A man lay in the bed, moving feebly in some restless dream, his gold hair faded and colorless where it lay in disorder over the embroidered pillows. His face was sunken and devoid of life, like the face of a man whom a vampire has kissed.

"It would serve her right if you left tonight!" Gareth stormed. "Rode back north and left her to deal with her own miserable worm, if she wanted it so badly!"

He swung around to pace the big chamber of the guest house again, so furious he could barely splutter. In his anger, he seemed to have forgotten his own fear of Zyerne and his desire for protection against her, forgotten his long quest to the Winterlands and his desperation to have it succeed. From her seat in the window, Jenny watched him fulminate, her own face outwardly calm but her mind racing.

John looked up from tinkering with the keys of the hurdy-gurdy. "It wouldn't do, my hero," he said quietly. "However and whyever it got here, the dragon's here now. As Zyerne said, the people hereabouts are no concern of mine, but I can't be riding off and leaving them to the dragon. Leaving out the gnomes, there's the spring planting to be thought of."

The boy stopped in his pacing, staring at him. "Hunh?"

John shrugged, his fingers stilling on the pegs. "The

harvest's gone," he pointed out. "If the dragon's still abroad in the land in the spring, there'll be no crop, and then, my hero, you'll see real starvation in this town."

Gareth was silent. It was something he had never thought of, Jenny guessed. He had clearly never gone short of food in his life.

"Besides," John went on, "unless the gnomes can reoccupy the Deep pretty quick, Zyerne will destroy them here, as Dromar said, and your friend Polycarp in the Citadel as well. For all Dromar's hedging about keeping us out of the heart of the Deep, the gnomes have done for us what they can; and the way I see it, Polycarp saved your life, or at least kept you from ending up like your father, so deep under Zyerne's spells he can't tell one week from the next. No, the dragon's got to be killed."

"But that's just it," Gareth argued. "If you kill the dragon, she'll be free to take over the Deep, and then the Citadel will fall because they'll be able to attack it from the rear." He looked worriedly over at Jenny. "*Could* she have summoned the dragon?"

Jenny was silent, thinking about that terrible power she had felt in the garden, and the dreadful, perverted lour of it in the lamplit room at Zyerne's hunting lodge. She said, "I don't know. It's the first time I've heard of human magic being able to touch a dragon—but then, Zyerne derives her magic from the gnomes. I have never heard of such a thing..."

"*Cock by its feet, horse by its hame*..." repeated John. "Could she be holding the dragon by his name? She knows it, right enough."

Jenny shook her head. "Morkeleb is only the name men give it, the way they call Azwylcartusherands Dromar, and Taseldwyn Mab. If she'd had his true name, his essence, she could send him away again; and she obviously can't, or she would have killed you in the garden tonight."

She hitched her shawl up over her shoulders, a thin

and glittering spiderweb of South Islands silk, the thick masses of her hair lying over it like a second shawl. Cold seemed to breathe through the window at her back.

Gareth went back to pacing, his hands shoved in the pockets of the old leather hunting breeches he'd put on to go burgling.

"But she didn't know its name, did she?"

"No," replied Jenny. "And in that case..." She paused, then frowned, dismissing the thought.

"What?" John wanted to know, catching the doubt in her voice.

"No," she repeated. "It's inconceivable that at her level of power she wouldn't have been taught Limitations. It's the first thing anyone learns." And seeing Gareth's incomprehension, she explained. "It's one of the things that takes me so long when I weave spells. You have to limit the effect of any spell. If you call rain, you must specify a certain heaviness, so as not to flood the countryside. If you call a curse of destruction upon someone or something, you have to set Limitations so that their destruction doesn't come in a generalized catastrophe that wipes out your own house and goods. Magic is very prodigal in its effects. Limitations are among the earliest things a mage is taught."

"Even among the gnomes?" Gareth asked. "You said their magic is different."

"It is taught differently—transmitted differently. There are things Mab has said that I do not understand and things that she refuses to tell me about how their power is formed. But it is still magic. Mab knows the Limitations—from what she has told me, I gather they are more important in the night below the ground. If she studied among the gnomes, Zyerne would *have* to have learned about them."

John threw back his head and laughed in genuine amusement. "Gaw, it must be rotting her!" He chuckled. "Think of it, Jen. She wants to get rid of the gnomes, so she calls down a generalized every-worst-curse she can think of upon them—and gets a dragon she can't get rid of! It's gie beautiful!"

"It's 'gie' frivolous," Jenny retorted.

"No wonder she threw fire at me! She must be that furious just thinking about it!" His eyes were dancing under his singed brows.

"It just isn't possible," Jenny insisted, in the cool voice she used to call their sons back from skylarking. Then, more seriously, "She can't have gotten to that degree of power untaught, John. It's impossible. All power must be paid for, somehow."

"But it's the sort of thing that would happen if it hadn't been, isn't it?"

Jenny didn't reply. For a long time she stared out the window at the dark shape of the battlements, visible beneath the chilly autumn stars. "I don't know," she said at last, stroking the spiderweb fringes of her gauze shawl. "She has so much power. It's inconceivable that she hasn't paid for it in some fashion. The key to magic is magic. She has had all time and all power to study it fully. And yet..." She paused, identifying at last her own feelings toward what Zyerne was and did. "I thought that someone who had achieved that level of power would be different."

"Ah," John said softly. Across the room, their eyes met. "But don't think that what she's done with her achievement has betrayed your striving, love. For it hasn't. It's only betrayed her own."

Jenny sighed, reflecting once again on John's uncanny ability to touch the heart of any problem, then smiled a little at herself; and they traded a kiss in a glance.

Gareth said quietly, "But what are we going to do? The dragon has to be destroyed; and, if you destroy it, you'll be playing right into her hands."

A smile flicked across John's face, a glimpse of the bespectacled schoolboy peeking out from behind the complex barricades raised by the hardships of the Winterlands and his father's embittered domination. Jenny felt his eyes on her again—the tip of one thick reddish brow and the question in the bright glance. After ten years, they had grown used to speaking without words.

A qualm of fear passed over her, though she knew he was right. After a moment, she drew her breath in another sigh and nodded.

"Good." John's impish smile widened, like that of a boy intent on doing mischief, and he rubbed his hands briskly. He turned to Gareth. "Get your socks packed, my hero. We leave for the Deep tonight."

CHAPTER IX

"Stop."

Puzzled, Gareth and John drew rein on either side of Jenny, who sat Moon Horse where she had halted her in the middle of the leaf-drifted track. All around them the foothills of Nast Wall were deathly silent, save for the trickle of wind through the charred trunks of what had once been woods to either side of the road and the faint jingle of brass as Osprey tugged at his leading-rein and Clivy began foraging prosaically in the sedges of the ditch-side. Lower down the hills, the woods were still whole, denuded by coming winter rather than fire; under the pewter-gray trunks of the beeches, the rust-colored underbrush lay thick. Here it was only a tangle of brittle stems, ready to crumble at a touch. Half-hidden in the weeds near the scorched paving stones of the road were the blackened bones of fugitives from the dragon's first attack, mixed with shattered cooking vessels and the silver coins that had been dropped in flight. The coins lay in the mud still. No one had ventured this close to the ruined town to retrieve them.

Up ahead in the weak sunlight of winter, the remains

of the first houses of Deeping could be seen. According to Gareth the place had never been walled. The road ran into the town under the archway below the broken clock tower.

For a long while Jenny sat listening in silence, turning her head this way and that. Neither of the men spoke—indeed, ever since they had slipped out of the Palace in the small hours before dawn, Jenny had been acutely conscious of John's growing silence. She glanced across at him now, where he sat withdrawn into himself on his riding horse Cow, and remembered for the dozenth time that day Zyerne's words—that without her assistance, neither he nor Jenny would be capable of meeting the dragon Morkeleb.

Beyond a doubt John was remembering them, too.

"Gareth," Jenny said at last, her voice little more than a whisper, "is there another way into the town? Some place in the town that is farther from the Gates of the Deep than we are now?"

Gareth frowned. "Why?"

Jenny shook her head, not certain herself why she had spoken. But something whispered across her nerves, as it had all those weeks ago by the ruins of the nameless town in the Winterlands—a sense of danger that caused her to look for the signs of it. Under Mab's tutelage she had become more certain of trusting her instincts, and something in her hated to go closer than the ruined clock tower into the sunlight that fell across Deeping Vale.

After a moment's consideration Gareth said, "The farthest point in Deeping from the Great Gates would be the Tanner's Rise. It's at the bottom of that spur over there that bounds the town to the west. I think it's about a half-mile from the Gates. The whole town isn't—wasn't—much more than a quarter-mile across."

"Will we have a clear view of the Gates from there?"

Confused by this bizarre stipulation, he nodded. "The

ground's high, and most of the buildings were flattened in the attack. But if we wanted a lookout on the gates, you can see there's enough of the clock tower left for a..."

"No," Jenny murmured. "I don't think we can go that near."

John's head came sharply around at that. Gareth faltered, "It can't—it can't *hear* us, can it?"

"Yes," Jenny said, not knowing why she said it. "No— it isn't hearing, exactly. I don't know. But I feel something, on the fringes of my mind. I don't think it knows we're here—not yet. But if we rode closer, it might. It is an old dragon, Gareth; it must be, for its name to be in the Lines. In one of the old books from the Palace library, it says that dragons change their skins with their souls, that the young are simply colored and bright; the mature are complex of pattern and the old become simpler and simpler again, as their power deepens and grows. Morkeleb is black. I don't know what that means, but I don't like what I think it implies—great age, great power—his senses must fill the Vale of Deeping like still water, sensitive to the slightest ripple."

"He pox-sure heard your father's knights coming, didn't he?" John added cynically.

Gareth looked unhappy. Jenny nudged her mare gently and took a step or two closer to the clock tower, casting her senses wide over all the Vale. Through the broken webs of branches overhead, the massive darkness of the westward-facing cliffs of Nast Wall could be seen. Their dizzy heights towered like rusted metal, streaked with purple where shadows hit; boulders flashed white upon it like outcroppings of broken bone. Above the line of the dragon's burning, the timber grew on the flanks of the mountain around the cliffs, up toward the mossed rocks of the cirques and snowfields above. The ice-gouged horns of the Wall's bare and ragged crest were veiled in cloud now, but beyond its hunched shoulder to the east a thin track of smoke could be seen, marking the Citadel of Halnath and the siege camps beneath it.

Below that wall of stone and trees, the open spaces of the Vale lay, a huge well of air, a gulf filled with pale, sparkly sunlight—and with something else. Jenny's mind touched it briefly and shrank from that living consciousness that she sensed, coiled like a snake in its dark lair.

Behind her, she heard Gareth argue, "But the dragon you killed up in the gully in Wyr didn't know you were coming." The very loudness of his voice scraped her nerves and made her want to cuff him into silence. "You were able to get around behind it and take it by surprise. I don't see how..."

"Neither do I, my hero," John cut in softly, collecting Cow's reins in one hand and the charger Osprey's lead in the other. "But if you're willing to bet your life Jen's wrong, I'm not. Lead us on to the famous Rise."

On the night of the dragon, many had taken refuge in the buildings on Tanner's Rise; their bones lay everywhere among the blackened ruin of crumbled stone. From the open space in front of what had been the warehouses, it had once been possible to overlook the whole thriving little town of Deeping, under its perpetual haze of smoke from the smelters and forges down below. That haze was gone now, burned off in the dragon's greater fire; the whole town lay open to the mild, heatless glitter of the winter sunlight, a checkerwork of rubble and bones.

Looking about her at the buildings of the Rise, Jenny felt cold with shock, as if she had been struck in the pit of the stomach; then, as she realized why she recognized the place, the shock was replaced by horror and despair.

It was the place where she had seen John dying, in her vision in the water bowl.

She had done divination before, but never so accurately as this. The precision of it appalled her—every stone and puddle and broken wall was the same; she remembered the way the looming line of the dark cliffs looked against the sky and the very patterns of the bones of the town below. She felt overwhelmed by a despairing urge to change something—to shatter a wall, to dig a hole, to clear away the brush at the gravelly lip of the Rise where it sloped down to the town—anything to make it not as it had been. Yet in her soul she knew doing so would change nothing and she feared lest whatever she did would make the picture she had seen more, rather than less, exact.

Her lips felt stiff as she spoke. "Is this the only point in the town this far from the Gates?" She knew already what Gareth would reply.

"It had to be, because of the smell of the tanneries. You see how nothing was built near it. Even the water tanks and reservoirs were put up in those rocks to the north, rather than here where the better springs were."

Jenny nodded dully, looking out toward the high rocks to the north of the town where he was pointing. Her whole soul was crying *No! No...*

She felt suddenly hopeless and stupid, overmatched and unprepared and incredibly naïve. *We were fools,* she thought bitterly. *The slaying of the first worm was a fluke. We should never have been so stupid as to presume upon it, never have thought we could do it again. Zyerne was right. Zyerne was right.*

She looked over at John, who had dismounted from Cow and was standing on the rocky lip of the Rise where the ground fell sharply to the dale below, looking across toward the opposite rise of the Gates. Cold seemed to cover her bones like a vast, winged shadow blocking the sun, and she heeled Moon Horse gently over beside him.

Without looking up at her, he said, "I figure I can just make it. The Temple of Sarmendes is about a quarter-mile along the Grand Passage, if Dromar was telling the truth. If Osprey and I go full-pelt, we should just about be able to catch the dragon in the Market Hall, just within the Gates. Saying he's able to hear me the minute I start down the Rise, I should still be able to catch him before he can get out into the air. I'll have room to fight him in the Market Hall. That will be my only chance."

"No," Jenny said quietly. He looked up at her, eyebrows quirking. "You have another chance, if we ride back now to Bel. Zyerne can help you take the thing from behind, deeper in the caves. Her spells will protect you, too, as mine can not."

"Jen." The closed wariness of his expression split suddenly into the white flash of teeth. He held up his hands to help her down, shaking his head reprovingly.

She made no move. "At least it is to her advantage to preserve you safe, if she wants the dragon slain. The rest is none of your affair."

His smile widened still further. "You have a point, love," he assented. "But she doesn't look to me like she can cook worth a row of beans." And he helped her down from her horse.

The foreboding that weighed on Jenny's heart did not decrease; rather, it grew upon her through the short afternoon. She told herself, again and again, as she paced out the magic circles and set up her fire in their midst to brew her poisons, that water was a liar; that it divined the future as crystal could not, but that its divinations were less reliable even than fire's. But a sense of impending doom weighed upon her heart, and, as the daylight dimmed, in the fire under her simmering kettle she seemed to see again the same picture: John's shirt of chain mail rent open by claws in a dozen places, the broken links all glittering with dark blood.

Jenny had set up her fire at the far end of the Rise, where the wind would carry the smoke and the vapors away from both the camp and the Vale, and worked throughout the afternoon spelling the ingredients and the steel of the harpoons themselves. Miss Mab had advised her about the more virulent poisons that would work upon dragons, and such ingredients as the gnome wizard had not had among her slender stocks Jenny had purchased in the Street of the Apothecaries in the Dockmarket in Bel. While she worked, the two men prowled the Rise, fetching water for the horses from the little well some distance into the woods, since the fountain house that had served the tanneries had been crushed like an eggshell, and setting up a camp. John had very little to say since she had spoken to him on the edge of the Rise; Gareth seemed to shiver all over with a mingling of excitement and terror.

Jenny had been a little surprised at John's invitation that Gareth join them, though she had planned to ask John to extend it. She had her own reasons for wanting the boy with them, which had little to do with his expressed desire—though he had not expressed it lately—to see a dragonslaying close at hand. She—and undoubtedly John as well—knew that their departure would have left Gareth unprotected in Bel.

Perhaps Mab had been right, she thought, as she turned her face from the ghastly choke of the steam and wiped it with one gloved hand. There were worse evils than the dragon in the land—to be slain by it might, under certain circumstances, be construed as a lesser fate.

The voices of the men came to her from the other side of the camp as they moved about preparing supper; she had noticed that neither spoke very loudly when they were anywhere near the edge of the Rise. John said, "I'll get this right yet," as he dropped a mealcake onto the griddle and looked up at Gareth. "What's the Market Hall like? Anything I'll be likely to trip over?"

"I don't think so, if the dragon's been in and out,"

Gareth said after a moment. "It's a huge hall, as Dromar said; over a hundred feet deep and even wider side to side. The ceiling's very high, with fangs of rock hanging down from it—chains, too, that used to support hundreds of lamps. The floor was leveled, and used to be covered with all kinds of booths, awnings, and vegetable stands; all the produce from the Realm was traded to the Deep there. I don't think there was anything there solid enough to resist dragon fire."

Aversin dropped a final mealcake on the griddle and straightened up, wiping his fingers on the end of his plaid. Blue darkness was settling over Tanner's Rise. From her small fire, Jenny could see the two of them outlined in gold against a background of azure and black. They did not come near her, partly because of the stench of the poisons, partly because of the spell-circles glimmering faintly in the sandy earth about her. The key to magic is magic—Jenny felt that she looked out at them from an isolated enclave of another world, alone with the oven-heat of the fire, the biting stench of the poison fumes, and the grinding weight of the death-spells in her heart.

John walked to the edge of the Rise for perhaps the tenth time that evening. Across the shattered bones of Deeping, the black skull-eye of the Gates looked back at him. Slabs of steel and splintered shards of burned wood lay scattered over the broad, shallow flight of granite steps below them, faintly visible in the watery light of the waxing moon. The town itself lay in a pool of impenetrable dark.

"It isn't so far," said Gareth hopefully. "Even if he hears you coming the minute you ride into the Vale, you should reach the Market Hall in plenty of time."

John sighed. "I'm not so sure of that, my hero. Dragons move fast, even afoot. And the ground down there's bad. Even full-tilt, Osprey won't be making much speed of it, when all's said. I would have liked to scout for the clearest route, but that isn't possible, either. The most I can hope for is that there's no uncovered cellar doors or privy pits between here and the Gates."

Gareth laughed softly. "It's funny, but I never thought about that. In the ballads, the hero's horse never trips on the way to do battle with the dragon, though they do it from time to time even in tourneys, where the ground of the lists has been smoothed beforehand. I thought it would be—oh, like a ballad. Very straight. I thought you'd ride out of Bel, straight up here and on into the Deep..."

"Without resting my horse after the journey, even on a lead-rein, nor scouting the lay of the land?" John's eyes danced behind his specs. "No wonder the King's knights were killed at it." He sighed. "My only worry is that if I miss my timing by even a little, I'm going to be spot under the thing when it comes out of the Gates..."

Then he coughed, fanning at the air, and said, "Pox blister it!" as he dashed back to pick the flaming meal-cakes off the griddle. Around burned fingers, he said, "And the damn thing is, even Adric cooks better than I do..."

Jenny turned away from their voices and the sweetness of the night beyond the blazing heat of her fire. As she dipped the harpoons into the thickening seethe of brew in her kettle, the sweat plastered her long hair to her cheeks, running down her bare arms from the turned-up sleeves of her shift to the cuffs of the gloves she wore; the heat lay like a red film over her toes and the tops of her feet, bare as they often were when she worked magic.

Like John, she felt withdrawn into herself, curiously separated from what she did. The death-spells hung like a stench in the air all around her, and her head and bones were beginning to ache from the heat and the effort of the magic she had wrought. Even when the powers she called were for good, they tired her; she felt weighed down by them now, exhausted and knowing that she had wrought nothing good from that weariness.

The Golden Dragon came to her mind again, the first heartstopping instant she had seen it dropping from the sky like amber lightning and had thought, This is beauty. She remembered, also, the butchered ruin left in the gorge, the stinking puddles of acid and poison and blood, and the faint, silvery singing dying out of the shivering air. It might have been only the fumes she inhaled, but she felt herself turn suddenly sick at the thought.

She had slaughtered Meewinks, or mutilated them and left them to be eaten by their brothers; she remembered the crawling greasiness of the bandit's hair under her fingers as she had touched his temples. But they were not like the dragon. They had chosen to be what they were.

Even as I have.

And what are you, Jenny Waynest?

But she could find no answer that fitted.

Gareth's voice drifted over to her from the other fire. "That's another thing they never mention in the ballads that I've been meaning to ask you. I know this sounds silly, but—how do you keep your spectacles from getting broken in battle?"

"Don't wear 'em," John's voice replied promptly. "If you can see it coming, it's too late anyway. And then, I had Jen lay a spell on them, so they wouldn't get knocked off or broken by chance when I *do* wear them."

She looked over at the two of them, out of the condensing aura of death-spells and the slaughter of beauty that surrounded her and her kettle of poison. Firelight caught in the metal of John's jerkin; against the blueness of the night it gleamed like a maker's mark stamped in gold upon a bolt of velvet. She could almost hear the cheerful grin in his voice, "I figured if I was going to break my heart loving a magewife, I might as well get some good from it."

Over the shoulder of Nast Wall the moon hung, a half-open white eye, waxing toward its third quarter. With a stab like a shard of metal embedded somewhere in her heart, Jenny remembered then that it had been so, in her vision in the water.

Silently, she pulled herself back into her private circle of death, closing out that outer world of friendship and love and silliness, closing herself in with spells of ruin and despair and the cold failing of strength. It was her power to deal death in this way, and she hated herself for it; though, like John, she knew she had no choice.

"Do you think you'll make it?" Gareth nattered. Before them, the ruins of the broken town were purple and slate with shadow in the early light. The war horse Osprey's breath was warm over Jenny's hand where she held the reins.

"I'll have to, won't I?" John checked the girths and swung up into the saddle. The cool reflection of the morning sky gleamed slimily on the grease Jenny had made for him late last night to smear on his face against the worst scorching of the dragon's fire. Frost crackled in the weeds as Osprey fidgeted his feet. The last thing Jenny had done, shortly before dawn, had been to send away the mists that seeped up from the woods to cloak the Vale, and all around them the air was brilliantly clear, the fallow winter colors warming to life. Jenny herself felt cold, empty, and overstretched; she had poured all her powers into the poisons. Her head ached violently and she felt unclean, strange, and divided in her mind, as if she were two separate people. She had felt so, she recalled, when John had ridden against the first dragon, though then she had not known why. Then she had not known what the slaughter of that beauty would be like. She feared for him and felt despair like a stain on her heart; she only wanted the day to be over, one way or the other.

The mail rings on the back of John's gloves rattled sharply as he reached down, and she handed him up his harpoons. There were six of them, in a quiver on his back; the steel of their barbed shafts caught a slither of the early light, save for the ugly black that covered their points. The leather of the grips was firm and tough under her palms. Over his metal-patched doublet, John had pulled a chain mail shirt, and his face was framed in a coif of the same stuff. Without his spectacles and with his shaggy hair hidden beneath it, the bones of his face were suddenly prominent, showing what his features could look like in an old age he might never reach.

Jenny felt she wanted to speak to him, but there was nothing she could think of to say.

He gathered the reins in hand. "If the dragon comes out of the Gate before I reach it, I want the pair of you to leg it," he said, his voice calm. "Get into cover as deep as you can, the higher up the ridge the better. Let the horses go if you can—there's a chance the dragon will go after them first." He did not add that by that time he would already be dead.

There was a momentary silence. Then he bent from the saddle and touched Jenny's lips with his own. His felt, as they always did, surprisingly soft. They had spoken little, even last night; each had already been drawn into an armor of silence. It was something they both understood.

He reined away, looking across the Vale to the black eye of the Deep, and to the black thing waiting within. Osprey fiddle-footed again, catching John's battle nerves; the open ground of Deeping seemed suddenly to stretch away into miles of enormous, broken plain. To Jenny's eye, every tumbled wall looked as tall as the house it had once been, every uncovered cellar a gaping chasm. He would never cross in time, she thought.

Beside her, John leaned down again, this time to pat

Osprey's dappled neck encouragingly. "Osprey, old friend," he said softly, "don't spook on me now."

He drove in his spurs, and the sharp crack of iron-shod hooves as they shot forward was like the chip of distant lightning on a summer noon. Jenny took two steps down the loose, rocky slope after him, watching the gray horse and the pewter-dark shape of the man as they plunged through the labyrinth of gaping foundations, broken beams, standing water who knew how deep, slipping down drifts of charred wood chips and racing toward the open black mouth of the Gates. Her heart hammering achingly in her chest, Jenny stretched her mageborn senses toward the Gate, straining to hear. The cold, tingling air seemed to breathe with the dragon's mind. Somewhere in that darkness was the slithery drag of metallic scales on stone...

There was no way to call the image of the dragon in her scrying-stone, but she sat down suddenly where she was on the loose, charred rubble of the slope and pulled the slip of dirty-white crystal upon its chain from her jacket pocket. She heard Gareth call her name from the top of the slope, but she vouchsafed neither answer nor glance. Across the Vale, Osprey leaped the split ruin of the demolished Gates on the granite steps, cool blue shadows falling over him and his rider like a cloak as the Gate swallowed them up.

There was a flick and a gleam, as the wan sunlight caught in the facets of the jewel. Then Jenny caught a confused impression of hewn stone walls that could have encompassed the entire palace of Bel, a cavern-ceiling bristling with stone teeth from which old lamp-chains hung down into vast, cobalt spaces of air... black doorways piercing the walls, and the greatest of them opening opposite....

Jenny cupped her hands around the jewel, trying to see into its depths, straining past the curtains of illusion that covered the dragon from her sight. She thought she saw the flash of diffuse sunlight on chain mail and saw Osprey trip on the charred debris of blackened bones and spilled coins and half-burned poles that littered the floor. She saw John pull him out of the stumble and saw the gleam of the harpoon in his hand... Then something spurted from the inner doors, like a drench of thrown bathwater, splattering viscously into the dry ash of the floor, searing upward in a curtain of fire.

There was a darkness in the crystal and in that darkness, two burning silver lamps.

Nothing existed around her, not the cool shift of the morning air, nor the sunlight warming her ankles in her buckskin boots where her heels rested on the chopped-up slope of gravel and weeds, not the wintry smell of water and stone from below, nor the small noises of the restless horses above. Cupped in her hands, the edges of the crystal seemed to burn in white light, but its heart was dark; through that darkness only fragmentary images came—a sense of something moving that was vast and dark, the swinging curve of John's body as he flung a harpoon, and the cloudy swirls of blinding fumes.

In some way she knew Osprey had gone down, smitten by the stroke of the dragon's tail. She had a brief impression of John on his knees, his eyes red and swollen from the acrid vapors that filled the hall, aiming for another throw. Something like a wing of darkness covered him. She saw flame again and, as a queer, detached image, three harpoons lying like scattered jackstraws in the middle of a puddle of blackened and steaming slime. Something within her turned to ice; there was only darkness and movement in the darkness, and then John again, blood pouring through the rips in his mail shirt, staring up at a towering shape of glittering shadow, his sword in his hand.

Blackness swallowed the crystal. Jenny was aware that her hands were shaking, her whole body hurting with a pain that radiated from a seed of cold under her breastbone, her throat a bundle of twisted wires. She thought blindly, *John*, remembering him striding with graceful insouciance into Zyerne's dining room, his armor of outrageousness protecting him from Zyerne's claws; she remembered the flash of autumn daylight on his specs as he stood ankle-deep in pig muck at the Hold, reaching up his hands to help her dismount.

She could not conceive of what life would be like without that fleeting, triangular grin.

Then somewhere in her mind she heard him call out to her: *Jenny*...

She found him lying just beyond the edge of the trapezoid of light that fell through the vast square of the Gates. She had left Moon Horse outside, tossing her head in fear at the acrid reek of the dragon that pervaded all that end of the Vale. Jenny's own heart was pounding, so that it almost turned her sick; all the way across the ruins of Deeping she had been waiting for the dark shape of the dragon to emerge from the Gates.

But nothing had come forth. The silence within the darkness was worse than any sound could have been.

After the brightness of the Vale, the blue vaults of the Market Hall seemed almost black. The air was murky with vapors that diffused what little light there was. The trapped fumes burned her eyes and turned her dizzy, mixed with the smoke of burning and the heavy reek of poisoned slag. Even with a wizard's sight, it took Jenny's eyes a moment to accustom themselves. Then sickness came over her, as if the blood that lay spread everywhere had come from her body, rather than John's.

He lay with his face hidden by his outflung arm, the mail coif dragged back and the hair beneath it matted with blood where it had not been singed away. Blood lay in a long, inky trail behind him, showing where he had crawled after the fight was over, past the carcass of the horse

Osprey, leading like a sticky path to the vast, dark bulk of the dragon.

The dragon lay still, like a shining mound of obsidian knives. Supine, it was a little higher than her waist, a glittering blacksnake nearly forty feet long, veiled in the white smoke of its poisons and the darkness of its magic, harpoons sticking from it like darts. One foreleg lay stretched out toward John, as if with its last strength it had reached to tear him, and the great talon lay like a skeleton hand in a pool of leaked black blood. The atmosphere all about it seemed heavy, filled with a sweet, clear singing that Jenny thought was as much within her skull as outside of it. It was a song with words she could not understand; a song about stars and cold and the long, ecstatic plunge through darkness. The tune was half-familiar, as if she had heard a phrase of it once, long ago, and had carried it since in her dreams.

Then the dragon Morkeleb raised his head, and for a time she looked into his eyes.

They were like lamps, a crystalline white kaleidoscope, cold and sweet and burning as the core of a flame. It struck her with a sense of overwhelming shock that she looked into the eyes of a mage like herself. It was an alien intelligence, clean and cutting as a sliver of black glass. There was something terrible and fascinating about those eyes; the singing in her mind was like a voice speaking to her in words she almost understood. She felt a calling within her to the hungers that had all of her life consumed her.

With a desperate wrench, she pulled her thoughts from it and turned her eyes aside.

She knew then why the legends warned never to look into a dragon's eyes. It was not only because the dragon could snag some part of your soul and paralyze you with indecision while it struck.

It was because, in pulling away, you left some shred of yourself behind, snared in those ice-crystal depths.

She turned to flee, to leave that place and those too-knowing eyes, to run from the singing that whispered to the harmonics of her bones. She would have run, but her booted foot brushed something as she turned. Looking down to the man who lay at her feet, she saw for the first time that his wounds still bled.

CHAPTER X

"HE CAN'T BE dying!" Gareth finished laying a heap of fresh-cut branches beside the low fire and turned to Jenny, his eyes pleading with her. As if, Jenny thought, with what power was left in her numbed mind, his saying could make it so.

Without speaking, she leaned across to touch the ice-cold face of the man who lay covered with plaids and bearskins, so close to the flickering blaze.

Her mind felt blunted, like a traveler lost in the woods who returned again and again to the same place, unable to struggle clear.

She had known that it would come to this, when first she had taken him into her life. She should never have yielded to the mischief in those brown eyes. She should have sent him away and not given in to that weak part of herself that whispered: I want a friend.

She stood up and shook out her skirts, pulling her plaid more tightly around her sheepskin jacket. Gareth was watching her with frightened dog eyes, hurt and pleading; he followed her over to the heap of the packs on the other side of the fire.

She could have had her fill of lovers. There were always those who would lie with a witch for the novelty of it or for the luck it was said to bring. Why had she let him stay until morning and talked to him as if he were not a man and an enemy whom she knew even then would fetter her soul? Why had she let him touch her heart as well as her body?

The night was dead-still, the sky dark save for the white disc of the waxing moon. Its ghostly light barely outlined the broken bones of the empty town below. A log settled in the dying fire; the spurt of light touched a spangle of red on the twisted links of John's mail shirt and glimmered stickily on the upturned palm of one blistered hand. Jenny felt her whole body one open wound of grief.

We change what we touch, she thought. Why had she let him change her? She had been happy, alone with her magic. The key to magic is magic—she should have held to that from the start. She had known even then that he was a man who would give his life to help others, even others not his own.

If he had waited for Zyerne...

She pushed the thought away with bitter violence, knowing Zyerne's magic could have saved him. All day she had wanted to weep, not only with grief, but with anger at herself for all the choices of the past.

Thin and plaintive as a child's, Gareth's voice broke into her circle of stumbling self-hate. "Isn't there anything that you can do?"

"I have done what I can," she replied wearily. "I have washed his wounds and stitched them shut, laid spells of healing upon them. The dragon's blood is a poison in his veins, and he has lost too much blood of his own."

"But surely there's *something*..." In the brief gleam of the fire, she could see that he had been weeping. Her own soul felt cold now and drained as John's flesh.

"You have asked me that seven times since it grew

dark," she said. "This is beyond my skills—beyond the medicines that I have—beyond my magic."

She tried to tell herself that, even had she not loved him, even had she not given up the time she could have spent studying, it would still have been so.

Would she have been able to save him, if she had not given him all those hours; if she had spent all those early mornings meditating among the stones in the solitude of the hilltop instead of lying talking in his bed?

Or would she only have been a little bleaker, a little madder—a little more like the worst side of herself—a little more like Caerdinn?

She did not know, and the hurt of that was almost as bad as the hurt of suspecting that she did know.

But she had only her own small powers—spells worked one rune at a time, patiently, in the smallest increments of thought. She slowed and calmed her mind, as she did when she worked magic, and realized she could not cure him. What then could she do for him? What had Mab said, when she had spoken of healing?

She ran her hands through her long hair, shifting the weight of it from her face and neck. Her shoulders hurt with cramp; she had not slept in two nights, and her body ached.

"The most we can do now is keep heating stones in the fire to put around him," she said at last. "We must keep him warm."

Gareth swallowed and wiped his nose. "Just that?"

"For now, yes. If he seems a little stronger in the morning, we may be able to move him." But she knew in her heart that he would not live until morning. Like a whispering echo, the vision in the water bowl returned to her, a bitter nightmare of failed hope.

Hesitantly, Gareth offered, "There are physicians up at Halnath. Polycarp, for one."

"And an army around its walls." Her voice sounded

very cold to her own ears. "If he's still alive in the morning ... I didn't want you to risk putting yourself once again where Zyerne might reach you, but in the morning, I think you should take Battlehammer and ride back to Bel."

Gareth looked frightened at the mention of Zyerne's name and at the thought of possibly facing her alone, but he nodded. Jenny was interested to note, in some detached portion of her tired soul, that, having sought all his life for heroism, while Gareth might now flinch from it, he did not flee.

She went on, "Go to the house of the gnomes and fetch Miss Mab here. The medicines of the gnomes may be locked away in the Deep, but..." Her voice trailed off. Then she repeated softly, "The medicines of the gnomes."

Like pins and needles in a numbed limb, the hurt of hope renewed as a sudden wash of agony. She whispered, "Gareth, where are John's maps?"

Gareth blinked at her uncomprehendingly, too preoccupied for the moment with his own fears of Zyerne to realize what she was getting at. Then he gave a start, and hope flooded into his face, and he let out a whoop that could have been heard in Bel. "The Places of Healing!" he cried, and threw his arms around her, sweeping her off her feet. "I knew it!" he shouted, with all his old forlorn cockiness. "I knew you could think of something! You can..."

"You don't know anything of the kind." She fought free of him, angry at him for expressing what was already surging through her veins like a swig of cheap brandy. She brushed past him and almost ran to John's side, while Gareth, gamboling like a large puppy, began to ransack the camp for the maps.

If there was anything worse than the pain of despair, she thought, it was the pain of hope. At least despair is restful. Her own heart was hammering as she brushed aside the russet hair from John's forehead, almost black-looking now against the bloodless flesh. Her mind was racing ahead, ticking off the remedies Mab had spoken of: distillations to slow and strengthen the thready heartbeat; salves to promote the healing of the flesh; and philters to counteract poison and give him back the blood he had lost. There would be spell-books, too, she thought, hidden in the Places of Healing, words with which to bind the soul to the flesh, until the flesh itself could recover. She could find them, she told herself desperately, she must. But the knowledge of what was at stake lay on her heart like stones. For a moment she felt so tired that she almost wished for his death, because it would require no further striving from her and threaten her with no further failure.

Holding his icy hands, she slid for a moment into the outer fringes of the healing trance and whispered to him by his inner name. But it was as if she called at the head of a descending trail along which he had long since passed—there was no answer.

But there was something else. In her trance she heard it, a soft touch of sound that twisted her heart with fright—the slur of scales on rock, the shiver of alien music.

Her eyes opened; she found herself shaking and cold.

The dragon was alive.

"Jenny?" Gareth came nattering over to her side, his hands full of creased bits of dirty papyrus. "I found them, but—but the Places of Healing aren't on them." His eyes were filled with worry behind the cracked, crazy specs. "I've looked..."

Jenny took them from his hand with fingers that shook. In the firelight she could make out passages, caverns, rivers, all marked in Dromar's strong, runic hand, and the blank spots, unmarked and unlabeled. *The affair of the gnomes.*

Anger wrenched at her, and she threw the maps from her. "Damn Dromar and his secrets," she whispered

viciously. "Of course the Places of Healing are the heart
of the Deep that they all swear by!"

"But—" Gareth stammered weakly. "Can you—can
you find them anyway?"

Fury welled up in her, of hope thwarted, first by fear
and now by one gnome's stubbornness, like molten rock
pouring through the cracks of exhaustion in her soul. "In
those warrens?" she demanded. For a moment anger,
weariness, and the knowledge of the dragon claimed her,
tearing at her so that she could have screamed and called
down the lightning to rive apart the earth.

As Zyerne did, she told herself, fighting for calm. She
closed her fists, one around the other, and pressed her
lips against them, willing the rage and the fear to pass;
and when they passed, there was nothing left. It was as
if the unvoiced scream had burned everything out of her
and left only a well of dark and unnatural calm, a universe
deep.

Gareth was still looking at her, his eyes pleading. She
said quietly, "Maybe. Mab spoke of the way. I may be
able to reason it out." Mab had also said that one false
step would condemn her to a death by starvation, wandering in darkness.

Like an answer, she knew at once what John would
have said to that—*God's Grandmother, Jen, the dragon'll eat you before you get a chance to starve.*

Trust John, she thought, to make me laugh at a time
like this.

She got to her feet, chilled to the bone and feeling a
hundred years old, and walked to the packs once more.
Gareth trailed along after her, hugging his crimson cloak
about himself for warmth and chattering on about one
thing and another; locked in that strange stasis of calm,
Jenny scarcely heard.

It was only as she slung her big satchel about her shoulder and picked up her halberd that he seemed to feel her

silence. "Jenny," he said doubtfully, catching the edge of her plaid. "Jenny—the dragon is dead, isn't it? I mean, the poison did work, didn't it? It must have, if you were able to get John out of there..."

"No," Jenny said quietly. She wondered a little at the weird silence within her; she had felt more fear listening for the Whisperers in the Woods of Wyr than she did now. She started to move off toward the darkness of the shadow-drowned ruins. Gareth ran around in front of her and caught her by the arms.

"But—that is—how long..."

She shook her head. "Too long, almost certainly." She put her hand on his wrist to move him aside. Having made up her mind what she must do, she wanted it over with, though she knew she would never succeed.

Gareth swallowed hard, his thin face working in the low ruby light of the fire. "I—I'll go," he volunteered shakily. "Tell me what I should look for, and I..."

For an instant, laughter threatened to crack all her hard-won resolve—not laughter at him, but at the wan gallantry that impelled him, like the hero of a ballad, to take her place. But he would not have understood how she loved him for the offer, absurd as it was; and if she began to laugh she would cry, and that weakness she knew she could not now afford. So she only stood on her toes and pulled his shoulders down so that she could kiss his soft, thin cheek. "Thank you, Gareth," she murmured. "But I can see in the darkness, and you cannot, and I know what I seek."

"Really," he persisted, torn visibly between relief at her refusal, awareness that she was in fact far better suited than he for the task, a lifetime of chivalric precept, and a very real desire to protect her from harm.

"No," she said gently. "Just see that John stays warm. If I don't come back..." Her voice faltered at the knowledge of what lay before her—the death by the dragon, or the death within the maze. She forced strength into her words. "Do what seems best to you, but don't try to move him too soon."

The admonition was futile, and she knew it. She tried to remember Mab's words regarding the lightless labyrinths of the Deep and they slid from her mind like a fistful of water, leaving only the recollection of the shining wheels of diamond that were the dragon's watching eyes. But she had to reassure Gareth; and while John breathed, she knew she could never have remained in camp.

She squeezed Gareth's hand and withdrew from him. Hitching her plaids higher on her shoulder, she turned toward the shadowy trails through the Vale and the dark bulk of Nast Wall that loomed against a sullen and pitchy sky. Her final glimpse of John was of the last glow of the dying fire that outlined the shape of his nose and lips against the darkness.

Long before she reached the Great Gates of the Deep, Jenny was aware of the singing. As she crossed the frost-skimmed stones of the ruins, bled of all their daytime color by the feeble wash of the moonlight, she felt it—a hunger, a yearning, and a terrifying beauty, far beyond her comprehension. It intruded into her careful piecing-together of those fragmentary memories of Mab's remarks about the Places of Healing, broke even into her fears for John. It seemed to float around her in the air, and yet she knew that it could only be heard by her; it shivered in her bones, down to her very finger ends. When she stood in the Gates with the blackness of the Market Hall lying before her and her own shadow a diffuse smudge on the scuffed and blood-gummed refuse of the floor, it was almost overwhelming.

There was no sound to it, but its rhythm called her blood. Braided images that she could neither completely sense nor wholly understand twisted through her consciousness—knots of memory, of starry darkness that sunlight had never seen, of the joyous exhaustion of physical love whose modes and motives were strange to her, and of mathematics and curious relationships between things that she had never known were akin. It was stronger and very different from the singing that had filled the gully when the Golden Dragon of Wyr lay gasping its last. There was a piled strength in it of years lived fully and of patterns comprehended across unknowable gulfs of time.

The dragon was invisible in the darkness. She heard the soft scrape of his scales and guessed him to be lying across the inner doors of the Market Hall, that led to the Grand Passage and so into the Deep. Then the silver lamps of his eyes opened and seemed to glow softly in the reflected moonlight, and in her mind the singing flowed and intensified its colors into the vortex of a white core. In that core words formed.

Have you come seeking medicines, wizard woman? Or is that weapon you carry simply what you have deluded yourself into thinking sufficient to finish what your poisons do too slowly for your convenience?

The words were almost pictures, music and patterns shaped as much by her own soul as by his. They would hurt, she thought, if allowed to sink too deeply.

"I have come seeking medicines," she replied, her voice reverberating against the fluted dripstone of the toothed ceiling. "The power of the Places of Healing was everywhere renowned."

This I knew. There was a knot of gnomes that held out in the place where they took all the wounded. The door was low, but I could reach through it like a wolf raiding a bury of rabbits. I fed upon them for many days, until they were all gone. They had the wherewithal to make poisons there, too. They poisoned the carrion, as if they did not think that I could see the death that tainted the meat. This will be the place that you seek.

Because he spoke partially in pictures, she glimpsed also the dark ways into the place, like a half-remembered dream in her mind. Her hope stirred, and she fixed the pictures in her thoughts—tiny fragments, but perhaps enough to serve.

With her wizard's sight she could distinguish him now, stretched before her across the doors in the darkness. He had dislodged the harpoons from his throat and belly, and they lay blackened with his blood in the muck of slime and ash on the floor. The thorny scales of his back and sides lay sleek now, their edges shining faintly in the dim reflection of the moon. The heavy ridges of spikes that guarded his backbone and the joints of his legs still bristled like weapons. The enormous wings lay folded neatly along his sides, and their joints, too, she saw, were armored and spined. His head fascinated her most, long and narrow and birdlike, its shape concealed under a mask of bony plates. From those plates grew a vast mane of ribbonlike scales, mingled with tufts of fur and what looked like growths of ferns and feathers; his long, delicate antennae with their glittering bobs of jet lay limp upon the ground around his head. He lay like a dog, his chin between his forepaws; but the eyes that burned into hers were the eyes of a mage who is also a beast.

I will bargain with you, wizard woman.

She knew, with chill premonition but no surprise what his bargain would be, and her heart quickened, though whether with dread or some strange hope she did not know. She said, "No," but within herself she felt, like a forbidden longing, the unwillingness to let something this beautiful, this powerful, die. He was evil, she told herself, knowing and believing it in her heart. Yet there was something in those silver eyes that drew her, some song of black and latent fire whose music she understood.

The dragon moved his head a little on the powerful

curve of his neck. Blood dripped down from the tattered ribbons of his mane.

Do you think that even you, a wizard who sees in darkness, can search out the ways of the gnomes?

The pictures that filled her mind were of the darkness, of clammy and endless mazes of the world underground. Her heart sank with dread at the awareness of them; those few small images of the way to the Places of Healing, those fragmentary words of Mab's, turned in her hands to the pebbles with which a child thinks it can slaughter lions.

Still she said, "I have spoken to one of them of these ways."

And did she tell the truth? The gnomes are not famed for it in matters concerning the heart of the Deep.

Jenny remembered the empty places on Dromar's maps. But she retorted, "Nor are dragons."

Beneath the exhaustion and pain, she felt in the dragon's mind amusement at her reply, like a thin spurt of cold water in hot.

What is truth, wizard woman? The truth that dragons see is not pleasant to the human eyes, however uncomfortably comprehensible it may be to their hearts. You know this.

She saw that he had felt her fascination. The silver eyes drew her; his mind touched hers, as a seducer would have touched her hand. She saw, also, that he understood that she would not draw back from that touch. She forced her thoughts away from him, holding to the memories of John and of their sons, against the power that called to her like a whisper of amorphous night.

With effort, she tore her eyes from his and turned to leave.

Wizard woman, do you think this man for whom you risk the bones of your body will live longer than I?

She stopped, the toes of her boots touching the hem

of the carpet of moonlight which lay upon the flagstoned floor. Then she turned back to face him, despairing and torn. The wan light showed her the pools of acrid blood drying over so much of the floor, the sunken look to the dragon's flesh; and she realized that his question had struck at her weakness and despair to cover his own.

She said calmly, "There is the chance that he will."

She felt the anger in the movement of his head, and the pain that sliced through him with it. *And will you wager on that? Will you wager that, even did the gnomes speak the truth, you will be able to sort your way through their warrens, spiral within spiral, dark within dark, to find what you need in time? Heal me, wizard woman, and I will guide you with my mind and show you the place that you seek.*

For a time she only gazed up at that long bulk of shining blackness, the dark mane of bloody ribbons, and the eyes like oiled metal ringing eternal darkness. He was a wonder such as she had never seen, a spined and supple shadow from the thorned tips of his backswept wings to the horned beak of his nose. The Golden Dragon John had slain on the windswept hills of Wyr had been a being of sun and fire, but this was a smoke-wraith of night, black and strong and old as time. The spines of his head grew into fantastic twisted horns, icy-smooth as steel; his forepaws had the shape of hands, save that they had two thumbs instead of one. The voice that spoke in her mind was steady, but she could see the weakness dragging at every line of that great body and feel the faint shiver of the last taut strength that fought to continue the bluff against her.

Unwillingly, she said, "I know nothing of the healing of dragons."

The silver eyes narrowed, as if she had asked him for something he had not thought to give. For a moment they faced one another, cloaked in the cave's darkness. She was aware of John and of time—distantly, like something urgent in a dream. But she kept her thoughts concentrated upon the creature that lay before her and the diamond-prickled darkness of that alien mind that struggled with hers.

Then suddenly the gleaming body convulsed. She felt, through the silver eyes, the pain like a scream through the steel ropes of his muscles. The wings stretched out uncontrollably, the claws extending in a terrible spasm as the poison shifted in his veins. The voice in her mind whispered, *Go*.

At the same moment memories flooded her thoughts of a place she had never been before. Vague images crowded to her mind of blackness as vast as the night outdoors, columned with a forest of stone trees that whispered back the echo of every breath, of rock seams a few yards across whose ceilings were lost in distant darkness, and of the murmuring of endless water under stone. She felt a vertigo of terror as in a nightmare, but also a queer sense of *déjà vu*, as if she had passed that way before.

It came to her that it was Morkeleb and not she who had passed that way; the images were the way to the Places of Healing, the very heart of the Deep.

The spined black body before her twisted with another paroxysm of anguish, the huge tail slashing like a whip against the rock of the wall. The pain was visible now in the silver eyes as the poison ate into the dragon's blood. Then his body dropped slack, a dry clatter of horns and spines like a skeleton falling on a stone floor, and from a great distance off she heard again, *Go*.

His scales had all risen in a blanket of razors at his agony; quiveringly, they smoothed themselves flat along the sunken sides. Jenny gathered her courage and strode forward; without giving herself time to think of what she was doing, she scrambled over the waist-high hill of the ebony flank that blocked the doorway of the Grand Tunnel. The backbone ridge was like a hedge of spears, thrust-

ing stiffly from the unsteady footing of the hide. Kilting
up her skirt, she put a hand to steady herself on the carved
stone pillar of the doorjamb and leaped over the spines
awkwardly, fearing to the last that some renewed con-
vulsion would thrust them into her thighs.

But the dragon lay quiet. Jenny could sense only the
echoes of his mind within hers, like a faint gleam of far-
off light. Before her stretched the darkness of the Deep.

If she thought about them, the visions she had seen
retreated from her. But she found that if she simply walked
forward, as if she had trodden this way before, her feet
would lead her. Dream memories whispered through her
mind of things she had seen, but sometimes the angle of
sight was different, as if she had looked down upon them
from above.

The upper levels of the Deep were dry, wrought by the
gnomes after the fashion of the tastes of men. The Grand
Passage, thirty feet broad and paved in black granite,
worn and runnelled with the track of uncounted generations of feet, had been walled with blocks of cut stone to
hide the irregularities of its shape; broken statues lying
like scattered bones in the dark attested the classical
appearance of the place in its heyday. Among the frag-
mented whiteness of the marble limbs lay real bones, and
with them the twisted bronze frames and shattered glass
of the huge lamps that had once depended from the high
ceiling, all scraped together along the walls, like leaves
in a gutter, by the passage of the dragon's body. Even in
the darkness, Jenny's wizard's sight showed her the fire-
blackening where the spilled oil had been ignited by the
dragon's breath.

Deeper down, the place had the look of the gnomes.
Stalagmites and columns ceased to be carved into the
straight pillars favored by the children of men, and were
wrought into the semblance of trees in leaf, or beasts, or

grotesque things that could have been either; more and more frequently they had simply been left to keep the original shape of pouring water which had been their own. The straight, handsomely finished water courses of the higher levels gave place to tumbling streams in the lower deeps; in some places the water fell straight, fifty or a hundred feet from distant ceilings, like a living pillar, or gushed away into darkness through conduits shaped like the skulls of gargoyles. Jenny passed through caverns and systems of caves that had been transformed into the vast, interconnected dwelling places of the great clans and families of the gnomes, but elsewhere she found halls and rooms large enough to contain all the village of Deeping, where houses and palaces had been built freestanding, their bizarre spires and catwalks indistinguishable from the groves of stalagmites that clustered in strange forests on the banks of pools and rivers like polished onyx.

And through these silent realms of wonder she saw nothing but the evidences of ruin and decay and the scraping track of the dragon. White ur-toads were everywhere, squabbling with rats over the rotting remains of stored food or month-old carrion; in some places, the putrescent fetor of what had been hoards of cheese, meat, or vegetables was nearly unbreathable. The white, eyeless vermin of the deeper pits, whose names she could only guess at from Mab's accounts, slipped away at her approach, or hid themselves behind the fire-marked skulls and dropped vessels of chased silver that everywhere scattered the halls.

As she went deeper, the air became cold and very damp, the stone increasingly slimy beneath her boots; the weight of the darkness was crushing. As she walked the lightless mazes, she understood that Mab had been right; without guidance, even she, whose eyes could pierce that utter darkness, would never have found her way to the heart of the Deep.

But find it she did. The echo of it was in the dragon's mind, setting up queer resonances in her soul, a lamination of feelings and awareness whose alien nature she shrank from, uncomprehending. Beside its doors, she felt the aura of healing that lingered still in the air, and the faint breath of ancient power.

All through that series of caverns, the air was warm, smelling of dried camphor and spices; the putrid stench of decay and the crawling vermin were absent. Stepping through the doors into the domed central cavern, where ghost-pale stalactites regarded themselves in the oiled blackness of a central pool, she wondered how great a spell it would take to hold that healing warmth, not only against the cold in the abysses of the earth, but for so long after those who had wrought the spell had perished.

The magic here was great indeed.

It pervaded the place; as she passed cautiously through the rooms of meditation, of dreaming, or of rest, Jenny was conscious of it as a living presence, rather than the stasis of dead spells. At times the sensation of it grew so strong that she looked back over her shoulder and called out to the darkness, "Is someone there?" though in her reason she knew there was not. But as with the Whisperers in the north, her feelings argued against her reason, and again and again she extended her senses through that dark place, her heart pounding in hope or fear—she could not tell which. But she touched nothing, nothing but darkness and the drip of water falling eternally from the hanging teeth of the stones.

There was living magic there, whispering to itself in darkness—and like the touch of some foul thing upon her flesh, she felt the sense of evil.

She shivered and glanced around her nervously once more. In a small room, she found the medicines she sought, row after row of glass phials and stoppered jars of the green-and-white marbled ware the gnomes made in such quantity. She read their labels in the darkness and stowed them in her satchel, working quickly, partly from a growing sense of uneasiness and partly because she felt time leaking away and John's life ebbing like the going-out of the tide.

He can't die, she told herself desperately, not after all this—but she had come too late to too many bedsides in her years as a healer to believe that. Still, she knew that the medicines alone might not be enough. Hastily, glancing back over her shoulder as she moved from room to dark and silent room, she began searching for the inner places of power, the libraries where they would store the books and scrolls of magic that, she guessed, made up the true heart of the Deep.

Her boots swished softly on the sleek floors, but even that small noise twisted at her nerves. The floors of the rooms, like all the places inhabited by gnomes, were never at one level, but made like a series of terraces; even the smallest chambers had two or more. And as she searched, the eerie sense of being watched grew upon her, until she feared to pass through new doors, half-expecting to meet some evil thing gloating in the blackness. She felt a power, stronger than any she had encountered—stronger than Zyerne's, stronger than the dragon's. But she found nothing, neither that waiting, silent evil, nor any book of power by which magic would be transmitted down the years among the gnome mages—only herbals, anatomies, or catalogs of diseases and cures. In spite of her uneasy fear, she felt puzzled—Mab had said that the gnomes had no Lines, yet surely the power had to be transmitted somehow. So she forced herself to seek, deeper and deeper, for the books that must contain it.

Exhaustion was beginning to weaken her like slow illness. Last night's watching and the night's before weighed her bones, and she knew she would have to abandon her search. But knowledge of her own inadequacy drove her, questing inward into the forbidden heart of the Deep, desperate to find what she might before she returned to the surface to do what she could with what she had.

She stepped through a door into a dark place that echoed with her breathing.

She had felt cold before, but it seemed nothing now; nothing compared to the dread that congealed around her heart.

She stood in the place she had seen in the water bowl, in the visions of John's death.

It shocked her, for she had come on it unexpectedly. She had thought to find an archive there, a place of teaching, for she guessed this to be the heart and center of the blank places on Dromar's ambiguous maps. But through a knotted forest of stalactites and columns, she glimpsed only empty darkness that smelled faintly of the wax of a thousand candles, which slumped like dead things in the niches of the rock. No living thing was there, but she felt again that sense of evil and she stepped cautiously forward into the open spaces of black toward the misshapen stone altar.

She laid her hands upon the blue-black, soapy-feeling stone. In her vision the place had been filled with muttering whispers, but now there was only silence. For a moment, dark swirlings seemed to stir in her mind, the inchoate whisperings of fragmentary visions, but they passed like a groundswell, leaving no more aftertaste than a dream.

Still, they seemed to take from her the last of her strength and her will; she felt bitterly weary and suddenly very frightened of the place. Though she heard no sound, she whirled, her heart beating so that she could almost hear its thudding echo in the dark. There was evil there, somewhere—she knew it now, felt it close enough to leer over her shoulder. Shifting the bulging satchel upon her shoulder, she hastened like a thief across the slithery darkness of the gnomes' dancing floor, seeking the ways that would lead her out of the darkness, back to the air above.

Morkeleb's mind had guided her down into the abyss, but she could feel no touch of it now. She followed the marks she had made, runes that only she could see, drawn upon the walls with her forefinger. As she ascended through the dark rock seams and stairs of amber flowstone, she wondered if the dragon were dead. A part of her hoped that he was, for the sake of the people of these lands, for the gnomes, and for the Master; a part of her felt the same grief that she had, standing above the dragon's corpse in the gully of Wyr. But there was something about that grief that made her hope still more that the dragon was dead, for reasons she hesitated to examine.

The Grand Passage was as dark as the bowels of the Deep had been, bereft of even the little moonlight that had leaked in to illuminate it before; but even in the utter darkness, the air here was different—cold but dry and moving, unlike the still, brooding watchfulness of the heart of the Deep.

Her wizard's sight showed her the dark, bony shape of the dragon's haunch lying across the doorway, the bristling spears of his backbone pointing inward toward her. As she came nearer she saw how sunken the scaled skin lay on the curve of the bone.

Listen as she would, she heard no murmur of his mind. But, the music that had seemed to fill the Market Hall echoed there still, faint and piercing, with molten shivers of dying sound.

He was unconscious—dying, she thought. *Do you think this man will live longer than I?* he had asked.

Jenny unslung her plaid from her shoulder and laid the thick folds over the cutting knives of the dragon's spine. The edges drove through the cloth; she added the heavy sheepskin of her jacket and, shivering as the outer cold sliced through the thin sleeves of her shift, worked her foot onto the largest of the spines. Catching the doorpost once again for leverage, she swung herself nimbly up and over. For an instant she balanced on the haunch, feeling the slender suppleness of the bones under the steel scales and the soft heat that radiated from the dragon's body; then she sprang down. She stood for a moment, listening with her ears and her mind.

The dragon made no move. The Market Hall lay before her, blue-black and ivory with the feeble trickle of starlight that seemed so bright after the utter night below the ground. Even though the moon had set, every pot sherd and skewed lampframe seemed to Jenny's eyes outlined in brightness, every shadow like spilled ink. The blood was drying, though the place stank of it. Osprey still lay in a smeared pool of darkness, surrounded by glinting harpoons. The night felt very old. A twist of wind brought her the smell of woodsmoke from the fire on Tanner's Rise.

Like a ghost Jenny crossed the hall, shivering in the dead cold. It was only when she reached the open night of the steps that she began to run.

CHAPTER XI

AT DAWN SHE felt John's hand tighten slightly around her own.

Two nights ago she had worked the death-spells, weaving an aura of poison and ruin—the circles of them still lay scratched in the earth at the far end of the Rise. She had not slept more than an hour or so the night before that, somewhere on the road outside Bel, curled in John's arms. Now the drifting smoke of the low fire was a smudge of gray silk in the pallid morning air, and she felt worn and chilled and strange, as if her skin had been sandpapered and every nerve lay exposed. Yet she felt strangely calm.

She had done everything she could, slowly, meticulously, step by step, following Miss Mab's remembered instructions as if the body she knew so well were a stranger's. She had given him the philters and medicines as the gnomes did, by means of a hollow needle driven into the veins, and had packed poultices on the wounds to draw from them the poison of the dragon's blood. She had traced the runes of healing where the marks of the wounds cut the paths of life throughout his body, touching them with his inner name, the secret of his essence, woven into the spells. She had called him patiently, repeatedly, by the name that his soul knew, holding his spirit to his body by what force of magic she could muster, until the medicines could take hold.

She had not thought that she would succeed. When she did, she was exhausted past grief or joy, able to think no further than the slight lift of his ribcage and the crease of his blackened eyelids with his dreams.

Gareth said softly, "Will he be all right?" and she nodded. Looking at the gawky young prince who hunkered at her side by the fire, she was struck by his silence. Perhaps the closeness of death and the endless weariness of the night had sobered him. He had spent the hours while she was in the Deep patiently heating stones and placing them around John's body as he had been told to do—a dull and necessary task, and one to which, she was almost certain, she owed the fact that John had still been alive when she had returned from the dragon's lair.

Slowly, her every bone hurting her to move, she put off the scuffed scarlet weight of his cloak. She felt scraped and aching, and wanted only to sleep. But she stood up, knowing there was something else she must do, worse than all that had gone before. She stumbled to her medicine bag and brought out the brown tabat leaves she always carried, dried to the consistency of leather. Breaking two of them to pieces, she put them in her mouth and chewed.

Their wringing bitterness was in itself enough to wake her, without their other properties. She had chewed them earlier in the night, against the exhaustion that she had felt catching up with her while she worked. Gareth watched her apprehensively, his long face haggard within the straggly frame of his green-tipped hair, and she reflected that he must be almost as weary as she. Lines that had existed only as brief traces of passing expressions were etched there now, from his nostrils to the corners of his mouth, and others showed around his eyes when he took off his broken spectacles to rub the inner corners of the lids—lines that would deepen and settle into his manhood and his old age. As she ran her hands through the loosened cloud of her hair, she wondered what her own face looked like, or would look like after she did what she knew she must do.

She began collecting medicines into her satchel once more.

"Where are you going?"

She found one of John's plaids and wrapped it about her, all her movements stiff with weariness. She felt threadbare as a piece of worn cloth, but the uneasy strength of the tabat leaves was already coursing through her veins. She knew she would have to be careful, for the tabat was like a usurer; it lent, but it had a way of demanding back with interest when one could least afford to pay. The moist air felt cold in her lungs; her soul was oddly numb.

"To keep a promise," she said.

The boy watched her with trepidation in his earnest gray eyes as she shouldered her satchel once more and set off through the misty silences of the ruined town toward the Gates of the Deep.

"Morkeleb?"

Her voice dissipated like a thread of mist in the stillness of the Market Hall. Vapor and blue morning shadow cloaked the Vale outside, and the light here was gray and sickly. Before her the dragon lay like a dropped garment of black silk, held to shape only by its bonings. One wing stretched out, where it had fallen after the convulsions of the night before; the long antennae trailed limp among the ribbons of the mane. Faint singing still lay upon the air, drawing at Jenny's heart.

He had given her the way through the Deep, she

thought; it was John's life that she owed him. She tried to tell herself that it was for this reason only that she did not want that terrible beauty to die.

Her voice echoed among the upended ivory turrets of the roof. "Morkeleb!"

The humming changed within her mind, and she knew he heard. One delicate, crayfish antenna stirred. The lids of silver eyes slipped back a bare inch. For the first time she saw how delicate those lids were, tinted with subtle shades of violet and green within the blackness. Looking into the white depths they partly shielded, she felt fear, but not fear for her body; she felt again the cross-blowing winds of present *should* and future *if*, rising up out of the chasms of doubt. She summoned calm to her, as she summoned clouds or the birds of the hawthorn brakes, and was rather surprised at the steadiness of her voice.

"Give me your name."

Life moved in him then, a gold heat that she felt through the singing of the air. Anger and resistance; bitter resistance to the last.

"I cannot save you without knowing your name," she said. "If you slip beyond the bounds of your flesh, I need something by which to call you back."

Still that molten wrath surged through the weakness and pain. She remembered Caerdinn saying, "Save a dragon, slave a dragon." At that time, she had not known why anyone would wish to save the life of such a creature, nor how doing so would place something so great within your power. Cock by its feet...

"Morkeleb!" She walked forward, forgetting her fear of him—perhaps through anger and dread that he would die, perhaps only through the tabat leaves—and laid her small hands on the soft flesh around his eyes. The scales there were tinier than the ends of needles. The skin felt like dry silk beneath her hand, pulsing with warm life. She felt again that sense, half-fright, half-awe, of taking a step down a road which should not be trodden, and wondered if it would be wiser and better to turn away and let him die. She knew what he was. But having touched him, having looked into those diamond eyes, she could more easily have given up her own life.

In the glitter of the singing within her mind, one single air seemed to detach itself, as if the thread that bound together the complex knots of its many harmonies had suddenly taken on another color. She knew it immediately in its wholeness, from the few truncated fragments Caerdinn had whistled for her in a hedgerow one summer day. The music itself was the dragon's name.

It slid through her fingers, soft as silken ribbons; taking it, she began to braid it into her spells, weaving them like a rope of crystal around the dragon's fading soul. Through the turns of the music, she glimpsed the entrance to the dark, starry mazes of his inner mind and heart and, by the flickering light of it, seemed to see the paths that she must take to the healing of his body.

She had brought with her the medicines from the Deep, but she saw now that they were useless. Dragons healed themselves and one another through the mind alone. At times, in the hours that followed, she was terrified of this healing, at others, only exhausted past anything she had ever experienced or imagined, even in the long night before. Her weariness grew, encompassing body and brain in mounting agony; she felt entangled in a net of light and blackness, struggling to draw across some barrier a vast, cloudy force that pulled her toward it over that same frontier. It was not what she had thought to do, for it had nothing to do with the healing of humans or beasts. She summoned the last reserves of her own power, digging forgotten strengths from the marrow of her bones to battle for his life and her own. Holding to the ropes of his life took all this strength and more that she did not have; and in a kind of delirium, she understood that if he died, she would die also, so entangled was her essence in the starry skeins of his soul. Small and clear, she got a glimpse of the future, like an image in her scrying-stone—that if she died, John would die within the day, and Gareth would last slightly less than seven years, as a husk slowly hollowed by Zyerne's perverted powers. Turning from this, she clung to the small, rock-steady strength of what she knew: old Caerdinn's spells and her own long meditations in the solitude among the stones of Frost Fell.

Twice she called Morkeleb by his name, tangling the music of it with the spells she had so laboriously learned rune by rune, holding herself anchored to this life with the memory of familiar things—the shapes of the leaves of plants, gentian and dog's mercury, the tracks of hares upon the snow, and wild, vagrant airs played on the pennywhistle upon summer nights. She felt the dragon's strength stir and the echo of his name return.

She did not remember sleeping afterward. But she woke to the warmth of sunlight on her hair. Through the open Gates of the Deep, she could see the looming rock face of the cliffs outside drenched with cinnabar and gold by the afternoon's slanted light. Turning her head, she saw that the dragon had moved and lay sleeping also, great wings folded once more and his chin upon his foreclaws like a dog. In the shadows, he was nearly invisible. She could not see that he breathed, but wondered if she ever had. Did dragons breathe?

Lassitude flooded her, burying her like silk-fine sand. The last of the tabat leaves had burned out of her veins, and that exhaustion added to the rest. Scraped, drained, wrung, she wanted only to sleep again, hour after hour, for days if possible.

But she knew it was not possible. She had saved Morkeleb, but was under no illusion that this would let her sleep safely in his presence, once he had regained a little of his strength. A detached thread of amusement at herself made her chuckle; Ian and Adric, she thought, would boast to each other and every boy in the village that their mother could go to sleep in a dragon's lair—that is, if she ever made it back to tell them of it. Even rolling over hurt her bones. The weight of her clothes and her hair dragged at her like chain mail as she stood.

She stumbled to the Gates and stood for a moment, leaning against the rough-hewn granite of the vast pillar, the dry, moving freedom of the air fingering her face. Turning her head, she looked back over her shoulder and met the dragon's open eyes. Their depths stared into hers for one instant, crystalline flowers of white and silver, like glittering wells of rage and hate. Then they slid shut again. She walked from the shadows out into the brilliance of the evening.

Her mind as well as her body felt numbed as she walked slowly back through Deeping. Everything seemed queer and changed, the shadow of each pebble and weed a thing of new and unknown significance to her, as if for years she had walked half-blind and now had opened her eyes. At the northern side of the town, she climbed the rocks to the water tanks, deep black pools cut into the bones of the mountain, with sun flashing on their opaque surfaces. She stripped and swam, though the water was very cold. Afterward she lay for a long time upon her spread-out clothing, dreaming she knew not what. Wind tracked across her bare back and legs like tiny footprints, and the sun-dance changed in the pool as shadows crept across the black water. She felt it would have been good to cry, but was too weary even for that.

In time she got up, put on her clothes again, and returned to camp. Gareth was asleep, sitting with his knees drawn up and his face upon them on his crossed arms, near the glowing ashes of the fire.

Jenny knelt beside John, feeling his hands and face. They seemed warmer, though she could detect no surface blood under the thin, fair skin. Still, his eyebrows and the reddish stubble of his beard no longer seemed so dark. She lay down beside him, her body against his beneath the blankets, and fell asleep.

In the drowsy warmth of half-waking, she heard John murmur, "I thought that was you calling me." His breath was no more than a faint touch against her hair. She blinked into waking. The light had changed again. It was dawn.

She said, "What?" and sat up, shaking back the thick weight of her hair from her face. She still felt tired to death, but ravenously hungry. Gareth was kneeling by the campfire, tousled and unshaven with his battered spectacles sliding down the end of his nose, making griddle-cakes. She noted that he was better at it than John had ever been.

"I thought you were never waking up," he said.

"I thought I was never waking up either, my hero," John whispered. His voice was too weak to carry even that short distance, but Jenny heard him and smiled.

She climbed stiffly to her feet, pulled on her skirt again over her creased shift, laced her bodice and put on her boots, while Gareth set water over the coals to boil for coffee, a bitter black drink popular at Court. When Gareth went to fetch more water from the spring in the woods beyond the wrecked well house, Jenny took some of the boiling water to renew John's poultices, welcoming the simplicity of human healing; and the smell of herbs soon filled the little clearing among the ruins, along with the warm, strange smell of the drink. John fell asleep again, even before Jenny had finished with the bandages, but Gareth fetched her some bannocks and honey and sat with her beside the breakfast fire.

"I didn't know what to do, you were gone so long," he said around a mouthful of mealcake. "I thought about following you—that you might need help—but I didn't want to leave John alone. Besides," he added with a rueful grin, "I've never managed to rescue you from anything yet."

Jenny laughed and said, "You did right."

"And the promise you made?"

"I kept it."

He let out his breath with a sigh and bowed his head, as if some great weight that had been pressing down upon him had been lifted. After a while he said shyly, "While I was waiting for you, I made up a song . . . a ballad. About the slaying of Morkeleb, the Black Dragon of Nast Wall. It isn't very good . . ."

"It wouldn't be," Jenny said slowly, and licked the honey from her fingers. "Morkeleb is not dead."

He stared at her, as he once had when she had told him that John had killed the Golden Dragon of Wyr with an ax. "But I thought—wasn't your promise to John to—to slay him if—if John could not?"

She shook her head, the dark cloud of her hair snagging in the grubby fleece of her jacket collar. "My promise was to Morkeleb," she said. "It was to heal him."

Collecting her feet beneath her, she rose and walked over to John once more, leaving Gareth staring after her in appalled and unbelieving bewilderment.

A day passed before Jenny returned to the Deep. She stayed close to the camp, taking care of John and washing clothes—a mundane task, but one that needed to be done. Somewhat to her surprise, Gareth helped her in this, fetching water from the spring in the glade, but without his usual chatter. Knowing she would need her strength, she slept a good deal, but her dreams were disquieting. Her waking hours were plagued with a sense of being watched. She told herself that this was simply because Morkeleb, waking, had extended his awareness across the Vale and knew where they were, but certain understandings she had found within the mazes of the dragon's mind would not allow her to believe this.

She was aware that Gareth was watching her, too, mostly when he thought she wasn't looking.

She was aware of other things, as well. Never had she felt so conscious of the traces and turnings of the wind, and of the insignificant activities of the animals in the surrounding woods. She found herself prey to strange contemplation and odd knowledge of things before unsuspected—how clouds grow, and why the wind walked the way it did, how birds knew their way south, and why, in certain places of the world at certain times, voices could be heard speaking indistinctly in empty air. She would have liked to think these changes frightened her because she did not understand them, but in truth the reason she feared them was because she did.

While she slept in the late afternoon, she heard Gareth speak to John of it, seeing them and understanding through the depths of her altered dreams.

"She healed him," she heard Gareth whisper, and was aware of him squatting beside the tangle of bearskins and plaids where John lay. "I think she promised to do so, in trade for his letting her past him to fetch the medicines."

John sighed and moved one bandaged hand a little where it lay on his chest. "Better, maybe, she had let me die."

"Do you think..." Gareth swallowed nervously and cast a glance at her, as if he knew that asleep, she still could hear. "Do you think he's put a spell on her?"

John was silent for a time, looking up at the gulfs of sky above the Vale, thinking. Though the air down here was still, great winds racked the upper atmosphere, herding piled masses of cloud, charcoal gray and blinding white, up against the shaggy flanks of the mountains. At length he said, "I think I'd feel it, if there were another mind controlling hers. Or I'd like to flatter myself to thinking

I'd feel it. They say you should never look into a dragon's eyes, lest he put a spell on you. But she's stronger than that."

He turned his head a little and looked at where she lay, squinting to focus his shortsighted brown eyes upon her. The bare flesh on either side of the bandages on his arms and chest was livid with bruises and pitted with tiny scabs where the broken links of the mail shirt had been dragged through it. "When I used to dream of her, she didn't look the same as in waking. When I was delirious, I dreamed of her—it's as if she's grown more herself, not less."

He sighed and looked back at Gareth. "I used to be jealous of her, you know. Not of another man, but jealousy of herself, of that part of her she'd never give me—though God knows, back in those days, what I wanted it for. Who was it who said that jealousy is the only vice that gives no pleasure? But that was the first thing I had to learn about her, and maybe the hardest I've ever learned about anything—that she is her own, and what she gives me is of her choosing, and the more precious because of it. Sometimes a butterfly will come to sit in your open palm, but if you close your hand, one way or the other, it—and its choice to be there—are gone."

From there Jenny slid into deeper dreams of the crushing darkness of Ylferdun and the deep magic she sensed slumbering in the Places of Healing. As if from a great distance, she saw her children, her boys, whom she had never wanted to conceive but had borne and birthed for John's sake, but loved uneasily, unwillingly, and with desperately divided heart. With her wizard's sight she could see them sitting up in their curtained bed in the darkness, while wind drove snow against the tower walls; not sleeping at all, but telling one another tales about how their father and mother would slay the dragon and ride back with pack trains and pack trains of gold.

She woke when the sun lay three-quarters down the sky toward the flinty crest of the ridge. The wind had shifted; the whole Vale smelled of sharp snow and pine needles from the high slopes. The air in the lengthening slaty shadows was cold and damp.

John was asleep, wrapped in every cloak and blanket in the camp. Gareth's voice could be heard in the woods near the little stone fountain, tunelessly singing romantic lyrics of passionate love for the edification of the horses. Moving with her habitual quiet, Jenny laced up her bodice and put on her boots and her sheepskin jacket. She thought about eating something and decided not to. Food would break her concentration, and she felt the need of every fragment of strength and alertness that she could muster.

She paused for a moment, looking around her. The old, uneasy sensation of being watched returned to her, like a hand touching her elbow. But she sensed, also, the faint tingling of Morkeleb's power in the back of her mind and knew that the dragon's strength was returning far more quickly than that of the man he had almost slain.

She would have to act and act now, and the thought of it filled her with fear.

"Save a dragon, slave a dragon," Caerdinn had said. Her awareness of how small her own powers were terrified her, knowing what it was against which she must pit them. So this, in the end, was what she had paid for John's love, she told herself, with a little wry amusement. To go into a battle she could not hope to win. Involuntarily another part of her thought at once that at least it wasn't John's life, but her own, that would be forfeit, and she shook her head in wonderment at the follies of love. No wonder those with the power were warned against it, she thought.

As for the dragon, she had a sense, almost an instinct, of what she must do, alien to her and yet terrifyingly clear.

Her heart was hammering as she selected a scruffy plaid from the top of the pile over John. The thin breezes fluttered at its edges as she slung it around her; its colors faded into the muted hues of weed and stone as she made her way silently down the ridge once more and took the track for the Deep.

Morkeleb no longer lay in the Market Hall. She followed the scent of him through the massive inner doors and along the Grand Passage—a smell that was pungent but not unpleasant, unlike the burning, metallic reek of his poisons. The tiny echoes of her footfalls were like far-off water dripping in the silent vaults of the passage—she knew Morkeleb would hear them, lying upon his gold in the darkness. Almost, she thought, he would hear the pounding of her heart.

As Dromar had said, the dragon was laired in the Temple of Sarmendes, some quarter-mile along the passage. The Temple had been built for the use of the children of men and so had been wrought into the likeness of a room rather than a cave. From the chryselephantine doors Jenny looked about, her eyes piercing the absolute darkness there, seeing how the stalagmites that rose from the floor had been cut into pillars, and how walls had been built to conceal the uneven shape of the cavern's native rock. The floor was smoothed all to one level; the statue of the god, with his lyre and his bow, had been sculpted of white marble from the royal quarries of Istmark, as had been his altar with its carved garlands. But none of this could conceal the size of the place, nor the enormous, irregular grandeur of its proportions. Above those modestly classical walls arched the ceiling, a maze of sinter and crystal that marked the place as nature's work timidly homesteaded by man.

The smell of the dragon was thick here, though it was clean of offal or carrion. Instead the floor was heaped with gold, all the gold of the Deep, plates, holy vessels, reliquaries of forgotten saints and demigods, piled between the pillars and around the statues, tiny cosmetic pots smelling of balsam, candlesticks quivering with pendant pearls like aspen leaves in spring wind, cups whose rims flashed with the dark fire of jewels, a votive statue of Salernesse, the Lady of Beasts, three feet high and solid gold . . . All the things that gnomes or men had wrought of that soft and shining metal had been gathered there from the farthest tunnels of the Deep. The floor was like a beach with the packed coins that had spilled from their torn sacks, and through it gleamed the darkness of the floor, like water collected in hollows of the sand.

Morkeleb lay upon the gold, his vast wings folded along his sides, their tips crossed over his tail, black as coal and seeming to shine, his crystal eyes like lamps in the dark. The sweet, terrible singing that Jenny had felt so strongly had faded, but the air about him was vibrant with the unheard music.

"Morkeleb," she said softly, and the word whispered back at her from the forest of glittering spikes overhead. She felt the silver eyes upon her and reached out, tentatively, to the dark maze of that mind.

Why gold? she asked. *Why do dragons covet the gold of men?*

It was not what she had meant to say to him, and she felt, under his coiled anger and suspicion, something else move.

What is that to you, wizard woman?

What was it to me that I returned here to save your life? It would have served me and mine better to have let you die.

Why then did you not?

There were two answers. The one she gave him was, *Because it was understood between us that if you gave me the way into the heart of the Deep, I should heal you and give you your life. But in that healing you gave me your name, Morkeleb the Black*—and the name she spoke in her mind was the ribbon of music that was his true name, his essence; and she saw him flinch. *They have said, Save a dragon, slave a dragon, and by your name you shall do as I bid you.*

The surge of his anger against her was like a dark wave, and all along his sides the knifelike scales lifted a little, like a dog's hackles. Around them in the blackness of the Temple, the gold seemed to whisper, picking up the groundswell of his wrath.

I am Morkeleb the Black. I am and will be slave to no one and nothing, least of all a human woman, mage though she may be. I do no bidding save my own.

The bitter weight of alien thoughts crushed down upon her, heavier than the darkness. But her eyes were a mage's eyes, seeing in darkness; her mind held a kind of glowing illumination that it had not had before. She felt no fear of him now; a queer strength she had not known she possessed stirred in her. She whispered the magic of his name as she would have formed its notes upon her harp, in all its knotted complexities, and saw him shrink back a little. His razor claws stirred faintly in the gold.

By your name, Morkeleb the Black, she repeated, *you shall do my bidding. And by your name, I tell you that you will do no harm, either to John Aversin, or to Prince Gareth, or to any other human being while you remain here in the south. When you are well enough to sustain the journey, you shall leave this place and return to your home.*

Ire radiated from his scales like a heat, reflected back about him by the thrumming gold. She felt in it the iron pride of dragons, and their contempt for humankind, and also his furious grief at being parted from the hoard that he had so newly won. For a moment their souls met and locked, twisting together like snakes striving, fighting for advantage. The tide of her strength rose in her, surging and sure, as if it drew life from the combat itself. Terror and exhilaration flooded her, like the tabat leaves, only far stronger, and she cast aside concern for the limitations of her flesh and strove against him mind to mind, twisting at the glittering chain of his name.

She felt the spew of his venomous anger, but would not let go. *If you kill me, I shall drag you down with me into death,* she thought; *for dying, I shall not release your name from my mind.*

The strength that was breaking the sinews of her mind drew back, but his eyes held to hers. Her thoughts were suddenly flooded with images and half-memories, like the visions of the heart of the Deep; things she did not understand, distracting and terrifying in their strangeness. She felt the plunging vertigo of flight in darkness; saw black mountains that cast double shadows, red deserts unstirred by wind since time began and inhabited by glass spiders that lived upon salt. They were dragon memories, confusing her, luring her toward the place where his mind could close around hers like a trap, and she held fast to those things of her own life that she knew and her memory of the piping of old Caerdinn whistling the truncated air of Morkeleb's true name. Into that air she twisted her own spells of breaking and exhaustion, mingling them with the rhythm of his heart that she had learned so well in the healing, and she felt once more his mind draw back from hers.

His wrath was like the lour of thunder-sky, building all around her; he loomed before her like a cloud harboring lightning. Then without warning he struck at her like a snake, one thin-boned claw raised to slash.

He would not strike, she told herself as her heart contracted with terror and her every muscle screamed to flee ... He could not strike her for she had his name and he knew it ... She had saved him; he must obey ... Her mind gripped the music of his name even as the claws hissed

down. The wind of them slashed at her hair, the saber
blades passing less than a foot from her face. White eyes
stared down at her, blazing with hate; the rage of him
beat against her like a storm.

Then he settled back slowly upon his bed of gold. The
tang of his defeat was like wormwood in the air.

*You chose to give me your name rather than die, Mor-
keleb.* She played his name like a glissando and felt the
surge of her own rising power hum in the gold against his.
You will go from these lands and not return.

For a moment more she felt his anger, resentment, and
the fury of his humbled pride. But there was something
else in the hoarfrost glitter of his gaze upon her, the knowledge that she was not contemptible.

He said quietly, *Do you not understand?*

Jenny shook her head. She looked around her once
again at the Temple, its dark archways piled high with
more gold than she had ever seen before, a treasure more
fabulous than any other upon earth. It would have bought
all of Bel and the souls of most of the men who dwelled
there. But, perhaps because she herself had little use for
gold, she felt drawn to ask again, *Why gold, Morkeleb?
Was it the gold that brought you here?*

He lowered his head to his paws again, and all around
them the gold vibrated with the whisper of the dragon's
name. *It was the gold, and the dreams of the gold,* he
said. *I had discontent in all things; the longing grew upon
me while I slept. Do you not know, wizard woman, the
love that dragons have for gold?*

She shook her head again. *Only that they are greedy
for it, as men are greedy.*

Rose-red light rimmed the slits of his nostrils as he
sniffed. *Men,* he said softly. *They have no understanding
of gold; no understanding of what it is and of what it can
be. Come here, wizard woman. Put your hand upon me
and listen with my mind.*

She hesitated, fearing a trap, but her curiosity as a mage drove her. She picked her way over the cold, uneven heaps of rings, platters, and candlesticks, to rest her hand once more against the soft skin below the dragon's great eye. As before, it felt surprisingly warm, unlike a reptile's skin, and soft as silk. His mind touched hers like a firm hand in the darkness.

In a thousand murmuring voices, she could hear the gold pick up the music of the dragon's name. The blended nuances of thought were magnified and made richer, distinct as subtle perfumes, piercing the heart with beauty. It seemed to Jenny that she could identify every piece of gold within that enormous chamber by its separate sounding, and hear the harmonic curve of a vessel, the melding voices of every single coin and hairpin, and the sweet tingling locked in the crystal heart of every jewel. Her mind, touching the dragon's, flinched in aching wonder from the caress of that unbearable sweetness as the echoes awoke answering resonances within her soul. Memories of dove-colored dusks on the Fell that was her home pulled at her with the deep joy of winter nights lying on the bearskins before the hearth at Alyn Hold, with John and her sons at her side. Happiness she could not name swept over her, breaking down the defenses of her heart as the intensity of the music built, and she knew that for Morkeleb it was the same in the chimeric deeps of his mind.

When the music faded, she realized she had closed her eyes, and her cheeks were wet with tears. Looking about her, though the room was as black as before, she thought that the memory of the dragon's song lingered in the gold, and a faint luminosity clung to it still.

In time she said, *That is why men say that dragon's gold is poisoned. Others say that it is lucky ... but it is merely charged with yearning and with music, so that even dullards can feel it through their fingers.*

Even so, whispered the voice of the dragon in her mind.

But dragons cannot mine gold, nor work it. Only gnomes and the children of men.

We are like the whales that live in the sea, he said, *civilizations without artifacts, living between stone and sky in our islands in the northern oceans. We lair in rocks that bear gold, but it is impure. Only with pure gold is this music possible. Now do you understand?*

The sharing had broken something between them, and she felt no fear of him now. She went to sit close to the bony curve of his shoulder and picked up a gold cup from the hoard. She felt as she turned it over in her hands that she could have chosen it out from a dozen identical ones. Its resonance was clear and individuated in her mind; the echo of the dragon's music held to it, like a remembrance of perfume. She saw how precisely it was formed, chastened and highly polished, its handles tiny ladies with garlands twined in their hair where it streamed back over the body of the cup; even microscopically fine, the flowers were recognizable as the lilies of hope and the roses of fulfillment. Morkeleb had killed the owner of this cup, she thought to herself, only for the sake of the incredible music which he could call from the gold. Yet his love for the gold had as little to do with its beauty as her love for her sons had to do with their—undeniable, she thought— good looks.

How did you know this was here?

Do you not think that we, who live for hundreds of years, would be aware of the comings and goings of men? Where they build their cities, and with whom they trade, and in what? I am old, Jenny Waynest. Even among the dragons, my magic is accounted great. I was born before we came to this world; I can sniff gold from the bones of the earth and follow its path for miles, as you follow ground water with a hazel twig. The gold-seams of the

Wall rise to the surface here like the great salmon of the north country rising to spawn.

The dragon's words were spoken in her mind, and in her mind she had a brief, distant glimpse of the Earth as the dragons saw it, spread out like a mottled carpet of purple and green and brown. She saw the green-black pelt of the forests of Wyr, the infinitely delicate cloud shapes of the crowns of the tall oaks, fragile and thready with winter, and saw how, toward the north, they were more and more replaced by the coarse spiky teeth of pine and fir. She saw the gray and white stones of the bare Winterlands, stained all the colors of the rainbow with lichen and moss in summer, and saw how the huge flashing silver shapes of eight- and ten-foot salmon moved beneath the waters of the rivers, under the blue, gliding shadow of the dragon's wings. For an instant, it was as if she could feel the air all about her, holding her up like water; its currents and countereddies, its changes from warm to cold.

Then she felt his mind closing around hers, like the jaws of a trap. For an instant she was locked into suffocating darkness, the utter darkness that not even the eyes of a wizard could pierce. Panic crushed her. She could neither move nor think, and felt only the acid gloating of the dragon all around her, and, opening beneath her, a bottomless despair.

Then as Caerdinn had taught her, as she had done in healing John—as she had always done within the circumscribed limits of her small magic—she forced her mind to calm and began to work rune by rune, note by note, concentrating singly and simply upon each element with her whole mind. She felt the wrath of the dragon smothering her like a hot sea of night, but she wedged open a crack of light, and into that crack she drove the music of the dragon's name, fashioned by her spells into a spear.

She felt his mind flinch and give. Her sight returned,

and she found herself on her feet among the knee-deep piles of gold, the monstrous dark shape backing from her in anger. This time she did not let him go, but flung her own wrath and her will after him, playing upon the music of his name and weaving into it the fires that scorched his essence. All the spells of pain and ruin she had wrought into the poison flooded to her mind; but, like her fury at the bandits at the crossroads these many weeks ago, her anger had no hate in it, offering him no hold upon her mind. He shrank back from it, and the great head lowered so that the ribbons of his mane swept the coins with a slithery tinkle.

Wrapped in a rage of magic and fire, she said, *You shall not dominate me, Morkeleb the Black—neither with your power nor with your treachery. I have saved your life, and you shall do as I command you. By your name you shall go, and you shall not return to the south. Do you hear me?*

She felt him resist, and drove her will and the strength of her newfound powers against him. Like a wrestler's body, she felt the dark, sulfurous rage slither from beneath the pressure of her will; she stepped back, almost instinctively, and faced him where he crouched against the wall like a vast, inky cobra, his every scale bristling with glittering wrath.

She heard him whisper, *I hear you, wizard woman*, and heard, in the cold voice, the reasonance not only of furious anger at being humbled, but of surprise that she could have done so.

Turning without a word, she left the Temple and walked back toward the square of diffuse light that marked the outer hall at the end of the Grand Passage and the Great Gates beyond.

CHAPTER XII

WHEN JENNY CAME down the steps of the Deep she was shaking with exhaustion and an aftermath of common sense that told her that she should have been terrified. Yet she felt curiously little fear of Morkeleb, even in the face of his treachery and his wrath. Her body ached— the power she had put forth against him had been far in excess of what her flesh was used to sustaining—but her head felt clear and alert, without the numbed weariness she felt when she had overstretched her powers. She was aware, down to her last finger end, of the depth and greatness of the dragon's magic, but was aware also of her own strength against him.

Evening wind dusted across her face. The sun had sunk beyond the flinty crest of the westward ridge, and though the sky still held light, Deeping lay at the bottom of a lake of shadow. She was aware of many things passing in the Vale, most of them having nothing to do with the affairs of dragons or humankind—the *skreak* of a single cricket under a charred stone, the flirt of a squirrel's tail as it fled from its hopeful mate, and the flutterings of the chaffinches as they sought their nighttime nests. Where the trail turned downward around a broken pile of rubble that had once been a house, she saw a man's skeleton lying in the weeds, the bag of gold he had died clutching split open and the coins singing softly to her where they lay scattered among his ribs.

She was aware, suddenly, that someone else had entered the Vale.

It was analagous to sound, though unheard. The scent of magic came to her like smoke on the shift of the wind. She stopped still in the dry tangle of broomsedge, cold shreds of breeze that frayed down from the timberline stirring in her plaids. There was magic in the Vale, up on the ridge. She could hear the slither and snag of silk on beech mast, the startled splash of spilled water in the dusk by the fountain, and Gareth's voice halting over a name...

Catching up her skirts, Jenny began to run.

The smell of Zyerne's perfume seemed everywhere in the woods. Darkness was already beginning to collect beneath the trees. Panting, Jenny sprang up the whitish, flinty rocks to the glade by the fountain. Long experience in the Winterlands had taught her to move in utter silence, even at a dead run; and thus, for the first moment, neither of those who stood near the little well was aware of her arrival.

It took her a moment to see Zyerne. Gareth she saw at once, standing frozen beside the wellhead. Spilled water was soaking into the beech mast around his feet; a half-empty bucket balanced on the edge of the stone trough beside the well itself. He didn't heed it; she wondered how much of his surroundings he was aware of at all.

Zyerne's spells filled the small glade like the music heard in dreams. Even she, a woman, felt the scented warmth of the air that belied the tingly cold lower down in the Vale and sensed the stirring of need in her flesh. In Gareth's eyes was a kind of madness, and his hands were shaking where they were clenched, knotted into fists, before him. His voice was a whisper more desperate than a scream as he said, "No."

"Gareth." Zyerne moved, and Jenny saw her, as she seemed to float like a ghost in the dusk among the birch trees at the glade's edge. "Why pretend? You know your love for me has grown, as mine has for you. It is like fire in your flesh now; the taste of your mouth in my dreams has tormented me day and night..."

"While you were lying with my father?"

She shook back her hair, a small, characteristic gesture, brushing the tendrils of it away from her smooth brow. It was difficult to see what she wore in the dusk— something white and fragile that rippled in the stirrings of the wind, pale as the birches themselves. Her hair was loosened down her back like a young girl's; and, like a young girl, she wore no veils. Years seemed to have vanished from her age, young as she had seemed before. She looked like a girl of Gareth's age, unless, like Jenny, one saw her with a wizard's eye.

"Gareth, I never lay with your father," she said softly. "Oh, we agreed to pretend, for the sake of appearances at Court—but even if he had wanted me to, I don't think I could have. He treated me like a daughter. It was you I wanted, you..."

"That's a lie!" His mouth sounded dried by fever heat.

She held out her hands, and the wind lifted the thin fabric of her sleeves back from her arms as she moved a step into the glade. "I could bear waiting no longer. I had to come, to learn what had happened to you—to be with you..."

He sobbed, "Get away from me!" His face was twisted by something close to pain.

She only whispered, "I want you..."

Jenny stepped from the somber shade of the trail and said, "No, Zyerne. What you want is the Deep."

Zyerne swung around, her concentration breaking, as

Morkeleb had tried to break Jenny's. The lurid sensuality that had dripped from the air shattered with an almost audible snap. At once, Zyerne seemed older, no longer the virgin girl who could inflame Gareth's passion. The boy dropped to his knees and covered his face, his body racked with dry sobs.

"It's what you've always wanted, isn't it?" Jenny touched Gareth's hair comfortingly, and he threw his arms around her waist, clinging to her like a drowning man to a spar. Oddly enough, she felt no fear of Zyerne now, or of the greater strength of the younger woman's magic. She seemed to see Zyerne differently, even, and felt calm as she faced her—calm and ready.

Zyerne uttered a ribald laugh. "So there's our boy who won't tumble his father's mistress? You had them both to yourself, didn't you, slut, coming down from the north? Enough time and more to tangle him in your hair."

Gareth pulled free of Jenny and scrambled to his feet, shaking all over with anger. Though Jenny could see he was still terrified of the sorceress, he faced her and gasped, "You're lying!"

Zyerne laughed again, foully, as she had in the garden outside the King's rooms. Jenny only said, "She knows it isn't true. What did you come here for, Zyerne? To do to Gareth what you've done to his father? Or to see if it's finally safe for you to enter the Deep?"

The enchantress's mouth moved uncertainly, and her eyes shifted under Jenny's cool gaze. Then she laughed, the mockery in it marred by her uncertainty. "Maybe to get your precious Dragonsbane at the same time?"

A week—even a day—ago, Jenny would have responded to the taunt with fear for John's safety. But she knew Zyerne had not gone anywhere near John. She knew she would have sensed it, if such magic had been worked so near—almost, she thought, she would have heard their voices, no matter how softly they spoke. And in any case, John was unable to flee; one deals with the unwounded enemy first.

She saw Zyerne's hand move and felt the nature of the spell, even as she smelled the singed wool of her skirts beginning to smoke. Her own spell was fast and hard, called with the mind and the minimal gesture of the hand rather than the labor it had once entailed. Zyerne staggered back, her hands over her eyes, taken completely by surprise.

When Zyerne raised her head again, her eyes were livid with rage, yellow as a devil's in a face transformed with fury. "You can't keep me from the Deep," she said in a voice which shook. "It is mine—it will be mine. I've driven the gnomes from it. When I take it, no one, *no one*, will be able to contend against my power!"

Stooping, she seized a handful of old leaves and beechnuts from the mast that lay all about their feet. She flung them at Jenny. In the air, they burst into flame, growing as they burned, a tangled bonfire that Jenny swept aside with a spell she had hardly been aware she'd known. The blazing logs scattered everywhere, throwing streamers of yellow fire into the blue gloom and blazing up in half-a-dozen places where they touched dry weeds. Doubling like a hare upon her tracks, Zyerne darted for the path that led down into the Vale. Jenny leaped at her heels, her soft boots in three strides outdistancing the younger woman's precarious court shoes.

Zyerne twisted in her grip. She was taller than Jenny but not physically as strong, even taking into account Jenny's exhaustion; for an instant their eyes were inches apart, the yellow gaze boring like balefire into the blue.

Like a hammerblow, Jenny felt the impact of a mind upon hers, spells of hurt and terror that gripped and twisted at her muscles, utterly different from the weight and living strength of the dragon's mind. She parried the spell, not so much with a spell as with the strength of her will, throwing it back at Zyerne, and she heard the younger woman curse her in a spate of fury like a burst sewer. Nails tore at her wrists as she sought the yellow eyes with her own again, catching Zyerne's silky curls in a fist like a rock, forcing her to look. It was the first time she had matched strength in anger with another mage, and it surprised her how instinctive it was to probe into the essence—as she had probed into Gareth's, and Mab into hers—not solely to understand, but to dominate by understanding, to give nothing of her own soul in return. She had a glimpse of something sticky and foul as the plants that eat those foolish enough to came near, the eroded remains of a soul, like an animate corpse of the young woman's mind.

Zyerne screamed as she felt the secrets of her being bared, and power exploded in the air between them, a burning fire that surrounded them in a whirlwind of tearing force. Jenny felt a weight falling against her, a blackness like the dragon's mind but greater, the shadow of some crushing power, like an ocean of uncounted years. It drove her to her knees, but she held on, sloughing away the crawling, biting pains that tore at her skin, the rending agony in her muscles, the fire, and the darkness, boring into Zyerne's mind with her own, like a white needle of fire.

The weight of the shadow faded. She felt Zyerne's nerve and will break and got to her feet again, throwing the girl from her with all her strength. Zyerne collapsed on the dirt of the path, her dark hair hanging in a torrent over her white dress, her nails broken from tearing at Jenny's wrists, her nose running and dust plastered to her face with mucus. Jenny stood over her, panting for breath, her every muscle hurting from the twisting impact of Zyerne's spells. "Go," she said, her voice quiet, but with power in her words. "Go back to Bel and never touch Gareth again."

Sobbing with fury, Zyerne picked herself up. Her voice shook. "You stinking gutter-nosed sow! I won't be kept from the Deep! It's mine, I tell you; and when I come there, I'll show you! I swear by the Stone, when I have the Deep, I'll crush you out like the dung-eating cockroach you are! You'll see! They'll all see! They have no right to keep me away!"

"Get out of here," Jenny said softly.

Sobbing, Zyerne obeyed her, gathering up her trailing white gown and stumbling down the path that led toward the clock tower. Jenny stood for a long time watching her go. The power Jenny had summoned to protect her faded slowly, like fire banked under embers until it was needed again.

It was only after Zyerne was out of sight that she realized that she should never have been able to do what she had just done—not here and not in the Deep.

And it came to her then, what had happened to her when she had touched the mind of the dragon.

The dragon's magic was alive in her soul, like streaks of iron in gold. She should have known it before; if she had not been so weary, she thought, perhaps she would have. Her awareness, like Morkeleb's, had widened to fill the Vale, so that, even in sleep, she was conscious of things taking place about her. A shiver passed through her flesh and racked her bones with terror and wonderment, as if she had conceived again, and something alive and alien was growing within her.

Smoke from the woods above stung her nose and eyes, white billows of it telling her that Gareth had succeeded in dousing the flames. Somewhere the horses were whinnying in terror. She felt exhausted and aching, her whole body wrenched by the cramp of those gripping spells, her wrists smarting where Zyerne's nails had torn them. She began to tremble, the newfound strength draining away under the impact of shock and fear.

A countersurge of wind shook the trees around her, as if at the stroke of a giant wing. Her hair blowing about her face, she looked up, but for a moment saw nothing. It was something she'd heard of—that dragons, for all their size and gaudiness, could be harder to see in plain daylight than the voles of the hedgerow. He seemed to blend down out of the dusk, a vast shape of jointed ebony and black silk, silver-crystal eyes like small moons in the dark.

He could feel my power nearing its end, she thought despairingly, remembering how he had turned on her before. The terrible, shadowy weight of Zyerne's spells still lay on her bones; she felt they would break if she tried to summon the power to resist the dragon. Wrung with a weariness close to physical nausea, she looked up to face him and hardened her mind once again to meet his attack.

Even as she did so, she realized that he was beautiful, as he hung for a moment like a black, drifting kite upon the air.

Then his mind touched hers, and the last pain of Zyerne's spells was sponged away.

What is it, wizard woman? he asked. *It is only evil words, such as fishwives throw at one another.*

He settled before her on the path, folding his great wings with a queerly graceful articulation, and regarded her with his silver eyes in the dusk.

He said, *You understand.*

No, she replied. *I think I know what has happened, but I do not understand.*

Bah. In the leaky gray twilight beneath the trees, she saw all the scale-points along his sides ruffle slightly, like the hair of an affronted cat. *I think that you do. When your mind was in mine, my magic called to you, and the dragon within you answered. Know you not your own power, wizard woman? Know you not what you could be?*

With a cold vertigo that was not quite fear she understood him then and willed herself not to understand.

He felt the closing of her mind, and irritation smoked from him like a white spume of mist. *You understand*, he said again. *You have been within my mind; you know what it would be to be a dragon.*

Jenny said, *No*, not to him, but to that trickle of fire in her mind that surged suddenly into a stream.

As in a dream, images surfaced of things she felt she had once known and forgotten, like the soaring freedom of flight. She saw the earth lost beneath her in the clouds, and about her was a vaporous eternity whose absolute silence was broken only by the sheer of her wings. As from great height, she glimpsed the stone circle on Frost Fell, the mere below it like a broken piece of dirty glass, and the little stone house a chrysalis, cracked open to release the butterfly that had slept within.

She said, *I have not the power to change my essence.*

I have, the voice whispered among the visions in her mind. *You have the strength to be a dragon, once you consent to take the form. I sensed that in you when we struggled. I was angry then, to be defeated by a human; but you can be more than human.*

Gazing up at the dark splendor of the dragon's angular form, she shook her head. *I will not put myself thus in your power, Morkeleb. I cannot leave my own form without your aid, nor could I return to it. Do not tempt me.*

Tempt? Morkeleb's voice said. *There is no temptation from outside the heart. And as for returning—what are you as a human, Jenny Waynest? Pitiful, puling, like all your kin the slave of time that rots the body before the mind has seen more than a single flower in all the meadows of the Cosmos. To be a mage you must be a mage, and I see in your mind that you fight for the time to do even that. To be a dragon . . .*

"To be a dragon," she said aloud, to force her own

mind upon it, "I have only to give over my control of you. I will not lose myself thus in the dragon mind and the dragon magic. You will not thus get me to release you."

She felt the strength press against the closed doors in her mind, then ease, and heard the steely rustle of his scales as his long tail lashed through the dry grasses with annoyance. The dark woods came back into focus; the strange visions receded like a shining mist. The light was waning fast about them, all the colors bled from straggly briar and fern. As if his blackness took on the softer hues of the evening, the dragon was nearly invisible, his shape blending with the milky stringers of fog that had begun to veil the woods and with the black, abrupt outlines of dead branch and charred trunk. Somewhere on the ridge above her, Jenny could hear Gareth calling her name.

She found she was trembling, not solely from weariness or the piercing cold. The need within her was terrifying—to be what she had always wished to be, to have what she had wanted since she had been fourteen, ugly, and cursed with a terrible need. She had tasted the strength of the dragon's fire, and the taste lingered sweet in her mouth.

I can give you this, the voice in her mind said.

She shook her head, more violently this time. *No. I will not betray my friends.*

Friends? Those who would bind you to littleness for their own passing convenience? The man who grudges you the essence of your soul out of mourning for his dinner? Do you cling to all these little joys because you are afraid to taste the great ones, Jenny Waynest?

He had been right when he had said that there is no temptation from outside the heart. She flung back her long hair over her shoulders and called to herself all the strength remaining in her, against the star-prickled darkness that seemed to draw upon the very marrow of her bones.

Get away from me, she told him. *Go now and return to the islands in the northern sea that are your home. Sing your songs to the rock-gold and the whales, and let be forever the sons of men and the sons of gnomes.*

As if she had struck a black log that, breaking, had revealed the living fire smoldering within, she felt the surge of his anger again. He reared back, his body arched against the dimming sky. The dark wire and silk of his wings rattled as he said, *Be it so then, wizard woman. I leave to you the gold of the Deep—take of it what you will. My song is in it. When old age comes, whose mortal frost you have already begun to feel upon your bones, press it to your heart and remember that which you have let pass you by.*

He gathered himself upon his haunches, his compact, snakelike shape rising above her as he gathered about him the glitter of magic in the air. Black wings unfurled against the sky, looming over her so that she could see the obsidian gleam of his sides, the baby-skin softness of the velvet belly, still puckered with the crimped, ugly mouths of harpoon wounds. Then he flung himself skyward. The great stroke of his wings caught him up. She felt the magic that swirled about him, a spindrift of enchantment, the star trail of an invisible comet. The last rays of sinking light tipped his wings as he rose beyond the blue shadow of the ridge. Then he was gone.

Jenny watched him go with desolation in her heart. All the woods seemed laden now with the smell of wet burning, and the murky earthiness of dead smoke. She became slowly aware that the hem of her skirt was sodden from kneeling in the wet path; her boots were damp and her feet cold. Listless weariness dragged upon her, from muscles pulled by exertion and Zyerne's spells and also from the words the dragon had spoken to her when she had turned away from what he had offered.

As a dragon, she would have no more hold upon him, nor would she wish any longer to drive him from the Deep. Was that, she wondered, why he had offered her the splendid and terrifying freedom of that form? They said that dragons did not entrap with lies but with truth, and she knew he had read accurately the desires of her soul.

"Jenny?" A smudged, dirty Gareth came hurrying toward her down the path. To her ears, used to the voice of the dragon, he sounded tinny and false. "Are you all right? What happened? I saw the dragon..." He had removed his specs and was seeking a sufficiently clean patch of his sooty, spark-holed shirt to wipe them on, without much success. Against the grime on his face the lenses had left two white circles, like a mask, in which his gray eyes blinked nakedly.

Jenny shook her head. She felt weary to the point of tears, almost incapable of speech. He fell into step with her as she began slowly climbing the path up the Rise once more.

"Did Zyerne get away?"

She looked at him, startled. After what had passed between herself and Morkeleb, she had nearly forgotten Zyerne. "She—she left. I sent her away." It seemed like days ago.

"You *sent her away*?" Gareth gasped, dumfounded.

Jenny nodded, too tired to explain. Thinking about it, she frowned, as something snagged at her mind. But she only asked, "And you?"

He looked away from her and reddened with shame. Part of Jenny sighed in exasperation at this foolishness, so petty after the force of the dragon's greater seduction; but part of her remembered what it was like to be eighteen, and prey to the uncontrollable yearnings of the body.

Comfortingly, she touched the skinny arm under the ripped lawn of his shirtsleeve.

"It is a spell she had on you," she said. "Nothing more. We are all tempted..." She pushed aside the echoing memory of the dragon's words. "...And what is in our deepest hearts is still not what we are judged on, but rather what we ultimately do. She only uses such spells to draw you to her, to control you as she controls your father."

They reached the clearing, soggy and dirty-looking, like a garment upon which acid had been spilled, with charred spots and little puddles of gleaming water which still steamed faintly from the smolder they had quenched.

"I know." Gareth sighed and picked up the bucket from the sodden ground to dip it once more into the well. He moved stiffly from pulled muscles and exertion but didn't complain of them as he once might have done. On the edge of the well trough, he found his tin cup and dipped water from the bucket to hand to her, the wetness icy against her fingers. She realized with a little start that she had neither eaten nor drunk since breakfast. There had been no time, and now she felt old and exhausted as she took the cup from his hand.

"You just sent her away?" Gareth asked again. "And she went? She didn't turn herself into a falcon...?"

"No." Jenny looked up, as it came to her what it was that had bothered her about the events of the evening. "Morkeleb..." She stopped, not wanting to speak of what Morkeleb had offered to her.

But even so, she thought, she could not have taken on a dragon's form without his help. His powers had broken through to the powers within her, but her powers were still raw and small. And Zyerne...

"I defeated her," she said slowly. "But if she's as shape-crafty as you have said—if she has that kind of strength—

I shouldn't have been able to defeat her, even though my powers have grown."

She almost said, "Even with the dragon's powers in me," but the words stuck on her lips. She felt the powers stir in her, like an alien child in the womb of fate, and tried to put aside the thought of them and of what they might mean. She raised the cup to her lips, but stopped, the water untasted, and looked up at Gareth again.

"Have you drunk any of the water from this well?" she asked.

He looked at her in surprise. "We've all been drinking it for days," he said.

"This evening, I mean."

He looked ruefully around at the clearing and his own soaked sleeves. "I was too busy throwing it about to drink any," he said. "Why?"

She passed her hand across the mouth of the cup. As things were visible to a wizard in darkness, she saw the viscid sparkle of green luminosity in the water.

"Has it gone bad?" he asked worriedly. "How can you tell?"

She upended the cup, dumping the contents to the ground. "Where was Zyerne when you came into the clearing?"

He shook his head, puzzled. "I don't remember. It was like a dream . . ." He looked around him, though Jenny knew that the clearing, soggy and trampled in the dismal gloom, was very different from the soft place of twilight enchantment if had appeared an hour or so ago.

At last he said, "I think she was sitting where you are now, on the edge of the wellhead."

Morkeleb had said, *They did not think that I could see the death that tainted the meat.* Was it Dromar who had remarked that dragons were impossible to poison?

She twisted her body and moved her hands across the

surface of the bucket that Gareth had drawn up. The reek of death rose from it, and she recoiled in disgust and horror, as if the water had turned to blood beneath her fingers.

CHAPTER XIII

"BUT WHY?" SQUATTING before the fire on his hunker-bones, Gareth turned to look at John, who lay in his nest of bearskin blankets and ratty plaids a few feet away. "As far as she was concerned, you'd slain her dragon for her." He unraveled the screw of paper in which they'd brought the coffee up from Bel, decided there wasn't enough to bother with measuring, and dumped it into the pot of water that bubbled over the fire. "She didn't know then that Jenny was any threat to her. Why poison us?"

"At a guess," John said, propping himself with great care up on one elbow and fitting his spectacles to his dirty, unshaven face, "to keep us from riding back to Bel with the news that the dragon was dead before she could get your dad to round up the remaining gnomes on some trumped-up charge. As far as she knew, the dragon was dead—I mean, she couldn't have seen him in a crystal or a water bowl, but she could see us all alive and chipper, and the inference is a pretty obvious one."

"I suppose." Gareth unrolled his turned-up sleeves and slung his cloak around his shoulders once more. The morning was foggy and cold, and the sweat he'd worked up clearing out the well house close to their camp in the ruined tanneries was drying.

"I doubt she'd have poisoned you," John went on. "If she'd wanted you dead, she'd never have waited for you."

Gareth blushed hotly. "That isn't why she waited," he mumbled.

"Of course not," John said. "Dead, you're not only no good to her—if you die, she loses everything."

The boy frowned. "Why? I mean, I can see her wanting me under her power so I'd no longer be a threat to her, the same reason she put Polycarp out of the way. And if she killed the two of you, she'd need me to back up her story about the dragon still being in the Deep, at least until she could get rid of the gnomes." He sniffed bitterly and held out his blistered hands to the fire. "She'd probably use Bond and me as witnesses to say eventually that *she* slew the dragon. Then she'd be able to justify having my father give her the Deep."

He sighed, his mouth tight with disillusionment. "And I thought Polycarp stretching a bit of cable over a fence sounded like the depths of perfidy." He settled the griddle over the fire, his thin face looking much older than it had in the jonquil pallor of the daytime flames.

"Well," John said gently, "it isn't only that, Gar." He glanced over at Jenny, who sat in the shadows of the newly cleared doorway of the well house, but she said nothing. Then he looked back to Gareth. "How long do you think your father's going to last with Zyerne alive? I don't know what her spells are doing to him, and I know a dying man when I see one. As it is, for all her power, she's only a mistress. She needs the Deep for a power base and fortress independent of the King, and she needs the Deep's gold."

"My father would give it to her," Gareth said softly. "And I—I suppose I'm just the contingency plan, in case he should die?" He poked at the softly sizzling cakes on the griddle. "Then she had to destroy Polycarp, whether or not he tried to warn me of her. The Citadel guards the back way into the Deep."

"Well, not even that." John lay back down again and folded his hands on his breast. "She wanted to be rid of Polycarp because he's an alternative heir."

"Alternative to whom?" Gareth asked, puzzled. "To me?"

John shook his head. "Alternative to Zyerne's child."

The horror that crossed the boy's face was deeper than fear of death—deeper, Jenny thought with the strange dispassion that had lain upon her all that morning and through the previous night, than fear of being subjugated to the enchantress's spells. He looked nauseated by the thought, as if at the violation of some dark taboo. It was a long time before he could speak. "You mean—my father's child?"

"Or yours. It would scarcely matter which, as long as it had the family looks." Bandaged hands folded, John looked shortsightedly up at the boy as, half-numbed, Gareth went through the automatic motions of forking griddlecakes from the skillet. Still in that gentle, matter-of-fact voice, he went on, "But you see, after this long under Zyerne's spells, your father may not be capable of fathering a child. And Zyerne needs a child, if she's to go on ruling."

Jenny looked away from them, thinking about what it would be, to be that child. The same wave of sickness Gareth had felt passed over her at the knowledge of what Zyerne would do to any child of hers. She would not feed upon it, as she fed upon the King and Bond; but she would raise it deliberately as an emotional cripple, forever dependent upon her and her love. Jenny had seen it done, by women or by men, and knew what manner of man or woman emerged from that smothered childhood. But even then, the twisting had been from some need of the parent's heart, and not something done merely to keep power.

She thought of her own sons and the absurd love she bore them. She might have abandoned them, she thought with sudden fury at Zyerne, but even had she not loved them, even were they got on her by rape, she would never have done that to them. It was a thing she would have liked to think she herself could scarcely conceive of anyone doing to an innocent child—except that in her heart she knew exactly how it could be done.

Anger and sickness stirred in her, as if she had looked upon torture.

"Jenny?"

Gareth's voice broke her from her thoughts. He stood a few paces from her, looking pleadingly down at her. "He will get better, won't he?" he asked hesitantly. "My father, I mean? When Zyerne is banished, or—or is killed—he will be the way he was before?"

Jenny sighed. "I don't know," she replied in a low voice. She shook her mind free of the lethargy that gripped her, a weariness of the spirit as much as the ache of her body left by the battering of Zyerne's spells. It was not only that she had badly overstretched her own newfound powers, not only that her body was unused to sustaining the terrible demands of the dragon's magic. She was aware now that her very perceptions were changing, that it was not only her magic that had been changed by the touch of the dragon's mind. *The dragon in you answered*, he had said—she was starting to see things as a dragon saw.

She got stiffly to her feet, staggering a little against the shored-up doorpost of the well house, feeling physically drained and very weak. She had watched through the night, telling herself it was for Zyerne that she watched, though in her heart she knew the enchantress would not be back, and it was not, in fact, for her that she waited. She said, "It isn't the spells that she holds him under that are harming him. Zyerne is a vampire, Gareth—not of the blood, like the Whisperers, but of the life-essence itself. In her eyes last night I saw her essence, her soul; a sticky and devouring thing, yes, but a thing that must feed to go on living. Miss Mab told me of the spells of the Places of Healing that can shore up the life of a dying man by taking a little of the life-energy of those who consent to give it. It is done seldom, and only in cases of great need. I am certain this is what she has done to your father and to Bond. What I don't understand is why she would need to. Her powers are such that..."

"You know," John broke in, "it says in Dotys' *Histories* ... or maybe it's in Terens... or is it the *Elucidus Lapidarus* ...?"

"But what can we *do*?" Gareth pleaded. "There must be something! I could ride back to Bel and let Dromar know it's safe for the gnomes to reoccupy the Deep. It would give them a strong base to..."

"No," Jenny said. "Zyerne's hold on the city is too strong. After this, she'll be watching for you, scrying the roads. She'd intercept you long before you came near Bel."

"But we have to do something!" Panic and desperation lurked at bay in his voice. "Where can we go? Polycarp would give us shelter in the Citadel..."

"You going to tell the siege troops around the walls you want a private word with him?" John asked, forgetting all about his speculations upon the classics.

"There are ways through the Deep into Halnath."

"And a nice locked door at the end of 'em, I bet, or the tunnels sealed shut with blasting powder to keep the dragon out—even if old Dromar *had* put them on his maps, which he didn't. I had a look for that back in Bel."

"Damn him..." Gareth began angrily, and John waved him silent with a mealcake in hand.

"I can't blame him," he said. Against the random browns and heathers of the bloodstained plaid folded beneath his head his face still looked pale but had lost its dreadful chalkiness. Behind his specs, his brown eyes were bright and alert. "He's a canny old bird, and he knows Zyerne. If she didn't know where the ways through to the Citadel hooked up into the main Deep, he wasn't going to have that information down on paper that she could steal. Still, Jen might be able to lead us."

"No." Jenny glanced over at him from where she sat cross-legged beside the fire, dipping the last bite of her griddlecake into the honey. "Even being able to see in darkness, I could not scout them out unaided. As for you going through them, if you try to get up in under a week, I'll put a spell of lameness on you."

"Cheat."

"Watch me." She wiped her fingers on the end of her plaid. "Morkeleb guided me through to the heart of the Deep; I could never have found it, else."

"What was it like?" Gareth asked after a moment. "The heart of the Deep? The gnomes swear by it..."

Jenny frowned, remembering the whispering darkness and the soapy feel of the stone altar beneath her fingertips. "I'm not sure," she said softly. "I dreamed about it..."

As one, the horses suddenly flung up their heads from the stiff, frosted grass. Battlehammer nickered softly and was answered, thin and clear, from the mists that floated on the fringes of the woods that surrounded Deeping Vale. Hooves struck the stone, and a girl's voice called out, "Gar? Gar, where are you?"

"It's Trey." He raised his voice to shout. "Here!"

There was a frenzied scrambling of sliding gravel, and the whitish mists solidified into the dark shapes of a horse and rider and a fluttering of dampened veils. Gareth strode to the edge of the high ground of the Rise to catch the bridle of Trey's dappled palfrey as it came stumbling up the last slope, head-down with exhaustion and matted with sweat in spite of the day's cold. Trey, clinging to the saddlebow, looked scarcely better off, her face scratched as if she had ridden into low-hanging branches in the wood and long streamers clawed loose from her purple-and-white coiffure.

"Gar, I knew you had to be all right." She slid from the saddle into his arms. "They said they saw the dragon—that Lady Jenny had put spells upon him—I knew you had to be all right."

"We're fine, Trey," Gareth said doubtfully, frowning at the terror and desperation of the girl's voice. "You look as if you've ridden here without a break."

"I had to!" she gasped. Under the torn rags of her white Court dress, her knees were trembling, and she clung to Gareth's arm for support; her face was colorless beneath what was left of its paint. "They're coming for you! I don't understand what's happening, but you've got to get out of here! Bond . . ." She stumbled on her brother's name.

"What about Bond? Trey, what's going on?"

"I don't know!" she cried. Tears of wretchedness and exhaustion overflowed her eyes, and she wiped them impatiently, leaving faint streaks of blue-black kohl on her round cheeks. "There's a mob on its way, Bond's leading it . . ."

"Bond?" The idea of the lazy and elegant Bond troubling himself to lead anyone anywhere was absurd.

"They're going to kill you, Gar! I heard them say so! You, and Lady Jenny, and Lord John."

"What? Why?" Gareth was growing more and more confused.

"More to the point, who?" John asked, propping himself up among his blankets once again.

"These—these people, laborers mostly—smelters and artisans from Deeping out of work, the ones who hang around the Sheep in the Mire all day. There are Palace guards with them, too, and I think more are coming—I don't know why! I tried to get some sense out of Bond, but it's as if he didn't hear me, didn't know me! He slapped me—and he's never hit me, Gar, not since I was a child..."

"Tell us," Jenny said quietly, taking the girl's hand, cold as a dead bird in her warm rough one. "Start from the beginning."

Trey gulped and wiped her eyes again, her hands shaking with weariness and the exertion of a fifteen-mile ride. The ornamental cloak about her shoulders was an indoor garment of white silk and milky fur, designed to ward off the chance drafts of a ballroom, not the bitter chill of a foggy night such as the previous one had been. Her long fingers were chapped and red among their diamonds.

"We'd all been dancing," she began hesitantly. "It was past midnight when Zyerne came in. She looked strange— I thought she'd been sick, but I'd seen her in the morning and she'd been fine then. She called Bond to her, into an alcove by the window. I—" Some color returned to her too-white cheeks. "I crept after them to eavesdrop. I know it's a terribly rude and catty thing to do, but after what we'd talked of before you left I—I couldn't help doing it. It wasn't to learn gossip," she added earnestly. "I was afraid for him—and I was so scared because I'd never done it before and I'm not nearly as good at it as someone like Isolde or Merriwyn would be."

Gareth looked a little shocked at this frankness, but John laughed and patted the toe of the girl's pearl-beaded slipper in commiseration. "We'll forgive you this time, love, but don't neglect your education like that again. You see where it leads you?" Jenny kicked him, not hard, in his unwounded shoulder.

"And then?" she asked.

"I heard her say, 'I must have the Deep. They must be destroyed, and it must be now, before the gnomes hear. They mustn't be allowed to reach it.' I followed them down to that little postern gate that leads to the Dock-market; they went to the Sheep in the Mire. The place was still full of men and women; all drunk and quarreling with each other. Bond went rushing in and told them he'd heard you'd betrayed them, sold them out to Polycarp; that you had the dragon under Lady Jenny's spells and were going to turn it against Bel; that you were going to keep the gold of the Deep for yourselves and not give it to them, its rightful owners. But they weren't *ever* its rightful owners—it always belonged to the gnomes, or to the rich merchants in Deeping. I tried to tell that to Bond..." Her cold-reddened hand stole to her cheek, as if to wipe away the memory of a handprint.

"But they were all shouting how they had to kill you and regain their gold. They were all drunk—Zyerne got the innkeeper to broach some more kegs. She said she was going to re-enforce them with the Palace guards. They were yelling and making torches and getting weapons. I ran back to the Palace stables and got Prettyfeet, here..." She stroked the exhausted pony's dappled neck, and her voice grew suddenly small. "And then I came here. I rode as fast as I dared—I was afraid of what might happen if they caught me. I'd never been out riding alone at night..."

Gareth pulled off his grubby crimson cloak and slung it around her shoulders as her trembling increased.

She concluded, "So you have to get out of here..."

"That we do." John flung back the bearskins from over his body. "We can defend the Deep."

"Can you ride that far?" Gareth asked worriedly, handing him his patched, iron-plated leather jerkin.

"I'll be gie in trouble if I can't, my hero."

"Trey?"

The girl looked up from gathering camp things as Jenny spoke her name.

Jenny crossed quietly to where she stood and took her by the shoulders, looking into her eyes for a long moment. The probing went deep, and Trey pulled back with a thin cry of alarm that brought Gareth running. But to the bottom, her mind was a young girl's—not always truthful, anxious to please, eager to love and to be loved. There was no taint on it, and its innocence twisted at Jenny's own heart.

Then Gareth was there, indignantly gathering Trey to him.

Jenny's smile was crooked but kind. "I'm sorry," she said. "I had to be sure."

By their shocked faces she saw that it had not occurred to either of them that Zyerne might have made use of Trey's form—or of Trey.

"Come," she said. "We probably don't have much time. Gar, get John on a horse. Trey, help him."

"I'm perfectly capable . . ." John began, irritated.

But Jenny scarcely heard. Somewhere in the mists of the half-burned woods below the town, she felt sudden movement, the intrusion of angry voices among the frost-rimmed silence of the blackened trees. They were coming and they were coming fast—she could almost see them at the turning of the road below the crumbling ruin of the clock tower.

She turned swiftly back to the others. "Go!" she said. "Quickly, they're almost on us!"

"How . . ." began Gareth.

She caught up her medicine bag and her halberd and vaulted to Moon Horse's bare back. "Now! Gar, take Trey with you. John, RIDE, damn you!" For he had wheeled back, barely able to keep upright in Cow's saddle, to remain at her side. Gareth flung Trey up to Battle-hammer's back in a flurry of torn skirts; Jenny could hear the echo of hooves on the trail below.

Her mind reached out, gathering spells together, even the small effort wrenching at her. She set her teeth at the stabbing pain as she gathered the dispersing mists that had been burning off in the sun's pallid brightness—her body was not nearly recovered from yesterday. But there was no time for anything else. She wove the cold and dampness into a cloak to cover all the Vale of Deeping; like a secondary pattern in a plaid, she traced the spells of disorientation, of *jamais vu*. Even as she did so, the hooves and the angry, incoherent voices were very close. They rang in the misty woods around the Rise and near the gatehouse in the Vale as well—Zyerne must have told them where to come. She wheeled Moon Horse and gave her a hard kick in her skinny ribs, and the white mare threw herself down the rocky slope in a gangly sprawl of legs, making for the Gates of the Deep.

She overtook the others in the gauzy boil of the mists in the Vale. They had slowed down as visibility lessened; she led them at a canter over the paths that she knew so well through the town. Curses and shouts, muffled by the fog, came from the Rise behind them. Cold mists shredded past her face and stroked back the black coils of her hair. She could feel the spells that held the brume in place fretting away as she left the Rise behind, but dared not try to put forth the strength of will it would take to hold them after she was gone. Her very bones ached from even the small exertion of summoning them; she knew already that she would need all the strength she could summon for the final battle.

The three horses clattered up the shallow granite steps. From the great darkness of the gate arch, Jenny turned to see the mob still milling about in the thinning fog, some fifty or sixty of them, of all stations and classes but mostly poor laborers. The uniforms of the handful of Palace guards stood out as gaudy splotches in the grayness. She heard their shouts and swearing as they became lost within plain sight of one another in territory they had all known well of old. That won't last long, she thought.

Moon Horse shied and fidgeted at the smell of the dragon and of the old blood within the vast gloom of the Market Hall. The carcass of the horse Osprey had disappeared, but the place still smelled of death, and all the horses felt it. Jenny slid from her mare's tall back and stroked her neck, then whispered to her to stay close to the place in case of need and let her go back down the steps.

Hooves clopped behind her on the charred and broken flagstones. She looked back and saw John, ashen under the stubble of beard, still somehow upright in Cow's saddle. He studied the Vale below them with his usual cool expressionlessness. "Zyerne out there?" he asked, and Jenny shook her head.

"Perhaps I hurt her too badly. Perhaps she's only remaining at the Palace to gather other forces to send against us."

"She always did like her killing to be done by others. How long will your spells hold them?"

"Not long," Jenny said doubtfully. "We have to hold this gate here, John. If they're from Deeping, many of them will know the first levels of the Deep. There are four or five ways out of the Market Hall. If we retreat further in, we'll be flanked."

"Aye." He scratched the side of his nose thoughtfully. "What's wrong with just letting them in? We could hide up somewhere—once they got to the Temple of Sarmendes with all that gold, I doubt they'd waste much energy looking for us."

Jenny hesitated for a moment, then shook her head. "No," she said. "If they were an ordinary mob, I'd say yes, but—Zyerne wants us dead. If she cannot break and overwhelm my mind with her magic, she's not going to give up before she has destroyed my body. There are enough of them that would keep hunting us, and we can't take a horse into the deeper tunnels to carry you; without one, we'd never be able to move swiftly enough to avoid them. We'd be trapped in a cul-de-sac and slaughtered. No, if we're to hold them, it has to be here."

"Right." He nodded. "Can we help you?"

She had returned her attention to the angry snarl of moving figures out in the pale ruins. Over her shoulder, she said, "You can't even help yourself."

"I know *that*," he agreed equably. "But that wasn't my question, love. Look . . ." He pointed. "That bloke there's figured out the way. Here they come. Gaw, they're like ants."

Jenny said nothing, but felt a shiver pass through her as she saw the trickle of attackers widen into a stream.

Gareth came up beside them, leading Battlehammer; Jenny whispered to the big horse and turned him loose down the steps. Her mind was already turning inward upon itself, digging at the strength in the exhausted depths of her spirit and body. John, Gareth, and the slender girl in the white rags of a Court gown, clinging to Gareth's arm, were becoming mere wraiths to her as her soul spiraled down into a single inner vortex, like the single-minded madness that comes before childbearing—nothing else existed but herself, her power, and what she must do.

Her hands pressed to the cold rock of the gate pillar, and she felt that she drew fire and strength from the stone itself and from the mountain beneath her feet and above her head—drew it from the air and the darkness that surrounded her. She felt the magic surge into her veins like a reined whirlwind of compressed lightning. Its power frightened her, for she knew it was greater than her body would bear, yet she could afford no Limitation upon these spells. It was thus, she knew, with dragons, but her body was not a dragon's.

She was aware of John reining Cow sharply back away from her, as if frightened; Gareth and Trey had retreated already. But her mind was out in the pale light of the steps, looking down over Deeping, contemplating in leisurely timelessness the men and women running through the crumbled walls of the ruins. She saw each one of them with the cool exactness of a dragon's eyes, not only how they were dressed, but the composition of their souls through the flesh they wore. Bond she saw distinctly, urging them on with a sword in his hand, his soul eaten through with abcesses like termite-riddled wood.

The forerunners hit the cracked pavement and dust of the square before the gates. Like the chirp of an insect in a wall, she heard Gareth nattering, "What can we do? We have to help her!" as she dispassionately gathered the lightning in her hands.

"Put that down," John's voice said, suddenly weak and bleached. "Get ready to run for it—you can hide in the warrens for a time if they get through. Here's the maps..."

The mob was on the steps. Incoherent hate rose around her like a storm tide. Jenny lifted her hands, the whole strength of rock and darkness funneling into her body, her mind relaxing into the shock instead of bracing against it.

The key to magic is magic, she thought. Her life began and ended in each isolate crystal second of impacted time.

The fire went up from the third step, a red wall of it, whole and all-consuming. She heard those trapped in the first rush screaming and smelled smoke, charring meat, and burning cloth. Like a dragon, she killed without hate, striking hard and cruel, knowing that the first strike must kill or her small group would all be dead.

Then she slammed shut before her the illusion of the doors that had long ago been broken from the gateway arch. They appeared like faded glass from within, but every nail and beam and brace of them was wrought perfectly from enchanted air. Through them she saw men and women milling about the base of the steps, pointing up at what they saw as the renewed Gates of the Deep and crying out in wonder and alarm. Others lay on the ground, or crawled helplessly here and there, beating out the flames from their clothes with frenzied hands. Those who had not been trapped in the fire made no move to help them, but stood along the bottom of the step, looking up at the gates and shouting with drunken rage. With the cacophony of the screams and groans of the wounded, the noise was terrible, and worse than the noise was the stench of sizzling flesh. Among it all, Bond Clerlock stood, staring up at the phantom gates with his hunger-eaten eyes.

Jenny stepped back, feeling suddenly sick as the human in her looked upon what the dragon in her had done. She had killed before to protect her own life and the lives of those she loved. But she had never killed on this scale, and the power she wielded shocked her even as it drained her of strength.

The dragon in you answered, Morkeleb had said. She felt sick with horror at how true his knowledge of her had been.

She staggered back, and someone caught her—John and Gareth, looking like a couple of not-very-successful brigands, filthy and battered and incongruous in their spectacles. Trey, with Gareth's tattered cloak still draped over her mud-stained white silks and her purple-and-white hair hanging in asymmetrical coils about her chalky face, wordlessly took a collapsible tin cup from her pearl-beaded reticule, filled it from the water bottle on Cow's saddle, and handed it to her.

John said, "It hasn't stopped them for long." A mist of sweat covered his face, and the nostrils of his long nose were marked by dints of pain from the mere effort of standing. "Look, there's Bond drumming up support for a second go. Silly bleater." He glanced across at Trey and added, "Sorry." She only shook her head.

Jenny freed herself and walked unsteadily to the edge of the shadow gate. Her head throbbed with exhaustion that bordered nausea. The voices of the men and her own voice, when she spoke, sounded flat and unreal. "He'll get it, too."

In the square below the gates, Bond was running here and there among the men, stepping over the charred bodies of the dying, gesticulating and pointing up at the phantom doors. The Palace guards looked uncertain, but the laborers from the Dockmarket were gathered about him, listening and passing wineskins among themselves. They shook their fists up at the Deep, and Jenny remarked, "Like the gnomes, they've had their taste of poverty."

"Yes, but how can they blame us for it?" Gareth objected indignantly. "How can they blame the gnomes? The gnomes were even more victims of it than they."

"Whether or no," John said, leaning against the stone pillar of the Gate, "I bet they're telling themselves the treasures of the Deep are theirs by right. It's what Zyerne will have told 'em, and they obviously believe it enough to kill for them."

"But it's silly!"

"Not as silly as falling in love with a witch, and we've both done that," John replied cheerfully. In spite of her exhaustion, Jenny chuckled. "How long can you hold them, love?"

Something in the sound of his voice made her look back quickly at him. Though he had dismounted from Cow to help her, it was obvious he could not stand alone; his flesh looked gray as ash. Shouting from below drew her attention a moment later; past the smoke still curling from the steps, she could see men forming up into a ragged line, the madness of unreasoning hate in their eyes.

"I don't know," she said softly. "All power must be paid for. Maintaining the illusion of the Gates draws still more of my strength. But it buys us a little time, breaking the thrust of their will if they think they'll have to break them."

"I doubt that lot has the brains to think that far." Still leaning heavily on the pillar, John looked out into the slanted sun of the square outside. "Look, here they come."

"Get back," Jenny said. Her bones hurt with the thought of drawing forth power from them and from the stone and air around her one more time. "I don't know what will happen without Limitations."

"I can't get back, love; if I let go of this wall, I'll fall down."

Through the ghost shape of the Gates, she saw them coming, running across the square toward the steps. The magic came more slowly, dredged and scraped from the seared core of her being—her soul felt bleached by the effort. The voices below rose in a mad crescendo, in which the words "gold" and "kill" were flung up like spars of driftwood on the rage of an incoming wave. She glimpsed Bond Clerlock, or what was left of Bond Clerlock, somewhere in their midst, his Court suit pink as a shell among the blood-and-buttercup hues of the Palace guards. Her mind locked into focus, like a dragon's mind; all things were clear to her and distant, impersonal as images in a divining crystal. She called the white dragon rage like a thunderclap and smote the steps with fire, not before them now, but beneath their feet.

As the fire exploded from the bare stone, a wave of sickness consumed her, as if in that second all her veins had been opened. The shrieking of men, caught in the agony of the fire, struck her ears like a slapping hand, as grayness threatened to drown her senses and heat rose through her, then sank away, leaving behind it a cold like death.

She saw them reeling and staggering, ripping flaming garments from charred flesh. Tears of grief and weakness ran down her face at what she had done, though she knew that the mob would have torn the four of them apart and had known, that time, that she could summon fire. The illusion of the Gates felt as tenuous as a soap-bubble around her—like her own body, light and drifting. John stumbled to catch her as she swayed and pulled her back to the pillar against which he had stood; for a moment they both held to it, neither strong enough to stand.

Her eyes cleared a little. She saw men running about the square in panic, rage, and pain; and Bond, oblivious to burns which covered his hand and arm, was chasing after them, shouting.

"What do we do now, love?"

She shook her head. "I don't know," she whispered. "I feel as if I'm going to faint."

His arm tightened around her waist. "Oh, do," he encouraged enthusiastically. "I've always wanted to carry you to safety in my arms."

Her laughter revived her, as he had no doubt meant it to. She pushed herself clear of his support as Gareth and Trey came up, both looking ill and frightened.

"Could we run for it through the Deep?" Gareth asked, fumbling the maps from an inner pocket and dropping two of them. "To the Citadel, I mean?"

"No," Jenny said. "I told John—if we left the Market Hall, they'd flank us; and carrying John, we couldn't outdistance them."

"I could stay here, love," John said quietly. "I could buy you time."

Sarcastically, she replied, "The time it would take them to pick themselves up after tripping over your body in the archway would scarcely suffice."

"*One* of us could try to get through," Trey suggested timidly. "Polycarp and the gnomes at the Citadel would know the way through from that side. They could come for the rest of you. I have some candles in my reticule, and some chalk to mark the way, and I'm no good to you here..."

"No," Gareth objected, valiantly fighting his terror of the dark warrens. "I'll go."

"You'd never find it," Jenny said. "I've been down in the Deep, Gareth, and believe me, it is not something that can be reasoned out with chalk and candles. And, as John has said, the door at the end will be locked in any case, even if they didn't blast it shut."

Down below them, Bond's voice could be heard dimly, shouting that the Gate wasn't real, that it was just a witch's trick, and that all the gold that had been lost was theirs by right. People were yelling, "Death to the thieves! Death to the gnome-lovers!" Jenny leaned her head against the stone of the pillar, a bar of sunlight falling through the Gate around her and lying like a pale carpet on the fire-black rubble of the Market Hall. She wondered if Zyerne had ever felt like this, when she had called upon the deep reserves of her powers, without Limitations—helpless before the anger of men.

She doubted it. It did something to you to be helpless. All power must be paid for. Zyerne had never paid.

She wondered, just for a moment, how the enchantress had managed that.

"What's that?"

At the sound of Trey's voice, she opened her eyes again and looked out to where the girl was pointing. The light filling the Vale glinted harshly on something up near the ruined clock tower. Listening, she could pick out the sound of hooves and voices and feel the distant clamor of anger and unthinking hate. Against the dull slate color of the tower's stones, the weeds of the hillside looked pale as yellow wine; between them the uniforms of half a company of Palace guards glowed like a tumble of hothouse poppies. The sun threw fire upon their weapons.

"Gaw," John said. "Reinforcements."

Bond and a small group of men were running up through the rubble and sedge toward the new company, flies swarming thick on the young courtier's untended wounds. Small with distance, Jenny saw more and more men under the shadow of the tower, the brass of pike and cuirass flashing, the red of helmet crests like spilled blood against the muted hues of the stone. Exhaustion ate like poison into her bones. Her skin felt like a single open, throbbing wound; through it, she could feel the illusion of the Gate fading to nothingness as her power drained and died.

She said quietly, "You three get back to the doors into the Grand Passage. Gar, Trey—carry John. Bolt the doors from the inside—there are winches and pulleys there."

"Don't be stupid." John was clinging to the gatepost beside her to stay upright.

"Don't *you* be stupid." She would not take her eyes from the swarming men in the square below.

"We're not leaving you," Gareth stated. "At least, I'm not. Trey, you take John . . ."

"No," Trey and the Dragonsbane insisted in approximate unison. They looked at one another and managed the ghost of a mutual grin.

"It's all of us or none of us, love."

She swung around on them, her eyes blazing palely with the crystalline coldness of the dragon's eyes. "None of you can be of the slightest use to me here against so many. John and Trey, all you'll be is killed immediately. Gareth . . ." Her eyes pinned his like a lance of frost. "You may not be. They may have other instructions concerning you, from Zyerne. I may have the strength for one more spell. That can buy you some time. John's wits may keep you alive for a while more in the Deep; you'll need Trey's willingness as well. Now go."

There was a short silence, in which she could feel John's eyes upon her face. She was conscious of the men approaching in the Vale; her soul screamed at her to get rid of these three whom she loved while there was yet time.

It was Gareth who spoke. "Will you really be able to hold the Gate against another charge? Even of—of my father's men?"

"I think so," Jenny lied, knowing she hadn't the strength left to light a candle.

"Aye, then, love," said John softly. "We'd best go." He took her halberd to use as a crutch; holding himself upright with it, he put a hand on her nape and kissed her. His mouth felt cold against hers, his lips soft even through the hard scratchiness of five days' beard. As their lips parted, their eyes met, and, through the dragon armor of hardness, she saw he knew she'd lied.

"Let's go, children," he said. "We won't shoot the bolts till we have to, Jen."

The line of soldiers was descending through the labyrinth of shattered foundations and charred stone. They were joined by the men and women of Deeping, those, Jenny noted, who had thrown garbage at Miss Mab in the fountain square of Bel. Makeshift weapons jostled pikes and swords. In the brilliance of daylight everything seemed hard and sharp. Every house beam and brick stood out to Jenny's raw perceptions like filigree work, every tangle of weed and stand of grass clear and individuated. The amber air held the stench of sulfur and burned flesh. Like a dim background to angry ranting and exhortation rose the keening of the wounded and, now and again, voices crying, "Gold . . . gold . . ."

They scarcely even know what it is for, Morkeleb had said.

Jenny thought about Ian and Adric, and wondered briefly who would raise them, or if, without her and John's protection of the Winterlands, they would live to grow up at all. Then she sighed and stepped forth from the shadows into the light. The pale sun drenched her, a small, skinny, black-haired woman alone in the vast arch of the shattered Gate. Men pointed, shouting. A rock clattered against the steps, yards away. The sunlight felt warm and pleasant upon her face.

Bond was screaming hysterically, "Attack! Attack now!

Kill the witch-bitch! It's our gold! We'll get the slut this time—get her..."

Men began to run forward up the steps. She watched them coming with a curious feeling of absolute detachment. The fires of dragon-magic had drained her utterly—one last trap, she thought ironically, from Morkeleb, a final vengeance for humiliating him. The mob curled like a breaking wave over the ruined beams and panels of the shattered gates, the sunlight flashing on the steel of the weapons in their hands.

Then a shadow crossed the sunlight—like a hawk's, but immeasurably more huge.

One man looked up, pointed at the sky, and screamed.

Again the sunlight was darkened by circling shade. Jenny raised her head. The aureate light streamed translucently through the black spread of bones and the dark veins of sable wings, sparkled from the spikes that tipped the seventy-foot span of that silent silk, and gilded every horn and ribbon of the gleaming mane.

She watched the dragon circling, riding the thermals like a vast eagle, only peripherally conscious of the terrified shouting of the men and the frenzied squeals of the guards' horses. Yelling and crashing in the rubble, the attackers of the Deep turned and fled, trampling upon their dead and dropping their weapons in their headlong flight.

The Vale was quite empty by the time Morkeleb lighted upon the heat-cracked steps of the Deep.

anger at having to ask the help of any human, anger at needing help, anger at admitting it, even to himself. But in the close-shielded mind, she felt other things—exhaustion approaching her own and the chill thread of fear.

By my name you drove me forth from this place, he said. *But something else, something beyond my name, draws me back. Like a jewel, one jet-bobbed antenna flicked in the wind. Like the discontented dreams that first brought me to this place, it will not let me rest; it is a yearning like the craving for gold, but worse. It tormented me as I flew north, mounting to pain, and the only ease I had was when I turned south again. Now all the torments of my soul and my dreams center upon this mountain. Before you entered my mind, it was not so— I came and went as I pleased, and naught but my own desire for the gold made me return. But this pain, this longing of the heart, is something I never felt before, in all my years; it is something I never knew of, until your healing touched me. It is not of you, for you commanded me to go. It is a magic that I do not understand, unlike the magic of dragons. It gives me no rest, no peace. I think of this place constantly, though, by my name, wizard woman, it is against my will that I return.*

He shifted upon his haunches, so that he lay as a cat will sometimes lie, his forelimbs and shoulders sphinx-like, but his hinder legs stretched out along the uppermost step. The spiked club of his tail lashed slightly at its clawed tip.

It is not the gold, he said. *Gold calls to me, but never with a madness like this. It is alien to my understanding, as if the soul were being rooted from me. I hate this place, for it is a place of defeat and disgrace to me now, but the craving to be here consumes me. I have never felt this before and I do not know what it is. Has it come from you, wizard woman? Do you know what is it?*

Jenny was silent for a time. Her strength was slowly

returning, and she felt already less weak and brittle than she had. Sitting on the steps between the dragon's claws, his head rose above hers, the thin, satiny ribbons of his mane brushing against her face. Now he cocked his head down; looking up, she met one crystalline silver eye.

She said, *It is a longing such as humans feel. I do not know why it should possess you, Morkeleb—but I think it is time that we found out. You are not the only one drawn to the Deep as if possessed. Like you, I do not think it is the gold. There is something within the Deep. I sense it, feel it within my bones.*

The dragon shook his great head. *I know the Deep*, he said. *It was my hold and dominion. I know every dropped coin and every soda-straw crystal; I heard the tread of every foot passing in the Citadel overhead and the slipping of the blind white fish through the waters deep below. I tell you, there is nothing in the Deep but water, stone, and the gold of the gnomes, sleeping in the darkness. There is nothing there that should draw me so.*

Perhaps, Jenny said. Then, aloud, she called into the echoing cavern behind her, "Gareth? John? Trey?"

The dragon lifted his head with indignation as soft footfalls scuffled within. Like speech without words, Jenny felt the sharp flash of his pride and his annoyance at her for bringing other humans into their counsels and she longed to slap his nose as she slapped her cat's when he tried to steal food from her fingers.

He must have felt the returning glint of her exasperation, for he subsided, his narrow chin sinking to rest upon the long-boned hooks of one black foreclaw. Beyond the spears of his backbone she saw the great tail lash.

The others came out, Gareth and Trey supporting John between them. He had slept a little and rested and looked better than he had. The spells of healing she had laid upon him were having their effect. He gazed up at the dark shape of the dragon, and Jenny felt their eyes meet and knew that Morkeleb spoke to him, thought she heard not what he said.

John replied in words. "Well, it was just as well, wasn't it? Thank you."

Their eyes held for a moment more. Then the dragon raised his head and turned it away irritably, transferring his cold silver gaze to Gareth. Jenny saw the young man flush with shame and confusion; whatever the dragon said to him, he made no reply at all.

They laid John down with his back to the granite door pillar, his plaid folded beneath his shoulders. His spectacles caught the starlight, rather like the silvery glow of the dragon's eyes. Jenny seated herself on the steps between him and the dragon's talons; Gareth and Trey, as if for mutual protection, sat opposite and close together, staring up in wonder at the thin, serpentine form of the Black Dragon of Nast Wall.

In time, Jenny's flawed, silver-shot voice broke the silence. "What is in the Deep?" she asked. "What is it that Zyerne wants so badly there? All her actions have been aimed toward having it—her hold over the King, her attempts to seduce Gareth, her desire for a child, the siege of Halnath, and the summoning of the dragon."

She did not summon me, retorted Morkeleb angrily. *She could not have done that. She has no hold upon my mind.*

"You're here, ain't you?" John drawled, and the dragon's metallic claws scraped upon the stone as his head swung round.

Jenny said sharply, "John! Morkeleb!"

The dragon subsided with a faint hiss, but the bobs of his antennae twitched with annoyance.

She went on, "Might it be that she is herself summoned?"

I tell you there is nothing there, the dragon said. *Nothing save stone and gold, water and darkness.*

"Let's back up a bit, then," John said. "Not what does Zyerne want in the Deep, but just what does she want?"

Gareth shrugged. "It can't be gold. You've seen how she lives. She could have all the gold in the Realm for the asking. She has the King..." He hesitated, and then went on calmly, "If I hadn't left for the north when I did, she would certainly have had me, and very probably a son to rule through for the rest of her life."

"She used to live in the Deep," Trey pointed out. "It seems that, ever since she left it, she's been trying to get control of it. Why did she leave? Did the gnomes expel her?"

"Not really," Gareth said. "That is, they didn't formally forbid her to enter the Deep at all until this year. Up until then she could come and go in the upper levels, just like any other person from Bel."

"Well if she's shapestrong, that's to say she had the run of the place, so long as she stayed clear of the mage-born," John reasoned, propping his specs with one forefinger. "And what happened a year ago?"

"I don't know," Gareth said. "Dromar petitioned my father in the name of the Lord of the Deep not to let her— or any of the children of men, for that matter..."

"Again, that's a logical precaution against a shape-shifter."

"Maybe." Gareth shrugged. "I didn't think of it then— a lot of the unpopularity of the gnomes started then, because of that stipulation. But they said Zyerne specifically, because she had..." He fished in his compendious, ballad-trained memory for the exact wording. "... 'defiled a holy thing.'"

"No idea what it was?"

The prince shook his head. Like John, he looked drawn and tired, his shirt a fluttering ruin of dirt and spark holes, his face sparkling faintly with an almost-invisible adolescent stubble. Trey, sitting beside him, looked little better.

With her typical practicality, she had carried a comb in her reticule and had combed out her hair, so that it hung past her hips in crinkled swaths, the smooth sheen of its fantastic colors softened to a stippling of snow white and violet, like the pelt of some fabulous beast against the matted nap of Gareth's cloak.

"'Defiled a holy *thing*." Jenny repeated thoughtfully. "It isn't how Mab put it. She said that she had poisoned the heart of the Deep—but the heart of the Deep is a place, rather than an object."

"Is it?" said John curiously.

"Of course. I've been there." The silence of it whispered along her memory. "But as for what Zyerne wants . . ."

"You're a witch, Jen," said John. "What do you want?"

Gareth looked shocked at the comparison, but Jenny only thought for a moment, then said, "Power. Magic. The key to magic is magic. My greatest desire, to which I would sacrifice all things else, is to increase my skills."

"But she's already the strongest sorceress in the land," Trey protested.

"Not according to Mab."

"I suppose there were gnome wizards in the Deep stronger," John said interestedly. "If there hadn't been, she wouldn't have needed to summon Morkeleb."

She did not summon me! The dragon's tail lashed again, like a great cat's. *She could not. Her power is not that great.*

"Somebody's is," John remarked. "Before you wiped out the Deep and the mages in it, the gnomes were strong enough to keep Zyerne out. But they all perished, or at least all the strong ones did . . ."

"No," Jenny said. "That's what has puzzled me. Mab said that she herself was stronger than Zyerne at some time in the past. That means that either Mab grew weaker, or Zyerne stronger."

"Could Mab's power have been weakened in some way

when Morkeleb showed up?" John glanced up at the dragon. "Would that be possible? That your magic would lessen someone else's?"

I know nothing of the magic of humans, nor yet of the magic of gnomes, the dragon replied. *Yet among us, there is no taking away of another's magic. It is like taking away another's thoughts from him, and leaving him with none.*

"That's another thing," Jenny said, folding her arms about her drawn-up knees. "When I met Zyerne yesterday ... My powers have grown, but I should not have been able to defeat her as I did. She is shapestrong—she should have far more strength than I did." She glanced over at Gareth. "But she didn't shift shape."

"But she can," the boy protested. "I've *seen* her."

"Lately?" asked John suddenly.

Gareth and Trey looked at one another.

"Since the coming of the dragon? Or, to put it another way, since she hasn't been able to enter the Deep?"

"But either way, it's inconceivable," Jenny insisted. "Power isn't something that's contingent upon any place or thing, any more than knowledge is. Zyerne's power couldn't have weakened any more than Mab's could. Power is within you—here, or in Bel, or in the Winterlands, or wherever you are. It is something you learn, something you develop. All power must be paid for..."

"Except that it's never looked as if Zyerne had paid for hers," John said. His glance went from Jenny to the dragon and back. "You said the magic of the gnomes is different. Is there a way she could have stolen power, Jen? That she could be using something she's no right to? I'm thinking how you said she doesn't know about Limitations—obviously, since she summoned a dragon she can't get rid of..."

She did not summon me!

"She seems to think she did," John pointed out. "At

least she's kept saying how she was the one who kicked the gnomes out of the Deep. But mostly I'm thinking about the wrinkles on her face."

"But she doesn't have any wrinkles," Trey objected, disconcerted at this lightning change of topic.

"Exactly. Why doesn't she? Every mage I've known—Mab, who isn't that old as gnomes go, old Caerdinn, that crazy little wander-mage who used to come through the Winterlands, and you, Jen—the marks of power are printed on their faces. Though it hasn't aged you," he added quickly, with a concern for her vanity that made Jenny smile.

"You are right," she said slowly. "Now that you speak of it, I don't think I've ever encountered a mage that—that sweet-looking. Maybe that's what first troubled me. And Mab said something about Zyerne stealing secrets. Zyerne herself said that when she is able to get into the Deep, she'll have the power to destroy us all." She frowned, some other thought tugging at her mind. "But it doesn't make sense. If you think she could have gained her powers by studying arts possessed by the gnomes—by breaking into and reading the books of their deeper magic—you're wrong. I searched through the Places of Healing in quest of just such books, and found none."

"That's a bit odd in itself, isn't it?" John mused. "But when you said power isn't contingent on any thing, any more than knowledge is—knowledge can be stored in a book. Is there any way power can be stored? *Can* a mage use another mage's power?"

Jenny shrugged. "Oh, yes. Power can be accumulated by breadth as well as by depth; several mages can focus their power together and direct it toward a single spell that lies beyond their separate strengths. It can be done by chanting, meditating, dancing..." She broke off, as the vision rose once more to her mind—the vision of the heart of the Deep. "Dancing..." she repeated softly, then shook her head. "But in any case, the power is controlled by those who raise it."

"Is it?" asked John. "Because in Polyborus it says..."

Morkeleb cut him off. *But if she were forbidden the Deep, Zyerne could have been nowhere near it when the power was raised that sent this yearning unto me and called me back. Nor, indeed, could she have been near the Deep to conjure the dreams that first brought me here. And no other mages would have combined to raise that power.*

"That's what I'm trying to tell you!" John broke in. "In Dotys—or Polyborus' *Analects*—or maybe it's the *Elucidus Lapidarus*..."

"What?" demanded Jenny, well aware that John was perfectly capable of fishing for the source of reference for ten minutes in the jackdaw-nest of his memory.

"Dotys—or Polyborus—says that it used to be rumored that mages could use a certain type of stone for a power-sink. They could call power into it, generation after generation, sometimes, or they could combine—and I think he mentioned dancing—and when they needed great power, for the defense of their realm or defeat of a dragon or a really powerful devil, they could call power out of it."

They looked at one another in silence—witch and prince, maiden and warrior and dragon.

John went on, "I think what the gnomes were guarding—what lies in the heart of the Deep—is a power sink."

"The Stone," Jenny said, knowing it for truth. "They swear 'by the Stone' or 'by the Stone in the heart of the Deep.' Even Zyerne does. In my vision, they were dancing around it."

John's voice was soft in the velvety darkness. "And in that case, all Zyerne would have needed to steal was the key to unlock it. If she was apprenticed in the Places of Healing near there, that wouldn't have been hard."

"If she's mentally in contact with it, she could use it somewhat, even at a distance," Jenny said. "I felt it, when I struggled with her—some power I have never felt. Not living, like Morkeleb—but strong because it is dead and does not care what it does. It must be the source of all her strength, for shapechanging and for the curse she sent to the gnomes, the curse that brought you here from the north, Morkeleb."

"A curse that's still holding good whether she wants it to or not." John's spectacles flashed in the starlight as he grinned. "But she must not be able to wield it accurately at a distance, even as Miss Mab can't use it against her. It would explain why she's so wild not to let them get even a chance of going back."

So what then? demanded Morkeleb grimly. *Did your estimable Dotys, your wise Polyborus, speak of a way to combat the magic of these stones?*

"Well," John said, a faint grin of genuine amusement touching the corners of his mouth, "that was the whole point of my coming south, you see. My copy of the *Elucidus Lapidarus* isn't complete. Almost nothing in my library is. It's why I agreed to become a Dragonsbane for the King's hire in the first place—because we need books, we need knowledge. I'm as much a scholar as I can be, but it isn't easy."

With the size of a human brain, it would not be! Morkeleb snapped, irrationally losing his temper. *You are no more scholar than you are Dragonsbane!*

"But I never claimed to be," John protested. "It's just there's all these ballads, see..."

The jet claws rattled again on the pavement. Jenny, exasperated with them both, began, "I really am going to let him eat you this time..."

Trey put in hastily, "Could you use the Stone yourself, Lady Jenny? Use it against Zyerne?"

"Of course!" Gareth bounced like a schoolboy on the hard step. "That's it! Fight fire with fire."

Jenny was silent. She felt their eyes upon her—Trey's, Gareth's, John's, the crystal gaze of the dragon turned down at her from above. The thought of the power stirred in her mind like lust—Zyerne's power. The key to magic is magic...

She saw the worry in John's eyes and knew what her own expression must look like. It sobered her. "What are you thinking?"

He shook his head. "I don't know, love."

He meant that he would not stand in the way of any decision she made. Correctly interpreting his look, she said gently, "I would not misuse the power, John. I would not become like Zyerne."

His voice was pitched to her ears alone. "Can you know that?"

She started to reply, then stilled herself. Shrill and clear she heard Miss Mab's voice saying, *She took the secrets of those greater than she, defiled them, tainted them, poisoned the very heart of the Deep*... She remembered, too, that sense of perverted power that had sparkled in the lamplight around Zyerne and the luckless Bond, and how the touch of the dragon's mind had changed her.

"No," she said at last. "I cannot know. And it would be stupid of me to meddle with something so powerful without knowing its dangers, even if I could figure out the key by myself."

"But," Gareth protested, "it's our only chance of defeating Zyerne! They'll be back—you know they will! We can't stay holed up here forever."

"Could we learn enough about the Stone for you to circumvent its powers somehow?" Trey suggested. "Would there be a copy of the Whatsus Howeverus you talked about in the Palace library?"

Gareth shrugged. His scholarship might extend to seven

minor variants of the ballad of the Warlady and the Red Worm of Weldervale, but it was a broken reed insofar as obscure encyclopedists went.

"There would be one at Halnath, though, wouldn't there?" Jenny said. "And if it didn't contain the information, there are gnomes there who might know."

"If they'd tell." John propped himself gingerly a little higher against the granite of the gate pillar, the few portions of his shirt not darkened with bloodstains very white in the rising moonlight against the metallic glints of his doublet. "Dromar's lot wouldn't even admit it existed. They've had enough of humans controlling the Stone, and I can't say as I blame them. But whatever happens," he added, as the others subsided from their enthusiasm into dismal reflection once more, "our next move had better be to get out of here. As our hero says, you know Bond and the King's troops will be back. The only place we *can* go is Halnath, and maybe not there. How tight are the siege lines, Gar?"

"Tight," Gareth said gloomily. "Halnath is built on a series of cliffs—the lower town, the upper town, the University, and the Citadel above that, and the only way in is through the lower town. Spies have tried to sneak in over the cliffs on the mountain side of the city and have fallen to their deaths." He readjusted his cracked spectacles. "And besides," he went on, "Zyerne knows as well as we do that Halnath is the only place we can go."

"Pox." John glanced over at Jenny, where she sat against the alien curves of the dragon's complicated shoulder bones. "For something that was never any of our business to begin with, this is looking worse and worse."

"I could go," Trey ventured. "The troops would be least likely to recognize me. I could tell Polycarp..."

"They'd never let you through," John said. "Don't think Zyerne doesn't know you're here, Trey; and don't think she'd let you off because you're Bond's sister or that Bond would risk Zyerne so much as pouting at him to get you off. Zyerne can't afford even one of us returning to the gnomes with word the dragon's left the Deep."

That, Morkeleb said thinly, *is precisely our problem. The dragon has NOT left the Deep. Nor will he, until this Zyerne is destroyed. And I will not remain here docile, to watch the gnomes carrying on their petty trafficking with my gold.*

"*Your* gold?" John raised an eyebrow. With a swift gesture of her mind Jenny stilled Morkeleb again.

Nor would they allow it, she said, *for the dragon alone. It would only be a matter of time until their distrust of you mastered them, and they tried to slay you. No—you must be freed.*

Freed! The voice within her mind was acrid as the stench of vinegar. *Freed to be turned like a beggar onto the roads?* The dragon swung his head away, the long scales of his mane clashing softly, like the searingly thin notes of a wind chime. *You have done this to me, wizard woman! Before your mind touched mine I was not bound to this place . . .*

"You were bound," Aversin said quietly. "It's just that, before Jenny's mind touched yours, you weren't aware of it. Had you tried to leave before?"

I remained because it was my will to remain.

"And it's the old King's will to remain with Zyerne, though she's killing him. No, Morkeleb—she got you through your greed, as she got poor Gar's dad through his grief and Bond through his love. If we hadn't come, you'd have stayed here, bound with spells to brood over your hoard till you died. It's just that now you know it."

That is not true!

True or not, Jenny said, *it is my bidding, Morkeleb, that as soon as the sky grows light, you shall carry me over the mountain to the Citadel of Halnath, so that I can send Polycarp the Master to bring these others to safety there through the Deep.*

The dragon reared himself up, bristling all over with rage. His voice lashed her mind like a silver whip. *I am not your pigeon nor your servant!*

Jenny was on her feet now, too, looking up into the blazing white deeps of his eyes. *No*, she said, holding to the crystal chain of his inner name. *You are my slave, by that which you gave me when I saved your life. And by that which you gave me, I tell you this is what you shall do.*

Their eyes held. The others, not hearing what passed between their two minds, saw and felt only the dragon's scorching wrath. Gareth caught up Trey and drew her back toward the shelter of the gateway; Aversin made a move to rise and sank back with a gasp. He angrily shook off Gareth's attempt to draw him to safety, his eyes never leaving the small, thin form of the woman who stood before the smoking rage of the beast.

All this Jenny was aware of, but peripherally, like the weave of a tapestry upon which other colors are painted. Her whole mind focused in crystal exactness against the mind that surged like a dark wave against hers. The power born in her from the touch of the dragon's mind strengthened and burned, forcing him back. Her understanding of his name was a many-pointed weapon in her hands. In time Morkeleb sank to his haunches again, and back to his sphinx position.

In her mind his voice said softly, *You know you do not need me, Jenny Waynest, to fly over the mountains. You know the form of the dragons and their magic. One of them you have put on already.*

The other I might put on, she replied, *for you would help me in that, to be free of my will. But you would not help me put it off again.*

The deeps of his eyes were like falling into the heart of a star. *If you wished it, I would.*

The need in her for power, to separate herself from all that had separated her from its pursuit, shuddered through her like the racking heat of fever. "To be a mage you must be a mage," Caerdinn had said.

He had also said, "Dragons do not deceive with lies, but with truth." Jenny turned her eyes from those cosmic depths. *You say it only because in becoming a dragon, I will cease to want to hold power over you, Morkeleb the Black.*

He replied, *Not 'only,' Jenny Waynest.*

Like a wraith he faded into the darkness.

Though still exhausted from the battle at the Gates, Jenny did not sleep that night. She sat upon the steps, as she had sat awake most of the night before, watching and listening—for the King's men, she told herself, though she knew they would not come. She was aware of the night with a physical intensity, the moonlight like a rime of molten silver on every chink and crack of the scarred steps upon which she sat, turning to slips of white each knotted weed-stem in the scuffed dust of the square below. Earlier, while she had been tending to John by the fire in the Market Hall, the bodies of the slain rioters had vanished from the steps, though whether this was due to fastidiousness on Morkeleb's part or hunger, she wasn't sure.

Sitting in the cold stillness of the night, she meditated, seeking an answer within herself. But her own soul was unclear, torn between the great magic that had always lain beyond her grasp and the small joys she had cherished in its stead—the silence of the house on Frost Fell, the memory of small hands that seemed to be printed on her palms, and John.

John, she thought, and looked back through the wide

arch of the Gate to where he lay, wrapped in bearskins beside the small glow of the fire.

In the darkness she made out his shape, the broad-shouldered compactness that went so oddly with the whippet litheness of his movements. She remembered the fears that had driven her to the Deep to seek medicines—that had driven her first to look into the dragon's silver eyes. Now, as then, she could scarcely contemplate years of her life that did not—or would not—include that fleeting, triangular smile.

Adric had it already, along with the blithe and sunny half of John's quirky personality. Ian had his sensitivity, his maddening, insatiable curiosity, and his intentness. His sons, she thought. My sons.

Yet the memory of the power she had called to stop the lynch mob on these very steps returned to her, sweetness and terror and exultation. Its results had horrified her, and the weariness of it still clung to her bones, but the taste that lingered was one of triumph at having wielded it. How could she, she wondered, have wasted all those years before this beginning? The touch of Morkeleb's mind had half-opened a thousand doors within her. If she turned away from him now, how many of the rooms behind those doors would she be able to explore? The promise of the magic was something only a mageborn could have felt; the need, like lust or hunger, something only the mageborn would have understood. There was a magic she had never dreamed of that could be wrought from the light of certain stars, knowledge unplumbed in the dark, eternal minds of dragons and in the singing of the whales in the sea. The stone house on the Fell that she loved came back to her like the memory of a narrow prison; the clutch of small hands on her skirts, of an infant's mouth at her breast, seemed for a time nothing more than bonds holding her back from walking through its doors to the moving air outside.

Was this some spell of Morkeleb's? she wondered, wrapping the soft weight of a bearskin more tightly around her shoulders and gazing at the royal blue darkness of the sky above the western ridge. Was it something he had sung up out of the depths of her soul, so that she would leave the concerns of humans and free him of his bondage to her?

Why did you say, "Not" 'only,'"Morkeleb the Black?

You know that as well as I, Jenny Waynest.

He had been invisible in the darkness. Now the moonlight sprinkling his back was like a carpet of diamonds and his silver eyes were like small, half-shut moons. How long he had been there she did not know—the moon had sunk, the stars moved. His coming had been like the floating of a feather on the still night.

What you give to them you have taken from yourself. When our minds were within one another, I saw the struggle that has tortured you all your life. I do not understand the souls of humans, but they have a brightness to them, like soft gold. You are strong and beautiful, Jenny Waynest. I would like it if you would become one of us and live among us in the rock islands of the northern seas.

She shook her head. *I will not turn against those that I love.*

Turn against? The sinking moonlight striped his mane with frost as he moved his head. *No. That I know you would never do, though, for what their love has done to you, they would well deserve it if you did. And as to this love you speak of, I do not know what it is—it is not a thing of dragons. But when I am freed of the spells that bind me here, when I fly to the north again, fly with me. This is something also that I have never felt—this wanting of you to be a dragon that you can be with me. And tell me, what is it to you if this boy Gareth becomes the slave of his father's woman or to one of his own choosing? What is it to you who rules the Deep, or how long this woman Zyerne can go on polluting her mind and her body until she dies because she no longer recalls enough about her own magic to continue living? What is it to you if the Winterlands are ruled and defended by one set of men or another, or if they have books to read about the deeds of yet a third? It is nothing, Jenny Waynest. Your powers are beyond that.*

To leave them now would be to turn against them. They need me.

They do not need you, the dragon replied. *Had the King's troops killed you upon these steps, it would have been the same for them.*

Jenny looked up at him, that dark shape of power—infinitely more vast than the dragon John had slain in Wyr and infinitely more beautiful. The singing of his soul re-echoed in her heart, magnified by the beauty of the gold. Clinging to the daylight that she knew against the calling of the dark, she shook her head again and said, *It would not have been the same.*

She gathered the furs about her, rose, and went back into the Deep.

After the sharpness of the night air, the huge cavern felt stuffy and stank of smoke. The dying fire threw weird flickers of amber against the ivory labyrinth of inverted turrets above and glinted faintly on the ends of the broken lamp chains that hung down from the vaulted blackness. It was always so, going from free night air to the frowsty stillness of indoors, but her heart ached suddenly, as if she had given up free air for a prison forever.

She folded the bearskin, laid it by the campfire, and found where her halberd had been leaned against the few packs they had brought with them from the camp. Somewhere in the darkness, she heard movement, the sound of someone tripping over a plaid. A moment later Gareth's voice said softly, "Jenny?"

"Over here." She straightened up, her pale face and

the metal buckles of her sheepskin jacket catching the low firelight. Gareth looked tired and bedraggled in his shirt, breeches, and a stained and scruffy plaid, as unlike as possible to the self-conscious young dandy in primrose-and-white Court mantlings of less than a week ago. But then, she noted, there was less in him now than there had been, even then, of the gawky and earnest young man who had ridden to the Winterlands in quest of his hero.

"I must be going," she said softly. "It's beginning to turn light. Gather what kindling you can, in case the King's men return and you have to barricade yourselves behind the inner doors in the Grand Passage. There are foul things in the darkness. They may come at you when the light is gone."

Gareth shuddered wholeheartedly and nodded.

"I'll tell Polycarp how things stand. He should come back here to get you, if they didn't blast shut the ways into the Deep. If I don't make it to Halnath..."

The boy looked at her, the heroically simple conclusions of a dozen ballads reverberant in his shocked features.

She smiled, the pull of the dragon in her fading. She reached up the long distance to lay a hand on his bristly cheek. "Look after John for me."

Then she knelt and kissed John's lips and his shut eyelids. Rising, she collected a plaid and her halberd and walked toward the clear slate-gray air that lay like water outside the darker arch of the Gate.

As she passed through it, she heard a faint north-country voice behind her protest, "Look after John, indeed!"

CHAPTER XV

LIGHT WATERED THE darkness, changing the air from velvet to silk. Cold cut into Jenny's hands and face, imbuing her with a sense of strange and soaring joy. The high cirques and hanging valleys of the Wall's toothy summits were stained blue and lavender against the charcoal gray of the sky; below her, mist clung like raveled wool to the bones of the shadowy town. For a time she was alone and complete, torn by neither power nor love, only breathing the sharp air of dawn.

Like a shift in perception, she became aware of the dragon, lying along the bottom step. Seeing her, he rose and stretched like a cat, from nose to tail knob to the tips of the quivering wings, every spine and horn blinking in the gray-white gloom.

Wrap yourself well, wizard woman. The upper airs are cold.

He sat back upon his haunches and, reaching delicately down, closed around her one gripping talon, like a hand twelve inches across the back and consisting of nothing but bone wrapped in muscle and studded with spike and horn. The claws lapped easily around her waist. She felt no fear of him; though she knew he was treacherous, she had been within his mind and knew he would not kill her. Still, a shivery qualm passed through her as he lifted her up against his breast, where she would be out of the airstream.

The vast shadow of his wings spread against the mauve gloom of the cliff behind them, and she cast one quick glance down at the ground, fifteen feet below. Then she looked up at the mountains surrounding the Vale and at the white, watching eye of the moon on the flinty crest of the ridge, a few days from full and bright in the western air as the lamps of the dragon's eyes.

Then he flung himself upward, and all the world dropped away.

Cold sheered past her face, its bony fingers clawing through her hair. Through the plaids wrapped around her, she felt the throbbing heat of the dragon's scales. From the sky she looked to the earth again, the Vale like a well of blue shadow, the mountain slopes starting to take on the colors of dawn as the sun brushed them, rust and purple and all shades of brown from the whitest dun to the deep hue of coffee, all edged and trimmed with the dark lace of trees. The rain tanks north of Deeping caught the new day like chips of mirror; as the dragon passed over the flanks of the mountain, circling higher, she saw the bright leap of springs among the pine trees, and the white spines of thrusting rock.

The dragon tilted, turning upon the air, the vast wings searing faintly at the wind. Occasional eddies of it whistled around the spikes that defended the dragon's backbone—some of them no longer than a finger, others almost a cubit, dagger-sharp. In flight the dragon seemed to be a thing made of silk and wire, lighter than his size would lead one to think, as if the flesh and muscle, like the mind and the shape of his bones, were different in composition from all things else upon the Earth.

This is the realm of the dragons, Morkeleb's voice said within her mind. *The roads of the air. It is yours, for the stretching out of your hand.*

In the slant of the light they laid no shadow upon the ground, but it seemed to Jenny that she could almost see the track of their passage written like a ship's wake upon the wind. Her mind half-within the dragon's, she could sense the variations of the air, updraft and thermal, as if the wind itself were of different colors. With the dragon's awareness, she saw other things in the air as well—the paths of energy across the face of the world, the tracks that traveled from star to star, like the lines of force that were repeated in the body, smaller and smaller, in the spreads of dealt cards or thrown runes or the lie of leaves in water. She was aware of life everywhere, of the winter-white foxes and hares in the patchy snowlines beneath the thin scrum of cloud below, and of the King's troops, camped far down upon the road, who pointed and cried out as the dragon's dark shape passed overhead.

They crossed the flank of the mountain to its daylight side. Before and below her, she saw the cliff and hill and Citadel of Halnath, a spiky conglomerate of thrusting gray ramparts clinging like a mud-built swallow's nest to the massive shoulder of a granite cliff. From its feet, the land lay crisscrossed with wooded ravines to the silver curve of a river; mist blended with the blue of woodsmoke to veil the straggling lines of tents and guard posts, horse lines and trenches raw with yellow mud, that made up the siege camps. An open ring of battered ground lay between the walls and the camp, ravaged by battle and bristling with the burned-out shells of the small truck farms that nestled around the walls of any town. Beyond, to the north, the green stretches of the Marches vanished away under a gauze of mists, the horse- and cattle-lands that were the Master's fief and strength. From the river marshes where pewter waters spread themselves, a skein of danglefoot herons rose through the milky vapors, tiny and clear as a pen sketch.

There. Jenny pointed with her mind toward the battlements of the high Citadel. *The central court there. It's narrow, but long enough for us to land.*

Wind and her long hair lashed her eyes as the dragon wheeled.

They have armored their walls, the dragon said. *Look*.

Men were running about the ramparts, pointing and waving at the enormous wings flashing in the air. Jenny glimpsed catapults mounted on the highest turrets, counterweighted slings bearing buckets that burst suddenly into red flame and massive crossbows whose bolts could point nowhere but at the sky.

We'll have to go in, Jenny said. *I'll protect you.*

By catching the bolts in your teeth, wizard woman? Morkeleb asked sarcastically, circling away as some overeager slinger slipped his ropes and a bucketful of naphtha described a curving trajectory, flames streaming like faded orange pennants against the brightness of the new day. *What protection can you, a human, offer me?*

Jenny smiled to herself, watching the naphtha as it broke into blazing lumps in falling. None of them landed in the town on the slopes below—they knew their mathematics, these defenders of Halnath, and how to apply them to ballistics. For herself, she supposed she should have been terrified, to be carried this high above the reeling earth—if she fell, she would fall for a long time before she died. But whether it was her trust in Morkeleb, or the dragon's mind that enveloped hers in the thoughts of those who lived in the airstream, she felt no fear of it. Indeed, she almost believed that, if she were to drop, she had only to spread out her own wings, as she did in dreams of flight.

Small as toys on the walls of the Citadel, the machines of defense were being cranked around to bear upon them. They looked, at this distance, like nothing so much as

John's little models. *And to think I grew impatient when he insisted upon showing me how every one of them fired.* She smiled, half to Morkeleb and half to herself. *Swing north, Morkeleb, and come at them from along that ridge. The problem with machines has always been that it requires only the touch of a wizard's mind to fox their balance.*

There were two engines guarding the approach she had set, a bolt-firing catapult and a spring-driven sling. She had thrown her magic before, conjuring images within her mind, to foul the bowstrings of bandits in the north and to cause their feet to find roots as they ran, or their swords to stick in their sheaths. Having seen the mechanisms of these weapons in John's models, she found this no harder. Ropes twisted in the catapult, jamming the knots when the triggering cord was jerked. With a dragon's awareness, she saw a man running in panic along the battlements; he knocked over a bucket into the mechanism of the sling so that it could not be turned to aim. The dragon swung lazily from the weapon's possible path, guided by the touch of Jenny's mind within his; and she felt, like a chuckle of dark laughter, his appreciation for the ease with which she thwarted the mechanical devices.

You are small, wizard woman, he said, amused, *but a mighty defender of dragons, nevertheless.*

Throwing her streaming hair back from her eyes, Jenny could see men on the battlements below them clearly now. They were clothed in makeshift uniforms, the black, billowing gowns of scholars covered with battered bits of armor, some of it stamped with the royal arms and obviously taken from prisoners or the slain. They fled in all directions as the dragon drew near, save for one man, tall, red-haired, and thin as a scarecrow in his ragged black gown, who was swinging something to bear upon them that looked for a moment like a telescope—a metal tube braced upon stakes. The walls swooped closer. At the last moment Jenny saw harpoons stacked beside him and, instead of glass in the tube's mouth, the glint of a metal point.

The lone defender had a burning spill in one hand, lighted from one of the naphtha buckets. He was watching them come in, taking aim—*Blasting powder*, thought Jenny; *the gnomes will have brought plenty up from the mines*. She remembered John's abortive experiments with rockets.

The scene rushed to meet them, until every chipped stone of the wall and every patch on the scholar's ragged gown seemed within reach of Jenny's hand. As he brought the spill down to the touch-hole, Jenny used her mind to extinguish the flame, as she would have doused a candle.

Then she spread out her arms and cried, "STOP!" at the top of her voice.

He froze in mid-motion, the harpoon he had snatched from the pile beside him cocked back already over his shoulder, though Jenny could tell by the way he held it that he had never thrown one before and could not have hit them. Even at that distance, she saw wonder, curiosity, and delight on his thin face. Like John, she thought, he was a true scholar, fascinated with any wonder, though it carried his death upon its wings.

Morkeleb braked in the air, the shift of his muscles rippling against Jenny's back. All men had fled the long, narrow court of the Citadel and the walls around it, save that single defender. The dragon hung for a moment like a hovering hawk, then settled, delicate as a dandelion seed, to perch on the wall above the shadowy well of the court. The great hind-talons gripped the stone as the long neck and tail counterbalanced, and he stooped like a vast bird to set Jenny on her feet upon the rampart.

She staggered, her knees weak from shock, her whole body trembling with exhilaration and cold. The tall, red-haired young man, harpoon still in one hand, moved forward along the walkway, black robe billowing beneath an outsize hauberk of chain mail. Though he was clearly cautious, Jenny thought from the way he looked at Morkeleb that he could have stood and studied the dragon for hours; but there was a court-bred politeness in the way he offered Jenny his hand.

It took her a moment to remember to speak in words. "Polycarp of Halnath?"

He looked surprised and disconcerted at hearing his name. "I am he." Like Gareth, it took more than dragons or bandits to shake his early training; he executed a very creditable Dying Swan in spite of the harpoon.

Jenny smiled and held out her hands to him. "I am Jenny Waynest, Gareth's friend."

"Yes, there is a power sink in the heart of the Deep." Polycarp, Master of the Citadel of Halnath and Doctor of Natural Philosophy, folded long, narrow hands behind his back and turned from the pointed arches of the window to look at his rescued, oddly assorted guests. "It is what Zyerne wants; what she has always wanted, since first she knew what it was."

Gareth looked up from the ruins of the simple meal which strewed the plain waxed boards of the workroom table. "Why didn't you tell me?"

The bright blue eyes flickered to him. "What could I have said?" he asked. "Up until a year ago I wasn't even sure. And when I was . . ." His glance moved to the gnome who sat at the table's head, tiny and stooped and very old, his eyes like pale green glass beneath the long mane of milk-white hair. "Sevacandrozardus—Balgub, in the tongue of men; brother of the Lord of the Deep who was slain by the dragon—forbade me to speak of it. I could not break his confidence."

Beyond the tall windows, the turrets of the lower Citadel, the University, and the town beneath could be glimpsed, the sunlight on them yellow as summer butter, though the buildings below were already cloaked in the shadows of the mountain as the sun sank behind its shoulder. Sitting on the end of the couch where John lay, Jenny listened in quiet to the debating voices. Her body ached for sleep and her mind for stillness, but she knew that both would be denied her. Neither the words of the impromptu council nor the recollection of the trip back through the Deep with Polycarp and the gnomes to fetch the others had eradicated from her thoughts the soaring memory of the dragon's flight.

She knew she ought not to let it hold her so. She ought to be more conscious of her own gladness that they were, at least for the moment, relatively safe and more preoccupied with their exchange of information with the Master and with plans for how to deal with the Stone and its mistress. Yet the flight and the memory of the dragon's mind had shaken her to the bones. She could not put that wild intoxication from her heart.

The old gnome was saying, "It has always been forbidden to speak of the Stone to outsiders. After it became clear that the girl Zyerne had heard of it somehow and had spied upon those who used it and learned its key, my brother, the Lord of the Deep, redoubled the anathema. It has from the darkness of time been the heart of the Deep, the source of power for our Healers and mages, and has made our magic so great that none dared to assault the Deep of Ylferdun. But always we knew its danger as well—that the greedy could use such a thing for their own ends. And so it was."

Jenny roused herself from her thoughts to ask, "How did you know she had used it?" Like the others, she had bathed and was now dressed like them all in the frayed black gown of a scholar of the University, too large for her and belted tight about her waist. Her hair, still damp from washing, hung about her shoulders.

The gnome's light eyes shifted. Grudgingly, he said,

"To take power from the Stone, there must be a return. It gives to those who draw upon it, but later it asks back from them. Those who were used to wielding its power—myself, Taseldwyn whom you know as Miss Mab, and others—could feel the imbalance. Then it corrected itself, or seemed to. I was content." He shook his head, the opals that pinned his white hair flashing in the diffuse light of the long room. "Mab was not."

"What return does it ask?"

For a moment his glance touched her, reading in her, as Mab had done, the degree of her power. Then he said, "Power for power. All power must be paid for, whether it is taken from your own spirit, or from the holding-sink of others. We, the Healers, of whom I was chief, used to dance for it, to concentrate our magic and feed it into the Stone, that others might take of its strength and not have their very life-essences drawn from them by it—the woman Zyerne did not know how to make the return of magic to it, did not even learn that she should. She was never taught its use, but had only sneaked and spied until she learned what she thought was its secret. When she did not give back to it, the Stone began to eat at her essence."

"And to feed it," said Jenny softly, suddenly understanding what she had seen in the lamplight of Zyerne's room, "she perverted the healing spells that can draw upon the essences of others for strength. She drank, like a vampire, to replace what was being drunk from her."

In the pale light of the window, Polycarp said, "Yes," and Gareth buried his face in his hands. "Even as she can draw upon the Stone's magic at a distance, it draws upon her. I am glad," he added, the tone of his light voice changing, "to see you're still all right, Gar."

Gareth raised his head despairingly. "Did she try to use you?"

The Master nodded, his thin, foxy face grim. "And when I kept my distance and made you keep yours, she turned to Bond, who was the nearest one she could prey upon. Your father..." He fished for the kindest words to use. "Your father was of little more use to her by that time."

The prince's fist struck the table with a violence that startled them all—and most of all Gareth himself. But he said nothing, and indeed, there was little he could say, or that any could say to him. After a moment, Trey Clerlock rose from the couch in the corner, where she had been lying like a child playing dress-up in her flapping black robe, and came over to rest her hands upon his shoulders.

"Is there any way of destroying her?" the girl asked, looking across the table to the tiny gnome and the tall Master who had come to stand at his side.

Gareth turned to stare up at her in shock, having, man-like, never suspected the ruthless practicality of women.

"Not with the power she holds through the King and through the Stone," Polycarp said. "Believe me, I thought about it, though I knew I truly would face a charge of murder for it." A brief grin flickered across his face. "But as I ended up facing one anyway..."

"What about destroying the Stone, then?" John asked, turning his head from where he lay flat on his back on a tall-legged sleeping couch. Even the little he had been able to eat seemed to have done him good. In his black robe, he looked like the corpse at a wake, washed and tended and cheerful with his specs perched on the end of his long nose. "I'm sure you could find a good Stonebane someplace..."

"Never!" Balgub's wrinkled walnut face grew livid. "It is the source of the healing arts of the gnomes! The source of the strength of the Deep! It is ours..."

"It will do you precious little good if Zyerne gets her hands on it," John pointed out. "I doubt she could break through all the doors and gates you locked behind us on our way up here through the Deep, but if the King's troops manage to breach the Citadel wall, that won't make much difference."

"If Jenny could be given the key to the use of the Stone..." suggested Gareth.

"No!" Balgub and Jenny spoke at once. All those in the Master's long, scrubbed stone workroom, John included, looked curiously at the witch of Wyr.

"No human shall touch it!" insisted the gnome with shrill fury. "We saw the evil it did. It is for the gnomes, and only for us."

"And I would not touch it if I could." Jenny drew her knees up close to her chest and folded her arms around them; Balgub, in spite of his protest, looked affronted that the greatest treasure of the Deep should be refused. Jenny said, "According to Mab, the Stone itself has been defiled. Its powers, and the spells of those that use it, are polluted by what Zyerne has done."

"That is not true." Balgub's tight little face set in an expression of obstinancy. "Mab insisted that the Stone's powers were becoming unpredictable and its influence evil on the minds of those who used it. By the heart of the Deep, this is not so, and so I told her, again and again. I do not see how..."

"After being fed chewed-up human essences instead of controlled spells, it would be a wonder if it didn't become unpredictable," John said, with his usual good-natured affability.

The gnome's high voice was scornful. "What can a warrior know of such things? A warrior hired to slay the dragon, who has," he added, with heavy sarcasm, "signally failed in even that task."

"I suppose you'd rather he'd signally succeeded?" Gareth demanded hotly. "You'd have had the King's troops coming at you the Deep by this time."

"Lad." John reached patiently out to touch the angry

prince's shoulder. "Let's don't fratch. His opinion does me no harm and shouting at him isn't going to change it."

"The King's troops would never have found their way through the Deep, even with the gates unbolted," Balgub growled. "And now the gates are locked; if necessary we will seal them with blasting powder—it is there and ready, within yards of the last gate."

"If Zyerne was leading them, they would have found the way," Polycarp returned. The links of the too-large mail shirt he wore over his gown rattled faintly as he folded his arms. "She knows the way to the heart of the Deep well enough from the Deeping side. As you all saw, from there to the underground gates of the Citadel it's an almost straight path. And as for the Stone not having been affected by what she has put into it . . ." He glanced down at the stooped back and round white head of the gnome perched in the carved chair beside him. "You are the only Healer who escaped the dragon to come here, Balgub," he said. "Now that the dragon is no longer in the Deep, will you go in and use the Stone?"

The wide mouth tightened, and the green eyes did not meet the blue.

"So," said the Master softly.

"I do not believe that Mab was right," Balgub insisted stubbornly. "Nevertheless, until she, I, and the remaining Healers in Bel can examine the thing, I will not have it tampered with for good or ill. If it came to saving the Citadel, or keeping Zyerne from the Deep, yes, I would risk using it, rather than let her have it." Little and white as two colorless cave shrimp, his hands with their smooth moonstone rings closed upon each other on the inkstained tabletop. "We have sworn that Zyerne shall never again have the use of the Stone. Every gnome—and every man . . ." He cast a glance that was half-commanding, half-questioning up at the Master, and Polycarp inclined his head slightly, "—in this place will die before she lays a hand upon what she seeks."

"And considering what her powers will be like if she does," Polycarp added, with the detached speculation of a scholar, "that would probably be just as well."

"Jen?"

Jenny paused in the doorway of the makeshift guest room to which she and John had been assigned. After the windy ramparts, the place smelled close and stuffy, as the Market Hall had last night. The mingled scents of dusty paper and leather bindings of the books stored there compounded with the moldery odors of straw ticks that had gone too long without having the straw changed; after the grass-and-water scents of the east wind, they made the closeness worse. The lumpish shapes of piles of books heaped along two walls and the ghostly scaffolding of scroll racks lining the third made her think of John's overcrowded study in the north; several of the volumes that had been put here to make room for refugees trapped by the siege had been taken from their places and already bore signs of John's reading. John himself stood between the tall lights of two of the pointed windows, visible only as a white fold of shirt sleeve and a flash of round glass in the gloom.

She said, "You shouldn't be out of bed."

"I can't be on the broad of my back forever." Through his fatigue, he sounded cheerful. "I have the feeling we're all going to be put to it again in the near future, and I'd rather do it on my feet this time."

He was silent for a moment, watching her silhouette in the slightly lighter doorway.

He went on, "And for a woman who hasn't slept more than an hour or so for three nights now, you've no room to speak. What is it, Jen?"

Like a dragon, she thought, he has a way of not being

lied to. So she did not say, "What is what?" but ran her hands tiredly through her hair and crossed to where he stood.

"You've avoided speaking to me of it—not that we've had time to do so, mind. I don't feel you're angry with me, but I do feel your silence. It's to do with your power, isn't it?"

His arm was around her shoulder, her head resting against the rock-hardness of his pectoral, half-uncovered by the thin muslin shirt. She should have known, she told herself, that John would guess.

So she nodded, unable to voice the turmoil that had been all day in her mind, since the dragon's flight and all the night before. Since sunset she had been walking the ramparts, as if it were possible to outwalk the choice that had stalked her now for ten years.

Morkeleb had offered her the realms of the dragons, the woven roads of the air. All the powers of earth and sky, she thought, and all the years of time. The key to magic is magic; the offer was the answer to all the thwarted longings of her life.

"Jen," John said softly, "I've never wanted you to be torn. I know you've never been complete and I didn't want to do that to you. I tried not to."

"It wasn't you." She had told herself, a hundred years ago it seemed, that it was her choice, and so it had been— the choice of doing nothing and letting things go on as they were, or of doing something. And, as always, her mind shrank from the choice.

"Your magic has changed," he said. "I've felt it and I've seen what it's doing to you."

"It is calling me," she replied. "If I embrace it, I don't think I would want to let go, even if I could. It is everything that I have wanted and worth to me, I think, everything that I have."

She had said something similar to him long ago, when

they had both been very young. In his jealous possessiveness, he had screamed at her, "But you are everything that I have or want to have!" Now his arms only tightened around her, as much, she sensed, against her grief as his own, though she knew the words he had spoken then were no less true tonight.

"It's your choice, love," he said. "As it's always been your choice. Everything you've given me, you've given freely. I won't hold you back." Her cheek was pressed to his chest, so that she only felt the quick glint of his smile as he added, "As if I ever could, anyway."

They went to the straw mattress and huddle of blankets, the only accommodation the besieged Citadel had been able to offer. Beyond the windows, moisture glinted on the black slates of the crowded stone houses below; a gutter's thread was like a string of diamonds in the moonlight. In the siege camps, bells were ringing for the midnight rites of Sarmendes, lord of the wiser thoughts of day.

Under the warmth of the covers, John's body was familiar against hers, as familiar as the old temptation to let the chances of pure power go by for yet another day. Jenny was aware, as she had always been, that it was less easy to think about her choices when she lay in his arms. But she was still there when sleep finally took her, and she drifted into ambiguous and unresolved dreams.

CHAPTER XVI

WHEN JENNY WAKENED, John was gone.

Like a dragon, in her dreams she was aware of many things; she had sensed him waking and lying for a long while propped on one elbow beside her, watching her as she slept; she had been aware, too, of him rising and dressing, and of the slow painfulness of donning his shirt, breeches, and boots and of how the bandages pulled painfully over the half-healed mess of slashes and abrasions on his back and sides. He had taken her halberd for support, kissed her gently, and gone.

Still weary, she lay in the tangle of blankets and strawticks, wondering where he had gone, and why she felt afraid.

Dread seemed to hang in the air with the stormclouds that reared dark anvil heads above the green distances north of Nast Wall. There was a queer lividness to the light that streamed through the narrow windows, a breathless sense of coming evil, a sense that had pervaded her dreams...

Her dreams, she thought confusedly. What had she dreamed?

She seemed to remember Gareth and the Master Polycarp walking on the high battlements of the Citadel, both in the billowing black robes of students, talking with the old ease of their interrupted friendship. "You must admit it was a singularly convincing calumny," Polycarp was saying.

Gareth replied bitterly, "I didn't have to believe it as readily as I did."

Polycarp grinned and drew from some pocket in his too-ample garments a brass spyglass, unfolding its jointed sections to scan the fevered sky. "You're going to be Pontifex Maximus one day, Cousin—you need practice in believing ridiculous things," And looking out toward the road that led south he had stared, as if he could not believe what he saw.

Jenny frowned, remembering the cloudy tangles of the dream.

The King, she thought—it had been the King, riding up the road toward the siege camps that surrounded the Citadel. But there had been something wrong with that tall, stiff form and its masklike face, riding through the sulfurous storm light. An effect of the dream? she wondered. Or had the eyes really been yellow—Zyerne's eyes?

Troubled, she sat up and pulled on her shift. There was a wash bowl in a corner of the room near the window, the surface of the water reflecting the sky like a piece of smoked steel. Her hand brushed across it; at her bidding, she saw Morkeleb, lying in the small upper courtyard of the Citadel, a small square of stone which contained nothing save a few withered apple trees, a wooden lean-to that had once held gardening equipment and now, like every other shelter in the Citadel, housed displaced books. The dragon lay stretched out like a cat in the pallid sunlight, the jeweled bobs of his antennae flicking here and there as if scenting the welter of the air, and beside him, on the court's single granite bench, sat John.

The dragon was saying, *Why this curiosity, Dragonsbane? That you may know us better, the next time you choose to kill one of us?*

"No," John said. "Only that I may know dragons better. I'm more circumscribed than you, Morkeleb—by a body that wears out and dies before the mind has seen half what it wants to, by a mind that spends half its time doing what it would really rather not, for the sake of the people who're in my care. I'm as greedy about knowledge as Jenny is—as you are for gold, maybe more so—for I know I have to snatch it where I can."

The dragon sniffed in disdain, the velvet-rimmed nostril flaring to show a surface ripple of deeper currents of thought; then he turned his head away. Jenny knew she ought to feel surprise at being able to call Morkeleb's image in the water bowl, but did not; though she could not have phrased it in words, but only in the half-pictured understandings of dragon-speech, she knew why it had formerly been impossible, but was possible to her now. Almost, she thought, she could have summoned his image and surroundings without the water.

For a time they were silent, man and dragon, and the shadows of the black-bellied thunderheads moved across them, gathering above the Citadel's heights. Morkeleb did not look the same in the water as he did face to face, but it was a difference, again, that could not be expressed by any but a dragon. A stray wind shook the boughs of the cronelike trees, and a few spits of rain speckled the pavement of the long court below them. At its far end, Jenny could see the small and inconspicuous—and easily defensible—door that led into the antechambers of the Deep. It was not wide, for the trade between the Citadel and the Deep had never been in anything bulkier than books and gold, and for the most part their traffic had been in knowledge alone.

Why? Morkeleb asked at length. *If, as you say, yours*

is a life limited by the constraints of the body and the narrow perimeters of time, if you are greedy for knowledge as we are for gold, why do you give what you have, half of all that you own, to others?

The question had risen like a whale from unguessed depths, and John was silent for a moment before answering. "Because it's part of being human, Morkeleb. Having so little, we share among ourselves to make any of it worth having. We do what we do because the consequences of not caring enough to do it would be worse."

His answer must have touched some chord in the dragon's soul, for Jenny felt, even through the distant vision, the radiant surge of Morkeleb's annoyance. But the dragon's thoughts sounded down to their depths again, and he became still, almost invisible against the colors of the stone. Only his antennae continued to move, restless, as if troubled by the turmoil in the air.

A thunderstorm? Jenny thought, suddenly troubled. In winter?

"Jenny?" She looked up quickly and saw the Master Polycarp standing in the tall slit of the doorway. She did not know why at first, but she shuddered when she saw hanging at his belt the brass spyglass he had used in her dream. "I didn't want to wake you—I know you've been without sleep..."

"What is it?" she asked, hearing the trouble in his voice.

"It's the King."

Her stomach jolted, as if she had missed one step of a stairway in darkness, the dread of her dream coalescing in her, suddenly hideously real.

"He said he'd escaped from Zyerne—he wanted sanctuary here, and wanted above all to talk to Gar. They went off together..."

"No!" Jenny cried, horrified, and the young philosopher looked at her in surprise. She snatched up and flung on the black robe she had been wearing earlier, dragging its belt tight. "It's a trick!"

"What...?"

She pushed her way past him, shoving up the robe's too-long sleeves over her forearms; cold air and the smell of thunder smote her as she came into the open and began to run down the long, narrow stairs. She could hear Morkeleb calling to her, faint and confused with distance; he was waiting for her in the upper court, his half-risen scales glittering uneasily in the sickly storm light.

Zyerne, she said.

Yes. I saw her just now, walking with your little prince to the door that leads down into the Deep. She was in the guise of the old King—they had already passed through the door when I spoke of it to Aversin. Is it possible that the prince did not know it, as Aversin said to me? I know that humans can fool one another with the illusions oj their magic, but are even his own son and his nephew whom he raised so stupid that they could not have told the difference between what they saw and what they knew?

As always, his words came as pictures in her mind— the old King leaning, whispering, on Gareth's shoulder for support as they walked the length of the narrow court toward the door to the Deep, the look of pity, involuntary repulsion, and wretched guilt on the boy's face—feeling repelled, and not knowing why.

Jenny's heart began to pound. *They know the King has been ill*, she said. *No doubt she counted upon their forgiveness of any lapses. She will go to the Stone, to draw power from it, and use Gareth's life to replace it. Where's John now? He has to...*

He has gone after them.

WHAT? Like a dragon, the word emerged only as a blazing surge of incredulous wrath. *He'll kill himself!*

He will likely be forestalled, Morkeleb replied cynically. But Jenny did not stay to listen. She was already running down the steep twist of steps to the lower court. The cobbles of the pavement there were uneven and badly worn, with tiny spangles of vagrant rain glittering among them like silver beads on some complex trapunto; the harshness of the stone tore at her feet as she ran toward that small, unprepossessing door.

She flung back to the dragon the words, *Wait for her here. If she reaches the Stone, she will have all power at her command—I will never be able to defeat her, as I did before. You must take her when she emerges...*

It is the Stone that binds me, the dragon's bitter voice replied in her mind. *If she reaches it, what makes you think I shall be able to do anything but her will?*

Without answering Jenny flung open the door and plunged through into the shadowy antechambers of the earth.

She had seen them the previous morning, when she had passed through with the gnomes who had gone to fetch John, Gareth, and Trey from the other side of the Deep. There were several rooms used for trade and business, and then a guardroom, whose walls were carved to three-quarters of their height from the living bone of the mountain. The windows, far up under the vaulted ceilings, let in a shadowy blue light by which she could just see the wide doors of the Deep itself, faced and backed with bronze and fitted with massive bars and bolts of iron.

These gates were still locked, but the man-sized postern door stood ajar. Beyond it lay darkness and the cold scent of rock, water, and old decay. Gathering up her robes, Jenny stepped over the thick sill and hurried on, her senses probing ahead of her, dragonlike, her eyes seeking the silvery runes she had written on the walls yesterday to mark her path.

The first passage was wide and had once been pleasant, with basins and fountains lining its walls. Now some were broken, others clogged in the months of utter neglect;

moss clotted them and water ran shining down the walls and along the stone underfoot, wetting the hem of Jenny's robe and slapping coldly at her ankles. As she walked, her mind tested the darkness before her; retracing yesterday's route, she paused again and again to listen. The way through the Deep ran near the Places of Healing, but not through them; somewhere, she would have to turn aside and seek the unmarked ways.

So she felt at the air, seeking the living tingle of magic that marked the heart of the Deep. It should lie lower than her own route, she thought, and to her left. Her mind returned uncomfortably to Miss Mab's words about a false step leaving her to die of starvation in the labyrinthine darkness. If she became lost, she told herself, Morkeleb could still hear her, and guide her forth . . .

But not, she realized, if Zyerne reached the Stone. The power and longing of the Stone were lodged in the dragon's mind. If she got lost, and Zyerne reached the Stone and gained control of Morkeleb, there would be no daylight for her again.

She hurried her steps, passing the doors that had been raised for the defense of the Citadel from the Deep, all unlocked now by Gareth and the one he supposed to be the King. By the last of them, she glimpsed the sacks of blasting powder that Balgub had spoken of, that final defense in which he had placed such faith. Beyond was a branching of the ways, and she stopped again under an arch carved to look like a monstrous mouth, with stalactites of ivory grimacing in a wrinkled gum of salmon-pink stone. Her instincts whispered to her that this was the place—two tunnels diverged from the main one, both going downwards, both to the left. A little way down the nearer one, beside the trickle of water from a broken gutter, a wet footprint marked the downward-sloping stone.

John's, she guessed, for the print was dragged and slurred. Further along that way, she saw the mark of a drier boot, narrower and differently shaped. She saw the tracks again, dried to barely a sparkle of dampness on the first steps of a narrow stair which wound like a path up a hillslope of gigantic stone mushrooms in an echoing cavern, past the dark alabaster mansions of the gnomes, to a narrow doorway in a cavern wall. She scribbled a rune beside the door and followed, through a rock seam whose walls she could touch with her outstretched hands, downward, into the bowels of the earth.

In the crushing weight of the darkness, she saw the faint flicker of yellow light.

She dared not call out, but fled soundlessly toward it. The air was warmer here, unnatural in those clammy abysses; she felt the subtle vibrations of the living magic that surrounded the Stone. But there was an unwholesomeness in the air now, like the first smell of rot in decaying meat or like the livid greenness that her dragon eyes had seen in the poisoned water. She understood that Miss Mab had been right and Balgub wrong. The Stone had been defiled. The spells that had been wrought with its strength were slowly deteriorating, perverted by the poisons drawn from Zyerne's mind.

At the end of a triangular room the size of a dozen barns, she found a torch, guttering itself out near the foot of a flight of shallow steps. The iron door at the top stood unbolted and ajar, and across its threshold John lay unconscious, scavenger-slugs already sniffing inquiringly at his face and hands.

Beyond, in the darkness, Jenny heard Gareth's voice cry, "Stop!" and the sweet, evil whisper of Zyerne's laughter.

"Gareth," the soft voice breathed. "Did you ever think it was possible that you could stop me?"

Shaken now with a cold that seemed to crystallize at the marrow of her bones, Jenny ran forward into the heart of the Deep.

Through the forest of alabaster pillars she saw them, the nervous shadows of Gareth's torch jerking over the white stone lace that surrounded the open floor. His face looked dead white against the black, baggy student gown he wore; his eyes held the nightmare terror of every dream, every encounter with his father's mistress, and the knowledge of his own terrifying weakness. In his right hand he held the halberd John had been using for a crutch. John must have warned him that it was Zyerne, Jenny thought, before he collapsed. At least Gareth has a weapon. But whether he would be capable of using it was another matter.

The Stone in the center of the onyx dancing floor seemed to glow in the vibrating dark with a sickly corpse light of its own. The woman before it was radiant, beautiful as the Death-lady who is said to walk on the sea in times of storm. She looked younger than Jenny had ever seen her, with the virgin fragility of a child that was both an armor against Gareth's desperation and a weapon to pierce his flesh if not his heart. But even at her most delicate, there was something nauseating about her, like poisoned marzipan—an overwhelming, polluted sensuality. Wind that Jenny could not feel seemed to lift the soft darkness of Zyerne's hair and the sleeves of the frail white shift that was all that she wore. Stopping on the edge of the flowstone glades, Jenny realized that she was seeing Zyerne as she had once been, when she first had come to this place—a mageborn girl-child who had run through these lightless corridors seeking power, as she herself had sought it in the rainy north; trying, as she herself had tried, to overcome the handicap of its lack in whatever way she could.

Zyerne laughed, her sweet mouth parting to show pearls of teeth. "It is my destiny," she whispered, her small hands caressing the blue-black shine of the Stone. "The gnomes had no right to keep it all to themselves. It is

mine now. It was meant to be mine from the founding of
the world. As you were."

She held out her hands, and Gareth whispered, "No."
His voice was thin and desperate as the wanting of her
clutched at his flesh.

"What is this *No*? You were made for me, Gareth.
Made to be King. Made to be my love. Made to father
my son."

Like a phantom in a dream, she drifted toward him
over the oily blackness of the great floor. Gareth slashed
at her with the torch, but she only laughed again and did
not even draw back. She knew he hadn't the courage to
touch her with the flame. He edged toward her, the halberd in his hand, but Jenny could see his face rolling with
streams of sweat. His whole body shook as he summoned
the last of his strength to cut at her when she came near
enough—fighting for the resolution to do that and not to
fling down the weapon and crush her in his arms.

Jenny strode forward from the alabaster glades in a
blaze of blue witchlight, and her voice cut the palpitant
air like a knife tearing cloth. She cried, "ZYERNE!" and
the enchantress spun, her eyes yellow as a cat-devil's in
the white blaze of the light, as they had been in the woods.
The spell over Gareth snapped, and at that instant he
swung the halberd at her with all the will he had left.

She flung the spell of deflection at him almost
contemptuously; the weapon rang and clattered on the
stone floor. Swinging back toward him, she raised her
hand, but Jenny stepped forward, her wrath swirling about
her like woodsmoke and phosphorous, and flung at Zyerne
a rope of white fire that streamed coldly from the palm
of her hand.

Zyerne hurled it aside, and it splattered, sizzling, on
the black pavement. Her yellow eyes burned with unholy
light. "You," she whispered. "I told you I'd get the Stone—
and I told you what I'd do to you when I did, you ignorant

bitch. I'll rot the stinking bones of your body for what you did!"

A spell of crippling and ruin beat like lightning in the close air of the cavern, and Jenny flinched from it, feeling all her defenses buckle and twist. The power Zyerne wielded was like a weight, the vast shadow she had only sensed before turned now to the weight of the earth where it smote against her. Jenny threw it aside and writhed from beneath it; but for a moment, she hadn't the strength to do more. A second spell struck her, and a third, cramping and biting at the muscles and organs of her body, smoking at the hem of her gown. She felt something break within her and tasted blood in her mouth; her head throbbed, her brain seemed to blaze, all the oxygen in the world was insufficient to her lungs. Under the ruthless battering she could do no more than defend herself; no counterspell would come, no way to make it stop. And through it all, she felt the weaving of the death-spells, swollen and hideous perversions of what she herself had woven, returning like a vengeance to crush her beneath them. She felt Zyerne's mind, powered by the force of the Stone, driving like a black needle of pain into hers; felt the grappling of a poisoned and vicious essence seeking her consent.

And why not? she thought. Like the black slime of bursting pustules, all her self-hatreds flowed into the light. She had murdered those weaker than herself; she had hated her master; she had used a man who loved her for her own pleasure and had abandoned the sons of her body; she had abandoned her birthright of power out of sloth and fear. Her body screamed, and her will to resist all the mounting agonies weakened before the scorching onslaught of the mind. How could she presume to fight the evil of Zyerne, when she herself was evil without even the excuse of Zyerne's grandeur?

Anger struck her then, like the icy rains of the Winterlands, and she recognized what was happening to her as a spell. Like a dragon, Zyerne deceived with the truth, but it was deception all the same. Looking up she saw that perfect, evil face bending over her, the golden eyes filled with gloating fire. Reaching out, Jenny seized the fragile wrists, the very bones of her hands hurting like an old woman's on a winter night; but she forced her hands to close.

Grandeur? her mind cried, slicing up once more through the fog of pain and enchantment. *It is only you who see yourself as grand, Zyerne. Yes, I am evil, and weak, and cowardly, but, like a dragon, I know what it is that I am. You are a creature of lies, of poisons, of small and petty fears—it is that which will kill you. Whether I die or not, Zyerne, it is you who will bring your own death upon yourself, not for what you do, but for what you are.*

She felt Zyerne's mind flinch at that. With a twist of fury Jenny broke the brutal grip it held upon hers. At the same moment her hands were struck aside. From her knees, she looked up through the tangle of her hair, to see the enchantress's face grow livid. Zyerne screamed "You! You..." With a piercing obscenity, the sorceress's whole body was wrapped in the rags of heat and fire and power. Jenny, realizing the danger was now to her body rather than to her mind, threw herself to the floor and rolled out of the way. In the swirling haze of heat and power stood a creature she had never seen before, hideous and deformed, as if a giant cave roach had mated with a tiger. With a hoarse scream, the thing threw itself upon her.

Jenny rolled aside from the rip of the razor-combed feet. She heard Gareth cry her name, not in terror as he would once have done, and from the corner of her eye she saw him slide the halberd across the glass-slick floor to her waiting hand. She caught the weapon just in time to parry a second attack. The metal of the blade shrieked on the tearing mandibles as the huge weight of the thing bore her back against the blue-black Stone. Then the thing turned, doubling on its tracks as Zyerne had done that evening in the glade, and in her mind Jenny seemed to hear Zyerne's distant voice howling, "I'll show you! I'll show you all!"

It scuttled into the forest of alabaster, making for the dark tunnels that led to the surface.

Jenny started to get to her feet to follow and collapsed at the foot of the Stone. Her body hurt her in every limb and muscle; her mind felt pulped from the ripping cruelty of Zyerne's spells, bleeding still from her own acceptance of what she was. Her hand, which she could see lying over the halberd's shaft, seemed no longer part of her, though, rather to her surprise, she saw it was still on the end of her arm and attached to her body; the brown fingers were covered with blisters, from some attack she had not even felt at the time. Gareth was bending over her, holding the guttering torch.

"Jenny—Jenny, wake up—Jenny *please*! Don't make me go after it alone!"

"No," she managed to whisper and swallowed blood. Some instinct told her the lesion within her had healed, but she felt sick and drained. She tried to rise again and collapsed, vomiting; she felt the boy's hands hold her steady even though they shook with fear. Afterward, empty and chilled, she wondered if she would faint and told herself not to be silly.

"She's going to get Morkeleb," she whispered, and propped herself up again, her black hair hanging down in her face. "The power of the Stone rules him. She will be able to hold his mind, as she could not hold mine."

She managed to get to her feet, Gareth helping her as gently as he could, and picked up the halberd. "I have to stop her before she gets clear of the caverns. I defeated her mind—while the tunnels limit her size, I may be able to defeat her body. Stay here and help John."

"But . . ." Gareth began. She shrugged free of his hold and made for the dark doorway at a stumbling run.

Beyond it, spells of loss and confusion tangled the darkness. The runes that she had traced as she'd followed John were gone, and for a few moments the subtle obscurity of Zyerne's magic smothered her mind and made all those shrouded ways look the same. Panic knotted around her throat as she thought of wandering forever in the darkness; then the part of her that had found her way through the woods of the Winterlands said, *Think. Think and listen.* She released magic from her mind and looked about her in the dark; with instinctive woodcraftiness, she had taken back-bearings of her route while making her rune-markings, seeing what the landmarks looked like coming the other way. She spread her senses through the phantasmagoric domain of fluted stone, listening for the echoes that crossed and recrossed in the blackness. She heard the muted murmur of John's voice speaking to Gareth about doors the gnomes had meant to bar and the clawed scrape of unclean chitin somewhere up ahead. She deepened her awareness and heard the skitter of the vermin of the caves as they fled, shocked, from a greater vermin. Swiftly, she set off in pursuit.

She had told Morkeleb to stand guard over the outer door. She prayed now that he had had the sense not to, but it scarcely mattered whether he did or not. The power of the Stone was in Zyerne—from it she had drawn the deepest reserves of its strength, knowing that, when the time came to pay it back, she would have lives aplenty at her disposal to do it. The power of the Stone was lodged in Morkeleb's mind, tighter now that his mind and hers had touched. With the dragon her slave, the Citadel would fall, and the Stone be Zyerne's forever.

Jenny quickened once more to a jog that felt ready to

break her bones. Her bare feet splashed in the trickling water, making a faint, sticky pattering among the looming shapes of the limestone darkness; her hands felt frozen around the halberd shaft. How long a start Zyerne had she didn't know, or how fast the abomination she had become could travel. Zyerne had no more power over her, but she feared to meet her now and pit her body against that body. A part of her mind thought wryly: John should have been doing this, not she—it was his end of the bargain to deal with monsters. She smiled bitterly. Mab had been right; there were other evils besides dragons in the land.

She passed a hillslope of stone mushrooms, an archway of teeth like grotesque daggers. Her heart pounded and her chilled body ached with the ruin Zyerne had wrought on her. She ran, passing the locks and bars the gnomes had set such faith in, knowing already that she would be too late.

In the blue dimness of the vaults below the Citadel, she found the furniture toppled and scattered, and she forced herself desperately to greater speed. Through a doorway, she glimpsed a reflection of the fevered daylight outside; the stench of blood struck her nostrils even as she tripped and, looking down, saw the decapitated body of a gnome lying in a pool of warm blood at her feet. The last room of the Citadel vaults was a slaughterhouse, men and gnomes lying in it and in the doorway to the outside, their makeshift black livery sodden with blood, the close air of the room stinking with the gore that splattered the walls and even the ceiling. From beyond the doorway, shouting and the stench of burning came to her; and, stumbling through the carnage, Jenny cried out *Morkeleb*! She hurled the music of his name like a rope into the sightless void. His mind touched hers, and the hideous weight of the Stone pressed upon them both.

Light glared in her eyes. She scrambled over the bodies

in the doorway and stood, blinking for an instant in the lower court, seeing all around the door the paving stones charred with a crisped muck of blood. Before her the creature crouched, larger and infinitely more hideous in the befouled and stormy daylight, metamorphosed into something like a winged ant, but without an ant's compact grace. Squid, serpent, scorpion, wasp—it was everything hideous, but no one thing in itself. The screaming laughter that filled her mind was Zyerne's laughter. It was Zyerne's voice that she heard, calling to Morkeleb as she had called to Gareth, the power of the Stone a tightening noose upon his mind.

The dragon crouched immobile against the far rampart of the court. His every spike and scale were raised for battle, yet to Jenny's mind came nothing from him but grating agony. The awful, shadowy weight of the Stone was tearing at his mind, a power built generation after generation, fermenting in upon itself and directed by Zyerne upon him now, summoning him to her bidding, demanding that he yield. Jenny felt his mind a knot of iron against that imperious command, and she felt it when the knot fissured.

She cried again, *Morkeleb*! and flung herself, mind and body, toward him. Their minds gripped and locked. Through his eyes, she saw the horrible shape of the creature and recognized how he had known Zyerne through her disguise—the patterning of her soul was unmistakable. Peripherally, she was aware that this was true for every man and gnome who cowered within the doorways and behind the protection of each turret; she saw things as a dragon sees. The force of the Stone hammered again at her mind, and yet it had no power over her, no hold upon her. Through Morkeleb's eyes, she saw herself still running toward him—toward, in a sense, herself—and saw the creature turn to strike at that small, flying rag of black-wrapped bones and hair that she knew in a detached way for her own body.

Her mind was within the dragon's, shielding him from the burning grip of the Stone. Like a cat, the dragon struck, and the creature that had been Zyerne wheeled to meet the unexpected threat. Half within her own body, half within Morkeleb's, Jenny stepped in under the sagging, bloated belly of the monster that loomed so hugely near her and thrust upward with her halberd. As the blade slashed at the stinking flesh, she heard Zyerne's voice in her mind, screaming at her the back-street obscenities of a spoiled little slut whom the gnomes had taken in on account of the promise of her power. Then the creature gathered its mismated limbs beneath it and hurled itself skyward out of their way. From overhead, Jenny felt the hot rumble of thunder.

Her counterspell blocked the bolt of lightning that would have come hurling down on the court an instant later; she used a dragon-spell, such as those who walked the roads of the air used to allow them to fly in storms. Morkeleb was beside her then, her mind shielding his from the Stone as his body shielded hers from Zyerne's greater strength. Minds interlinked, there was no need of words between them. Jenny seized the knife-tipped spikes of his foreleg as he raised her to his back, and she wedged herself uncomfortably between the spearpoints that guarded his spine. More thunder came, and the searing breathlessness of ozone. She flung a spell to turn aside that bolt, and the lightning—channeled, she saw, through the creature that hovered in the livid air above the Citadel like a floating sack of pus—struck the tubular harpoon gun on the rampart. It exploded in a bursting star of flame and shattered iron, and the two men who were cranking another catapult to bear on the monster turned and fled.

Jenny understood then that the storm had been summoned by Zyerne, called by her powers through the Stone from afar, and the Stone's magic gave her the power to direct the lightning when and where she would. It had been her weapon to destroy the Citadel—the Stone, the storm, and the dragon.

She pulled off her belt and used it to lash herself to the two-foot spike before her. It would be little use if the dragon turned over in flight, but would keep her from being thrown off laterally, and that was all she could hope for now. She knew her body was exhausted and hurt, but the dragon's mind lifted her out of herself; and in any case, she had no choice. She sealed herself off from the pain and ripped the Limitations from mind and flesh.

The dragon hurtled skyward to the thing waiting above.

Winds tore at them, buffeting Morkeleb's wings so that he had to veer sharply to miss being thrown into the highest turret of the Citadel. From above them, the creature spat a rain of acid mucus. Green and stinking, it seared Jenny's face and hands like poison and made smoking tracks of corrosion on the steel of the dragon's scales. Furiously keeping her mind concentrated against the searing agony, Jenny cast her will at the clouds, and rain began to sluice down, washing the stuff away and half-blinding her with its fury. Long black hair hung stickily down over her shoulders as the dragon swung on the wind, and she felt lightning channeling again into the hovering creature before them. Seizing it with her mind, she flung it back. It burst somewhere between them, the shock of it striking her bones like a blow. She had forgotten she was not a dragon, and that her flesh was mortal.

Then the creature fell upon them, its stumpy wings whirring like a foul bug's. The weight of it rolled the dragon in the air so that Jenny had to grasp the spikes on either side of her, below the blades and yet still cutting her fingers. The earth rolled and swung below them, but her eyes and mind locked on the thing above. Its stink was overpowering, and from the pullulant mass of its flesh, a sharklike head struck, biting at the massive joints of the dragon's wings, while the whirlwind of evil spells sucked and ripped around them, tearing at their linked minds.

Ichorous yellow fluid burst from the creature's mouth as it bit at the spikes of the wing-joints. Jenny slashed at the eyes, human and as big as her two fists, gray-gold as mead—Zyerne's eyes. The halberd blade clove through the flesh—and from among the half-severed flaps of the wound, other heads burst like a knot of snakes among spraying gore, tearing at her robe and her flesh with suckerlike mouths. Grimly, fighting a sense of nightmare horror, she chopped again, her blistered hands clotted and running with slime. Half her mind called from the depths of the dragon's soul the healing-spells against the poisons she knew were harbored in those filthy jaws.

When she slashed at the other eye, the creature broke away from them. The pain of Morkeleb's wounds as well as her own tore at her as he swung and circled skyward, and she knew he felt the burning of her ripped flesh. The Citadel dropped away below them; rain poured over them like water from a pail. Looking up, she could see the deadly purplish glow of stored lightning rimming the black pillows of cloud so close above their heads. The battering of Zyerne's mind upon theirs lessened as the sorceress rallied her own spells, spells of wreckage and ruin against the Citadel and its defenders below.

Mists veiled the thrusting folds of the land beneath them, the toy fortress and the wet, slate-and-emerald of the meadows beside the white stream of the river. Morkeleb circled, Jenny's eyes within his seeing all things with clear, incredible calm. Lightning streaked down by her and she saw, as if it had been drawn in fine lines before her eyes, another catapult explode on the ramparts, and the man who had been winding it flung backward over the parapet, whirling limply down the side of the cliff.

Then the dragon folded his wings and dropped. Her mind in Morkeleb's, Jenny felt no fear, clinging to the spikes while the wind tore her sopping hair back and her bloody, rain-wet robes plastered to her body and arms. Her mind was the mind of a stooping falcon. She saw, with precise pleasure, the sacklike, threshing body that was their target, felt the joy of impending impact as the dragon fisted his claws...

The jar all but threw her from her precarious perch on the dragon's backbone. The creature twisted and sagged in the air, then writhed under them, grabbing with a dozen mouths at Morkeleb's belly and sides, heedless of the spikes and the monstrous slashing of the dragon's tail. Something tore at Jenny's back; turning, she hacked the head off a serpentine tentacle that had ripped at her, but she felt the blood flowing from the wound. Her efforts to close it were fogged and slow. They seemed to have fallen into a vortex of spells, and the weight of the Stone's strength dragged upon them, trying to rend apart the locked knot of their minds.

What was human magic and what dragon she no longer knew, only that they sparkled together, iron and gold, in a welded weapon that attacked both body and mind. She could feel Morkeleb's growing exhaustion and her own dizziness as the Citadel walls and the stone-toothed cliffs of Nast Wall wheeled crazily beneath them. The more they hacked and cut at the awful, stinking thing, the more mouths and gripping tentacles it sprouted and the tighter its clutch upon them became. She felt no more fear than a beast might feel in combat with its own kind, but she did feel the growing weight of the thing as it multiplied, getting larger and more powerful as the two entwined bodies thrashed in the sea of streaming rain.

The end, when it came, was a shock, like the impact

of a club. She was aware of a booming roar somewhere in the earth beneath them, dull and shaking through her exhausted singlemindedness; then, more clearly, she heard a voice like Zyerne's screaming, multiplied a thousandfold through the spells that suffocated her until it axed through her skull with the rending echo of indescribable pain.

Like the passage from one segment of a dream to another, she felt the melting of the spells that surrounded them and the falling-away of the clinging, flaccid flesh and muscle. Something flashed beneath them, falling through the rainy air toward the wet roof crests of the Citadel below, and she realized that the plunging flutter of streaming brown hair and white gauze was Zyerne.

The instantaneous *Get her* and Morkeleb's *Let her fall* passed between them like a spark. Then he was plunging again, as he had plunged before, falconlike, tracking the falling body with his precise crystal eyes and plucking it from the air with the neatness of a child playing jacks.

Charcoal-gray with rain, the walls of the Citadel court rose up around them. Men, women, and gnomes were everywhere on the ramparts, hair slicked down with the pouring cloudburst to which nobody was paying the slightest attention. White smoke poured from the narrow door that led into the Deep, but all eyes were raised skyward to that black, plummeting form.

The dragon balanced for a moment upon the seventy-foot span of his wings, then extended three of his delicate legs to touch the ground. With the fourth, he laid Zyerne on the puddled stone pavement, her dark hair spreading out around her under the driving rain.

Sliding from the dragon's back, Jenny knew at once that Zyerne was dead. Her mouth and eyes were open. Distorted with rage and terror, her face could be seen to be pointy and shrewish with constant worry and the cancerous addiction to petty angers.

Trembling with weariness, Jenny leaned against the

dragon's curving shoulder. Slowly, the scintillant helix of
their minds unlinked. The rim of brightness and color that
had seemed to edge everything vanished from her vision.
Living things had solid bodies once more, instead of incorporeal ghosts of flesh through which shone the shapes of
souls.

A thousand pains came back to her—of her body and
of the stripped, hurting ruin of her mind. She became
aware of the blood that stuck her torn robe to her back
and ran down her legs to her bare feet—became aware
of all the darkness in her own heart, which she had accepted
in her battle with Zyerne.

Holding to the thorned scales for support, she looked
down at the sharp, white face staring upward at her from
the rain-hammered puddles. A human hand steadied her
elbow, and turning, she saw Trey beside her, her frivolously tinted hair plastered with wet around her pale face.
It was the closest, she realized, that she had seen any
human besides herself come to Morkeleb. A moment later
Polycarp joined them, one arm wrapped in makeshift
dressings and half his red hair burned away by the creature's first attack upon the door.

White smoke still billowed from the door of the Deep.
Jenny coughed, her lungs hurting, in the acrid fumes.
Everyone in the court was coughing—it was as if the
Deep itself were in flames.

More coughing came from within. In the shadowy slot,
two forms materialized, the shorter leaning upon the taller.
From soot-blackened faces, two pairs of spectacle lenses
flashed whitely in the pallid light.

A moment later they emerged from the smoke and
shadow into the stunned silence of the watching crowd
in the court.

"Miscalculated the blasting powder," John explained
apologetically.

CHAPTER XVII

IT WAS NOT for several days after John and Gareth blew up the Stone that Jenny began to recover from the battle beneath and above the Citadel.

She had cloudy recollections of them telling Polycarp how they had backtracked to the room by the gates where the blasting powder had been left, while her own consciousness darkened, and a vague memory of Morkeleb catching her in his talons as she fell and carrying her, catlike, to the small shelter in the upper court. More clear was the remembrance of John's voice, forbidding the others to go after them. "She needs a healing we can't give her," she heard him say to Gareth. "Just let her be."

She wondered how he had known that. But then, John knew her very well.

Morkeleb healed her as dragons heal, leading the body with the mind. Her body healed fairly quickly, the poisons burning themselves out of her veins, the slashed, puckered wounds left by the creature's mouths closing to leave round, vicious-looking scabs the size of her palm. Like John's dragon-slaying scars, she thought, they would stay with her for what remained of her life.

Her mind healed more slowly. Open wounds left by her battle with Zyerne remained open. Worst was the knowledge that she had abandoned the birthright of her power, not through the fate that had denied her the ability or the circumstances that had kept her from its proper teaching, but through her own fear.

They are yours for the stretching-out of your hand, Morkeleb had said.

She knew they always had been.

Turning her head from the shadows of the crowded lean-to, she could see the dragon lying in the heatless sun of the court, a black cobra with his tasseled head raised, his antennae flicking to listen to the wind. She felt her soul streaked and mottled with the mind and soul of the dragon and her life entangled with the crystal ropes of his being.

She asked him once why he had remained at the Citadel to heal her. *The Stone is broken—the ties that bind you to this place are gone.*

She felt the anger coiled within him stir. *I do not know, wizard woman. You cannot have healed yourself—I did not wish to see you broken forever.* The words in her mind were tinted, not only with anger, but with the memory of fear and with a kind of shame.

Why? she asked. *You have often said that the affairs of humankind are nothing to dragons.*

His scales rattled faintly as they hackled, then, with a dry whisper, settled again. Dragons did not lie, but she felt the mazes of his mind close against her.

Nor are they. But I have felt stirring in me things that I do not understand, since you healed me and shared with me the song of the gold in the Deep. My power has waked power in you, but what it is in you that has waked its reflection in me I do not know, for it is not a thing of dragons. It let me feel the grip of the Stone, as I flew north—a longing and a hurt, which before was only my

*own will. Now because of it, I do not want to see you
hurt—I do not want to see you die, as humans die. I want
you to come with me to the north, Jenny; to be one of
the dragons, with the power for which you have always
sought. I want this, as much as I have ever wanted the
gold of the earth. I do not know why. And is it not what
you want?*

But to that, Jenny had no reply.

Long before he should have been on his feet, John
dragged himself up the steps to the high court to see her,
sitting behind her on the narrow makeshift cot in her little
shelter, brushing her hair as he used to at the Hold on
those nights when she would come there to be with him
and their sons. He spoke of commonplaces, of the dis-
mantling of the siege troops around the Citadel and of the
return of the gnomes to the Deep, of Gareth's doings, and
of the assembling of the books they would take back to
the north, demanding nothing of her, neither speech, decision, nor thought. But it seemed to her that the touch of
his hands brought more bitter pain to her than all Zyerne's
spells of ruin.

She had made her choice, she thought, ten years ago
when first they had met; and had remade it every day
since then. But there was, and always had been, another
choice. Without turning her head, she was aware of the
thoughts that moved behind the diamond depths of Morkeleb's watching eyes.

When he rose to go, she laid a hand on the sleeve of
his frayed black robe. "John," she said quietly. "Will you
do something for me? Send a message to Miss Mab, asking
her to choose out the best volumes of magic that she
knows of, both of the gnomes and of humankind, to go
north also?"

He regarded her for a moment, where she lay on the
rough paillasse on her narrow cot which for four nights
now had been her solitary bed, her coarse dark hair hang-

ing over the whiteness of her shift. "Wouldn't you rather look them out for yourself, love? You're the one who's to be using them, after all."

She shook her head. His back was to the light of the open court, his features indistinct against the glare; she wanted to reach out her hand to touch him, but somehow could not bring herself to do so. In a cool voice like silver she explained, "The magic of the dragon is in me, John; it is not a thing of books. The books are for Ian, when he comes into his power."

John said nothing for a moment. She wondered if he, too, had realized this about their older son. When he did speak, his voice was small. "Won't you be there to teach him?"

She shook her head. "I don't know, John," she whispered. "I don't know."

He made a move to lay his hand on her shoulder, and she said, "No. Don't touch me. Don't make it harder for me than it already is."

He remained standing for a moment longer before her, looking down into her face. Then, obedient, he silently turned and left the shed.

She had come to no further conclusion by the day of their departure from the Citadel, to take the road back to the north. She was conscious of John watching her, when he thought she wasn't looking; conscious of her own gladness that he never used the one weapon that he must have known would make her stay with him—he never spoke to her of their sons. But in the nights, she was conscious also of the dark cobra shape of the dragon, glittering in the moonlight of the high court, or wheeling down from the black sky with the cold stars of winter prickling upon his spines, as if he had flown through the heart of the galaxy and come back powdered with its light.

The morning of their departure was a clear one, though bitterly cold. The King rode up from Bel to see them off, surrounded by a flowerbed of courtiers, who regarded John with awe and fear, as if wondering how they had dared to mock him, and why he had not slain them all. With him, also, were Polycarp and Gareth and Trey, hand-fast like schoolchildren. Trey had had her hair redyed, burgundy and gold, which would have looked impressive had it been done in the elaborate styles of the Court instead of in two plaits like a child's down her back.

They had brought with them a long line of horses and mules, laden with supplies for the journey and also with the books for which John had so cheerfully been prepared to risk his life. John knelt before the tall, vague, faded old man, thanking him and swearing fealty; while Jenny, clothed in her colorless northlands plaids, stood to one side, feeling queerly distant from them all and watching how the King kept scanning the faces of the courtiers around him with the air of one who seeks someone, but no longer remembers quite who.

To John the King said, "Not leaving already? Surely it was only yesterday you presented yourself?"

"It will be a long way home, my lord." John did not mention the week he had spent waiting the King's leave to ride forth against the dragon—it was clear the old man recalled little, if anything, of the preceding weeks. "It's best I start before the snows come on heavy."

"Ah." The King nodded vaguely and turned away, lean-ing on the arms of his tall son and his nephew Polycarp. After a pace or two, he halted, frowning as something surfaced from the murk of his memory, and turned to Gareth. "This Dragonsbane—he did kill the dragon, after all?"

There was no way to explain all that had passed, or how rightness had been restored to the kingdom, save by the appropriate channels, so Gareth said simply, "Yes."

"Good," said the old man, nodding dim approval. "Good."

Gareth released his arm; Polycarp, as Master of the Citadel and his host, led the King away to rest, the courtiers trailing after like a school of brightly colored, ornamental fish. From among them stepped three small, stout forms, their silken robes stirring in the ice winds that played from the soft new sky.

Balgub, the new Lord of the Deep of Ylferdun, inclined his head; with the stiff unfamiliarity of one who has seldom spoken the words, he thanked Lord Aversin the Dragonsbane, though he did not specify for what.

"Well, he hardly could, now, could he?" John remarked, as the three gnomes left the court in the wake of the King's party. Only Miss Mab had caught Jenny's eye and winked at her. John went on, "If he came out and said, 'Thank you for blowing up the Stone,' that would be admitting that he was wrong about Zyerne not poisoning it."

Gareth, who was still standing hand-in-hand with Trey beside them, laughed. "You know, I think he does admit it in his heart, though I don't think he'll ever completely forgive us for doing it. At least, he's civil to me in Council—which is fortunate, since I'm going to have to be dealing with him for a long time."

"Are you?" A flicker of intense interest danced in John's eye.

Gareth was silent for a long moment, fingering the stiff lace of his cuff and not meeting John's gaze. When he looked up again, his face was weary and sad.

"I thought it would be different," he said quietly. "I thought once Zyerne was dead, he would be all right. And he's better, he really is." He spoke like a man trying to convince himself that a mended statue is as beautiful as it was before it broke. "But he's—he's so absentminded. Badegamus says he can't be trusted to remember edicts he's made from one day to the next. When I was in Bel, we made up a Council—Badegamus, Balgub, Polycarp, Dromar, and I—to sort out what we ought to do; then I tell Father to do it—or remind him it's what he was going to do, and he'll pretend he remembers. He knows he's gotten forgetful, though he doesn't quite remember why. Sometimes he'll wake in the night, crying Zyerne's name or my mother's." The young man's voice turned momentarily unsteady. "But what if he never recovers?"

"What if he never does?" John returned softly. "The Realm will be yours in any case one day, my hero." He turned away and began tightening the cinches of the mules, readying them for the trek down through the city to the northward road.

"But not now!" Gareth followed him, his words making soft puffs of steam in the morning cold. "I mean—I never have time for myself anymore! It's been months since I worked on my poetry, or tried to complete that southern variant of the ballad of Antara Warlady..."

"There'll be time, by and by." The Dragonsbane paused, resting his hand on the arched neck of Battlehammer, Gareth's parting gift to him. "It will get easier, when men know to come to you directly instead of to your father."

Gareth shook his head. "But it won't be the same."

"Is it ever?" John moved down the line, tightening cinches, checking straps on the parcels of books—volumes of healing, Anacetus' works on greater and lesser demons, Luciard's *Firegiver*, books on engineering and law, by gnomes and men. Gareth followed him silently, digesting the fact that he was now, for all intents and purposes, the Lord of Bel, with the responsibilities of the kingdom—for which he had been academically prepared under the mental heading of "some day"—thrust suddenly upon his unwilling shoulders. Like John, Jenny thought pityingly, he would have to put aside the pursuit of his love of knowledge for what he owed his people and return to it only when he could. The only difference was that his realm was at peace and that John had been a year younger than Gareth was when the burden had fallen to him.

"And Bond?" John asked gently, looking over at Trey. She sighed and managed to smile. "He still asks about Zyerne," she said softly. "He really did love her, you know. He knows she's dead and he tries to pretend he remembers it happening the way I told him, about her falling off a horse...But it's odd. He's kinder than he was. He'll never be considerate, of course, but he's not so quick or so clever, and I think he hurts people less. He dropped a cup at luncheon yesterday—he's gotten very clumsy—and he even apologized to me." There was a slight wryness to her smile, perhaps to cover tears. "I remember when he would not only have blamed me for it, but gotten me to blame myself."

She and Gareth had been following John down the line, still hand in hand, the girl's rose-colored skirts bright against the pewter grayness of the frosted morning. Jenny, standing apart, listened to their voices, but felt as if she saw them through glass, part of a life from which she was half-separated, to which she did not have to go back unless she chose. And all the while, her mind listened to the sky, hearing with strange clarity the voices of the wind around the Citadel towers, seeking something...

She caught John's eye on her and saw the worry crease between his brows; something wrung and wrenched in her heart.

"Must you go?" Gareth asked hesitantly, and Jenny, feeling as if her thoughts had been read, looked up; but it was to John that he had spoken. "Could you stay with me, even for a little while? It will take nearly a month for the troops to be ready—you could have a seat on the Council. I—I can't do this alone."

John shook his head, leaning on the mule Clivy's withers. "You are doing it alone, my hero. And as for me, I've my own realm to look after. I've been gone long as it is." He glanced questioningly at Jenny as he spoke, but she looked away.

Wind surged down around them, crosswise currents swirling her plaids and her hair like the stroke of a giant wing. She looked up and saw the shape of the dragon melting down from the gray and cobalt of the morning sky.

She turned from the assembled caravan in the court without a word and ran to the narrow stair that led up to the walls. The dark shape hung like a black kite on the wind, the soft voice a song in her mind.

By my name you have bidden me go, Jenny Waynest, he said. *Now that you are going, I too shall depart. But by your name, I ask that you follow. Come with me, to the islands of the dragons in the northern seas. Come with me, to be of us, now and forever.*

She knew in her heart that it would be the last time of his asking; that if she denied him now, that door would never open again. She stood poised for a moment, between silver ramparts and silver sky. She was aware of John climbing the steps behind her, his face emptied of life and his spectacle lenses reflecting the pearly colors of the morning light; was aware, through him, of the two little boys waiting for them in the crumbling tower of Alyn Hold—boys she had borne without intention of raising, boys she should have loved, she thought, either more or less than she had.

But more than them, she was aware of the dragon, drifting like a ribbon against the remote white eye of the day moon. The music of his name shivered in her bones; the iron and fire of his power streaked her soul.

To be a mage you must be a mage, she thought. The key to magic is magic.

She turned and looked back, to see John standing on the root-buckled pavement between the barren apple trees behind her. Past him, she glimpsed the caravan of horses in the court below, Trey and Gareth holding the horses' heads as they snorted and fidgeted at the scent of the dragon. For a moment, the memory of John's body and John's voice overwhelmed her—the crushing strength of his muscles and the curious softness of his lips, the cold slickness of a leather sleeve, and the fragrance of his body mixed with the more prosaic pungence of woodsmoke and horses that permeated his scruffy plaids.

She was aware, too, of the desperation and hope in his eyes.

She saw the hope fade, and he smiled. "Go if you must, love," he said softly. "I said I wouldn't hold you, and I won't. I've known it for days."

She shook her head, wanting to speak, but unable to make a sound, her dark hair swirled by the wind of the dragon's wings. Then she turned from him, suddenly, and ran to the battlements, beyond which the dragon lay waiting in the air.

Her soul made the leap first, drawing power from the wind and from the rope of crystal thought that Morkeleb flung her, showing her the way. The elements around the nucleus of her essence changed, as she shed the shape that she had known since her conception and called to her another, different shape. She was half-conscious of spreading her arms against the wind as she strode forward over the edge of the battlement, of the wind in her dark hair as she sprang outward over the long drop of stone and cliff and emptiness. But her mind was already speeding toward the distant cloud peaks, the moon, the dragon.

On the walls behind her, she was aware of Trey whispering, "She's beautiful . . ."

Against the fading day moon, the morning's strengthening light caught in the milk-white silk of her spreading wings and flashed like a spiked carpet of diamonds along the ghost-pale armor of the white dragon's back and sides.

But more than of that, she was conscious of John,

Dragonsbane of ballad and legend, watching her with silent tears running down his still face as she circled into the waiting sky, like a butterfly released from his hand. Then he turned from the battlements, to the court where the horses waited. Taking the rein from the stunned Gareth, he mounted Battlehammer and rode through the gateway, to take the road back to the north.

CHAPTER XVIII

THEY FLEW NORTH together, treading the woven roads of the sky.

The whole Earth lay below her, marked with the long indigo shadows of morning, the bright flash of springing water, and the icy knives of the glaciers. She saw the patterns of the sea, with its currents of green and violet, its great, gray depths, and the scrum of white lace upon its surface, and those of the moving air. All things were to her as a dragon sees them, a net of magic and years, covering the Earth and holding it to all the singing universe in a crystal web of time.

They nested among the high peaks of Nast Wall, among the broken bone ends of the world, looking eastward over the gorges where the bighorn sheep sprang like fleas from rock to rock, past dizzying drops of green meltwater and woods where the dampness coated each tree in pillows of emerald moss, and down to the woods on the foothills of the Marches, where those who swore fealty to the Master dwelt. Westward, she could look past the glacier that lay like a stilled river of green and white through the gouged gray breakers of the cliffs, past cold and barren rocks, to see the Wildspae gleaming like a sheet of brown silk beneath the steam of its mists and, in the glimmering bare woods along its banks, make out the lacework turrets of Zyerne's hunting lodge among the trees.

Like a dragon, she saw backward and forward in time; and like a dragon, she felt no passion at what she saw.

She was free, to have what she had always sought— not only the power, which the touch of Morkeleb's mind had kindled in her soul, but freedom to pursue that power, released from the petty grind of the work of days.

Her mind touched and fingered that knowledge, wondering at its beauty and its complexity. It was hers now, as it had always been hers for the taking. No more would she be asked to put aside her meditations, to trek ten miles on foot over the wintry moors to deliver a child; no more would she spend the hours needed for the study of her power ankle-deep in a half-frozen marsh, looking for frogwort for Muffle the smith's rheumatism.

No more would her time—and her mind—be divided between love and power.

Far off, her dragon's sight could descry the caravan of horses, making their antlike way along the foothills and into the woods. So clear was her crystal sight that she could identify each beast within that train—the white Moon Horse, the balky roans, the stupid sorrel Cow, and the big liver-bay Battlehammer—she saw, too, the flash of spectacle lenses and the glint of metal spikes on a patched old doublet.

He was no more to her now than the first few inches upon the endless ribbon of dragon years. Like the bandits and the wretched Meewinks—like his and her sons—he had his own path to follow through the labyrinth patterns of darkening time. He would go on with his fights for his people and with his dogged experiments with rock salts and hot-air balloons, his model ballistas and his quest for lore about pigs. One day, she thought, he would take a boat out to the rough waters of Eldsbouch Cove to search for the ruins of the drowned breakwater, and she would not be waiting for him on the round pebbles of the gravel beach . . . He would ride out to the house beneath the standing stones on Frost Fell, and she would not be standing in its doorway.

In time, she knew, even these memories would fade. She saw within herself, as she had probed at the souls of others. Trey's, she recalled, had been like a clear pool, with bright shallows and unsuspected depths. Zyerne's had been a poisoned flower. Her own soul she saw also as a flower whose petals were turning to steel at their outer edges but whose heart was still soft and silky flesh. In time, it would be all steel, she saw, breathtakingly beautiful and enduring forever—but it would cease to be a flower.

She lay for a long time in the rocks, motionless save for the flick of her jeweled antennae as she scried the colors of the wind.

It was thus to be a dragon, she told herself, to see the patterns of all things from the silence of the sky. It was thus to be free. But pain still poured from some broken place inside her—the pain of choice, of loss, and of stillborn dreams. She would have wept, but there was nothing within dragons that could weep. She told herself that this was the last time she would have to feel this pain or the love that was its source. It was for this immunity that she had sought the roads of the sky.

The key to magic is magic, she thought. And all magic, all power, was now hers.

But within her some other voice asked, For what purpose? Afar off she was aware of Morkeleb, hunting the great-horned sheep in the rocks. Like a black bat of steel lace, he passed as soundlessly as his own shadow over the snowfields, wrapping himself in the colors of the air to drop down the gorges, the deceptive glitter of his magic hiding him from the nervous, stupid eyes of his prey. Magic was the bone of dragon bones, the blood of their blood; the magic of the cosmos tinted everything they perceived and everything they were.

And yet, in the end, their magic was sterile, seeking nothing but its own—as Zyerne's had been.

Zyerne, Jenny thought. The key to magic is magic. For it Zyerne had sacrificed the men who loved her, the son she would have borne, and, in the end, her very humanity—even as she herself had done!

Caerdinn had been wrong. For all his striving to perfect his arts, in the end he had been nothing but a selfish, embittered old man, the end of a Line that was failing because it sought magic for magic's sake. The key to magic was not magic, but the use of magic; it lay not in having, but in giving and doing—in loving, and in being loved.

And to her mind there rose the image of John, sitting beside Morkeleb in the high court of the Citadel. *Having so little, we shared among ourselves to make any of it worth having . . . the consequences of not caring enough to do it would have been worse . . .*

It had been John all along, she thought. Not the problem, but the solution.

Shadow circled her, and Morkeleb sank glittering to the rocks at her side. The sun was half-down the west and threw the shimmer of the blue glacier light over him like a sparkling cloak of flame.

What is it, wizard woman?

She said, *Morkeleb, return me to being what I was.*

His scales bristled, flashing, and she felt the throb of his anger deep in her mind. *Nothing can ever return to being what it was, wizard woman. You know that. My power will be within you forever, nor can the knowledge of what it is to be a dragon ever be erased from your mind.*

Even so, she said. *Yet I would rather live as a woman who was once a dragon than a dragon who was once a woman. On the steps of the Deep, I killed with fire, as a dragon kills; and like a dragon, I felt nothing. I do not want to become that, Morkeleb.*

Bah, Morkeleb said. Heat smoked from the thousand razor edges of his scales, from the long spikes and the folded silk of his wings. *Do not be a fool, Jenny Waynest. All the knowledge of the dragons, all their power, is yours, and all the years of time. You will forget the loves of the earth soon and be healed. The diamond cannot love the flower, for the flower lives only a day, then fades and dies. You are a diamond now.*

The flower dies, Jenny said softly, *having lived. The diamond will never do either. I do not want to forget, and the healing will make me what I never wanted to be. Dragons have all the years of time, Morkeleb, but even dragons cannot roll back the flow of days, nor return along them to find again time that they have lost. Let me go.*

No! His head swung around, his white eyes blazing, his long mane bristling around the base of his many horns. *I want you, wizard woman, more than I have ever wanted any gold. It is something that was born in me when your mind touched mine, as my magic was born in you. Having you, I will not give you up.*

She gathered her haunches beneath her and threw herself out into the void of the air, white wings cleaving the wind. He flung himself after, swinging down the gray cliffs and waterfalls of Nast Wall, their shadows chasing one another over snow clefts dyed blue with the coming evening and rippling like gray hawks over the darkness of stone and chasm. Beyond, the world lay carpeted by autumn haze, red and ochre and brown; and from the unleaved trees of the woods near the river, Jenny could see a single thread of smoke rising, far off on the evening wind.

The whiteness of the full moon stroked her wings; the stars, through whose secret paths the dragons had once come to the earth and along which they would one day depart, swung like a web of light in their unfolding patterns above. Her dragon sight descried the camp in the woods and a lone, small figure patiently scraping burned bannocks off the griddle, books from a half-unpacked box stacked around him.

She circled the smoke, invisible in the colors of the air, and felt the darkness of a shadow circling above her.

Wizard woman, said the voice of the dragon in her mind, *is this truly what you want?*

She did not reply, but she knew that, dragon-wise, he felt the surge and patterns of her mind. She felt his bafflement at them, and his anger, both at her and at something within himself.

At length he said, *I want you, Jenny Waynest. But more than you, I want your happiness, and this I do not understand—I do not want you in grief.* And then, his anger lashing at her like a many-tailed whip, *You have done this to me!*

I am sorry, Morkeleb, she said softly. *What you feel is the love of humans, and a poor trade for the power that the touch of your mind gave me. It is what I learned first, from loving John—both the pain and the fact that to feel it is better than not to be able to feel.*

Is this the pain that drives you? he demanded.

She said, *Yes.*

Bitter anger sounded in his mind, like the far-off echo of the gold that he had lost. *Go, then*, he said, and she circled down from the air, a thing of glass and lace and bone, invisible in the soft, smoky darkness. She felt the dragon's power surround her with heat and magic, the pain shimmering along her bones. She leaned into the fear that melted her body, as she had leaned into the winds of flight.

Then there was only weariness and grief. She knelt alone in the darkness of the autumn woods, the night chill biting into all the newly healed wounds of her back and arms. Through the warty gray and white of the tree boles, she could see the red glow of fire and smell the familiar odors of woodsmoke and horses; the plaintive strains of a pennywhistle keened thinly in the air. The bright edge of color had vanished from all things; the evening was raw and misty, colorless, and very cold. She shivered and drew her sheepskin jacket more closely about her. The earth felt damp where her knees pressed it through her faded skirts.

She brushed aside the dark, coarse mane of her hair and looked up. Beyond the bare lace of the trees, she could see the black dragon still circling, alone in the sounding hollow of the empty sky.

Her mind touched his, with thanks deeper than words. Grief came down to her, grief and hurt, and rage that he could feel hurt.

It is a cruel gift you have given me, wizard woman, he said. *For you have set me apart from my own and destroyed the pleasure of my old joys; my soul is marked with this love, though I do not understand what it is and, like you, I shall never be able to return to what I have been.*

I am sorry, Morkeleb, she said to him. *We change what we touch, be it magic, or power, or another life. Ten years ago I would have gone with you, had I not touched John, and been touched by him.*

Like an echo in her mind she heard his voice. *Be happy, then, wizard woman, with this choice that you have made. I do not understand the reasons for it, for it is not a thing of dragons—but then neither, any longer, am I.*

She felt rather than saw him vanish, flying back in the darkness toward the empty north. For a moment he passed before the white disk of the moon, skeletal silk over its stern face—then he was gone. Grief closed her throat, the grief of roads untaken, of doors not opened, of songs unsung—the human grief of choice. In freeing her, the dragon, too, had made his choice, of what he was and would be.

We change what we touch, she thought. And in that, she supposed, John—and the capacity to love and to care that John had given her—was, and forever would be, Morkeleb's bane.

She sighed and got stiffly to her feet, dusting the twigs and leaves from her skirts. The shrill, sweet notes of the pennywhistle still threaded the evening breeze, but with them was the smell of smoke, and of bannocks starting to burn. She hitched her plaid up over her shoulder and started up the path for the clearing.

About the Author

At various times in her life, Barbara Hambly has been a high-school teacher, a model, a waitress, a technical editor, a professional graduate student, an all-night clerk at a liquor store, and a karate instructor. Born in San Diego, she grew up in Southern California, with the exception of one high-school semester spent in New South Wales, Australia. Her interest in fantasy began with reading *The Wizard of Oz* at an early age and has continued ever since.

She attended the University of California, Riverside, specializing in medieval history. In connection with this, she spent a year at the University of Bordeaux in the south of France and worked as a teaching and research assistant at UC Riverside, eventually earning a Master's Degree in the subject. At the university, she also became involved in karate, making Black Belt in 1978 and competing in several national-level tournaments.

Her books include THE DARWATH TRILOGY: *Time of the Dark*, *The Walls of Air*, and *The Armies of Daylight*; *The Ladies of Mandrigyn*; and a historical whodunit, *The Quirinal Hill Affair*, set in ancient Rome.

From the lairs of darkness comes...

THE DARWATH TRILOGY

Barbara Hambly